# Searching for the Truth

## A Legacy of Light

## Book Three

I0670457

## Kyah Merritt

ISBN: 978-1-7355459-2-9

Cover art created using postermywall.com

Published by Northern Horizon Books

# Table of Contents

# Introduction

Far back in the mists of time (or at least 2011), at the age of sixteen, I wrote a short school paper about Pharaoh Tutankhamun and his unexpected death, which, at that point, was believed to have been the result of a chariot accident. In 2014, a new "virtual autopsy" of his remains strengthened the theory that he had lived with a clubfoot and several other physical challenges, which made a chariot wreck somewhat less likely, but presented the opportunity for other types of drama. Then, in 2015, Spike TV produced a highly-fictionalized biographical miniseries simply titled *Tut*.

My earlier interest in this historical figure, the compelling new information about him, and the entertaining Shakespearean soap opera converged in a story of my own. Through 2018-20, this story grew into a piece of historical fiction that has captivated me, kept me company through the coronavirus pandemic— this generation's historical event— and taught me more about Egyptian history, the Bible, and myself, than I ever could have dreamed.

During the writing process, I found more kinship with Tutankhamun and his family than I ever would have expected. And I am honored, grateful for, and moved by the experience of getting to know a person who was, in some ways, very much like me, and whose family was, in some ways, very much like mine. I hope my readers will be as intrigued as I have been as I seek to answer the questions of this famous Pharaoh's life and death.

# 1   The Proclamation

The way that the Pharaoh's body had changed since his return from Kadesh was driven home even more painfully the next day, the thirtieth and final day of the month of Sholiak. A royal audience was about to be conducted. With Grand Vizier Ay, the man who had betrayed Tutankhamun and his whole family. So the Pharaoh sat up in bed, a comfortable red robe over his sleeping-tunic, while Semerkhet, the valet who had become the best friend he'd ever had, brought out pieces of jewelry he had not worn in so very long. Not since weeks before he'd broken both his legs on that faraway battlefield.

Gently Sem took one thin arm, then the other, sliding bracelets onto the Pharaoh's wrists and a ring onto his finger. Tut paused as he felt Semerkhet slipping the jewelry on. Because… it felt so heavy. So much heavier than last time he had worn it. And… looking down at his hand, at his wrists, Tut could see that the ring, the bracelets, no longer fit properly. The ring fit loosely on his slender finger, as though it was about to slide off, and when he lifted his arms, with a little difficulty with the weight of the bracelets, the blue-and-gold cuffs seemed too big. They, too, hung loosely on his bony wrists, encircling his stick-thin forearms. It was as if they had been made for another person.

Tut looked down at his gaunt, wasted hands with a shudder. Slowly he moved each finger, watching them move. They were his, attached to his arms as they always had been, but they were no longer recognizable as *his* hands. They were as thin and frail as the hands of the oldest grandfather. As skeletal… He shuddered again. As skeletal as the fleshless hands of a mummy.

He shook his head. The life he had hoped for had been stolen from him. And his body... his body was no longer the one that had belonged to him for the past nineteen years.

Bracelets and ring in place, Semerkhet carefully settled a pectoral necklace over Tut's chest and shoulders as he sat there in bed, propped up on soft pillows.

Suddenly the Pharaoh felt as though he was trapped under a millstone; the necklace was compressing his lungs and weighing him down, pressing him into the bed.

"Take— take it off—" he coughed, gesturing with his thin hands. "Too— too much." Quickly, Sem removed the necklace, and Tut gasped, feeling his lungs fill with air again as the terrible weight was lifted.

"I'm sorry," the valet said quickly, hurriedly setting the necklace aside. "Are you all right?"

"Be fine," Tut whispered, pressing his hand to his chest as his heart pounded in fear and confusion. "Just too... too heavy."

Semerkhet nodded with a concerned frown. "Do you want... do you want your crown?"

The Pharaoh considered. And finally he nodded. He would probably never wear it again. "One... one more time."

Solemnly, Semerkhet went and got the heavy, red-and-white double crown, symbol of the unity of Egypt, holding it carefully in both hands. But as he held it out, ready to carefully place it on Tut's head, the King shook his head. He knew that the moment it touched him, he would collapse under its weight. "Maybe... maybe not," he said with a sigh. "My circlet might look nice, though."

Carefully Semerkhet put away the double crown and the heavy pectoral necklace. And he came back with the small, simple circlet with its tiny golden *uraeus*. Gently, he set it on the Pharaoh's head, taking a moment to brush the tiny braids of Tut's favorite wig out of his eyes.

"Do you want your makeup done?" Sem asked as he stepped back, satisfied with his work.

Tut smiled, giving his friend a nod. "I think I would. Thank you, Sem." And he closed his eyes as Semerkhet traced his eyes with kohl and painted his lids with blue-green paint. Just like old times.

And just like old times, Sem handed him his mirror to check out the finished look.

And Tutankhamun smiled. He looked like a Pharaoh.

When the Pharaoh was ready, Queen Ankhesenamun stood, heart pounding, as Ay was formally welcomed into the Pharaoh's chamber. Two days had passed since Meresankh's Granny Merneith had agreed to help them.

"Vizier, the Queen and Lady Merneith have a special announcement," Tut said stiffly. Although with as much of a smile as he could manage. They were announcing a joyous event, after all. And of course, for such an occasion, he had had Semerkhet and Raherka transfer him into his chair.

Merneith stepped forward, a little clay pot in her wrinkled old hands.

"I wish to announce the conception of a son by the Queen and the Pharaoh," the old midwife said with a smile. "As you can see, the barley has sprouted after being watered with the Queen's fluids. The heir to the throne should be born in the next Season of Inundation."

For a moment even Ay was speechless. He just stared at them, a completely blank look on his wrinkled face. Tut smiled as he watched the Vizier witness his own defeat.

Carefully the Queen watched the old midwife as she delivered the news. She could see the lie, but only just. Merneith was good.

"Barley," the Vizier repeated slowly, pushing the word out of his mouth as if it were sour. "For a son. How wonderful... how absolutely wonderful." He pursed his lips, his nostrils flaring, old hand clutching his cane as he processed what he was hearing. "My congratulations," he continued, his voice barely rising above a murmur. "My congratulations."

Ankh rested her hands on her flat belly and tried to glow. Her purple outer robe concealed its flatness; seemed to give the impression of a nonexistent curve. And Tut reached out and took her hand, willing happy tears to shimmer in his eyes. If only. Although... maybe.

The Grand Vizier looked down at the Queen's belly with an ugly sneer. "I cannot even begin to express the joy that fills my heart to hear this announcement," he said in a tone of poorly-disguised disgust. He gave a little bow. "My congratulations."

And he excused himself, with an insincere wish for the royal family's long life, health, and prosperity.

"Thank you, Granny," Ankh whispered as the old healer put away the sprouting pot. "Do you think he believed us?"

Merneith shook her head. "Who can say, dearie?" Then she gave a wise old chuckle. "Don't think that you're the first ones to ask me to fake a pregnancy test." She lowered her voice to a whisper. "Midwives keep lots of secrets."

"I'm just glad that Kemsit was willing to pee on the seeds for us," the Queen said with a little chuckle of her own. Then she

10

sighed, face falling slightly. "And I hope she and her husband are happy."

With a nod, Merneith excused herself, the righteous, lying midwife just like Shiprah and Puah back in the days of the Hebrew Prince.

Tut gave a heavy sigh, lying back in his chair. All this was getting tiring.

"I wonder if it is a boy or a girl," he mused. Then he smiled. "But if it really does happen… we've told the truth either way. The heir to the throne will be born next Inundation." And his wife squeezed his hand as together they pledged that boy or girl, their child would succeed his or her father as Pharaoh.

Then he sighed again. "Do you think that will be enough?" he asked. Slowly he took off the heavy bracelets and ungainly ring, then his circlet, handing them to Semerkhet to be put away again. Even wearing them for that length of time was enough.

Ankhesenamun shrugged. "Well, if I am pregnant, our prayers have been answered. If not… either Zannanza will get here in time for… me to try again… or, if I have to…" She sighed, clenching her hands as memories ached in her heart. "I will tell them that another royal child has left this world."

Tutankhamun reached out and took her hand. He didn't want her to have to tell a story about a heartbreak she had endured for real… twice. But he knew that if she had to, she would. She was brave. And she was strong.


"Usermontu will be excited," Tut said a moment later. "He loves babies."

His sister smiled. "Yes, he will. He's such a sweet old grandpa."

"I hope he gets back from Thebes soon," he said. "I can't wait to tell him."

Meresankh was formal today, the Queen thought. Prim and proper, she bowed every time she came or went, stiffly addressing Ankh as *Your Majesty* and carefully avoiding eye contact.

She knew why. Ankh had been mulling it over, comparing the results of the mission she had sent Meresankh on with her reaction. And she knew… she knew she had gone too far. She knew that on the day that she and the Pharaoh had gone out into Memphis, they had barely scratched the surface of the enormous city. How could she reasonably demand for two servants to comb the entire city and locate one child; a child about whom they had absolutely no information?

"Meresankh?" she said. The handmaiden looked up from stiffly rearranging wigs on their stands.

"Yes, Your Majesty?" she asked, keeping her eyes carefully lowered.

Ankhesenamun walked over to her. And she offered her hand.

"Meresankh," she said softly. "I'm sorry. I'm sorry I overreacted yesterday. It wasn't reasonable of me to expect you to be able to find one specific person in one of the largest cities in Egypt. I *was* asking the impossible. You and Hannu did your best. You blessed four children with shawls and sandals, and those apples and loaves of bread fed even more children; children who got to go to sleep with full stomachs for once. Your mission was a success."

Meresankh looked up. And she smiled. Slowly, she took the Queen's hand.

"Thank you," she said. She sighed. "I am sorry we didn't find her. But I suppose that means… we can do the same thing again next week."

Ankh smiled. "And the week after that… and the week after that."

The King and Queen thought about Usermontu all day; how delighted he would be to hear their news. Maybe their parents were no longer here, but in Vizier Usermontu, their baby would find a grandfather.

That afternoon, the priests returned from their visit to Thebes. But Amenmose, who had joined their trip to deliver the Pharaoh's letter to Usermontu, was not among them. Instead, another letter had come from Ay's secretary, who had also joined the delegation. A letter that told the Pharaoh and the Queen that both Vizier Usermontu and Amenmose had died of… overnight ague.

Ankh sat with her brother's head in her lap, his hand held tightly in hers, her tiny, delicate fingers laced with his. The letter from Thebes lay on the table. Usermontu could not help them.

They were running out of options.

"What else can we do?" Tut whispered into the hollow silence of dwindling options. "Other than letting Sem kill him? But if we did that, we'd all be dead an hour later. Too many people are loyal to him. But what else is there?"

"Regency, maybe," she said. "Between you and me, or between…" She chuckled. "And there's always the Prince."

The Pharaoh nodded. She was right. Their options were growing slimmer by the moment, but all was not lost.

All they could do was hope that Usermontu and Amenmose had died painlessly. But they knew that they would never learn the truth.

Ankh shifted where she sat on the bed, her brother's head in her lap. Her breasts were still sore. And now she was crampy, as she had been about three weeks ago. Three weeks ago had made sense. But now…

The Queen looked down at her belly. And wondered.

And then the tears began to flow.

## 2    Justice

Ankh was crying. Tut opened his eyes and saw his wife sobbing as she cradled him in her lap, her strong arms warm and soft around him.

"Can we win this game?" she whispered through her tears. "This horrible game of thrones? This is just like the days before Father died. All this maneuvering. All this cruelty. Every time we make a move, they make a stronger one. And even I don't know what will happen next."

Tut tried to smile. "But we have the last move in this game. You will marry the Prince and save Egypt from him." He gave a breathy little chuckle, extending a thin, shaking hand for her to take. For once, he could be the one to encourage his sister. "What do you always say..." he whispered, "that life is about what is... what you can change, and what you can't, and dealing with it all..."

She nodded, tears slowly rolling down her pretty brown face.

He sighed, giving her another half a smile. "That's what we're doing. And that's what we'll keep doing... until the end."

"Could we make me your co-regent?" the Queen asked, taking his hand and lacing her fingers with his. "I know we've talked about it before, but could we? Could we argue that under... under the circumstances, it's necessary?"

"You tell me," Tutankhamun said, and in his words, there was no sarcasm. Only an honest question for the greatest politician he knew. "What... what would we need to do to make that happen? Prepare a proclamation... thign it and theal it... and then what?"

Ankh looked down at their hands, entwined on the edge of the bed. "And then... we make the announcement. And the Vizier steals it or rewrites it, and I write another one and another one, and we fight until the funeral, and if he still hasn't found a way around me by then, he'll get rid of me." She laid her hand on her stomach. "Of us." The Queen shook her head. "I know I could. That's not the question. The question is… can I evade, push back, and escape everyone who wants to stop me for long enough to establish myself? The Vizier and his followers won't fight fair. And I'm not sure that murdering everyone who stands in my way is the best strategy."

The King sighed. And he knew that despite everything, despite his wife's courage, strength, and bravery and the wisdom and compassion with which she would continue to lead their country, the answer was *no*.


"They killed Usermontu," Ankhesenamun said simply, sitting down in her favorite chair in her own room. "The only one who still supported us."

Meresankh set down the stack of freshly-laundered sleeping-tunics and hurried over. Without thinking, she held out her hands, and the Queen took them gratefully. She did not seem to notice either— that this was something neither of them could have imagined doing a year ago.

Was there anything to say? Meresankh just shook her head sadly, placing sympathy on her face as within her heart, she asked I-AM how she could help her friend. Together, they sighed.

Then the handmaiden gave a little smile as a bit of inspiration touched her heart. She knew what to say.

"Remember your grandmothers," she said softly, smiling at Ankhesenamun. "Remember Tetisheri, remember Neith-hotep. Remember… remember Merneith. Both of them." They shared a

16

chuckle. Meresankh squeezed the Queen's hands, continuing even as tears began to gleam in her friend's eyes. "They came through things just like this. Men who tried to corner them; tried to limit them. Enemies who went after their families, tried to take Egypt for themselves.

"But they got through," she said, her voice breaking as she felt tears come to her eyes. "They did whatever it took to keep Egypt in one piece, to pull it through, whoever was against them. And with what you've learned from them... you know what to do. You know... you know more than any Queen before you."

Ankh was crying now, tears welling in her eyes and rolling slowly down her cheeks, taking her makeup with them.

"So what am I to do?" she asked, her voice broken.

Meresankh shook her head, blinking away her own tears. She wouldn't let go of the Queen's hands to wipe them away. "Endure," she whispered. "Have courage. Remember what you know. Be courageous and cunning, civil and sneaky, sweet and deadly. Be... everything you've taught me how to be. And remember what you've been through before. Things..."

Meresankh swallowed, asking in silent prayer what to say next. "Things that would kill someone else. But they haven't killed you," she said, taking the Queen's forearms as Ankh bent forward, sobbing. Meresankh fought back her own sobs. "They haven't. And they won't. You know they won't. Nothing... nothing could be worse than what you've already been through. Nothing. You've lost loved ones before... and made it through. You have... you have your little girls in your heart, and your sisters, and your parents, and the Pharaoh will be there too." Meresankh swallowed. "They say... they say what doesn't kill you makes you stronger. And that makes you the strongest Queen Egypt has ever seen."

The Queen didn't look up. She shook with sobs, threatening to fall out of the chair as Meresankh struggled to keep her upright with the supportive hold on her forearms. Finally Meresankh got her arms around her, holding her tight. Ankhesenamun clung to her, her sobs becoming wails.

Meresankh didn't say anything else. Just held her, and prayed, and let her cry it out.

They could hear it from the next room. Tutankhamun and Semerkhet looked up from their game of *seega*, then back at each other. The Queen was wailing.

They shared a sigh. And then they put the game aside. They didn't really feel like playing any longer.

"He was a good man," Semerkhet said hollowly.

Tut looked up from silently petting the cat as he stared into space, mind and heart aching with pleasant memories of the kind old man.

"Yes… yes, he was," he said softly.

Semerkhet gave a heavy sigh, a pensive gleam shining in his eyes. "I'm sorry," he said.

The Pharaoh nodded. "So am I."

When there were no more tears, no more clean handkerchiefs, and the peppermint tea was completely exhausted, Ankh looked up at her friend. Or tried to. Her eyes were so puffy she could hardly look at anything. And her nose was sore and raw from blowing it so much.

"Thank you," she whispered in a broken voice. Sitting here in her chair, she was shorter than Meresankh. But not by much.

Meresankh just nodded. "You're welcome, My Lady."

And she came in for another hug.

Meresankh noticed a change. Walking down the hall to or from an errand, she saw that the rest of the staff seemed to have divided into camps, whispering together in consistent little groups. And she saw that half of them bowed to Semerkhet when the Sole Companion walked by... and the other half bowed to the Grand Vizier and his son.

Was civil war brewing in the palace staff?

Semerkhet noticed it too. And although he wasn't offended that half of them weren't bowing to him anymore, far from it, he was disturbed by the change. What did it mean for the future of Egypt?

But he could see that Raherka was in their camp. And so were Khenut and Rahonem and Nuya. They were faithful to his Master; to the future of Egypt. And he knew that they could be trusted.

As he had since the Pharaoh's injury, the Vizier continued to send daily reports of his activities; reports that Tut did not know whether or not to trust— although he hoped that he still had Ay cornered. But with his own signet-ring, he approved transactions and agreements, the administration that a Grand Vizier was supposed to conduct for a Pharaoh. And life went on.

Meresankh and Hannu, the Queen's faithful handmaiden and the Pharaoh's loyal bodyguard, went out on another mission into town. And they kept their eyes peeled for the blue-and-purple shawl that would help them find the little girl the Queen was looking for. They sifted through a sea of white and tan adorned with occasional bursts of red or green or gold; a scarf, a piece of jewelry. But no blue-and-purple shawl.

Suddenly, Meresankh's heart jumped into her mouth. There it was, fluttering around a corner. The only blue-and-purple shawl she had seen all week.

"Hello, little girl!" she called, trying to get the child's attention. The tiny little girl stopped, looking up fearfully at the neatly-dressed handmaiden and the spear-bearing bodyguard. "It's all right," Meresankh said softly, bending down and holding out her hand. The little girl stepped forward cautiously, finally offering hers for a brief clasp.

But she... she was much too small to be the child the Queen had described. This child could scarcely be older than four, and they were looking for an eight-year-old.

"Where... where did you get that shawl, sweetheart?" Meresankh asked gently.

"N... Nefertiti gave it to me," the little girl stammered, backing away and pulling the warm shawl closer as if she was afraid that this courtly personage was about to accuse her of having stolen it.

Nefertiti? Was that the name of the little girl Meresankh's Mistress was searching for? How perfect, that this beautiful little girl should be named after her Lady's mother.

"What's your name?" Meresankh asked.

"Iset," she replied, huddling into the shawl as if it were armor. Her eyes flickered back and forth as they spoke, and she did not meet Meresankh's eyes. She dug the toes of one dirty little foot into the ground, poised to fly in a heartbeat. The other dirty little foot was wrapped very neatly in a linen bandage. So neatly, in fact, that its presence seemed inconsistent with the rest of her appearance— if a homeless child had access to such professional medical care, why had she remained homeless?

Meresankh was curious. But she put the question away for later.

"Iset," she said. "Nice to meet you. I'm Meresankh," she said, "and this is Hannu." The guard leaned on his spear like a staff, giving the little girl a smile and a friendly wave. "Do you... do you know where Nefertiti lives?"

"By the weavers," the tiny little girl said, still avoiding eye contact. She looked a little less anxious, but still suspicious; still ready to run if either of them made a false move. "She... she put the bandage on my foot. And Ineni's hand when he burned it making jewelry."

So they were searching for a little doctor. "Thank you, Iset," Meresankh said. She reached into her bag, pulling out a small loaf of bread. "This is for you."

Iset stared, as if not convinced that this stately person really meant to offer her a meal. But silently, Meresankh continued holding it out until Iset snatched it up in her dirty little hand, hiding it under the shawl so they couldn't take it back. And without even a smile, she turned tail, pushed off with her tiny little foot, and disappeared into the crowd, the heavy shawl billowing behind her.

Meresankh watched her go with a sigh. How sad that she was still afraid of them. That life had built such a wall around her heart, protecting her from the dangerous world she lived in. How sad that they had not been able to make her feel safe.

But they had given her a meal. And now, they had some information; information that would help them locate the other little girl the Queen wanted to find.

Tut rolled back and forth in bed during the long afternoon, heart aching. So many thoughts filled his heart, his mind; thoughts of pain, thoughts of fear, thoughts of anger. He punched his pillow into shape, giving an angry sigh.

His sister got up from her chair, coming to sit beside him. She didn't say "What is it?" She just rested her cool hand on his feverish cheek with a questioning little frown.

The Pharaoh sighed again. "What can we do?" he asked into the stubborn silence of the gods.

She shook her head, loving concern creasing her forehead. "You know," she whispered.

He nodded. "Endure. Change what we can and get through what we can't. I know. But it's not good enough. It's not good enough, Ankh!" Tut slammed his fist down onto his pillow, feeling it bounce as the pillow released a puff of dust. "It's what you always tell me, and it's right, I know it's right, but it's not enough... how am I supposed to accept this? Why is it right for me to accept this? I don't want the courage to accept the things I can't change; I want to be strong enough to change them!

"None of this ever should have happened, Ankh," he said, his voice softening into a tear-filled whisper. "None of it. Our parents... our sisters... our children... the war... our friends... none of this. Not even... not even my feet, Meritaten's feet. None of it."

He swallowed back his tears, wiping them away with his hand. "Why?" he whispered plaintively. Then, "Why?" loudly, insistently. He pushed the pillow onto the floor, rolling himself painfully onto his other side and hiding his face in the crook of his arm. His free hand clutched his blanket, knuckles showing white as if by strangling the blanket, he could change everything. And his body shook as he poured out the angry tears.

22

"You're right," his sister said, and he heard her beads tinkle as she shook her head. "It's not good enough." She swallowed. "So what... what else can we say?"

Tut released a heavy sigh, wiping his eyes again. "You tell me," he whispered. "I have nothing. Nothing."

Ankhesenamun shook her head as she bent to pick up the pillow. And she searched through a thousand years of history for the wisdom she and her brother needed.

Then she had it. And she gave a little smile. "There is... there is always something you can change," she whispered, slipping the pillow under his head again. "No matter what. Even... even if it seems small." The Queen chuckled. "Remember the ripples?"

Tutankhamun rolled back over with a wince and gave his sister half a smile. But then it faded. "But what about the past?" he asked softly. "I know... I know we'll have an impact on the future, but what about the past? That's what needs to change."

He found his words rising in volume again, his voice harsh and raw. "It's not fair— it's... it's wrong! All wrong! And it'll never be right until we fix it... and there's no way to fix it, but it seems like if we accept it, we're not fixing it even more. It's my goal... fixing everything for everyone... all the way back to the beginning... but there's no strategy that will get me there. The way things are will never be enough. And I will never be able to do enough."

Ankh considered the brick wall her brother had introduced into the debate. And she looked down into her empty arms. And pain filled her heart. And anger. Even at her brother, for forgetting her pain. She looked at him, unshed tears shining in her eyes.

"Do you think there has ever been a day when I didn't want to go back in time?" she whispered harshly. "Do you think you're the only one whose heart has ever broken? The only one who was ever hurt by things outside their control? The only one…" She blinked back the tears. "Who wonders every day how things might have been?"

Guilt filled his heart as the same pain… and the pain he felt for her… filled his own heart. He reached for her hand, and she let him take it. "I'm sorry," he said softly.

She squeezed his hand until her nails dug into it, then let it go. And she looked at him.

"I know you're hurting," she said softly. "So am I. So we have to count our blessings."

"Is that the answer?" he asked, giving her almost half a little smile.

"That someone else always knows how you feel?" she asked. "That there's always something to be grateful for?" She bit her lip as another truth rose in her heart, but she kept it inside. The truth that someone else always had it worse, and that no matter what, things could be worse. Those statements were true. But right now, they were neither kind nor necessary. Slowly, she nodded. "Yes, love. That is the answer."

Tutankhamun sighed. It was the answer. But what kind of answer was that? It didn't give him the power to change things, fix the past, make things the way he knew they always should have been. All it did was remind him of what he already knew… that he wasn't alone. And that he had a lot to be grateful for.

It wasn't the answer he wanted. But it would help.

# 3    Faithfulness

Ankh sat with her brother hour upon hour, stroking his head, watching over him as he ate a snack or drank a cup of tea, adjusting blankets and pillows to maximize the comfort that was becoming so elusive.

"I always liked Horemheb," he said as she sat with him around lunchtime, handing him a bowl of yogurt. How many weeks had it been? Four since he'd gotten home. Over one long month since he had been able to do so much as walk across his room. The month of Tybi had begun, each day shorter than the last. Soon, it would pass into Meshir, the darkest month of the year.

"So did I," she said. "For a soldier."

"He does tend to be serious," Tut agreed, taking a bite of yogurt. "Classic soldier." He sighed, looking back into the good old times that now only existed in memory. The time before all this. "But he could always be fun, too, when the time was right. And I could always trust him. There are secrets I've told him that I know he'll take to his grave." Tut shook his head. "He was the one who taught me to hunt, taught me to fight, all the way back to when I was twelve, thirteen. He made me a soldier. And I would have hoped…" He bit his lip. "That would have mattered."

"He failed us," Ankh agreed, shaking her head so the blue beads of her wig jingled. "Ay got to him."

"He was my Crown Prince, until and unless," the Pharaoh said, "tho he knew he was high on the list of being in line for the throne. But I thought it was working. I thought I was gaining credibility in his eyes; that he was starting to see that my peace strategy had worked and that maybe I knew what I was doing. But I fink I would have had to have gotten to him earlier. Or been older." He swallowed. "I just think... if I'd gotten Horemheb on my side before it was too late, I would have been safe. And Pentu and User-montu and Amenmose would have been thafe." A lump came to his throat. "I trusted him. Why didn't he wait; see if maybe he'd become my heir anyway? What did I ever do... that was worth killing me over?"

His sister took his hand, looking down at it as she slowly moved her thumb back and forth over his prominent knuckles.

"He wants power," she said slowly. "But at the same time, he wants to execute someone else's vision. And Ay got to him first. He knew Ay longer, and so he took him more seriously. And... he thought the Vizier was a stronger leader, because he wanted to take over lands that have never been part of Egypt, instead of focusing on being friends with our neighbors and improving human rights, education, and the economy right here at home. His... his priorities lined up with the Vizier's better than with yours. And the desire to stretch the borders of Egypt from Nubia to Babylon was too much for him."

The Pharaoh just sighed, looking down into the almost-empty bowl of yogurt and stirring what was left. As a politician, Ankh deeply understood the plan that Ay himself had revealed to Tutankhamun on the day Tut had told the Vizier he knew everything.

"And I..." he said in a choked voice, gripping the handle of the spoon until his knuckles turned white, "I had to die before I had an heir of my own. Before we had a son, or before... before I chose a second wife."

His sister didn't say anything. Just silently brushed the braids of his wig out of his eyes.

"What will you say to him when he gets back?" Ankh asked a moment later.

He sighed as he took the last bite of yogurt. "If I tell everyone that I know about the plot, I can have Ay, Horemheb, and Maya all banished or executed if I want. But that would only throw the whole country into even more chaos." He shook his head. "And I'll probably be dead before I'll see any of the benefits of getting rid of their corruption."

Ankh swallowed back the lump in her throat. "So what will you say?" she asked. "Knowing the General betrayed you— knowing Ay has promised the next throne to both Horemheb and Nakhtmin— knowing Ay and Horemheb made their move so you wouldn't have an heir of your own— knowing Horemheb believed in the Vizier more than he believed in you; believes in gold and conquest more than in creating a future of peace and prosperity?"

"I'll tell Horemheb I know everything," Tut said with a yawn, handing her the empty bowl and lying back in the bed. Sitting up to eat yogurt was exhausting. And almost without his noticing it, his lisp had taken over. "He knowth I know everything; he knowth I thaw him blow the trumpet. But I know he'll be thorry for everything when I tell him I know, and that he'll be a good perthon to have on our thide… keep Ay and Maya from juth slitting my throat. He might even be worthy of being Pharaoh someday after all. But it only workth…" Tut bit his lip. "It only workth if I'm still alive when he gets back."

Ankh closed her eyes. "Or it will be between me and Ay," she finished for him. "With or without the Prince."

Tut nodded, remembering his prior conversation with the Vizier. "If I'm gone before Horemheb gets back, the Vithier will make his move, even if you thend the letter to the Hittites. And if thomehow, Ay gets the throne, I don't fink Horemheb will fight him for it. He'll wait. Ay doethn't have many yearth ahead of him. But…" he continued, fighting back another yawn, "you and Thannantha are my heir. Not Horemheb. And I'll make that clear to the Vithier… if it really is the last thing I do." Tut blinked his sleepy eyes, struggling to keep them open. "Would you be willing to deal with Horemheb as Vithier when you become Pharaoh?"

He sighed and closed his eyes, relaxing into the pillows. Long conversations were tiring. And he was due for a nap. What time was it anyway? Early afternoon, he thought. Not that it mattered. He was getting too sleepy to think. But Ankh was there. That made everything all right.

Without a word, Ankh lay down next to him on the bed, taking him in her arms, letting him rest his head on her chest. Tut sighed, feeling himself supported by her small strength, encircled by her protective arms. She was every woman in his life, wife, sister, and sometimes mother. She was all he needed.

She was proud of herself, Ankh thought as he snored in her arms. And of her brother. Together, they had considered what still needed to be done to keep their country safe from the snakes that wanted to take it from them. Just like a King and Queen should.

But even as she held him in her arms, feeling his bones more clearly than even last week, she felt that he was slipping away from her. And that even with all her love, she would not be able to hang onto him forever.

Then she thought of what he had said. Horemheb as Vizier? It was a clever move, offering the General a reward he would not wish to refuse in exchange for his loyalty to Tut's memory and to the Queen.

28

When the time came, she would consider it.

"What will we do when we find her?" Ankh asked after her brother woke up from his nap.

Tut looked at his sister with a confused frown. "When we find who?" he said.

"The little girl," she said with a little sigh and a little smile. "Will we… or will I… could I adopt her?"

Tut reached out and placed his hand over his sister's. "You could," he said. "You really could."

She nodded, giving another little sigh. "I would love… I would love to," she said, her voice breaking. "I know she could help me if I became Pharaoh or married Zannanza; her inside knowledge of what it's like to live on the streets would help me create the best policies to fight poverty… but… with all the politics… all the danger… would that really be in her best interest, bringing her into this situation? Even if…" She touched her stomach, and her brother nodded. "Even this child will be born… right into the middle of an adventure. So as much as I would love to… I don't think that's the best way to help."

"So what would be best?" Tutankhamun asked.

The Queen paused. "Maybe… I can use the resources we've been blessed with to help her find her own way." She smiled. "When we find her, I'll ask her what she's good at and wants to be when she grows up. Then I can set her up with an apprenticeship. Even… even if she doesn't become mine, I can help her reach the future she wants for herself."

The Pharaoh smiled. And he nodded. "I think that sounds like a good plan."

A royal baby, Semerkhet thought. He was too shy to ask her any questions after bashfully congratulating her, but he kept an eye on the Queen, sneaking peeks at her belly, trying to see the curve growing as the baby got bigger. Nothing yet. Well, it wouldn't be born for another seven or eight months— it was still too small to see. Someday. Someday soon. And he promised himself that he would be the best uncle that had ever lived.

Granny was just as excited as Semerkhet was. About the hope that they had just revealed to the Vizier. And she promised Meresankh that she would take care of the Queen, just as she had hundreds of other mothers over five decades of midwifery. And together they prayed. And they waited.

Merneith was there for the Pharaoh, too. Her hands were old, and wrinkled, but they were sure and steady; hands that had delivered thousands of babies, welcoming them into new life. Faithfully she examined Tut's dying leg twice a day, cleaning it as necessary, wrapping it in fresh bandages, applying a new infection-fighting poultice, and returning it to its splint. These days it just lay there attached to him, itching, burning, and twinging with pain, barely a part of him anymore. He could hardly even move it. But he knew that even if Merneith could not cure him, she would provide the full measure of care… until the end.

And then the Queen realized something. She knew how Meryt felt, with two beautiful daughters who could not carry on their father's name. Her own mother had been Pharaoh, of course, but that had been made possible by Nefertiti's long co-regency with Akhenaten. Between Ankh and Tut, such a co-regency would make no difference, as no one who mattered would honor it. And without the support of Usermontu or Pentu, they would find it difficult, if not impossible, to change the law and make a daughter their heir. Even if they signed and sealed such a proclamation now, by the time those nine months had passed, Tut would be dead and buried, and the Queen knew that Ay would not honor his wishes.

And so, for her dynasty to go on, Ankh had to bear a son. She would love a third daughter with all her heart, and raise her up into the strong leader her mother already knew she could be, but only a son had even a chance of becoming his dead father's heir.

Tut wanted to get up. He thought about it every half-hour or so, and he would sit up in bed, stretching his arms and neck as he tried to get up the gumption to ask to be put in his chair.

Each time, he would be just about to ask; the request on his very lips. But then the pain, the weakness, would push him back down, making him settle back down under his blankets for a few more minutes, too tired and weak to make the effort just now.

Each time, he would be sure that this time, he would do it. But each time, he found himself forced to give up.

Ankh sat beside her brother as he drowsed, the cat curled up at his side. And as she had so many hundreds and thousands of times, she rested her hands on her belly. And wondered.

And prayed.

*Give us an heir. Bless us with a son. And bless him with health.*

But the only response was the familiar silence. And the questions that grew larger every day, just as she hoped the heir to the throne of Egypt was doing.

"My Lady?"

Ankh looked up, her hands still on her belly. And she smiled to see her friend Meresankh, coming into the room with a cup of tea.

"Hello, Meresankh." Smiling, her handmaiden approached, offering the tea.

"This is from Merneith," she said softly. "Another blend. It's good for mothers and babies."

The Queen returned the smile, accepting the tea. "Thank you, Meresankh," she said softly. "And thank Granny for me."

"I will, My Lady." And with a bow, she was gone, leaving the Queen to drink the tea that would strengthen both her and the child… if indeed, a tiny baby was growing bigger every day. She sipped the tea and wondered.

They waited all day, Ankh, Sem. Waited for Tut to ask to be put in his chair. The hours passed. But he didn't ask. He talked, chatted, even chuckled. He ate his meals. And he cuddled with his cat. And the day passed.

But he never asked.

"I miss Pentu," Tut said softly as he and Ankh played *seega*.

She made a move and nodded. "So do I."

"He was… he was another young politician," the Pharaoh said with a wistful sigh. "He knew that our ideas were good… and that age is no measure of wisdom." Tut smiled at his sister.

Ankhesenamun nodded. "Just like Meritaten," she said.

They looked down at the board, the unfinished game. And they both realized they didn't feel like playing any longer.

"Did you want to get up today?" Ankh asked a little later.

Tut's eyes brightened for a moment as he slowly sat up, beginning to push the bedclothes aside. And then he paused, shoulders seeming to sag. He sat as if in thought, then looked up at her with a sad, tired expression on his face. A look… of resignation.

"Not today," he said softly. And he lay back down and pulled the covers up to his chin.

The Queen felt uncertainty touch her heart as she turned away. *Not today…* He always wanted to get up. Always pushed himself to spend time in his chair, even just a few minutes. Even when she told him to stay in bed, to rest, to save his strength. He always made himself do it.

But not today. What… did that mean?

As Ankh clenched her hands, she wondered how many days they had left.

# 4    Loyalty

**A**nkh closed her eyes, trying to feel. Trying to feel the baby. And she thought of what its life would be like. A child who would call Zannanza *Father*. And who would never meet the Pharaoh who, as the brother of his mother, had been his uncle. Although Ankh knew that every time she looked into that child's eyes, Tut would be there.

She would tell her child Tut's story. Whether her brother was her child's uncle, or whether they had been blessed in the way they had hoped and she would carry him into the future in her womb, she would tell her son about the brave, compassionate young Pharaoh for whom he had been named. And in some way… Tut would never leave them. When she told his story, he would be there. And whenever she spoke her child's name, he would be there in the name of the son who was the image of his mother's brother, or the daughter who would remember, every time she heard her name, how much her uncle had loved her. As long as they remembered him, he would never really die.

But as she told the story to her child, she knew that her Hittite husband would be listening too. And again she wondered… if she would love him. And if he would be a good husband. The husband she had never had.

Everyone was working so hard to take care of the Pharaoh. But as one day blurred into the next, it could be hard to remember to be grateful.

"Why isn't his lunch here yet?" Ankh asked a little less sweetly than she meant to. Semerkhet popped up from his chair, bobbing his head respectfully as he headed out to the hallway.

"I'll go check," he said, and he was off with a wish for life, health, and prosperity.

The Queen rested her tired head on her hand. And she knew that Semerkhet would forgive her. He understood. After all, he was in exactly the same boat.

"So… you and Zannanza are my heirs," the Pharaoh said.

His sister looked up. And she took his hand.

"Yes, we are," she said.

"Tho," he said, "I thuppose… we should make it official. Becauth if there's one fing I've learned, it'th that juth thaying something won't make the Vithier honor it. We have to thign it and theal it."

The Queen nodded. "You're right," she said. Then she smiled. "Let's take care of that." Getting up, she brought him a piece of papyrus, a pen, and his signet-ring. And carefully, he dictated a royal proclamation.

"By order of the Pharaoh," he said, "Prince Zannanza of Hattusa and Queen Ankhesenamun of Egypt are declared as joint heirs to the throne of Egypt. Upon the death of Pharaoh Tutankhamun, they shall take their place as Pharaoh and Queen, ruling Egypt together."

Tutankhamun smiled at the proclamation, satisfied. Carefully, he pressed his signet-ring into the drop of wax his sister had applied. And when the ink dried, he asked his sister to hide the document until the time came to reveal it.

Every day, the Queen sent a little group of servants into town with gifts of food, clothing, sandals, blankets. Gifts for the children they encountered, the children who needed them, the little girl she still dreamed of and all the children like her. Gifts for the children whom she, through her rank as Queen, had the power, authority, and privilege to help. She knew that she herself had told her brother that distributing bread was not the way to address the root of poverty in their country. But that was true of adults; adults who would be much better served by being provided with the opportunity to work and earn a wage.

It did not apply to tiny children.

There was a knock at the door. Semerkhet got up from perusing a volume of history as he oversaw the catnap the Pharaoh was taking. Who could that be? Someone safe, he trusted; Minnefer wouldn't let anyone suspicious in. But whose visit was important enough for them to get as far as actually knocking on the royal bedroom door?

"Yes?" he asked shortly, opening the door. An older woman stood there, her eyes trained nervously on her feet. Had he looked like that, Sem wondered, during the first months he'd spent as the Pharaoh's valet; the months when he had been a servant rather than a friend?

"I… I just had a…" she stammered, struggling to formulate a coherent sentence as she hugged the folded blanket she was carrying in her arms.

"Can you come back later?" he interrupted. "The Pharaoh can't see anyone right now." Visibly withdrawing, she shuffled away with a wish for the Sole Companion's life, health, and prosperity, eyes still downcast. He watched her go, then closed the door behind her.

Fifteen minutes later, the Pharaoh woke up.

36

"Where's Satiah?" he asked. "She wath thuppothed to bring me the new blanket the royal weaverth just finished."

Semerkhet paused as his mind decoded the Pharaoh's words. And he hung his head. Shame, shame on him and his efforts to protect his little brother from all that was annoying in the world.

And gritting his teeth as he muttered, "She was actually just here," Semerkhet went to retrieve her. And apologize to her.

Ay still maintained the formality of bringing the Pharaoh a report each day of decisions to approve. But that meant that he was scared; that he knew that faithful servants were breathing down his neck wherever he went, and would report the slightest discrepancy between an official decision and its application to the King and Queen. So in general, he played it straight, not entering into open warfare with another attempt at deception.

It got harder for Tut to answer the questions and approve the different judgments. So his sister helped him, and when they had decided together, he made their judgment official with his signet-ring, stamping the Vizier's reports as the old man looked on, not always noticing a strange, hungry expression in his eyes, an expression that would suddenly disappear as Ay blinked, looking away. And the Pharaoh trusted that Ankh would use all her wisdom to guide Egypt in the right direction, just as she always had.

Semerkhet was grateful for Meresankh, for everything she did for them, for her cheerful smiles and kind questions that brought joy even amid the darkness, for the way that their visits always left him refreshed, ready to face the rest of the difficult day.

Sometimes… sometimes she would even rub his shoulders for a few minutes.

Now he knew why his Master enjoyed his massages so much. It struck him that he was the one giving a massage so much of the time that he had actually forgotten how good it felt. Now he remembered.

Meresankh watched the Queen carefully. And she brought her the herbal tea that Merneith made with herbs from her own garden; teas proven over generations to strengthen babies and their mothers. And she watched, and she prayed, and she waited. One day soon, they would be sure.

"So… how has everyone been?" the Queen asked. The long, weary day was not over, but she needed a short break; needed to clear her head with a short, sweet update from Meresankh on whatever her friend wanted to tell her about.

Meresankh poured her a cup of tea with a little smile. "Well," she said, "poor old Hori, you remember him, his gout's been playing up, and Persenet burned her hand in the kitchen a couple of days ago, but Granny and I have been taking good care of them. We made Hori some crocus extract, and we fixed up a honey-and-aloe poultice for Persenet. Aside from that, it's the usual; headaches, toothaches, backaches…" She shrugged with another little smile. "I like taking care of them. I like… knowing I'm making a difference."

Ankhesenamun took her hand, trying to put all of her gratitude into the small gesture. "More than you'll ever know."

Merneith and Meresankh continued to pray for Prince Zannanza. Prayed that the Lord of Light would bring him to Egypt safely. And prayed that he and the Queen would be the leaders their country needed.

Semerkhet sat with his Master hour by hour, reading to him, helping him take a sip of water or tea, humming old songs. Sometimes his Pharaoh would drift off, and he would have an hour of pain-free peace. That was all his valet wanted for him.

It was still so strange, though. For it to be normal to sit at the Pharaoh's side, holding his hand; to simply, casually reach out to comfortingly stroke his burning head. For all the boundaries of formality, all the rigid, royal propriety, to be gone. And to simply reach out and touch the best friend he cared about so much.

Tut closed his eyes. He hadn't been able to get out of bed today to sit in his chair. He had wanted to, and he had thought many times about trying… but something had stopped him. Something had told him that today, trying would only end in disaster and more broken bones.

He sighed. He knew what it meant. That he had gotten out of bed… for the very last time.

The Pharaoh reached out, beckoning to his sister. She got up from her chair, sitting beside him on the bed.

"Yes, love?"

"Hold me?" he whispered. She nodded with a smile, carefully lying down beside him so he could rest his head on her heart. "Not such a good day," he said.

"No?"

"No. I wanted to get up… but I don't fink… I just don't fink it'th a good idea. And I don't know… I don't know what that means."

"You could ask Merneith what she thinks," the Queen said. "Or maybe… maybe you just need someone else to help you. Who's been helping you, Kamose? Maybe you could ask Raherka, or even Neferkare; they're big and strong…"

Tut felt exhausted tears filling his eyes as his sister's helpful words washed over him. "I don't know," he sniffled. "And I don't— fank you, but— not helpful. You don't have to fix it. Juth… juth hold me."

She nodded. And silently, she held him close.


Again, Tut looked at his arms, his chest; looked at his face in the mirror.

And what he saw was bones. Sticking out, almost as if they were about to poke through his skin, a fragile framework that was all that was keeping his body together. He could count each rib; could identify the two separate bones of his forearms. Behind him, the prominences of his shoulderblades and vertebrae made it even more difficult than ever to get comfortable. Just looking at his hipbones frightened him.

*Weak*, he found himself thinking. *Pathetic*. His dream from so long ago came back to him; the dream in which the portrait of Grandfather Thutmose had come to life and called him a failure. And the words his ancestor had spoken rang in his heart. *Scrawny, pathetic Boy-King; feeble little cripple.*

He put the mirror aside, rolling onto his side and squeezing his eyes shut before the tears could fall.

*Who am I*, he asked himself. *Who is that?*

40

He thought of Ankh and Sem, his beloved sister and brother who faithfully cared for him; did everything they could to keep him comfortable. And he thought... he must scare them, this ugly, ghostly shadow of the young man he'd once been.

Because he scared himself.

The Pharaoh lay curled on his side that evening, ready to try to sleep. His sister sat down beside him, reaching out to gently touch his back.

And he tried to roll away from her. "No," he said softly. "Thank you."

Ankh pulled back in confusion, frowning down at her baby brother. "What? What's wrong?" She paused, trying to think what could possibly cause him to reject his favorite thing in the world. "Does it hurt?" she asked finally. "I'll be gentle. Just... just tell me what you need." She sighed. "Come on."

He looked up at her sadly. "It's not that," he said softly. "It's..." He held out his hands, thin and frail as those of the oldest grandfather. "Look at me, Ankh. I'm... I'm not me anymore. I'm this ugly... skeleton. And I don't..." He fought back tears. "Want you to touch me."

The Queen paused, tears filling her own eyes. Gently, she placed both hands on her brother's face, wiping away his tears with her thumbs. And he placed his hands, frail as they were, over hers.

"You..." she said gently, searching for the words, "you are the same as you always were. Who you really are. My..." She chuckled through her tears. "My little brother, who I love so much. And I... that person on the inside is the person that I love."

Tut sighed, blinking back his own tears. "I feel... I feel like this..." He gestured at the broken legs that lay motionless under the blanket, "is me. And I am this." He bit his lip, lowering his head and hiding his face. "B-broken."

Ankhesenamun shook her head, the golden beads of her wig murmuring a soft *no* as they jingled. "Look at me," she said gently, touching his chin with her soft, warm little hand. Slowly he raised his face to look at her, tears glimmering in his weary, shadowed eyes.

"You've always been more than your legs," she said softly. "Just like Meritaten." Softly, she laid a hand on his chest. "It's your mind… and your heart… that define you. Your choices. The way you treat people. The l… the legacy you leave behind. Not how fast you can get down to the wig-makers' workshop. You… who you really are, on the inside… aren't broken. And… inasmuch as the legs you have, the feet you have, do matter, they have made you a stronger person. It's like we said…" Again, she blinked back tears. "What doesn't kill us makes us stronger. And if what we've already come through together hasn't broken you, nothing ever will.

"But this…" She took his hand, looking down at the spidery fingers, the knobby wrist, "I would hold you and kiss you and cuddle you and rub your back if you really were a skeleton. I… I hope you know that." Gently, she squeezed his hand, running her thumb over his prominent knuckles. And carefully, so carefully, she reached out and ran her warm hand over each of his cold feet. He felt his heart warm as she touched them; the mismatched feet that she had always both loved and ignored. "I love you on the inside, and I love you on the outside. I love your heart and I love this, right here. All of you. I always have. And I always will."

Tutankhamun swallowed back more tears, looking gratefully at his sister. And as she wrapped her arms around him, lifting him and holding him to her heart, he accepted her love. This failing exterior… didn't matter. Truly didn't. Her love for him, his love for her, was what mattered. And that love would last forever.

And with a grateful sigh, he lay down again on his side, feeling her warm hands gently touch his back. Bones and all.

They established a new normal. Ankhesenamun and Semerkhet took it in turns to begin, sitting at Tut's side as evening fell. And they would stroke his head or rub his back as he did his best to drift off, their warm, loving hands making him feel safe and connected.

They guided him through the weary, restless nights, Nut's starry sky slowly turning above them as they hummed old songs— sometimes to the accompaniment of Semerkhet's lute— whispered funny riddles, told endless stories, trying to while away the hours as the three of them settled into a sort of weary tranquility. Letting him know with their hands, their voices, their presence, that he wasn't alone. As the night wore on they would switch back and forth every hour, one tapping the other on the shoulder as they crept away to steal a few minutes of rest. Hour by hour by hour. Sometimes when morning came, no one had slept at all.

As he suffered, Tut tried to focus on them, on these loved ones who were giving their all to make these days and nights as comfortable as possible. He was so loved. So incredibly loved. And he found it in his heart to be grateful.

Things had changed so much. Tut almost chuckled as he thought back to six months ago, when the process of Semerkhet putting him to bed consisted of nothing more than straightforwardly helping him with his shower, assisting him into his sleeping-tunic, and settling him into bed. It was simple, professional, mature, Semerkhet's help based mostly on what the Pharaoh strictly needed, with moments here and there of warm friendship. It was one adult helping another get ready for bed.

But now Tut felt like a little child again; the child who had been fussed over by sweet old Hetty back in the days, months, and years before being Pharaoh had meant anything more than occasionally wearing a tiny crown made specially to fit him, or ceremonially approving a piece of paperwork handed to him by the all-knowing Grand Vizier. The procedure was much more… juvenile now; significantly more juvenile than it had been since before his coronation. The nineteen-year-old could hardly have imagined before Kadesh how bedtime would have devolved back into bedtime stories, back rubs, and, yes, lullabies.

But that was what he needed right now. And he was grateful.

# 5    Politics

There was a knock on the door, just before lunchtime on the second day of Tybi. Confident that whoever stood on the other side had been approved by the bodyguard, Semerkhet went to answer it, and determine whether their visitor really needed a personal audience with the Pharaoh.

Nuya the scribe stood before him, looking rather chilly in the simple kilt that comprised the entirety of his uniform. "Your Excellency," he said, offering a bow. Semerkhet just tried to smile graciously.

"Yes, Nuya?"

Nuya looked down, shifting his weight uncomfortably. "Your Excellency," he said, "there's been a development." He swallowed. "The Grand Vizier has possession of the Pharaoh's signet-ring, and he's using it to sign proclamations of his own in the name of the Pharaoh. Proclamations that our Pharaoh would never have written."

Semerkhet closed his eyes. That snake. "Just a moment," he said. And leaving Nuya standing in the doorway, he hurried to the desk where the Pharaoh always kept his signet-ring, sorting through pens and sheets of papyri, hoping that at any moment, he would find the missing ring. He checked the nearby shelves. And he checked the floor. The ring was nowhere to be found.

Semerkhet returned to the doorway. "Come in, Nuya," he said.

"Presenting Nuya." Tutankhamun looked up from the story Meresankh was telling to see Semerkhet opening the door for the faithful scribe he had not seen in days. His heart immediately filled with anxious curiosity— he knew that Nuya would only have

45

come, and Semerkhet would only have admitted him, if there was something serious to report.

"What's going on?" the Pharaoh asked immediately, sitting up in bed as well as he could.

Nuya offered a deep bow to the Pharaoh and the Queen, then began. "Your Majesties, I heard the General, the Vizier's son, I mean, talking to the Treasurer about you signing a proclamation that if the Hittite Prince didn't get here before you... well... but even before the funeral, the Vizier would take back his regent duties until the Prince got here. I saw the declaration. Something like 'If the Pharaoh's chosen successor is not present when he takes his final breath, power will revert temporarily to the Grand Vizier until Pharaoh's designated heir arrives.' I know you wouldn't have signed any such thing, but he used your signet-ring, so it's as good as official."

The Pharaoh's heart jumped into his throat as his sister sat bolt upright in her chair. "He what?" Tut gasped.

"Is nothing beneath this man?" the Queen groaned. "Nothing?"

"But when did he take it?" the Pharaoh asked. "I'm alwayth here, and tho are you, or Sem."

His sister shook her head. And then she tapped her chin. "The last time he was in here... I remember him looking at it. And then..." She shook her head. "He sent his secretary, and Minnefer let him knock on the door. And the secretary said he'd been sent to check something; to double-check a date or a figure from the financial records for the new school. He must have taken it then." Ankh hung her head, resting her forehead in her hands. "And we didn't think anything of it."

Nuya swallowed, looking anxiously at the King. "What can we do, My Lord?"

46

Tutankhamun looked at his sister. And she smiled.

"What should we do?" he asked.

She tapped her chin again. "Let's see... we have to get the signet-ring back, but the Vizier knows we're on to him, and he'll be keeping an eye out for either me or Semerkhet sneaking into his office. So the two of us can't go after it."

The Queen paused. Tut knew she'd done it on purpose; left a space for him to use whatever mind-power he had left, to put that mind, that knowledge, that... that growing wisdom... to work.

She was wiser and more experienced, yes, but he was becoming a politician in his own right. He had learned a lot. And maybe... maybe he knew more than he thought he did.

He thought. And haltingly, he began to add to her plan as ideas pieced themselves together in his mind. "But we have to get it back... tho... what if we distracted the Vizier; maybe thent someone to talk to him while thomeone else goes in and gets it back. Maybe... could Granny help?"

"This sounds like a job for Amenia and Mutnedjmet," his sister said with a smile. "And Granny. Meresankh, will you do the honors? I'll receive the ladies in my sitting room."

"With pleasure, My Lady," the handmaiden said with a smile. And she was off.

"How'd I do?" Tut asked his sister.

She gave a little chuckle, reaching over to squeeze his hand. "You sound like a Pharaoh."

Tutankhamun lay back, closing his eyes. Another battle lay before them; another battle in the war against the Grand Vizier. Would they ever be able to defeat him? Would they ever be able just to stop him from destroying the Egypt they loved?

Although, whatever happened next, Tut could take pride in the plan he had just developed with no time to prepare, only the knowledge of what he had already learned. He was learning. And he was growing in wisdom. Figuring out how to apply lessons and concepts that had worked in previous situations to completely new scenarios.

He was becoming a wise Pharaoh.

Soon Ankhesenamun was waiting in her sitting room, having just put on a fresh, neat wig and diadem and slipped into a clean, unwrinkled gown. As she changed, she also consciously switched over from sister and wife to Queen. Because the Queen was what she needed to be right now.

A moment later, there was a knock at the door, and Meresankh came in, leading the two wives of Horemheb, dressed warmly in soft outer robes, Mutnedjmet's red, Amenia's yellow. They looked appreciatively around the Queen's room, then gave graceful, matching bows. Beside them, Granny's bent back bent even further as she also showed her respect to the Queen. And Meresankh locked the door, protecting the conversation they were about to have from any who might wish to listen in.

Ankh smiled at her friends. But before she gave them their instructions, she had to greet them, the sweet friends she had not seen for so long. And both found themselves being hugged by the Queen of Egypt.

"Oh, I've missed you," she whispered as she gave each of them a squeeze. "We were so delighted at the baskets you sent. So glad to know... that my friends are thinking of me." Both of Horemheb's wives looked slightly embarrassed at being hugged, but pleased at the same time.

"We think of you every day," Amenia said.

"And pray for you every night," Mutnedjmet added.

"How is the Pharaoh?" Amenia asked a moment later, face full of concern.

The Queen's face fell. And she reached out to take their hands. They just sighed. They knew what she meant.

"There's not much time," she said softly, and they bowed their heads. Then she gave half a smile. "Which is why we need your help."

Mutnedjmet looked at the Queen. "What can we do for you, Your Majesty?" she asked.

"You can help by being your sweet selves," Ankhesenamun said with a smile.

She paused. For their own safety, the less they knew, the better. "Someone... someone needs to be kept away from their office for awhile. It's just..." She smiled to herself. "Just politics."

"Who, My Lady?" Amenia asked.

Ankh sighed. "The Grand Vizier. All we need you to do is keep him talking. You don't have to say *yes*... I'm not ordering you as Queen; I'm asking you... as my friends." The Queen smiled at her friends; a smile full of hope. "Will you help us?"

"Of course, My Lady," Mutnedjmet said sincerely. "Anything."

"We could invite him to tea," Amenia suggested. "Tell him we're worried about our husband..." She took Mutnedjmet's hand, and the Queen could tell that that would be no deceit. "Tell him we want an official update on the campaign... and his status."

"Would tomorrow be all right?" Mutnedjmet asked the Queen.

Ankh nodded. "That shouldn't make much of a difference. Just tell us when you schedule it for... and do your best to keep him chatting for an hour or so." Then she paused. "And try to set it for halfway across the palace, if you can. There's… there's a secondary library, not far from the workshops, where the shoe-makers and wig-makers work."

"I'm not even sure I know where that is," Amenia said thought-fully, tapping her chin.

"Semerkhet made a map," the Queen said. She began shuffling through papyri to find it, then handed it to Amenia.

Amenia studied the map for a minute, then nodded. "So we're here…" she said, pointing. "Why don't we meet in the audience chamber across from the scribe department?"

"And if we run out of things to talk about, we can go see what the scribes are doing, and he can check their work for mistakes!" Mutnedjmet said with a chuckle.

Amenia nodded. "And if we do get lost, having to ask for di-rections will just make us even less suspicious! Or we could ask Rekhetre and Beket. They'll know. We'll get there one way or another!"

Ankh smiled. "Perfect. Thank you, ladies." She opened her arms again, and, looking a little surprised, they stepped toward her, allowing her to put one arm around each of them in a quick, one-armed hug. "Thank you for being my friends." Then she turned to Merneith, who was also wrapped warmly in a soft outer robe of dark blue. "You know what to do."

Granny gave a nod, a slow smile creeping over her old, lined face. "Meresankh told me." Then she winked. "No one ever suspects the Granny."

And they all chuckled.

The two wives smiled, again giving matching bows. Granny, too, bowed again.

And they were gone. The mission would take place tomorrow.

The Queen smiled as she watched her friends go. No matter what… even in a strange, terrible future in which she lost her crown and all her status; was thrown from the palace and became an anonymous citizen, they would be her friends. And they would do whatever they could to help her. Always.

Guilt filled the pit of Semerkhet's stomach as he crept over to the Pharaoh's bedside, hanging his head.

"I'm sorry, Morning Star," he whispered, looking down at his feet as he dug the toe of his sandal into the floor. "I should have known the Vizier's secretary was up to something; I should have paid more attention—"

The King shook his head, and Semerkhet fell silent.

"It'th all right," Tut said softly, gently shaking his head. "He wath careful. Careful enough to get past uth that one time. But that makes it my fault as well. And now… now we just know to be even more careful in the future. But Merneith will get the ring back. And we'll go back to thigning our own proclamations."

Semerkhet nodded with a grateful sigh. Maybe he wasn't a completely unforgivable failure.

Meresankh and Hannu searched the district where the weavers worked. As they searched, they offered apples or loaves of bread to any homeless child they saw, knowing that even if they didn't find her today, they had allowed a few children to go to bed with stomachs that were not empty.

Movement caught Meresankh's eye. And she looked up… and a warm whisper like the touch of the Sun told her that their search was over.

A little girl stood there, maybe about ten. Wrapped only in a tattered linen shift against the cold day, feet bare and dirty and scratched, face thin and smudged with dirt, wavy hair wild and tangled, eyes... large, catlike eyes haunted with a life no child should ever have to navigate alone.

There she was... the little girl the Queen had been looking for for so long. And now they finally knew her name.

"Nefertiti!" Meresankh called softly. Looking startled, the little girl looked up. And gently, Meresankh beckoned to her.

The day went on, and the Queen thought about what would be accomplished tomorrow. Felt her heart warm with pride at the politics in which her brother had participated with such wisdom, ill as he was. And prayed, to Whomever was listening, for tomorrow's mission to be blessed.

Then there was a knock at the door. "For you, My Lady," Semerkhet said a moment later. "Hannu."

Ankhesenamun got up and crossed to her brother's bedroom door. "Yes, Hannu?" she said with a little smile. The guard she'd sent into town with Meresankh in the hopes of finding the little girl she'd never stopped thinking of was standing in the hallway, a smile on his craggy face and a spring of joy in his usually-weary step. A smile and a lightness that made her wonder why he was so happy.

"My Lady," he said, his smile growing even brighter, "I have a report for you. The child you've been looking for... has been found. She's here. Waiting for you in your sitting room."

The Queen gasped, hands flying to her mouth as her heart began to pound. Giving a breathless smile to Tut and Semerkhet, she flew out the door, adjusting her wig as she hurried across the hall to her own suite.

She paused at the door, taking a deep breath, straightening her dress, trying to compose herself. Was she really about to meet the little girl she had been dreaming of for so long?

The Queen opened the door. And there she was, standing in the sitting room, the same tiny little girl Ankh and her brother had seen on that chilly day in Pharmouthi; the day they had ventured into town. She was taller than when they'd seen her that day; even thinner, if that was possible. All cleaned up, she had been given a warm robe and a pair of sandals, and her long, wavy hair had been neatly combed.

And she was here.

Fighting back tears, Ankhesenamun gently approached the child.

"Hello there, dear," she whispered, extending her hand. Solemnly, the child extended her own for a brief clasp, staring up at the Queen with the same wonder in her eyes as Ankh had seen on that day out in town. Those beautiful, catlike eyes that had haunted the Queen in her dreams ever since that day. "What's… what's your name?"

"N… Nefertiti, My Lady," the little girl whispered. "After Your Lady's mother."

Ankh blinked back more tears as she heard the name. Yes. It was so fitting. Her own mother's name belonging to this precious little girl. A beautiful woman had come. And a beautiful woman would grow up and change the world.

"Nefertiti," Ankh whispered in a choked voice. "I'm so glad to finally meet you…"

"I remember you, My Lady," the girl said with a little smile. "Thank you for the shawl."

The Queen nodded. "Oh, you're welcome; you're welcome. I wanted to do so much more…"

"But I would have been cold without it," Nefertiti said gratefully. "And it kept me warm… and now it's keeping Iset warm."

Ankh smiled, her heart warming as the tears filled her eyes. After so many months of longing to see this precious child once more, she was finally getting to meet her. Finally.

"Where do you live, Nefertiti?" she asked.

She sighed. "In a doorway, My Lady."

"And do you… do you have brothers and sisters?"

"I used to," Nefertiti said sadly. "But they died of the ague. Mommy died when my baby brother was born, and he died, too. And then Daddy didn't come home. They told me his boat flipped. Now I'm the only one left."

The only one left. The same situation the Queen herself was facing. She swallowed, finding the strength to smile down at the little girl.

"I want to help you… help you find a home," she said softly. "And a family."

"That's all I want, My Lady," Nefertiti whispered back. Tears sparkled in her eyes.

"You will have one," the Queen promised. "And you will be safe here." Then she smiled. "What do you want to be when you grow up?"

Nefertiti returned the smile. "A doctor, My Lady. I bandaged up Iset's foot for her when she stepped on a nail. And my friend Ineni's hand when he burned it pouring the gold for a necklace— he's going to be a goldsmith when he grows up, just like the great

Ranofer of Thebes. And I fix knees. Lots of knees, when my friends fall or get into fights... I... I like helping people."

The Queen nodded as she thought to herself. A sense of direction was warming her heart. And she knew whose apprentice Nefertiti should become.

"Hannu," she said, and the guard snapped to attention. "Please take Nefertiti down to Merneith. And tell her that our guest is in need of a good, hot meal."

"Yes, My Lady," he said, giving a bow. Ankhesenamun reached out to squeeze Little Nefertiti's hand, and, after offering her own bow, the child was gone.

The Queen wiped away tears, smudging her makeup, as the little girl walked away. Finally. Finally. After so many days of thinking of her, so many nights of dreaming of her, the little girl had been found.

And she would live a good life.

# 6    The Mission

Amenia and Mutnedjmet came back in the morning. And they told the King and Queen that their invitation had been accepted, and that they would be having tea with Ay that afternoon. The trap was set.

The hour came. And off they went, Mutnedjmet and Amenia; off to conduct their tactical assault. The battle was on.

They waited, Tutankhamun, Ankhesenamun, Semerkhet, Meresankh. Waited to see if this next move in the game would succeed; if they could parry this attack by the Vizier. The document he had prepared would allow him to take power the moment Tut took his final breath, and his next move would surely be to ensure that Prince Zannanza never arrived to claim his bride and carry the dynasty of Amenhotep and Thutmose into the next generation. But if they could get the proclamation, there was hope. Still hope.

"How do you think it'll go?" Tut asked into the tense silence.

Ankh blinked, coming out of her reverie. Then she gave half a smile. "I don't know... but they're clever. And they're sweet. I'm sure they'll keep him talking until Granny's done."

"And Granny..." Tut said.

The Queen chuckled as she thought of the tiny old woman. "Is so sweet and adorable that no one will ever even notice her sneaking in and out of the office. No one ever suspects the Granny," she said, remembering Merneith's own words.

"But she's the most dangerous of all," the Pharaoh said with a chuckle.

Ankhesenamun smiled. "Yes. She is."

Sem got out his lute and plucked out a plaintive old ballad while Tut and the Queen played *seega* and Meresankh played with the cat. No one spoke, but every time they heard a footstep in the hallway, they sat up straight, hearts leaping into their throats. But each time, it was only a servant walking by.

Finally, there was a knock at the door. And Semerkhet let Granny in, Granny, who was holding something within the folds of her warm outer robe.

"Your Majesties," she said, offering the document and signet-ring with a bow. Tut gave a heavy sigh of relief as he accepted the papyrus, looking down at it to see Ay's latest attempt at twisting the future to meet his ends. As Nuya had recounted, it outlined the way in which upon Tutankhamun's death, Ay would become King in all but name. With a nod, the Pharaoh put on his signet-ring. It was safest on his hand.

They smiled at one another, Tutankhamun, Ankhesenamun, Semerkhet, Meresankh, Merneith. And they reached out to clasp one another's hands, forming a circle. A circle of friends.

They shared another sigh, the five of them, a sigh that ended in a collective chuckle. That had been exhausting.

Then there was another knock at the door. And Amenia and Mutnedjmet stood there, matching smiles of satisfaction on their faces, as well as smiles of amazement at being in the Pharaoh's chambers.

"Did you do it?" Mutnedjmet whispered as they entered the room, Sem locking the door behind them. "The politics?"

"Yes," Tut whispered back with a smile, showing them the back of Ay's letter, which would remain anonymous, giving them only the general idea that the "politics" had involved confiscating a document. "All taken care of." They grinned, giving silent little claps of excitement. "Thank you," he said sincerely, making eye contact with Amenia, then Mutnedjmet. "Thank you."

The two looked at the Pharaoh. Really looked at him. And they smiled politely, bowing gracefully as they gave silent, sad sighs. They saw that the Queen had spoken the truth. There was not much time.

"How did it go?" Ankh asked with a little smile.

With another little sigh, Amenia smiled too, wrapping her yellow robe closer as a chilly breeze blew in through the window. "Pretty well," she said. "We got a good report on the campaign. Our husband..." She paused, face glowing with admiration as she clasped Mutnedjmet's hand. "Our husband is doing just fine. The Vizier told us," she said, glowing even brighter as she kept hold of Mutnedjmet's hand, "that victory has been won in Amurru, and Kadesh has been reclaimed for Egypt. The Mitanni and all the people of Amurru are safe, and so are our borders. The scout said he should be home on the seventeenth!"

Amenia squealed with delight, turning to Mutnedjmet and throwing her arms around her as they both gave a hop of excitement. Ankh and Meresankh laughed too, to see their sweet, simple joy.

"The seventeenth?" the Pharaoh asked from the bed. Blushing, the ladies stood at attention, their eyes lowered respectfully, as they remembered that they were in the Pharaoh's room. "That makes... what does that make?"

"Two more weeks, Great Morning Star," Semerkhet said. He, too, was standing at attention, the stiff, formal side of the Chief Valet resurfacing in the presence of the wives of General Horemheb.

58

Tut nodded. And he wondered... when Horemheb returned in another fortnight... would he be alive or dead?

Then Mutnedjmet took up the story. "And then after we had our tea, the Vizier found a lot of imperfections in the scribes' work. I think we could have kept him there all day!" Then she sighed, face shining like Amenia's. "Two more weeks."

"We can never thank you enough," Ankh said, holding out her hands. They clasped them, standing for a moment like three sisters, undivided by rank or position, united by purpose, loyalty, and friendship.

Then Amenia gave a curious smile. "I don't think I've met you," she said, extending her hand. Meresankh took it, dipping her head respectfully.

"I'm Meresankh, My Lady," she said politely. "And this is my granny, Merneith the midwife." Gracefully, the old woman inclined her head.

Horemheb's wife grinned. "So you're the best friend," she said, and Meresankh blushed. "The Queen is lucky to have someone like you."

Mutnedjmet nodded sincerely. "Absolutely. It's... it's good to know you're here. Even if... we can't do as much as we used to." Regretfully, she looked away, and the Queen knew that if things were different, the wife of the General would come visit her every day.

"I miss studying together," Amenia said wistfully. "We learned so much. And it's honestly changed things— how we see our-selves; how we see one another. And we've become so much more than we ever would have imagined."

"Nebet was my favorite on the Queens List," Mutnedjmet said. "The Vizier. And that's what it's all about. Being wise, and using your wisdom to help others. Being influential, even if you're not the Pharaoh." She smiled. "And we... we've been spending more time with our handmaidens, Rekhetre and Beket. And we've started telling them about what we've learned from you."

Ankh felt a catch in her throat. Already the ripples of her afternoons with her friends were spreading.

The cat stood up and stretched, padding down to the foot of the Pharaoh's bed to curl up in a pool of sunshine. And silently, Semerkhet poured a cup of tea for the Pharaoh, then for the Queen, Meresankh, and their guests.

There was a slight pause as they all sipped their tea. Meresankh glanced at the ladies' faces, then the Queen's. "The Queen and I have been studying too," she said. "I loved learning about Ahhotep the First. She kept Egypt in one piece... just like someone else I know." She smiled at the Queen, and Ankhesenamun reached out to take her hand. "I think it's kept us both strong," Meresankh said softly. "Remembering them." She swallowed, and together, she and the Queen remembered Ankhesenamun's moment of despair, and the strength that Meresankh had offered her in reminding her of those who had gone before. Meresankh smiled. "Because they got through. And so can we."

The ladies sighed, Mutnedjmet and Amenia looking away reflectively, Ankh and Meresankh silently squeezing one another's hands, Granny and her wisdom offering a concrete link to the matriarchs of the past, Tut and Semerkhet feeling two thousand years of strength like a tangible atmosphere hanging in the air. And they knew that because they had a past, they had a future.

Then the Queen chuckled. "Are we ready?" she asked. And taking up the proclamation the Vizier had prepared, she laid it on the incense-burner. And together, they watched it burst into flames.

And seeing the Pharaoh give a yawn, the wives of Horemheb excused themselves, elaborate beaded braids jingling as they made their way out of the room, ready to get back to their day, their regularly scheduled lives. Ready to get back to waiting for their big, strong, wonderful, handsome husband to come home. And ready to keep learning about the world they lived in and taking an interest in how it functioned… and in influencing how it functioned.

Their subterfuge, their multilayered secret mission, had been successful. And now the enemies of Ay were one step closer to victory.

Tutankhamun smiled up at his sister as she squeezed his hand. Had they won?

"What'll he say when he finds out?" Tut asked with a chuckle, glancing at the rising smoke that was all that was left of the Vizier's latest move in this unending battle.

Ankh bent and kissed his forehead. "He'll say 'the Pharaoh and the Queen are better opponents than I thought!'"

Tut nodded. They were.

Then he smiled as he thought of Mutnedjmet and Amenia's report on the campaign. The Mitanni and all the little towns and villages of Amurru were safe. Even though it had cost a war, so much death, his own death, even, Tutankhamun had kept his promise to that dark-bearded envoy, back in the good days in Paophi when he had been running his own meetings, ruling his own country, to help protect the Mitanni and their neighbors from the Hittites. And in that, he had been a King of peace.

Ankh smiled as she watched the ladies go, glowing with excitement. With their help, they now had a chance. A real chance to win. By being civil and sneaky, sweet and deadly, courageous and cunning, Amenia and Mutnedjmet had directed the attention of the Vizier so effectively that he had not even realized that they were distracting him. They had great power.

The Queen felt a glow of satisfaction inside her heart as she thought of the ways in which Mutnedjmet and Amenia were growing. Now that they really grasped, and had truly embraced the fact that they were people in their own right, with their own cares and interests, taking to heart the fact that they were more than extensions of their husband. They loved him as much as ever, but their adoration of him was no longer "big, strong, wonderful man syndrome." So their cooing, squealing, and glowing at the news that he was soon to be home was perfectly natural. And it made the Queen smile.

Then another thought touched her heart. Through her authority as Queen, she could have ordered them to help her. But… She smiled. Because she knew that that would never, ever be necessary. Because they were true friends.

Something moved at the window. Ankh got up, hurrying over to investigate. Someone was jogging away from peering inside; someone she recognized as one of Ay's secretaries. The Vizier knew something had happened.

But he couldn't do anything about it.

The Pharaoh shook his head, even as satisfaction at the promise he'd kept filled his heart. He had pledged Egypt's help to the Mitanni back in the month of Paophi… and he was amazed at how long ago that felt. Three months, and everything that had happened within them, felt like a lifetime.

"There's someone… I want you to meet," Tut's wife said softly.

He opened his eyes with a smile. She was smiling too, and there was something… something in her eyes. Something that made him curious.

"Who?" he asked.

"Meresankh and Hannu found her," Ankh said in a voice that ached with happy tears. "The little girl," she explained to her brother's questioning look. "Who we saw the day we went out into town. They found her. And they brought her to the palace."

Weak as he was, the Pharaoh struggled to sit up as he smiled, his excitement washing away the pain for a moment as his heart began to pound.

"Where is she?" he asked.

"Meresankh?" the Queen called. And the door opened.

As Tut watched, his sister's faithful handmaiden entered the room, followed by… the same precious little girl they had seen so long ago. She looked older; even thinner than before. But now… now she had on a fresh, clean linen gown, a soft, warm, green outer robe, and a solid pair of sandals, her face and hair were clean, and in one little hand, she had a half-eaten honey-cake.

"Your Majesties," Meresankh said gracefully. And as they watched, the child gave a little bow. "Presenting Nefertiti," the handmaiden said, and the little girl stepped into the room, taking her place close to the Queen.

The Pharaoh gave a little gasp when he heard her name. And he smiled at her, gently holding out a thin hand.

"This is the Pharaoh," Ankh said softly. And with a little smile, Nefertiti shook his hand.

"I remember you," she said with a friendly smile. "Thank you for the kebab."

He just shook his head. "You can have all the kebabs you want. Anything you want, anything you need… consider it done."

All she could do was smile.

Then Meresankh stepped forward, gently taking Nefertiti's hand. "Merneith will be her Granny, too, and take her on as an apprentice," she said. And she smiled, showing the dimple in her cheek. "I have a little sister."


"Master," Semerkhet said one morning as he brought his Pharaoh a bowl of sweet, yellow jujubes, "there's something… concerning me."

Tut took the bowl of fruit and looked up at his friend with an anxious frown. "What's going on?" he asked.

The valet sat down in the chair beside the bed, stretching his leg, feeling his healing knee twinge as the stiff muscle lengthened. It was healing well, but it still had a ways to go.

"There's division," he said finally. "Among the staff. Between the servants who can't wait for you to get better and spend the next fifty years being the greatest Pharaoh who ever lived… and the servants who want to see what it would be like if Ay took the throne. You can see it in their faces; people are frowning at each other, sitting in little groups, whispering… they're split, and they don't like each other anymore. And I'm…"

Semerkhet swallowed, looking down at his folded hands, the red ring gleaming on his hand. "I'm getting afraid of what might happen when the General gets home. Which… whichever side he stands on. Because this is starting to smell like civil war. They've drawn a line in the sand, and people are figuring out which side they stand on. I know our friends are on our side of it, but I'm afraid of what might happen. If they raided the armory... even if they raided the kitchens or the stables... blood could spill. All it would take would be one person getting angry enough to rile their side up, and the division would catch fire."

Semerkhet sighed, looking at his Pharaoh. "So I want to know... what you want me to do. What I can do to keep this from flaring up. I just... I don't want the palace to become a battlefield when the day... the day comes." He fought against choking up, and Tut sighed. He knew the day his friend was referring to.

Tutankhamun gave a deep sigh. This was not good. But he was grateful to his brother for having brought him this information. Now, as Pharaoh, he could decide what to do with it. Just like when Ankh had told him about the building projects getting de-layed and the minimum wage being canceled. He could rely on his loyal friend. And his own growing wisdom.

He reached out, and Sem gave him his hand. Tut looked down at their entwined hands; the hands of two friends, two brothers, working together for the same goals. Toward the same future. And together, they would make that future as good as possible.

"Here'th what I want you to do," he said finally. Semerkhet looked at him, ready and waiting for his instructions. "Sleep with a knife under your pillow, first of all. But be... be kind to the people on the other side of the split. And use your influence to encourage your friends to stay civil to them.

"Tell people... tell them that unity is the most important fing right now, as we move toward... toward the future. Whatever it holdth. And there should be only one side. A side that loves Egypt.

Whoever… whoever sits on the throne next, tell the staff that all we can do is wait and thee what will happen. And that anyone who can't abide these politicth any longer has permission to resign their position. I don't want to hold anyone to a career here against their will. It would be better for people to quit and be happy somewhere elth than to keep working here and get so angry that they resort to violence."

Tut smiled at his friend. "So that's what I want you to tell them. That if they can't stand the water, they don't have to be fishermen. And that I would rather see the staff shrink than see it turn on itself."

Semerkhet nodded, giving his brother a little smile as he squeezed his hand one more time and got up. "Thank you, Master," he said with a satisfied sigh. "I'll do that."

# 7    Trust

The day was chilly, but Meresankh followed her Granny out into the herb garden, bending down to gather the many herbs that they needed for the Pharaoh's leg. And even as her heart ached, Meresankh was proud that through following in her Granny's footsteps, she could help make his journey one tiny bit less awful.

The Queen wrapped her warm, green outer robe closer as she walked out into the garden, breathing in the fresh air, feeling the crisp breeze on her face, blowing the braids of her wig. At a respectful but safe distance stood Hannu, the guard who always accompanied her and her brother on walks, his spear in his hand, dagger within easy reach at his belt.

Suddenly Ankhesenamun's heart began to pound as an idea trickled down her spine like an icy raindrop.

Could she trust him? Was he truly loyal to her and the Pharaoh, or had the Vizier gotten to him, too? And if so... were their lives safe in his hands? Especially... She looked at his spear, his knife, and swallowed back the taste of fear. Since he was armed?

Not knowing what else to do, she sent up a quick prayer for protection, as well as for guidance. To Whoever happened to hear it. And she took a deep breath as a conviction settled in her heart. To discover whether he was loyal, all she had to do was ask.

"Hannu?" she asked into the silence that was broken only by the soft twittering of the birds in the trees and bushes.

He looked up, then stepped toward her and dropped to one knee. "Yes, My Lady?"

She extended her hand, inviting him to rise. He stood at attention, waiting to answer her question.

"What do you plan to do?" she asked. "When the next Pharaoh takes the throne?"

Hannu looked slightly taken aback; then his face fell as sadness seemed to weigh on his shoulders.

"Stay here with you, My Lady," he said finally. "For as long as you need me. Protect you..." He swallowed, looking this way and that for traitors who might be listening, his hand never far from his dagger. "Protect you from anyone who might wish you harm. And protect..." He looked down at her belly, at the secret that had quickly been whispered through the entire staff. "Protect the heir to the throne."

Ankhesenamun smiled up at him, feeling gratitude swell in her heart as the fear that he might present a threat fell away, replaced by security in the knowledge that he would work hard, risk his own safety, in fact, to keep her and her brother safe. As well as their future. Whatever happened.

"Thank you, Hannu," she said, offering her hand again. Looking embarrassed, he took it, kissing it like the Governor of Kush might have. "I'm just glad to know... that there's someone we can trust."

"Always, My Lady." And with another bow, Hannu kept walking, leaving her to her stroll, and to her thoughts.

The Queen waited for her blood as the month of Tybi went on. She watched her body's signs closely, waiting to see whether her body would go through its monthly purification... or whether it would retain her blood in preparation for a child.

She waited. And she prayed that it would not come; that her womb even now was embracing a tiny baby who would spend the next eight months growing big and strong… She prayed. And she waited.

She didn't bleed. She didn't know Whom to thank, but she breathed countless prayers of gratitude as the hope grew within her, the hope that the heir of Egypt was soon to be born.

Meresankh peeked into her Pharaoh's room. Semerkhet was sitting silently in his chair by the royal bed, staring into space. Much as he had been four hours ago.

Quietly she stepped into the doorway. She had asked the Queen's permission to relieve him. Time to take action.

"Sem?"

The Pharaoh's valet looked up to see Meresankh standing in the doorway of the bedroom. Although… if Semerkhet let his tired eyes relax, there were two of her, and they were both fuzzy.

"Hmm?"

"How long have you been sitting there?" she asked softly.

Slowly Sem turned his head, looking down at his Master sleeping quietly in the bed. He chuckled in slight embarrassment as he heard the nickname. No one but his Pharaoh ever called him *Sem*.

"I don't know…" He rubbed his face, pressing the heels of his hands against his closed eyes until he saw stars. "Doesn't really matter."

Suddenly she was at his side, resting her tiny, soft, warm little hand on his weary shoulder. How had she moved so quickly?

"Yes, it does," she whispered, dropping a kiss on his forehead. "It's a beautiful day. Go out in the garden, just for a few minutes. Get some air. Look at the flowers. Listen to the birds. I'll sit with

69

him, and if he wakes up, I'll come get you." She squeezed Semerkhet's hand. "Go on. Mother knows best. Go bring back some flowers. Brighten it up in here; freshen up the air."

He shook his head. It took a moment to remember the garden, remember the lotus-pools, remember the feeling of the sun on his face. Spending so long inside, and keeping such strange hours, he had not even been sure whether it was daytime outside.

Slowly Semerkhet rose and stretched, his hamstrings groaning as they straightened out after so many hours at a right angle. Oh, his neck and shoulders were stiff. He shook one foot, then the other, trying to get his circulation moving again. His feet were actually cold, and they prickled as he shook them.

Meresankh sat in Sem's chair, smiling sadly as she looked at the sleeping Pharaoh. Semerkhet bent over him and ran his hand over his head, whispering, "I'll be back soon." Then, with a wish for life, prosperity, and health, he was off, off to the garden, finding his way out of the room that had become his whole world.

His feet found their way to the entrance, and he was outdoors, the cool breeze touching his face, the warm Sun making him squint in the sudden brightness, the twittering of the birds making him smile in spite of himself, the chrysanthemums glowing like garnet and topaz. He wrapped his warm, red outer robe closer around himself as the cool air hit him, making him shiver. Tybi was such a lovely time of year, the days cool, almost crisp, the nights cold, the humidity comfortably low, the mosquitoes absent. Again he caught a glimpse of something; felt a moment of love as the Sun touched him. Sem picked a path and took off at a jog, even as his knee twinged with every stride. He would milk this break for all it was worth.

70

Now she was the one sitting with their Pharaoh, her Pharaoh. Meresankh sat silently in the chair, which was still warm from Semerkhet sitting in it for so long. Silently she watched Tutankhamun sleeping, shaking her head. Never in her life would she have imagined being the one to sit with him.

And she stared at him in wonder, her heart starting to pound in awe at the honor she had been given; the trust that had been placed in her. This was the Pharaoh, the sacred king whose people saw him as a god on Earth. And not only was she allowed to step into his room, but she was allowed to sit here completely alone with him, watching over him. In this moment, she was the one responsible for him... the one defending him. Little old her.

And yet... she knew he wasn't a god. He was a glorious king, but more than that, in this moment, he was a man. A... a boy. A vulnerable, defenseless, dying, motherless young boy, sleeping here under her care.

And she wished so dearly that his mother was here. The Queen would care for him, Semerkhet, Granny, even Meresankh would care for him, but as he lay dying, his mother was the one he needed. His mother, and the dear old nurse, Hetepheres, who had looked after him for so long.

Meresankh looked at him, his profile, so like the Queen's, with a long, graceful nose and a small chin, much less prominent than Semerkhet's. And she looked at his legs. He'd always walked with a cane; all the servants knew that. But now both of his legs were broken, carefully splinted and bandaged. Blanket carefully tucked so as to cause the least pain, his left leg was uncovered to the hip, lying thin and wasted on the mattress, the skin around the edges of the supportive splint an angry red. His right leg, less sensitive to the touch of the blanket, was covered, and Meresankh could just make out its thin shape, a slender stick under the sheets. It would be awhile before he walked on those legs again.

Meresankh gave a little shudder, clutching her robe in her hand as a thought hit her. *If* he walked again. If he ever got better at all.

And as she had a hundred thousand times before, she bowed her head to pray.


"I've been thinking," Ankh said softly.

Meresankh looked up from the continual tidying with which she had been busying herself these past weeks. The Queen was stealing a few precious moments of rest in her chambers.

"About what?" she asked.

Ankh sighed. And silently Meresankh watched her, waiting for what she would say. And she continued with her patient reorganization of her Lady's jewelry.

"Politics," she said simply. Meresankh set down the last bracelet and turned toward her, again waiting for her to continue. Ankhesenamun sighed again, looking away. "And marriage," she said. "And the future. About… about Zannanza. And about… about the Pharaoh." She fiddled with the bracelet on her wrist, one of Meritaten's.

"Our marriage… has been all about politics. Just politics." She gave a wry chuckle as the ever-present words came back to her. "Him, me, our marriage, everything in our entire lives, has been… just politics. That's all it's ever been. And I…" She bit her lip. "I want more. Maybe he never did, but I did. I want… I want a husband." Her voice broke, and quickly Meresankh offered her hand for her friend to clasp. Ankh flashed her a quick smile, then continued. "I have a brother. And I love him. So much. But I… is it so wrong to want a husband? Even if it means…" She gave a sob, covering her face with her free hand. And Meresankh just looked on.

Ankh swallowed, wiping away her tears. "It's never been about what we wanted. Either of us. But is this… is this the way that I will get…" Again, she paused to swallow back tears. "Do I have to lose my brother to gain a real husband?"

Meresankh had no answers.

As she waited, as she hoped, the Queen remembered. For so long, she had been the one walking beside her little brother, teaching him, encouraging him, mentoring him and helping him become the Pharaoh she had always known he could be.

He had been the one walking with her, however, when the dark days had come and hello had so suddenly turned to goodbye, their two tiny, precious daughters torn from their arms by mysterious afflictions no doctor could diagnose… or treat. Tutankhamun told her that neither of them had failed… that neither of them were at fault… that she was not broken… that she was not inadequate as a Queen… and that just as she had always told him, life was about living each day with the things you could change… and the things you could not. They could not change the past. So bravely, they had continued walking together into the future. And with each tragedy they lived through, they came through even stronger than before.

And what would happen in the chapter of life that was now unfolding before them, as the well-loved, expected future was torn from their unwilling grasp to be replaced by unknowns that threatened the very lives of those who would be left behind, remained to be seen.

"It wouldn't work, would it?" Tut asked his sister.

She looked up from shelling a bowl of pistachios. "Hmm?"

"A co-regenthy," he said. "You mentioned it, and it'th a good idea— really, it'th our best idea, but it wouldn't really change anything, would it? I mean, we could announth it, but what good would that do? We'd… we'd need people who thupported uth. And all those people are gone."

Ankh looked at her brother. And pride ached in her heart. He was right. For all its tragedy and unfairness, he understood the political situation they were facing.

"You're right," she said simply. "It wouldn't make a difference." Then she sighed, reaching out to squeeze his hand with half a smile. "But that doesn't mean we're out of hope."


"How could you betray me?"

Semerkhet stopped outside the Grand Vizier's quarters later that day as he heard a loud, angry voice.

"You knew the plan," Ay's voice continued, "and you turned back. Who talked to you? Or was I not paying you enough? Pray tell what led to this decision."

"I am loyal to my Pharaoh," a soft voice said resolutely. Semerkhet recognized it as Raherka's.

"I am your Pharaoh," Ay spat, and Sem thought he heard a blow land.

There was a shaky breath. Then Semerkhet heard Raherka say, "No, Vizier, you are not. You are the betrayer. And I realized I could no longer bring him poisoned wine on your orders."

"Then you are no longer of any use to me," Ay said bitterly. "Or anyone else." There was the sound of old fingers snapping.

74

"Guards," Ay said, "get this scum out of my sight. Is the wine ready?"

"Yes, Glorious Lord," another voice said. And Semerkhet had to get out of the way as Ay's door opened and two guards appeared, hustling Raherka down the hall. He recognized them as two of the six guards he'd met during his own brush with the law. The red mark of a stinging blow was splashed across one of Raherka's cheeks, and there was fear on his face. But also pride.

*Could he save Raherka?* Semerkhet wondered. If he charged in right now and demanded in the name of the Pharaoh, or by dint of his own rank as Sole Companion, that Raherka be set free, would it work?

No, he realized. If he stepped in, revealed to Ay and his followers that he had heard everything, not only would Raherka still die, but Semerkhet would be killed too.

And then who would protect the Pharaoh?

Shaking, heart pounding, Semerkhet turned and walked away. He regretted it a thousand, thousand times, but he could do nothing for Raherka. His duty was to his Master.

The Pharaoh shuddered as Semerkhet bowed and excused himself after telling him what he'd overheard. This was war. And Tut could not save everyone. First Pentu... then Usermontu and Amenmose... and now Raherka... casualties in the war for the next throne of Egypt. Friends who had paid the ultimate price for loyalty.

Who would be next?

Tut told Ankh. And Sem told Meresankh. And Ankh and Meresankh talked until there was nothing more to say. And they shuddered, both at what the Vizier was willing to do to those who displeased him, and at the power he still held. Pentu. Usermontu. Amenmose. Raherka. Meritaten. Nefertiti. Akhenaten. All gone for doing what was right.

And they wondered what the future held.

The Grand Vizier made an announcement in the courtyard just outside the palace, in front of most of the servants. The palace staff were all wrapped warmly in their outer robes against the cool of the early evening, a rainbow of red, yellow, green, and blue fabric. Semerkhet stood with his arm around Meresankh as they waited in the chilly breeze, wondering what that snake had to say.

"It is with great sadness that we mourn the unexpected death of Raherka, a loyal servant to the crown, during this unusually virulent ague season," Ay said solemnly. "Shortly after the death of Amenmose, another servant whose loyal heart was not strong enough to overcome the illness carried by the mosquitoes. This year has also seen the passing of Vizier Pentu and Vizier Usermontu, also taken by ague, just like our beloved Princess Meritaten, who left us in the first year of the reign of our glorious Pharaoh, our glorious Pharaoh who even now is recovering from ague. The priests are praying for relief from this outbreak of illness, and anyone suffering symptoms of ague is urged to seek the advice of a physician immediately. Thank you."

The lying jackal stepped down from the dais that had been set up for his speech, and the crowd of servants began to make their way back to the palace, ready to get back to work. Some of them appeared to be checking the surrounding air for mosquitoes, squinting into the middle distance and brushing nervously at their arms. They were the source of every problem Egypt was currently facing, of course.

And there *were* no mosquitoes at all. It was too cold for them; their season was long since passed, and there had been only one unseasonably warm spell that had allowed for their brief return. *Virulent ague season, my foot*, Sem thought. His Master's case was the only one he was aware of since the Season of Inundation had ended.

Ay paused when he saw Semerkhet. And the Vizier inclined his bald head. "Your Excellency."

"Vizier," Semerkhet said stiffly. He swallowed. "Thank you for such a lovely speech. What a good way to commemorate those who have died so… suddenly." He lowered his voice, assuming that same deadly whisper his Master had practiced on him back in the days before this; the days when it had seemed that nothing could stand in the way of the glorious future into which their Pharaoh was leading them. "You never can tell with ague… who will live… who will die… and who will benefit."

A hint of a sneer touched the Vizier's lips as his nostrils flared. "Be careful, Your Excellency," he whispered, "that you are not also… bitten. That would be… most unfortunate."

Then he continued on his way.

Semerkhet clenched his fists.


"What a terrible season for ague," Nakhtmin drawled. Semerkhet pulled up short on his trip down the hall, back to his Pharaoh's room. He looked down at the little General, trying to sneer down his nose at him like Nakhtmin always did to everyone. He actually deserved it. "First Pentu… then Raherka… and Usermontu… and Amenmose… I wonder who will be next."

"It does seem to have been… quite a season," Sem said curtly. His Master had told the Grand Vizier what he knew, and Semerkhet had just told Ay that he knew too; would it be wrong for him to say something to Nakhtmin? He decided to go for it, vent his feelings on this son of a snake. "And how strange that the mosquitoes seem to have political motives. Good day, General."

And before Nakhtmin could say anything else, the Sole Companion had kept walking.

# 8  Miracles

"What do you want me to do, Master?" Semerkhet said in a rush, hurrying into his Pharaoh's room without so much as a bow.

Tutankhamun blinked up at him from sitting propped up on pillows, letting Ankh help him eat his soup, which had been tested by Nuya. He was a bit tired today.

"About what, Sem?" he asked.

"About that jackal and his son," the valet panted. And breathlessly, he described the insincere memorial service and the conversations that had followed it, confessing that he had told Ay and Nakhtmin that he knew of their treachery. He swallowed, pressing his palms into his eyes to stop the red haze that was rising as his heart continued to pound. "I just feel like I'm this close to doing something we'll all regret."

Tutankhamun reached out and gently touched his valet's shoulder. Semerkhet lowered his hands and looked at him with a little smile, tense, angry shoulders slowly dropping as his righteous indignation faded. Slowly the redness began to dissipate.

"What do you think you should do?" the Pharaoh asked softly. "If it's too much right now, you can tell Ptahmose and Nuya, and they can step in; you can step back." He swallowed. "You could… go see how things are in the scribe department. It's up to you," he said calmly.

Semerkhet laughed. But it was a real laugh, a laugh that released all the heavy anger that had been weighing him down. He knew his Master wasn't threatening him; wasn't firing him. He just knew the best thing to bring up to get his attention; shake him out of this frame of mind. And yet at the same time, he was serious. If his valet needed to step away, he was being given the opportunity.

Semerkhet gave a heavy sigh. "Thank you," he whispered with half a little smile. "I think I'll be all right."

Tut nodded. "I know you will... Brother."


Meresankh sat with her Granny in her workshop as she prepared another medicine for the poor Pharaoh early on the morning of the fifth day of Tybi.

"He may not understand yet," Merneith was saying as her gnarled old hands worked a mortar and pestle, "but he will."

"Understand what, Granny?" Meresankh asked, petting the old black cat, which, as usual, was sleeping on the table.

"An idol is an idol is an idol, no matter how much gold you paint on it," she said firmly as she ground a dried herb into powder. "I've seen too much, my family saw too much, to set any stock in a piece of painted wood set up in a temple. Our Pharaoh's father may have called Him the Aten, but he had the right idea. He came very close to finding I-AM."

Meresankh looked up from petting the cat. She scooted closer— she loved this story. And her Granny smiled. "Oh, yes, dearie. He is our God, too, the God of the Hebrews, Who came to the Prince in the burning bush when he became a shepherd in Midian."

Merneith sighed, bowing her head as she folded her wrinkled old hands. Meresankh listened closely— she knew this story, but it was so strange, so fascinating, that she didn't want to miss a word.

"I saw the plagues, dearie. I was nineteen when it started; same as our Pharaoh is now. We heard that the Prince had returned, but it wasn't long before things started getting... so strange. The Nile..." She trembled. "Blood as far as the eye could see. And the insects after that, and the frogs… It wasn't long before my family went to Goshen and hid with a Hebrew family while all our own neighbors, all our own family, suffered plague after plague. But we saw what was happening, and we saw that the God Who was doing all this was the only true one. And we learned of Abraham, Isaac, Grand Vizier Joseph, the history of this mysterious chosen people who had been our slaves for so many generations."

Granny sighed again. "My cousins died, two of them, on that last terrible night, the night of the Angel of Death. I'll never forget lying awake in the middle of the night, knowing something was coming and that the lamb's blood my friend's father had daubed on the lintel and doorposts of the house was our only hope. And praying it would work. And the sounds… we heard that night. And the next day. All those mothers…" Granny shuddered. "It was the great cry, such as had never been heard in Egypt, and has never been heard again. After that it was over. Pharaoh said he wanted nothing more to do with the Hebrews. He changed his mind a day or two later, but the army he sent after them never came back."

"I remember the old rhyme you always told me when I was little," Meresankh said.

*Proud old Pharaoh stood so tall*
*Proud old Pharaoh had a great fall*
*All Pharaoh's horses and all Pharaoh's men*
*Went after the Hebrews and were never seen again.*

"And they never were," Merneith said grimly. She shook her head, folding her hands again. "The army never came back, and neither did the Hebrews, but somehow, the stories did. And we marveled at what was perhaps the greatest miracle of all… I-AM causing the sea itself to divide into two parts so that the Hebrews could cross on dry land. And then closing it again as the army began to follow them." She shook her head. "I'm sure there are still broken pieces of chariots on the bottom of the Red Sea."

Granny swallowed. "It hurt my mother and father so much not to go with the Hebrews when they left for the Promised Land, but they knew in their hearts that we were needed here."

Meresankh sighed. She remembered another song, a sad one sometimes sung as a lullaby in the families of those who knew the truth of what had really happened all those years ago.

*O sisters too, how may we do*
*For to preserve this day*
*These poor younglings for whom we sing,*
*"Lai, lai, lully, lullay"?*

*Pharaoh the king, in his raging,*
*Chargèd he hath this day*
*His men of might in his own sight*
*Each Hebrew son to slay*

And the other one, an Egyptian one which had also come from the story of the baby Hebrew Prince, the half-remembered story of the Princess finding him floating down the Nile in a tiny basket. To some, the story was no more than legend, but it seemed that no one could forget it— it had been passed down, in some form, in families both Hebrew and Egyptian.

*Rock-a-bye baby*
*Float down the Nile*

*Hope you don't get eaten*
*By a crocodile*
*Gift from the river*
*Sent from above*
*Drawn from the water*
*Chosen with love*

Then Merneith seemed to draw her thoughts back to the present. She sat up straighter with a wistful little smile and finished the story.

"My grandmother was a midwife in Memphis, alongside the Hebrew midwives Shiprah and Puah. And my mother was a midwife, and myself, and my sister, and my sister's daughters and granddaughters. We've never forgotten the power of what we saw… the God Who could kill the heir to the throne of Egypt, turn the Nile to blood, kill every soldier in Pharaoh's army, set His chosen people free no matter what the Pharaoh did… was the only One. We've kept those traditions alive… and we've also kept the Light alive, even here in Egypt. The Light that shone from the burning bush; the Light that Akhenaten saw in the Sun. The true Light of the World." She swallowed. "And if this Pharaoh can see it… maybe the Light will shine in all of Egypt." Merneith smiled. "You can close your eyes, or you can draw the curtains, but the Sun still shines. And the Light will shine in our hearts as long as we remember."

Sitting in her room, Meresankh took off the little silver necklace. She looked down at Isis, a pagan idol, nothing more than a story. Should she even wear such a thing?

Then she smiled. It was not wrong to cherish a gift. Even though she knew the truth. This necklace may have depicted a figure from nothing more than a fairy-tale, but it was a gift from her beloved; a symbol of his love for her. And that was what mattered.

The Queen had returned to the old religion when her father had died; even changed her name back to the -amun form, rejecting the Aten as false even though in reality, He was the closest Egypt had ever come to finding I-AM. They were friends now, something Meresankh never could have imagined a year ago, and maybe, when the time was right, she would ask her Mistress more about her faith. In the meantime, she would continue to pray for her, to the true God Whose Light she carried in her heart.

With every week, every day, every night that passed, Semerkhet's Master grew weaker, thinner. Semerkhet had to bite back the pain as he helped him bathe, gently running the cloth over his friend's stick-thin arms, dabbing it over what he could of the poor, broken legs, patting it gently over the Pharaoh's ribcage and tracing his spine and shoulderblades. And when he gently supported his brother's arm in one hand as he carefully rubbed on his moisturizer, there was no weight to it. It felt… it felt like helping a child.

Even Tutankhamun's favorite thing in the whole wide world was becoming more difficult. Semerkhet had to be so much more careful now, so much gentler, as he rubbed the frankincense-and-spikenard ointment onto his friend's thin back to put him to sleep, feeling every rib, every vertebra. With every night that passed, Tut asked him to use less pressure, until Sem felt like he was barely touching his brother's back. Long ago, so long ago, were the days when the Pharaoh had brought him his stiff neck or knotted-up shoulders, asking him to press harder until the stiffness finally eased. Now, the slightest pinch was painful. So Semerkhet was gentle. He didn't want to hurt his brother.

Ankhesenamun looked up from her midmorning break as Meresankh came into her private sitting room with a cup of tea, the tea Merneith had prepared. She accepted it with a smile, and sat sipping it, enjoying the warmth on this cool day, the refreshing flavor of the herbs.

A veil had been removed over the past year. She and Meresankh had always been so separate; the handmaiden was "one of the servants," and therefore, not in the same category as the Queen, barely even human. She had hardly spoken to Meresankh; barely acknowledged her. And Meresankh had hardly interacted with her, either. And even after she had started viewing her servant as human, there had still been a separateness.

Not anymore. They were sisters now; sisters in womanhood. And Ankhesenamun was grateful for every moment of it.

Meresankh served the Queen a cup of tea, then stood there quietly watching her drink it. For so long they had been utterly separate from one another, the Queen barely speaking to her, which prevented her from speaking back. Not that she had even wanted to; after all, the King and Queen were just the high-up bosses who only cared about themselves. Not really people Meresankh really cared to get to know. It was her honor and privilege to serve them, but that was it.

But now they were sisters. And Meresankh was delighted to count the Queen as one of her friends.

She smiled at her Mistress, and Ankh smiled back. And shyly, Meresankh asked,

"Any new signs?"

The Queen chuckled and gave a little nod, braids softly swaying. "I still haven't bled," she whispered.

Meresankh took her hand. And together they smiled.

Semerkhet stepped out into the hall outside his Pharaoh's room, just to stretch his legs for a minute. He'd hardly moved for the past four hours, and his legs were getting cold and stiff.

Meresankh was standing there, looking up at him with the smile that always warmed his heart. He walked over to her, holding out his hands. She took them and squeezed them, her little smile turning into a grin.

"How are you?" she asked.

He sighed, giving a shrug. "The same." He bowed his head. "What am I going to do?"

"You're going to keep taking care of him," she said. "And yourself, too. You're going to keep being the greatest brother anyone ever had."

Semerkhet shook his head sadly. "I mean after."

She paused. She knew what he meant. She kept his hands in hers, looking down at them. "You could work with Merneith," she said. "She'll teach you how to make herbal remedies that actually work, instead of things with crocodile eyeballs and dead mice."

"The granny?" he asked, his eyebrows rising.

"She's *my* Granny," Meresankh said just a little pointedly, and Sem shrank back from saying anything disrespectful. Then she chuckled, and his shoulders dropped as he joined her. "You'd be an excellent nurse. You already are. And from what I gather, you're the greatest massage therapist from here to Babylon."

He looked down with just a hint of a blush. "I do what I can."

She nodded, looking down at their entwined hands. "It's a gift. And… it's a gift you could share with other people as life goes on." Meresankh sighed. "And life will go on. But…" She swallowed. "You might… want… to start thinking… about your career options. Because someday, all of this… good and bad… will be in our memories."

She looked up at him, the next words coming out in a rush. "And I see this in you, and I want you to make it grow. Bless dozens of people, hundreds of people, with what you can do. You've learned so much here… where could you be using it five, ten years from now?" She gave him half a smile. "Do you really want to go into scribe work?"

Semerkhet laughed, shaking his head. "No. One day was enough. I'm still not sure I ever got all that ink off my fingers."

Then Sem chuckled again as a question popped into his mind. "Meresankh…" he asked slowly, knowing he was treading dangerously, "how… how old is Granny? I've… I've always wondered… I can't think of ever seeing anyone as old as her!"

Meresankh laughed and playfully elbowed him. "Old and wise enough to see a set of triplets born and bring all three of them through just like any baby," she said proudly.

Semerkhet's eyes went wide. "Trip… you mean, *three?* All at once?"

Meresankh grinned. "Three. All at once."

Sem shook his head with a shudder. "I didn't even know that was possible. Three…" He shook his head again. "But all three of them…"

"All fine," Meresankh said with a proud smile. "She's told me that story so many times. And that was forty-five years ago, not long after she became a midwife. And she was older than me then... she's over seventy years old."

Semerkhet just stared. "Seventy years..." Then he chuckled. "So does that mean she saw them build the pyramids?"

And with her own laugh, Meresankh just elbowed him again.

Meresankh also wondered what her future would hold. But with the blessing and guidance of I-AM, and the lessons she had learned, the inspiration she had taken, from the Queens her Mistress had taught her about— and the life her Lady herself was living— Meresankh knew she could do it.

And whatever her future held, she hoped that in it, she would be holding Semerkhet.

# 9 The Letter

Ankhesenamun looked up from taking a short break in her private sitting room, staring into space as she slowly sipped a hot cup of Merneith's tea. It tasted good. It felt good to sit down, to be alone for a moment, to know that safe in her own bedroom, she could sit and think.

Then the sound of a footstep made the hairs on the back of her neck prickle. The Queen set her teacup down and got up from her chair to see Grand Vizier Ay standing there in her bedroom. He had not knocked. The Vizier was brushing his fingers through the braids of her various displayed wigs; running his hands over her furniture. As if he was… looking for something.

She stood there in the doorway between the sitting room and the bedroom, silently watching him. He had not seen her. He carried on with his search, gnarled old claws picking through her belongings for his prey.

"What do you want, Vizier?" she asked coldly.

Ay stood straight up with a guilty start. Slowly he turned to her, bowing deeply with an obsequious smile.

"To see how you are, My Lady," he simpered. "And how you are feeling. Managing a pregnancy along with all the stress of the Pharaoh's deteriorating condition must be… challenging. How are you and your son on this fine day?"

Oh. Right. Ankh was pretending that she knew for a fact that she was pregnant. Quickly she put her hand on her stomach and smiled, trying to put the sparkling joy of motherhood into her eyes, the baby glow into her face.

"Pretty well so far," she said. "Although Lady Merneith says that I will probably start experiencing morning sickness soon. But so far, I'm…" She gave what she hoped was an exhilarated sigh. "Excellent." She paused. "And I know that no matter what happens, the future of Egypt is secure."

She stared at Ay for a moment, giving him just a hint of the eyes of Isis.

He dropped his gaze. "Indeed, My Lady." And the Vizier bowed again. "I wish you a pleasant day."

And he was gone.

As soon as he was out of sight, Ankh locked the door behind him. And, shaking her head, she retrieved the letter from its place among her toiletries. It was no longer safe in her room.

"Meresankh?" she called. Her handmaiden appeared from the storage room, dipping her head as she always did.

"Yes, My Lady?" The handmaiden dropped her voice to a whisper, forehead crinkling in a concerned frown. "Are you all right? What was he doing in here?"

Ankh shook her head. "I'm all right." She held out the letter. "This… isn't safe in my room. The letter to the Hittites. That's what the Vizier was looking for. Can you… can you keep it safe for me? If he finds it, who knows what he'll do… burn it, rewrite it, try to— try to stop me from ever writing another letter…"

Slowly Meresankh took the scroll in her dimpled little fingers. And she paused. Where could she keep it that no one would ever look? Then she looked up with a smile.

"Can I take it down to Granny?" she asked.

Ankh returned the smile. "I think that would be perfect."

Meresankh chuckled. "Yes, anyone who tries to steal it will know the wrath of her broom!"

Ankh sighed as she watched her handmaiden, her sister, leave her chambers, the letter tucked safely inside her gown. She could trust her friend. The letter would be safe.

Then she closed her eyes, giving a little sigh as the memories came. Telling Ay that she would soon be dealing with morning sickness... reminded her of the mornings she had spent four years ago, two years ago, losing her breakfast. And yet filled with joy at the same time, for the joy that was ahead of her, waiting beyond all the discomfort. The joy that had been stolen when hello had turned so suddenly to goodbye, the very breath stolen from within her as her world had shattered. And now to be pretending that joy, that hope... brought back the pain.

The Queen clenched her hands, nails digging into her palms. And again, she hoped. It was possible... just possible... that she was not pretending. And she hung all her hopes and prayers on that possibility; the breathless, exhilarating possibility that her story would come true.

When Tut woke up from his nap, it was to a painful cough. He pressed his hand to his chest, fishing through his blankets for a handkerchief. And when he was done coughing... when he was done coughing, whatever he had just forced from his lungs was pink.

"It's safe," Ankh told her brother as she sat down with his lunch of broth.

He looked up at her as she spooned up a bite for him. "The letter?" he whispered. Silently she nodded. He looked around, making sure that the door was closed. Then he leaned closer and whispered, "Where is it?"

91

"With Granny," she whispered back with a smile.

Tut accepted a bite of broth and nodded. "Good."


It was getting closer. The day that he would leave this world, no matter how hard he had been fighting to stay. The day... the day that his sister would marry Zannanza.

Tut bit his lip as he thought again of the big, strong, handsome Hittite, the man who could give Ankhesenamun everything he had not been able to. And Grandfather Thutmose's words came back. *Feeble little cripple... pathetic little Boy-King... weak... failure.*

And he felt the pain, which had been aching in his heart and prickling behind his eyes as sadness, begin to simmer into anger.

Slowly he turned his head, looking at her where she sat beside him, attentive as always. And he sighed.

"I don't... I don't want you to marry Zannanza," he said in a choked whisper. "I know you have to," he said before she could reply, "but I don't... *want* you to."

She sighed as well. But it was not the sad, sympathetic sigh he was expecting. It was a huff that made her nostrils flare.

"What do you want me to do?" she asked. And to his surprise, her voice was clipped.

Not knowing what else to do, he went on. "I don't know," he moaned. "There'th nothing elth for you *to* do. And I know it's the right thing... I just wish..."

Ankh took his hand. And she looked at him quite frankly. So frankly that he almost shrank back into the pillows. She was looking at him rather like Mother did when he had gotten into something he shouldn't.

And she replied.

"You're my brother," she said. And there was love in her voice, but he could tell that she wasn't going to leave it at that. "You're my brother, and I love you. Always have, always will. And nothing will ever change that. You know that."

He nodded. "I do."

Ankhesenamun looked down at their hands, then back at his face. "But…" she said, biting her lip. "Don't you ever want more? Is it… so wrong to want more?"

Tut shook his head. "I want a lot of things. But I never wanted to take another wife."

His sister gave another frustrated sigh. "I know. But I…" She shook her head, beaded braids jangling with a hint of anger. "I want more."

He just looked at her. And discovered too late that his silence had been too much.

His sister was shouting at him— Ankh was shouting at him, raising her voice at him, pouring out angry words that confused him and stung his heart.

"Do you ever think about what *I* want? That's all it's ever been, and I want more. You, me, our marriage, everything in our entire lives, is *just politics!* It's not fair! And I…" She stopped shouting, the next words seeming to catch in her throat as she blinked back angry tears. "I want a husband."

The words rang into silence as the Pharaoh looked at his sister, his wife. He let them echo; let them settle into his heart. He looked at their hands, then back up at her face, her forehead, still crinkled with anger, her eyes, still leaking tears that were getting makeup all over her face. And he thought of what to say.

"And I want you to have one. I know… I know this hathn't alwayth been what you wanted. I know we didn't get to choose.

But I know…" Now his voice was the one that was breaking as he continued to hold her hand, looking up at her. Slowly, her face was beginning to soften. "I know that I love you. And I know that I want… I want what's best for you. And the baby. Tho…" He sighed, a sad, heavy sigh. "I wish everything was different. But I want my sister to be happy."

Ankhesenamun sighed. And in her face, there was no more anger. Only sadness. And… what looked like gratitude. Gently she reached out, placing her soft, warm, little hand on his cheek. And bending forward, she kissed him on the forehead.

The Queen went for a walk. And she let the words she had spoken, her brother had spoken, echo again inside her heart. She hadn't meant to go too far; hadn't meant to hurt him like she had. But she had… spoken the truth.

The Pharaoh closed his eyes. Again, his sister's words had stung him. And again, they had all been true. Their marriage had, indeed, been *just politics*. But again, he reminded himself… that that was not his fault. And he promised himself that he would be the best brother he could to his sister. Even… even as she prepared her heart for the arrival of a second husband.

The truth hung in the air. But the anger dissipated. Even as the pain lingered. And as the day went on, brother and sister found their way back to one another.

She held him. Ankh lay beside her brother as the fifth day of Tybi passed into afternoon, wrapping her arms around him as he rested his head on her chest, his breathing, his heartbeat, in rhythm

94

with hers. And she remembered. Remembered all the years of their life together.

"Tell me a story, Ankh," he said softly. And she smiled.

"Where should I start?" she whispered.

"Start at the beginning."

Ankh nodded. "All right." She sighed, images, sensations coming back as her heart moved backward in time, back to the good old days. "It was the end of the Season of Emergence, the month of Pharmouthi. It was still chilly, and we had matching warm robes, all six of us girls. And Mother gathered us around, and she told us that in a few months, there would be seven of us.

"I was so excited," she continued. "All through the Season of the Harvest, the first half of Inundation, all through the heat of the year. And by the time the days started to get cool again, Mother's belly was as big as a watermelon.

"We were all so happy," Ankh said. "All six of us, and Father, too. We touched her belly every day as it got bigger, and we were so amazed when the day came that we could actually feel you moving around inside her, and you kicked against our hands. And we sang to you, and read poetry to you, and told you how much we loved you."

Ankhesenamun ran her hand over her brother's back, and he smiled. He knew what was coming next.

"And then the day came," his sister said proudly. "And we all waited together. We were so excited, and we were all whispering. Meritaten was sitting in the special chair they made for her, with the cushions that kept her skin from getting irritated from sitting so long, and little Setepenre didn't really know what was going on, but she was excited too. Father had gone to the birthing pavilion with Mother, so he could encourage her. And we waited.

95

"He loved Mother so much," Ankh said softly. "She was his beauty in motion. And he called her the Lady of All Women.

"And then the nurse came out to tell us you were here, and that you were a boy," she said. "We were so excited. A little brother to love and cuddle and play mother with. What fun it was going to be."

Tutankhamun sighed. And he took up the story. "But it was hard, sometimes," he said. "None of the doctors could explain it, but my feet didn't match, and it was hard for me to swallow."

Ankh nodded. "And Mother and Father named you *Tutankhaten*, the Living Image of Aten. And they were proud of you. If they were sad over your foot, we never saw their sadness. And there was never the slightest hint that either one of them blamed the other, just like there was no blame to be placed for Meritaten's feet."

"But the other politicians in Mother and Father's court didn't feel the same way, did they?" Tut asked.

She shook her head. "No. They didn't. Some of them… they would look at you and frown, because they didn't think you'd be able to take the throne. And they even asked our parents…" She swallowed, not wanting to hurt his feelings by repeating the harsh words. But he was an adult now. And he was strong enough to hear them. "They asked…" she began, "they asked them, 'Are you really making your crippled child your heir?' They asked our parents, 'Are you sure he can do it?' They even said… they even told them they could try again." Ankh closed her eyes, clenching her hands as the pain of that insult jabbed into her heart. "They told them… that they were young. And that with six daughters… *six*… surely this time it would be another boy. A strong son. A son who could lead Egypt."

96

Ankhesenamun looked up. "But our parents were firm. I remember Father told them, 'No.' And he sounded just like you when you make a proclamation. He said, 'We will not try again. We have been given six strong, beautiful daughters, and now a son, and when the day comes, Tutankhaten will be Pharaoh.'"

Ankh remembered how her father had smiled. "And Father said, 'Aten gave him to us, made according to His plan. There is purpose in all of this. And we choose to trust in that purpose.'

"And I always looked for that purpose," Ankh said, tears coming to her eyes. "And I always will. Until we find it.

"So you got bigger," she continued. "And the wet-nurses fed you until you were five, and you drank milk from the nanny-goat we had brought in. And you learned to walk, and you got around just fine. Just as well as the rest of us. When you came upon an obstacle, you found a way around it. And when you fell, you got up again."

"I remember my first cane," Tut said with a wistful little smile. He held out his skinny arms, indicating the length he remembered. "It was only about that long, wasn't it?"

Ankh just chuckled.

"Well, I was only twelve when they made it," Tut continued. Then he sighed again. "And my shoes… I always had special shoes, as long as I can remember." Now he shook his head, thinking sadly of how long it had been since he had worn shoes. And wondering if he ever would again.

Ankh smiled. "The first pair you had was just a plain pair. And you walked right out of them. But the royal shoemakers came up with a special design with different straps that kept them on your feet, and away you went."

Tut shook his head, chuckling as he pictured himself as a tiny little two- or three-year-old, toddling around the palace at Akhetaten, doing his best to keep up with his big sisters and getting into everything he could get his chubby little hands on. How far he had come.

His sister continued. "Then when I was eight and you were three, things changed. That was the year Father named Mother as his co-regent." Her heart ached as she said the words. Their mother had become their father's co-regent, just as at this very moment, she should be her brother's co-regent. If not for the other politicians who circled like vultures around them.

Tut smiled as he remembered the great *durbar*. The whole city had gathered for the beautiful ceremony, the announcement that the Queen was to be made co-regent. Dressed in her finest linen robe, wearing the blue-and-gold cap crown, Nefertiti had stood before the people as Akhenaten had handed her the crook and flail, declaring her his equal. And as he had bowed before her and kissed her hand, all of Egypt had thrown itself facedown before the new ruler, shouting out "all hail's" and their hopes for her long life, prosperity, and health. And the seven royal children had cheered for their mother as Father invoked the blessings of the Aten upon her reign.

Taking the name Ankhkheperure Neferneferuaten, Queen Nefertiti ruled alongside her husband as a Pharaoh of equal stature, sharing the kingship as Father served his nation as priest and Mother served it as leader. Side-by-side, they worked as one Pharaoh, guiding their nation according to their individual strengths. And Ankh had seen it all. It had shown her what a marriage, even a marriage between cousins, could look like. A true partnership, two sets of strengths balancing one another as two people who loved one another set out to achieve the same goals.

But their parents had not been able to lead Egypt into a golden future of peace. Even their strength and wisdom could not prevent the days of sickness from coming the year after Mother had become co-regent. Together Ankh and Tut went through all the events that had brought them to this place; the years of the Aten, the eclipse, the deaths of their sisters and their grandmother and their parents. And they remembered together.

"They got old, Mother and Father," Tutankhamun said.

Looking back, he could see it, the weariness that had grown in them. And with what he knew now, he thought he could catch a glimpse of what had made them that way. Now that he knew, in many small ways, what it meant to be a politician.

The war between the old false gods of the past and the Light of Aten had wearied them; endless politics, deception, and threats had worn them down. Mother was still graceful, beautiful, loveliness in motion, but her face grew lined, her eyes mature, their brightness sharpened into diamond points of political savvy. Father grew bent, his strength fading as pains in his chest came and went, shortness of breath slowed him down, and his tired legs sometimes became swollen. But always, he trusted in his God. Until the day he died.

"And when Mother died, we got married," Ankhesenamun continued. "And we were the little King and Queen, technically, at least. And the Grand Vizier and the General and the Treasurer 'helped' us, and Usermontu and Pentu when they joined the team."

"And we agreed to change our names, and we reopened the temples," Tut said. "And had more built. And we... we were some-how in charge of it all." He sighed, thinking back to his mention of his first cane. "It was when I was around twelve," he said again, "that it started getting harder to get around. I grew a lot that year, and I kept losing my balance. That left foot…" He sighed as the challenges that had once frustrated him shone in the golden past, happy memories of simpler times. "That left foot just wouldn't keep me up anymore. So they made me a cane… and now I have a hundred and thirty-nine of them."

Ankh just took his hand and kissed it.

"There was a lot going on in our lives," Tut summed up. "So we had to be brave."

"We did," Ankh said with a little sigh. She squeezed his hand. "And we were. And we still are. And we always will be."

Tut yawned, and Ankh smiled. Storytime was over. Time for a nap.

"Thank you," he said softly as his eyes began to close.

"Mm-hmm." She lay back on the bed, getting comfortable with her arm around him, his head still resting on her chest. And together, they settled in for a rest.

As Tut lay in her arms, Ankh let herself drift away into her own memories. And thoughts… thoughts of the future. She had lost five siblings in the past, two parents, two daughters. She had survived that. And she trusted that somehow, she would be able to survive the loss that was coming.

# 10  War

He kept praying, Semerkhet. For the Pharaoh, for the Queen, for the new baby. He remembered the terrible days, four years ago, two years ago, when he had mourned with the rest of Egypt, and he prayed that it would be protected; that this child would be strong and healthy. And he imagined having a new niece or nephew.

He hardly knew to Whom he was praying, but he could feel the same answering warmth in his heart as had carried him home from Kadesh. Someone was listening. Someone Who loved them. Somehow the gods had faded away within his heart; their names, their roles, their personalities. What really made one so different from another? He was gaining a strange sense of something bigger; of a Light that was stronger than any name. That Light was real. And it was full of love.

Was that enough?

Things would be hard in the future, he knew. When his Master… when his Master was gone, things would get ten times more dangerous for those who were left. So Semerkhet promised himself that he would protect this child from whoever might wish it harm. Whatever it took.

His friend hadn't gotten out of bed to sit in his chair for several days. And with each passing day, he seemed to grow weaker. Semerkhet closed his eyes, trying to hold back the pain so it didn't hit him square in the heart and knock him flat.

Had the day come when the Pharaoh would never get out of bed again?

Ankh paged through the familiar Queens List with a little smile. And very softly, she began to read out loud. She began to read to the tiny little Prince or Princess who she prayed was growing a little bigger each day. The Prince or Princess who was already part of a legacy older than the pyramids. This child would know how Egypt had come to be what it was; how his or her family had come to be where they were. And knowing who they were and where they came from, this Royal Son or Daughter would find strength.

Strength that they would need.

As the days came and went, each cooler and shorter than the last as the nights grew long and cold, Meresankh continued to do her best. She continued to keep her Lady's room tidy and her shoes and jewelry nicely organized; continued to keep an eye out for her friends when they would take a break from sitting with the Pharaoh who seemed to grow worse every day. She continued to encourage them, continued to hold their hands as they fought back tears, continued to listen to their frustrations and offer what comfort and encouragement she could, continued to try to bring light into the darkness with a cheerful word or a funny story. And if they had time, and they wanted to clear their heads, she would join them in a game of *seega*.

Anything she could do to remind them that she was there, and that she loved them with all her heart. Anything she could do to support them. Anything she could do to keep them strong. Anything she could do to bring them joy. Because, as she reminded herself with a smile, if she was keeping them strong and helping them take care of the Pharaoh, that meant that she was taking care of him, too.

And that was just another thing to be proud of.

102

Every night, Merneith brought the King a new blend of herbs in a cup of hot tea. They helped him settle as bedtime approached, but still he struggled to sleep through the night. So every night she brought a new combination of herbs, or a combination they had tried before but with different proportions. Maybe twice as much lavender as last night would do the trick. Maybe only half as much chamomile. Maybe the tea needed to steep longer before he drank it. Maybe it was better to drink it in three small portions over the two hours before bedtime; maybe it was better to take all of it just before turning in. Maybe some night they would find a combination and dose that worked.

Even now, Tut and Ankh still played *seega*. It was harder for him, and he couldn't play more than a game or two at a time, but he could still play. And he could still win.

"I think I really might be," Ankh said to Tut and Granny as Merneith tied a fresh poultice of lavender and rosemary over the Pharaoh's wound. It didn't look any better today… but at least it didn't look any worse. "I still haven't bled."

Merneith smiled, reaching out to take the Queen's hand as Tut laid his hand on her still-flat stomach.

"Praise be," Granny whispered. Tut just smiled at his sister's belly, his eyes full of hope.

"And I've been crampy, and I just feel… different. And my breasts are sore, too."

Merneith's smile grew wider. "Those are signs," she confirmed.

"Another month and I'll be sure?" Ankh asked the midwife.

Granny nodded. "Another month and we can do the wheat and barley test for real. And we'll be sure."

"Thank you for watching the letter," Tut whispered as Merneith turned back to readjust the bandage and poultice she'd just tied in place.

She smiled as she tightened the knot in the bandage, bright eyes disappearing in smile wrinkles.

"It's my honor, Your Majesty," she said.

Tut reached out and patted her wrinkled old hand. "You're helping save the future of Egypt."


Semerkhet had plenty of time to think as the Pharaoh rested. And he thought of the other losses they had suffered at the hands of the Grand Vizier.

Pentu. Usermontu. Raherka. Amenmose. Brave, loyal men who should not have died. Victims all of Ay's coldhearted cruelty; his single-minded ambition for the throne.

Sem closed his eyes. He had not called any of these men *Brother*. But someone did. And how could they be dead? How could they so suddenly have disappeared from this world, awakening to find themselves in the next while those who had loved and cared about them were left to mourn?

They had not deserved to die like that. It was... it wasn't fair. It was as unfair as the way that even now, his Pharaoh lay on his deathbed, condemned to death by the same man who had killed Amenmose, Raherka, Usermontu, Pentu.

They should not have died. But they had.

Semerkhet sighed. And silently, he said a prayer for their souls.

Ankh sighed, looking down at the letter in her hand. After asking Meresankh to bring her the letter that had been hidden in Granny's workshop, she had taken it to Nuya, the only scribe they could trust, who had copied it out in the graceful script of the priests. The Queen wanted to make sure her husband saw it before she sent it.

First, she had tested the scribe, making sure beyond sure that they could trust him with this important task. She had asked Nuya about children. And without her having made even the slightest suggestion that he was disloyal, she had confirmed his loyalty when he had congratulated her on her good news and gushed over how proud he would be to serve the new Prince or Princess; how honored he would be to protect them from all that was evil in the world. She had breathed a sigh of relief, a prayer of gratitude. And then she had asked Nuya to copy the letter for her.

She would remember the date that the letter had been prepared. The sixth day of Tybi.

"I have the letter," she whispered, gently stroking her brother's face with her soft little hand. The bedroom door was locked, so they were safe to discuss the future.

Slowly Tut opened his eyes. More and more naps were happening completely by accident. "Mmm?"

"I wanted you to know what it said," she said. She walked to the table and picked up a piece of papyrus, upon which the scribe had recorded her letter in hieratic script. Ankh cleared her throat and began.

"My husband…" Ankh paused, choking on her tears and pressing the back of her hand against her mouth. Tut offered his hand and she took it, swallowing as she prepared to start again. "My husband has died and there is no one I can trust. I am afraid. It is said that you have many sons. If you send me one of your sons, I will marry him and make him Pharaoh of Egypt. I do not wish to marry a servant... I have written to no other country; only to you. Send me one of your sons so that Egypt and the Kingdom of Hattusa may stand together as allies for all eternity."

Ankh put the letter down before she dropped tears onto the papyrus. Through his own tears, Tut barely saw her sit down beside him, wrapping her arms around him, half-lifting him. He hugged her back as tightly as he could, pressing his face against her shoulder as slowly, they breathed together. Nine years together was not enough.

He did not want her to marry a servant— that old vulture— either. But if she could marry a Prince, Egypt's future would be secure.

Time was becoming short.

Time was indeed becoming short, Ankh thought as she wiped away her tears. And there was no longer time to cry.

It was time to focus. And share every moment they had left.

Ankh burned her initial copy of the letter, exchanging the final draft of the letter with Merneith. Granny would keep it safe.

The Vizier knew that such a letter existed. But he didn't know where it was. It would wait in the midwife's workshop until the moment came for it to be sent.

On her way back from the kitchen with a bowl full of sliced melon for her Pharaoh and her Queen, Meresankh heard voices inside Ay's chambers. She paused in the shadows, standing so she

106

could just see through the half-open door; hear what they were saying.

The Vizier appeared to be dictating a letter to his secretary.

"The young Pharaoh was a naïve child, and if his Queen is allowed to rule, things will not be much better," he was saying. Meresankh gritted her teeth, forcing herself to remain silent as anger pulsed in her temples. How dare he talk about her Mistress and her Pharaoh that way. "A marriage between myself, or my son, and your daughter Princess Muwatti, therefore seems advantageous to both our kingdoms. My superior experience and wisdom would remain at the head of Egypt, while the union of our two nations would bolster both our economies, turn two former enemies into allies, and perhaps, one day, allow us to expand our combined territories into the lands of Nubia and Mitanni. I await your response."

He was writing to King Suppiluliuma too.

Meresankh tightened her grip on the bowl of fruit and hurried back to her Pharaoh's room as quick as she could trot. Politics just never ended, did it?

But as she went, she prayed her thanks to I-AM that she had been sent to the kitchen at the precise moment that would allow her to hear the Vizier's plan… so her Mistress and her Pharaoh could do something about it.

The Queen would know what to do. There was still hope.

"We have to send the letter," Meresankh panted, staggering into the Pharaoh's room without so much as a knock, a few juicy slices of melon slipping out of the bowl she carried and onto the floor. Bastet hopped out of Ankhesenamun's lap to investigate. "Right now."

"What happened?" the Pharaoh asked, sitting up straighter. He looked weary, looked worse than he had yesterday, but now he was alert, readying his heart and mind for battle.

"The Vizier's written his own letter," the handmaiden said, setting the bowl of fruit on the table and trying to catch her breath, one rounded little hand pressed to her pounding heart, the other resting on the table for support. Darting behind her, Semerkhet ran to the door to lock it, keeping her words inside the room in which they stood. "He's written to the Hittites, too. And he's asked King Suppiluliuma for the hand of Princess Muwatti, for either him or Nakhtmin. We have to do something."

Tut closed his eyes. They had sought Usermontu's help, they had promised that an heir was on the way, they had foiled Ay's attempt to give himself the right to claim the next throne, and they had prepared their own letter. But Ay was still one step ahead of them.

Ankhesenamun had stared silently at her handmaiden all through this breathless account, mind clearly working a mile a minute. But she didn't look afraid. She looked amused. Confident. Even... a little excited. And ready for the next battle.

She smiled at Tut. And yet, this time, she didn't place the decision of how to salvage the situation into his hands. He was weaker today even than on the day when he had helped create the plan of how to reclaim their signet-ring. To burden him with this task felt cruel. And so today, his big sister would step into the gap.

"Don't you worry about a thing," she said. "After all... it's just politics. Semerkhet," she asked, and the valet straightened up to stand at attention before her, "can you bring in Nuya, please? And Meresankh, can you get Granny?"

A few minutes later the scribe was bowing before the royal couple. His scribe's kilt was neatly starched, although as usual, he had ink on his fingers. And he looked cold, bare-chested on a day when most everyone was wrapped warmly in an outer robe. But as chilly as he was, the look of general satisfaction in his eyes (although of course he was anxiously ready for anything the Pharaoh might need) reminded Tut of what a good decision it had been to get Nuya moved to the scribe department.

"We need your help," Tutankhamun said from where he sat in the bed, wrapped up in blankets and propped on pillows. He was still as commanding, as regal, as he could manage.

"Anything, My Lord," Nuya said, inclining his head. Tut smiled to see that with all the respect the servant was offering, he didn't seem afraid; hadn't thrown himself facedown on the floor before the Pharaoh. He was even making eye contact. On the right people, Meresankh's gossiping campaign had worked.

"Your Majesty." Tut smiled to see Merneith coming into the room, a scheming little smile on her wise old face. Quickly, Semerkhet locked the door behind her. The old woman produced the precious letter, which had been waiting in her workshop, from inside her green outer robe, and placed it in the Pharaoh's hand. Ankhesenamun applied a wax seal, and, accepting a pen and his signet-ring from Semerkhet, Tutankhamun applied his royal signature to the letter that was to be their next move in this game.

"Fank you, Granny," Tut said gratefully. He turned back to Nuya, who was waiting for his orders. "I need you to go to the royal post-box and switch this letter, the one you just copied out for the Queen, with one that the Grand Vithier has written to King Suppiluliuma before the messengerth take it."

109

Then he smiled. He had another idea. Another level of comeuppance that could be added to this day of victory. "Granny... can you stall the Vizier while we make the switch? With all your medical ekthperienth, there must be something you could, er, offer him, that would slow him down a little. Or maybe..." He smiled again. "Even Nakhtmin."

"With pleasure. Castor oil in the General's drink should do nicely," she said, returning the smile a little mischievously. And she was off.

The Pharaoh handed the message to Nuya, carefully rolled up and tied with the same blue thread the Vizier always used. "It hath to go out today," he said softly. "And without the Vizier seeing. We don't have much time."

"I'll go at once," Nuya said with another bow. And before they could thank him, he was gone.

They waited for what felt like a very long time, palms sweating, stomachs twisting, hearts pounding. Bastet hunted for bugs; Semerkhet paged through a historical account. Ankhesenamun played *seega* with Meresankh, who Tut had never realized was a champion at the game. There was nothing to do but wait for Nuya to return.

But soon, their hearts leapt to hear a soft knock at the door. And Nuya came in, a broad smile on his face, and a letter tucked into his belt.

"Great Morning Star," he said, presenting it with a bow.

Tutankhamun took the scroll triumphantly, popped off the wax seal, and unrolled it. Ay's words were clear on the papyrus; Tut saw the words "advantageous" and "expand." So Nakhtmin was

110

not the only one who wanted to take over their neighbors' lands. He had gotten that lovely trait from his father. Daddy's little politician indeed.

"Thank you, Nuya," Tut said, reaching out his hand for a clasp. Looking surprised, Nuya shook his hand. "You just helped save Egypt." And the Pharaoh put Ay's letter under his pillow.

Then he lay back against his pillows, tired but satisfied. This was starting to feel like some sort of victory.


A little while later, Semerkhet went back out for another trip to the kitchen. And when he came back, he was smiling.

"The post just went out," he announced, offering a bowl of almonds to the Pharaoh.

Ankh hurried to the window, pulling back the gauzy linen curtains and smiling as she saw the guards carrying the box of letters on poles as if it were a palanquin. They would take it to a delivery boat, and off it would go down the Nile, all the way to the Hittites.

And she sent up a grateful prayer to Whoever was listening.

"It's gone," she said, turning back into the room with a smile. She bent over her brother, squeezing his hand and kissing him on the forehead. "It's on its way."

# 11    Revenge

Tut lay back with a smile. Their last hope was on its way. Then he sighed, thinking about the contents of Ankh's letter; the words she had written. *My husband has died,* she had told the Hittites, *and there is no one I can trust.* But he wasn't dead yet. How strange, how... spooky... that she had sent the letter while he still breathed; how strange that he himself had gotten to read the letter in which she had announced that he was dead. And how sad. Because he knew that by the time the letter reached the Hittites, or by the time their reply reached Egypt, he would be.

But in this letter, whatever happened, lay their final chance for victory.

And the opportunity for a mean chuckle as he imagined Nakhtmin suffering from Granny's sabotage. With enough castor oil, the effects on one's digestive system could be far-reaching and dramatic, although of course, Merneith's carefully measured dose would do no lasting harm. Only make the next hour or two seriously unpleasant, a punishment for being a generally unpleasant person, as well as a tactical distraction of the Vizier. The Pharaoh nodded. He deserved it, the little snake.

It wasn't long before the King and Queen saw the Vizier again— before they, in fact, invited him into the royal chambers. Tut tried to hide his smile as Ay came in, an insincere smile on his own face.

"How are you, my dear Pharaoh?" he asked, sneaking up on the conversation like a hunting jackal.

"Not so bad," Tutankhamun replied, giving the traitor a serene look of satisfaction. For a moment, Ay almost seemed to wonder why the Pharaoh looked so content. Then the look passed, replaced by smug satisfaction of his own.

"Egypt is in safe hands," the Vizier sneered. "I've prepared my own letter. When I, or perhaps Nakhtmin, marry Princess Muwatti, Egypt will be united with Hattusa just as you suggested… but with me on the throne." He gave an ugly smile, wrinkled face twisting with delight as he gloated over his victory. "The post went out an hour ago. Although unfortunately, I did not have the opportunity to watch it go out, as my dear son was suddenly taken with an upset stomach, and I had to assist him to the physicians' quarters." Ay pursed his lips, as though the memory of his son's symptoms was unpleasant. Then he smiled again. "The letter is on its way to Hattusa as we speak."

"Oh, you mean this letter?" Tut asked casually, producing the Vizier's message from underneath his pillow.

Ay just stared, ugly smile slowly melting away like a scented wax cone.

"Then which…" he stuttered, clutching his walking-stick. The Grand Vizier himself was beyond words.

"Ours," Tut said with a sweet little smile. "Prince Zannanza should be on his way soon. And a royal marriage between Egypt and Hattusa will occur… as previously discussed. My dear?" He looked up at the Queen. Triumphantly, Ankh took the Vizier's letter and laid it in an incense burner, where it burst into flames. Soon all that was left of Ay's scheme was the smell of burning paper.

"How did you…" Ay asked, actually blinking in shock. Not something Tutankhamun had ever expected to see, the Grand

Vizier blinking in shock. "You can't leave your bed," he said, looking at Tut with his old forehead wrinkled in confusion, "and you never leave his side," he said to the Queen. "How could you even have known about my letter, much less exchanged it for yours?"

"We have friends," Tut said simply. "Loyal friends." He did not elaborate, remembering Ankh's wisdom from so long ago, not to name names. But this simple statement would be enough. And he would say nothing of the loyal friends who had played a key role in the mission to restore the Pharaoh's signet-ring to its rightful place. The signet-ring that even now rested safely on the King's finger, for the Vizier to see. Tutankhamun folded his hands, making sure that it was in plain sight.

The Pharaoh raised a dark eyebrow, giving the traitor just a hint of the thunder and lightning as he let his nostrils flare threateningly. "What we do, Vizier," Tutankhamun said softly as the fire in the incense burner crackled, the papyrus curling and blackening as the flames licked it, "we do for Egypt."

"And what may happen," Ankh continued, standing rather like a lioness about to pounce on a gazelle and tear its throat out, "remains to be seen."

Ay stared as his plan crumbled into ash and smoke before his very eyes, his own words coming back around to betray him. He stared at the signet-ring he had stolen gleaming calmly on the Pharaoh's hand. And silently, he walked out of the room.

They let him go. What would they get by arresting him, other than an uprising by the servants whose loyalty lay with him? If he was back again tomorrow with another scheme, they would deal with that tomorrow.

Tut grinned up at his sister, the weight of the pyramids seeming to lift from his shoulders. And laughing, she bent to hug him. It felt good to laugh together.

Who knew what the Vizier would do in the future. But they knew that for now, in this, he was defeated. And that he and Nakhtmin would never know that Granny had been behind the little General's sudden rather horrifying digestive distress... which he was probably still dealing with at this very moment.

How many days, how many hours, had they just stolen back from the unforgiving future?

Ankhesenamun imagined the letter traveling by boat, by cart, by equestrian courier, all the way to the royal court of Hattusa. She imagined a tall, faceless Hittite King in glorious royal robes receiving the letter, reading it, pondering whether her plea was sincere or whether it was a trick intended to bring down Hattusa.

She had spoken the truth to Ay. What happened remained to be seen.

Her brother's cough was getting worse. Ankh winced as she watched him struggling to clear his lungs, producing stained handkerchiefs that became a more and more frightening red by the hour.

Everything was already wrong. But here was one more thing to face.

Meresankh saw Semerkhet less and less. He took fewer breaks and didn't eat in the servants' hall as much. She wondered how much he was eating at all.

But every now and then, when she had time, Meresankh would quietly stand in the doorway of her Pharaoh's room, and if the Queen was there too, she would smile at Meresankh and nod. And Meresankh would take Sem's hand and take him away for five or ten minutes, and they would share a cup of tea and a few minutes of conversation or companionable silence. She would encourage him. Try to cheer him up until at last he cracked a smile. And imagine what it would be like to look after him as his wife.

"That's not the blanket I want," Tut whined as Semerkhet brought him a heavy linen blanket. "Don't you pay any attention to anything? I want the soft one— the one I got for my birthday."

Semerkhet sighed. And as he fought back the impulse to shake his head, he smiled to himself. And remembered. Remembered the joys of being a big brother.

Ankh caught a glimpse of herself in her husband's bronze mirror as she brought him a bowl of broth for dinner. And she almost chuckled. She looked funny without makeup; she had not had the time to let Meresankh do her makeup for days. Hadn't even been in her own room long enough to let Meresankh put her makeup on. When was the last time she had slept in her own bed? And she had worn the same short, relatively simple wig, and the same old blue outer robe, for days. Not only was she not wearing eye makeup; she had dark circles under her eyes, and they were bloodshot with weariness. She glanced down at her hands; the red henna she usually wore on her fingernails was fading. And the only jewelry she had on, or had worn for over a week, was a simple pendant necklace, one of Mother's. Her diadems, too, were gathering dust in her room.

116

She didn't look like a Queen. But she looked like a wife and a sister.

The worst watch was two hours before morning came, Semerkhet found. Too late for there to be really any chance of getting any more sleep, or any sleep at all, some nights. Almost too late to even try to get back to sleep. But at the same time, still too early to give up. Every other night, Semerkhet had that watch. And when he didn't, the Queen did.

It was hard. There was so much sacrifice in taking care of the King, even the rare moment when Sem wondered what life would be like if he had simply become a scribe. But he couldn't really imagine being anywhere else. Taking care of his Pharaoh was his job, his responsibility, as Royal Valet, even at the expense of his own sleep. And making sure that his little brother knew he wasn't alone was his responsibility as a big brother. And through it all, it was his honor to take care of him.

Meresankh studied. At odd moments here and there with the Queen; on her own time in the royal library. There was so much to learn about the wise, courageous women who had blazed their path.

Then she smiled. One day, her Lady would be in these documents. Because she was the bravest, wisest Queen of all.

"How far is it to Hattusa?" Meresankh asked Semerkhet as they sat together at dinner.

Semerkhet took a bite of beans and pondered. "Kadesh is about three-fourths of the way to the city they're probably coming from," he estimated. "Might take a month on horseback, if they're not riding hard enough to kill the horses."

Meresankh nodded, then sipped her beer. "Do you think the Prince will come?" she asked in a small voice.

Sem just gave a heavy sigh. And he reached out and squeezed her hand.

"What if..." she began, then paused, biting her lip. She looked up at him, eyes big. "What if he doesn't?"

Semerkhet sighed, looking down at their entwined hands as he thought. Finally he looked up with half a smile. "Well, that's up to the Queen, isn't it?"

And Meresankh smiled.


They kept turning him, Semerkhet, Kamose, even Nuya, sometimes. Tut would hold his breath when they did it, feeling the fire scream through what was left of his broken legs, a breath away from gasping, "stop!" But each time, the moment when it became too painful was the moment that it was over. And they would leave him, gasping and panting, to lie in his new position; get a slightly different perspective on the room that had become his whole universe.

And he would rest. And try, as the pain slowly subsided, to be grateful for the fact that because he was being moved every two hours, he would not get bedsores.

But did it even matter at this point?


Tut could no longer play the lute, the new hobby he had enjoyed toying with only a few short weeks ago. But Semerkhet could, and he played day and night for his friends, whiling away the hours with songs happy and sad, old, contemporary, and made up on the

118

spot. And the King and Queen smiled as Semerkhet's music touched their hearts.

But even as she encouraged her friends, Meresankh could not fix everything. And sometimes… sometimes, they were having a bad day. Sometimes, when they came to sit with her, it was with tears in their eyes. And as she comforted them, her heart ached with heaviness. Because shouldn't she be able to make them feel better?

There were so many tears to be shed. Every day, it seemed, something would tug so painfully at Semerkhet's heart that the pain would begin to leak from his eyes. And he would turn away, hide his face, so the Pharaoh wouldn't see. He would bite his lip, clench his fist, bite his knuckle; anything so his brother wouldn't see he had been crying.

He didn't want his friend to know.

With everything she did, Tut got worse. Ankh poured every bit of her energy into looking after her husband, bringing him the things he needed, keeping him as comfortable as possible. But even if she could make him smile with a bouquet of flowers, help him while away the hours with a story, soothe him to sleep with a lullaby, it was never enough.

Because nothing she could do could heal him. No matter what she did, no matter how hard she worked, no matter how hard she tried, he was still going to die.

And the Queen of Egypt, who could prevent a war with the right words or begin one with the wrong ones, felt helpless.

Tut smiled as Semerkhet helped him get ready for bed as the sixth day of Tybi ended, dabbing a cool cloth over his neck and arms; helping him change into a fresh sleeping-tunic. Even with everything that was going on, it felt good to be looked after by a friend.

Then he felt a little ache in his heart. It was ending, he knew. And every time he spent time with Semerkhet, every time his valet got him up in the morning, put him to bed at night, sang to him, bathed him, told him a joke, made him smile… there was one time fewer remaining in the future.

And one day, there would be a day… that was the very last day of all.

Granny had a look at Tutankhamun that evening after faithfully examining what was left of his leg and gently wrapping a fresh bandage around it. This time, she was listening to his lungs. Sitting by him on the bed as he sat propped up on pillows, she laid her ear on his chest, carefully listening to him breathing in and out. Then she listened at his back.

When she sat up, it was with a grim face. "So many days unable to leave your bed have resulted in an infection in your lungs. I'm sorry, dear boy." She got up to make him a cup of infection-fighting tea. But she did not say whether this was something with which she could contend.

They hit another milestone that week. As Semerkhet put his Pharaoh to bed one night, he gently began to assist him onto his stomach as always. But the pain was too great. So Semerkhet stopped, and instead placed a few pillows against Tut's chest and stomach. And with Tutankhamun lying on his side, Semerkhet was

120

able to soothe him to sleep with gentle touch and the sleepy fragrances of spikenard and frankincense. Just like always.

Even though… Before Sem crept away, leaving his friend to sleep, he saw a tear sliding down his brother's warm, brown cheek. Biting back his own pain, he turned back to gently wipe it away. He understood. Tut was trapped. Imprisoned not only in his room, not only in his bed, but in the position in which he lay. Another of a thousand small losses had come. And every day, every night, brought them closer to the great loss that was yet to come.

Ankh settled down in her chair and closed her eyes. She had an hour before it was time to trade places with Semerkhet, and she wanted to make the most of it.

But her sleep was not filled with the warm, empty silence of comfortable, restful oblivion. It was filled with dreams.

*She sat on the throne, the double crown of Egypt weighing heavily on her head, the crook and flail cold in her hands, the jutting false beard of magnificence tied to her chin. Before her, courtiers from all over the country prostrated themselves on the floor with utterances of "All hail, Pharaoh Nefermaatet, the Morning and the Evening Star, the Lady of the Two Lands! All life, prosperity, and health!"*

*She looked around the room. And despite the pain, the strangeness, the uncertainty, she smiled.*

*Because she knew she could do it.*

Ankh woke up. And again, she blinked back tears. That wouldn't really happen, would it? They wouldn't really allow her to take the throne after her brother? Without a co-regency, without a son in her arms, taking the throne herself really was little more than a dream.

But she smiled. Because just as she had thought in the dream… if the opportunity came to her…

She knew she could do it.

# 12 Darkness

Ankh accepted a plate of homemade spicy chicken from Meresankh for lunch and inhaled the fragrant steam as her stomach growled. Until suddenly… the contented, hungry rumbling of her stomach turned into roiling and she set the plate on the side table just to keep from throwing up.

"What's wrong, My Lady?" Meresankh asked, frowning in concern.

Ankh put her hand on her churning stomach. "Just nauseated all of a sudden… thanks… I love your spicy chicken… but can you just… just get me some porridge?"

Meresankh nodded. "Of course, My Lady." And taking the plate of chicken, the handmaiden went to go find her Mistress something else to eat.

As Meresankh left the room, Ankh looked down at her belly. And smiled. It was time to talk to the midwife.

Semerkhet's stomach rumbled. He had just fed the King, but he hadn't had lunch yet. And suddenly he couldn't remember if he had had breakfast. There wasn't really time for all of that. Not anymore. Not now, when he couldn't bring himself to leave his Master's side.

Now the King was asleep, his chest slowly rising and falling as he lay there in the bed, the cat curled up at his side. His valet smiled as he watched his Master quietly sleeping, enjoying a few minutes of pain-free peace.

The Queen was taking a break, retiring to her own chambers for a few minutes. And so Semerkhet sat alone, silently guarding his brother as he slept. So late in the game, would any amount of sleep bring about any healing at all?

There was a soft knock at the door. Glancing at the drowsing Pharaoh, Semerkhet got up to answer it.

"Thanks; I couldn't have got the door with my hands full," Meresankh said with a smile, carefully entering with two plates of her Granny's famous spicy chicken. "Thought you'd be hungry, but I thought you wouldn't want to go to lunch. Didn't see you at breakfast."

He accepted the plate of chicken. "I really appreciate it. And you're right... I don't really feel comfortable leaving him." He looked at her a little sideways, and she smiled up at him, that adorable dimple appearing in her cheek. "You could have lunch with me in here, if you want. If the Queen doesn't need you for a few minutes."

"Our Queen's asleep," Meresankh said. "It's catching up with all of us." She looked pointedly up at Semerkhet.

He sighed. When was the last time any of them had slept through the night? Really... when had it been? He paged back through the past several nights in his mind, and couldn't find one. It had been awhile.

Then he smiled at his friend. "It would feel good to sit down for a few minutes." He reached out slightly with his free hand, and his heart began to pound as she took his hand in her tiny one. "With you."

Meresankh smiled again, and again he saw her sweet dimple. "It would." They crept into the King's sitting room and sat down again at the little table; in here, they could chat softly without waking him, but Sem could still see him through the doorway. Watch him sleep.

"You're used to tasting things," she said, nodding at the plate she'd offered him. "Tell me if it tastes all right, like I always make it."

Sem chewed his bite thoughtfully, then nodded with a little shrug. "Tastes fine to me. Tastes good."

Meresankh smiled at him. "Good." She shook her head. "My confidence in my own cooking has been shaken. The Queen just smelled it and she almost threw up."

Semerkhet looked up as he took another bite of chicken. "Isn't that a sign?" he asked.

Meresankh just smiled. Then she sighed. She looked up at him, feeling a tugging in her heart; a leading. "Sem," she said softly, "what... will happen, someday, a long time from now? When..." She glanced sideways at the sleeping King.

Semerkhet's jaw tightened. "He will be judged by Ma'at, and when his heart is weighed and found lighter than the feather in her hair, he will go to the Field of Reeds and be at peace."

Meresankh nodded. So he was still firmly founded in the polytheistic faith celebrated by most of the Egyptians she knew.

"What if..." she said slowly, wondering and praying how to go on, "what if Merneith is right? She did see everything that happened when Pharaoh Akhenaten was a child, and she believes that the Hebrew Prince was right; that the God of the Hebrews made all those things happen. Just like Pharaoh Akhenaten, who called Him the Aten." Meresankh felt the Light in her heart pushing her forward. She swallowed, then boldly went on. "I believe she's right." She looked down. "I've always believed. Ever since I was a little girl."

Semerkhet looked up, the spicy sauce of the bite of chicken he was about to eat dripping drop by drop back onto the plate. "You have?"

She glanced up at him, then down again, suddenly not at all sure how he would respond. "I have," she said finally.

He looked down, not meeting her eye. And he kept eating, the silence as thick as a sandstorm. But she couldn't take another bite. Not until he said something.

"Do you want to keep that, then?" he asked, his eyes flickering to her necklace under lowering eyebrows. His voice was hard; almost angry. She had never heard it like that before. "If it's a pagan idol?"

She reached up to stroke the necklace, gently shaking her head. Then she nodded, trying to give him the same smile she always did. "I do want to keep it. Even if I don't believe Isis exists... it's a gift that represents your love for me. And that's why I treasure it."

Meresankh reached out to touch Semerkhet's hand, but he didn't offer his. So she took hers back.

He sighed heavily. But his face was a little less hard, the anger in his eyebrows fading. He looked a little sad, a little... confused.

"You've given me a lot to think about," he said shortly. And he took another bite of chicken.

Meresankh finished her meal in silence. There was not much to do but wait and see what he decided. Pray that his heart would be opened. But she knew what her decision was.

Ankh had gone to meet with the midwife, to find out from the old woman if there was a real chance that they had told the truth to Ay and the others. And Semerkhet was quietly busying himself with the endless sorting and rearrangement of stacks of papyrus,

126

baskets of fresh cloths, and pieces of well-loved jewelry. So there was no one for Tut to talk to but his own heart.

And it hit him. With an impact that almost made him gasp, it hit him square in the heart.

He was never going to have an adulthood. He would never live to see thirty, forty, or fifty. Or even… even twenty. He would not have five more children with Ankh and see them have their own children. This… this, right here, was it. The body in which he was currently trapped, crippled, broken, but so young, barely more than that of a child, was the body in which he would die. Not the old man's body he had always imagined.

Tutankhamun closed his eyes as the truth soaked through him like cold rain. That meant… that meant that he would not have thirty years to lead his country into a glorious future. He would never live to become the strong, glorious Pharaoh, the true successor of Thutmose the First, that he had always dreamed of being. Would never— He bit his lip. Would never have the time to develop true wisdom. And he would never see his Sed Festival… he would probably never see the completion of the schools he and Ankh were having built. And he… he would never meet the baby who he hoped with every particle of his being was growing big and strong inside his wife's belly.

He didn't have thirty more years. He didn't have thirty more weeks… he might not even have thirty more days.

It was all cut short. Just as he was beginning to grasp his future in his hands, just as he was beginning to step out into adulthood, it was vanishing before his eyes, torn from his grasp. His reign, his life itself, were ending before they had begun. And it was too late for even the greatest doctor in Egypt to heal the wounds that were killing him.

He was alone. And he let the tears flow as he mourned for the future and the life and the time he would never have.

The Queen adjusted her dress and stood up from where she'd been sitting on her bed. Her examination by the midwife was complete.

She looked at Merneith, whose face was inscrutable.

"Well?" she asked. "What do you think? Do you think…" She touched her belly. "Could I be?"

Granny smiled up at her with bright eyes and took one of Ankh's hands in her wrinkled old hand.

"We'll just have to see."

Semerkhet made his way back to the Pharaoh's room that afternoon, keeping to himself as he always did. As before, half the other servants offered respectful nods as he passed, while the others stood in silence that looked almost angry.

"Don't bow, you fool!" one man whispered to his friend, who had hastily bobbed his head as Sem walked by. "He's not Crown Prince Nakhtmin."

"He's not the Crown Prince yet!" the second man hissed back, elbowing the other as they took their conversation to another part of the room. "And if Zannanza gets here on time, he never will be!"

"If that Hittite so much as steps onto the palace grounds, you know what will happen," the first man sneered. The other just pouted at him and walked away. But Semerkhet saw that the man who had called Nakhtmin the Crown Prince had had his hand on his knife.

Sem shook his head. Just like the news of the little Prince or Princess had spread like wildfire throughout the staff, so had the Pharaoh's revelation to the Vizier that the Queen had invited the Hittite Prince to stand beside her as the next page of history turned. Everyone in the palace knew of her daring plan. And everyone, clearly, had an opinion on it.

The lessons Mother and Grandmother had taught her filled Ankh's heart as she sat with her brother, watching him take a nap before dinner. Of all the women who had come before. Their power, their grace, their wisdom that she relied on, their legacy that lived in her now. Thoughts of Mother herself, reigning as Smenkhkare for three good years, keeping Egypt in one piece during its greatest upheaval.

And for the first time, she wondered.

Would she be joining them?

Pride swelled in Ankhesenamun's heart as she thought of it, her name being added to the Queens List that Mother and Grandmother had prepared. And she caught a glimpse of future Royal Daughters being inspired as they read her story, just as she had been inspired by stories of Neith-hotep, Tetisheri, Sobekneferu.

She imagined her baby growing up, watching its mother reigning as Pharaoh.

If she could marry the Hittite Prince and rule from beside the throne, she would. But if not...

She could take the throne herself. She knew she could. And through her authority and power, she would continue the legacy of her family as she made Egypt a better place.

And her throne name would be *Nefermaatet*. Because she would reign in beauty and in truth.

They took turns through the nights, Ankh and Sem, to sit with the Pharaoh and guide him through the restless hours. And through the days, they took turns, too. Took turns in weeping.

Meresankh rolled over in bed late that evening with a sigh. It was getting late; getting up to check her water-clock, she could see that she'd been in bed for three hours and hadn't slept a wink. But she couldn't. Not when she knew that in the other room, her Lady and Semerkhet were taking turns sitting up with the Pharaoh, trying to help him catch the sleep that was becoming so elusive to him. Sometimes, she knew, when the sun rose, no one had slept at all.

Fourth hour of night. In her mind Meresankh could see the Queen sitting at her brother's side, hear Semerkhet's gentle snores as he took the hour of sleep that was allotted to him, imagine the Pharaoh wincing every time a stab of pain jangled through what was left of his leg. She hadn't seen his leg for days, but she knew it was getting worse. And she knew it would only continue to get worse until the day he died. None of them could change that.

She rolled over again, still wide awake. And she sighed again. Why, she asked in her heart, why couldn't she do more? Why couldn't she truly fix any of this, rather than just tagging along with her Mistress and her friend, offering what little support she could? Why couldn't she truly do something? Something that would change all of this for the better?

A cup of tea and a smile was nothing in the face of the endless sleepless nights and rising stress the Queen was facing as the uncertain future grew ever nearer. A hand-clasp and the words "you're so brave" couldn't change the fact that Semerkhet was about to lose a second brother, as well as his career. Even the kindest gestures she could come up with could not change the future. Even the cleanest room would not solve the problems her Lady was facing.

And then the answer touched her heart, as warm and gentle as a soft ray of sunshine in the dark depths of the night. *You* are *doing something*, it told her. *There is always something you can do, even if it seems small. Always a way you can help. Always something that matters. Life is full of things you can change and things you can't, and you are changing everything you can for the better. What you are doing* is *important. These things may seem small, but they are worthwhile. And they are enough.*

And she remembered the cleaning she had done today; the thorough reorganization of the Queen's off-season wardrobe. Something so small, so insignificant, meaningless, even, in the face of the impending death of the Pharaoh. And yet... Meresankh felt herself smiling; felt her heart warm with gratitude. Because she knew that even that small thing mattered. She was making a difference.

And with that encouraging thought, she finally felt drowsiness begin to descend. Maybe she would get some sleep tonight after all.

Semerkhet lay silently on his cot late that night, wishing he could sleep. His Master had been asleep for an hour, which was a good run, and the Queen was taking her turn to sit beside him, but now Sem was the one who lay awake, staring into the blackness.

Meresankh. His sweet love, suddenly telling him she didn't believe in the gods of Egypt; that she loved the God of the Hebrews, the Aten his Master's father had worshiped. She'd kept his necklace as a token of love, but the figure of Isis on it was meaningless to her, nothing more than a pretty picture.

He wanted her to know that she was as beautiful as the Queen of all the goddesses. But she didn't believe any of them existed.

Although, the way things had been going these past few weeks… he wasn't sure if he was sure whether they existed either. Someone was there… but were They among the gods and goddesses he had been raised to worship?

And inside his aching heart, he realized that he no longer knew what he believed.

Semerkhet rolled over, hearing his Pharaoh shifting in bed and wondering if in a few moments he would be murmuring for attention, needing Sem as well as the Queen. In the meantime, he could keep gazing into his own thoughts. Wondering what to do… and wondering what was true.

Ankhesenamun struggled to sleep. She rolled back and forth in her chair, hand always resting on her belly. Her belly that was still so flat… but that might be blossoming with new life.

She thought back. And she blinked back the tears. The joy. The hope. And then… the silence. Emptiness.

She thought of them, the fleeting moments they had shared, brief moments of love and pain, moments too brief to put into words, and yet which seemed to stretch out into eternity. And she thought of the names she had whispered in her heart.

"Mereneferet," she had said, kissing the silent face of the tiny Princess who had been born so early, born sweetly, heartbreakingly sleeping. *Love and Beauty.* "Senebhenas," she had murmured two years later, being so careful as she held her second precious daughter, trying not to hurt her back. *Health is with her.* She had whispered their names when she and their father had laid them to rest. And she had whispered them through the days and nights that had separated them in time and space.

She wondered what it would be like to have the opportunity to raise the children she had carried inside. The children she had loved for so many months, and would love until the end of time.

And the hope that filled her heart now felt fragile. She… felt fragile. Because it had happened before. And it could happen again.

All she could do was pray. To Whoever was listening.

And hope. And wait.


It was so dark. Tutankhamun wasn't afraid of the dark; of course it was dark. It was the middle of the night. Time to be sleeping… if only he could.

Beside him, Semerkhet sat silently, occasionally reaching out to stroke his head. They weren't talking. Sem didn't want to keep him up, on the off-chance that he did drift off.

So he was free to think. About the darkness. And about the Light. About what he remembered, from the days of his parents, from more recent days, standing in the Sun and feeling the warmth of its Light touch his face. The silence of the temple. The cold, and the dark, standing before the mute, impassive gods and goddesses who had never once answered any one of his fervent prayers. As if they didn't care. Or as if they had no power to answer his prayers… no power to act. As if… they didn't exist. As if these cold stone statues, as cold as this Tybi night, were nothing more than artwork; as if they did not represent anything real. Only the hopes of an artist seeking a way to connect to the Divine.

Then he felt it. Gentle as a whisper; soft and warm as a ray of Sun gently touching his face. They did not exist. And they never had. But Someone did.

The Pharaoh shuddered again, lying in the dark, as the Truth touched him. Osiris, Horus, Amun-Ra himself... none of them real. Not at all. That was why they were so silent. They were nothing but stone. Nothing but stories. Stories... like his Father's, of the Aten?

Could those, maybe just, be more than stories? Could they? There were no answers, lying here in bed with so many hours to go before morning came with the Sun.

But he wasn't alone. That much he knew. As he lay there in the darkness of the middle of the night, he wished he could feel the touch of the Sun on his face, and he wished he could feel the same peace and love that his father had known.

He wished he knew the answers. But now another question was rising in his heart, alongside all the others. Whatever the answer to this mystery was... would he discover it before he took his final breath? And after his final breath... would he awaken to darkness, or to Light?

Tutankhamun shivered under his warm blankets. And for the first time, he was afraid of the dark.

# 13  Endurance

The next morning, the morning of the eighth of Tybi, the valet sat quietly watching the King being tended by his sister, the Queen bringing him a cup of tea and some simple porridge for breakfast; porridge that Semerkhet had faithfully checked and declared free of poison.

And it hit him. Hit him as hard as the solid ground had hit him when he had jumped from the chariot in Kadesh. With the same shock. The same impact.

Because suddenly he could see the emptiness that stretched out before him. The emptiness that he would face when his Master was gone. When his friend, his brother, was gone. The wall of busyness that had protected him since Amurru was beginning, brick by brick, to fall. And one day, it would come crashing down.

His friend would soon be gone. And all of this would be over. Everything that had defined his life for the past fourteen months, his day job, his night job, everything he did, everything that mattered to him, would be over. There would be no more Pharaoh to look after.

Or there would… but it would be a different Pharaoh. And who it would be was not yet certain— as was what they would do with Egypt after his dear Morning Star was gone.

Without ever really thinking about it seriously, Sem had always envisioned working at the palace as his Pharaoh's valet all his life, until they were both old. He had simply assumed that that was how his life would go, and that expected future, the prospect of spending his life at his Pharaoh's side, had made him happy.

But it wasn't going to happen that way. The future ahead of him was strange and unknown, and his brother was not in it. Now their

135

approaching separation was one of the only sure things in this strange, unfriendly future that Semerkhet was facing. Everything that had given his life meaning over the past year was about to be taken from him.

Images of Nedjes flashed through his heart; pictures of the smiling, happy little boy whom Semerkhet had taught to play hockey, who had loved his little dog, Scout, who had gotten ready to go hunting that morning just after his thirteenth birthday without knowing he would never come back. And a sandstorm of guilt buried Sem as it hit him again that once more, he was unable to protect his little brother.

He wouldn't stay, he decided. Couldn't stay. Couldn't imagine himself fetching shoes, doing makeup, facilitating a meal, assisting with bed, bath, and beyond, for anyone other than the Living Image of Amun. Even if the next Pharaoh was a good one, they wouldn't be his friend. Wouldn't be his brother. And in the strange, hoped-for event that the Queen took her place as the next Pharaoh, she wouldn't need a male valet. She would keep Meresankh.

He would study under Merneith, as Meresankh had suggested. Maybe, once he'd graduated, he could join a medical practice out in the city, sharing his skills with the population. Helping people find their way back to health, even people he didn't know, would bring him joy. Maybe his hands could bless others.

And maybe... someday... he would ask Meresankh to marry him. It wouldn't be until after all this was over, he was sure, but someday, he would ask her. And maybe... someday... they could find happiness. Even during the reign of whoever sat on the next throne. The thought of her standing beside him gave him a little hope. He would be lonely, but he would not be alone. And they

136

could find meaning, embrace joy, as they walked hand-in-hand into the unknown future. As long as they could balance their beliefs. As much as his love for her still warmed his heart, and as much as his questions, his doubts, about the way he had been raised to worship grew with each passing day, part of him still wasn't sure about her faith in the God of the Hebrews.

He clenched his hands. Philosophical differences between him and Meresankh aside, he might not get to marry her at all. He was about to lose his job; the good job he had had for over a year and would gladly have remained in for the rest of his life. And he was about to lose the home he was so grateful for; the comfortable, secure suite he had lived in for the past good year. Even studying with Granny, moving toward his specific goals for his new career, he would face an in-between time; a time with no income, no house of his own. But without a job, without a home, how could he provide for the woman he loved? Even if she wanted to marry him with all her heart, would it make sense for her to marry him if he was not able to provide?

He sighed. Maybe they would walk into this strange future side-by-side. And maybe they would be truly happy. But even if they could find happiness, he thought, it would take some finding. They would have to search for it. Because it was not going to simply appear.

There were hard days ahead.


Semerkhet was trying not to cry. Weakly extending his hand, Tut beckoned to him. Ankh scooted slightly so he could join them on the bed, then set aside the half-empty porridge-bowl. The Pharaoh had eaten all the breakfast he could manage.

Tut reached out to take Semerkhet's hand, squeezing it as hard as he could. Forcing his eyes open, he looked up at his friend, meeting his eyes.

"Fank you, dear Sem," he whispered through dry lips. "For everything." For getting him up and dressed every single morning, for putting him to bed at night, for being a listening ear, for keeping his secrets, for being loyal and brave and patient and compassionate and a beloved brother as well as a servant. For truly being, as his name suggested, an attentive friend. Tutankhamun wished he could sit up and give Semerkhet a hug, improper as it would be, but a few moments of solid, friendly eye contact would have to be enough.

Sem just gave a wistful smile and nodded. "It's my honor, Morning Star."

Semerkhet looked after his Pharaoh. And Tutankhamun was grateful. And yet they sighed through the days they spent together; felt their hearts ache as they sat together, read together, ate together. And they blinked back tears as the same thought touched each of their hearts. Just as they were becoming lifelong friends, it was all being ripped away. With agonizing slowness, day by day they moved closer to the hour when they would finally be separated. And they were powerless to do anything… but treasure every moment they had left.

He couldn't move. Tut lay on his side, the side he hadn't slept on, and stared at the wall until tears blurred his vision, a lump aching in his throat. His body was stiff, his neck sore, his back and limbs aching from the hard work of being trapped in the same position for hours on end. He couldn't get out of bed. Couldn't sit up. Couldn't even roll over without help. With every breath, there was the unyielding pain in his legs, pain that made him wince every time he tried to wiggle into a more comfortable position. With every breath, pain knifed through his chest as he struggled to draw air into his rattling lungs. And with every breath, there was the rising fever; the fever that made him bitterly resent the fact that even the cool weather of his favorite time of year had been stolen from him as he lay there sweating as though it was the middle of Epiphi.

He was trapped. Anger rose in his heart; agonizing, helpless frustration. Because it was so unfair. He should be in the prime of his life, racing horses, leading his armies to victory on the battlefield, hunting ostriches, going to hockey games… at the very least, going out to the garden at will; running his own daily meetings in the throne room. But he could not do any of those things. Because he was trapped inside the palace, inside his room, in his bed, in the position in which he lay, as effectively as a prisoner chained to the wall of their cell. And with each passing day, he knew that he was traveling slowly, inexorably toward a destination of death, with no hope of recovery. There was no escape.

Then the anger melted into sadness. What was there left to hope for, imprisoned in his room, with no chance— no chance of ever getting up again? What was the point— what was the point of trying anymore? And the emptiness of his future filled his aching heart with echoing despair. What was the point of going on?

And he lay there in bed with tears running down his face, wondering how many more awful things he would have to endure before the day he died.

Later that morning, Tut looked across his room at the graceful paintings on the walls, wishing he could look out the window at the cold Tybi day.

"How have we endured?" he whispered to his sister, who was in her chair as always, browsing through a papyrus of history. "Gotten through all this? We've lost both parents, all five sisters... and two daughters. How have we survived?"

Ankh reached over and patted his hand with a sad little sigh, a sad little smile. "Everything we've endured has made us stronger. And we have each other."

He looked up at her and took her hand. "I fink... together, we must be the strongest people in the world."

His sister nodded. "I think we are."

Tut swallowed, thinking back to their previous conversation. "Tho... what should my goal be?" he asked softly. "If I can't change the past?"

"How about changing the future?" she said with a little smile. "And... if you think about it, you have changed the past... for the people who will live a dynasty from now. Your policies— your minimum wage, your tax cuts, your limitations on slavery, your new schools, will change the past for the grandchildren who haven't been born yet. Because their parents and grandparents will have had opportunities they never would have otherwise. And they will grow up in a better world— a world you gave them. A world..." She smiled. "We gave them."

The Pharaoh blinked. "You're getting cosmic on me... but you're right. I never... thought of it that way. But you're right. Wow. That ith... what a thought."

Ankh nodded with a hint of a chuckle. "So that's your goal," she said. "Set our generation up for a good future, and Semerkhet's

140

great-grandchildren will live on the foundation of the past you provided for them."

Tutankhamun nodded. And he pressed his sister's hand to his lips. "Sounds like a plan."

Tut hadn't seen Ay in days, or Maya. Hadn't seen the treacherous Chief Physician in the weeks since he'd fired him and banished him from town, or Horemheb for even longer, when they had last met in Kadesh. He hadn't seen Usermontu since the beginning of Sholiak; Pentu since Paophi. So he had not heard the obsequious, worshipful intonations of all the traditional titles— Glorious Lord, King for Whom the Nile Floods, Lord of Perfect Laws, Lord of the Two Lands, Ruler of Truth— for many days. His sister called him "darling," Granny called him "my dear boy," and Sem called him "Morning Star," which was sounding less like a title and more like a nickname, a term of brotherly affection. Every time Ankh, Semerkhet, Merneith spoke to him, Tutankhamun knew how much he was loved.

The Queen smiled as her friend's merry chatter took her mind off the weary struggles of day-to-day life, Meresankh's delicate fingers deftly untangling an elaborate wig as she regaled her Mistress with a new story.

"...and Tentamun's had such a sore throat, now that the weather's getting cold."

"What should she be taking?" Ankhesenamun asked her.

Meresankh looked up and smiled. "Sage tea with honey," she said.

Ankh nodded, returning her smile. "I knew you'd know."

141

Through it all, Semerkhet had his lute. And he played what was in his heart, finding fewer old ballads or traditional folksongs pouring from his fingertips as he strummed to fill the silence. Fewer songs any of them knew, but more improvisation, melodies that came straight from his heart. Songs of sorrow. Songs of fear. Songs of hope. And as his lute gently wept, wept when his eyes no longer had tears to cry, the others sighed and nodded to hear the feelings in their own hearts transformed into heartfelt, heartbreaking melody. His lute wept for everyone.

Ankh sipped her tea and stared into space, thinking about the life she had shared with her little brother. As Pharaoh, he had looked to her for wisdom, for guidance, for a listening ear, a voice he could always trust. She had given it to him, guiding him through the world of politics as best she could, helping him navigate the dangerous waters of trust and betrayal. Through it all, she had kept him safe.

Except that this time, she hadn't.

And now still she stood beside him, guiding him through the pain, the weariness, the politics that would surely rage until the very last days of their life together. His big sister had always been with him. And she always would be. Until the very end.

And always... she had searched for a purpose; a purpose for the pain, the struggle, the indignity he faced every day of being unable to meet his own needs, unable to walk, even stand, without his cane. The struggle that had grown tenfold over the past weeks, as he lay in bed, unable to get up at all. She tried to hang onto it, the hope in what she had not yet seen. Why had the gods sent him to them like this? What was he intended to do?

And would he be able to do it before it was too late?

142

Ankh squared her shoulders. Here she stood, ready to step into the gap between two dynasties. But whether she would do it as Queen... or as Pharaoh... remained to be seen.

The light was waning; the Season of Emergence progressing. Soon they would come to the shortest day of the year. And then the days would wax again as they moved through the Season of Growth, toward the next harvest. Although where they would be when the next harvest came... and how many of them would see it... they were not sure.

Tut stared out the window at the dark, cloudy day, aching, cycling miserably between shivering with cold and radiating heat, just like he did every few days. In his pounding, fuzzy mind, he tried to reflect. His name meant "The Living Image of Amun." He felt his mouth twist in a wry chuckle. Pretty soon he would be the Dead Image of Amun.

He had been so blessed. *Before the battle, I could walk, even if I always had to have my cane,* he thought with a sigh. *Now, with two broken legs, I can't even get out of bed. If I could have the things I used to complain about, I would build a hundred temples out of gratitude.*

*Although to which god would I dedicate them?*

As the Pharaoh slept, the Queen watched him. And silent pain filled her heart as her previous thoughts returned to her. Here he was, just embarking upon adulthood, ready to take on the world. And yet now... here he was, lying upon his deathbed with two broken legs and worsening ague.

She looked down at her ring; at the bracelet she wore on her other wrist. Royal jewels that identified her as Queen. She thought of the diadems carefully stored in her room. And of the authority they communicated. Authority she bore as Queen— authority she had used in firing the treacherous Chief Physician; in sending the letter to the Hittite Prince. Authority she would be more than able to wield on a whole new level in succeeding her brother as Pharaoh.

And yet… Again, the Queen looked at her brother. All the authority she could ever bear, whether as Queen of Egypt or Pharaoh of the entire world, could not keep her brother from dying.

# 14    Doubt

"Tell me, Granny," Meresankh said as she stood beside Merneith in the herbalist's workshop, holding a basket into which the old woman was piling linen packets of herbs; parceled-out doses ready to be prepared into poultices for their Pharaoh's festering leg. "Is she?"

Granny looked at her as her old fingers carefully tied one of the tiny bundles of rosemary that Meresankh had helped gather from the herb garden. "Even I can't say yet," she said gently. "It's only been two weeks since the date she gave me." Merneith sighed. "Our Queen... wants to have a child. So badly. She and our Pharaoh, they've been through so much. And now... an heir would change everything. There are signs... but we can't be sure yet. We will just have to wait and see... and pray." She smiled at Meresankh, holding out her old, wrinkled hand with its bent fingers.

Meresankh took her hand and nodded. "Always pray." Then she sighed. "But this one..." The handmaiden looked down, remembering the dark days. "Will it be all right? Isn't there anything you can do... anything to give her to make the baby strong, if it really is on its way? To keep it... keep it safe?"

Merneith closed her eyes. She hadn't been the attending physician, but she remembered too.

Then Granny nodded, and in her little smile, there was hope. "There are things. Things I can make; things she can do. She's already started the tea I made up. If I-AM has answered our prayers, there are many things we can do to keep the Queen strong and support the baby's health. Don't you worry, dearie. I've been a midwife for fifty years. I know a thing or two."

Meresankh chuckled, and her Granny pulled her in for a hug, thin old arms wrapped around her with more strength than a stranger might expect. And she knew that Granny was right. If anyone could get the Queen to the birthing bricks safely, it was her. And that was the promise she had made.

He was thirsty. Tutankhamun asked Semerkhet for a cup of licorice tea, and, lying there propped up on pillows, reached out to take it.

Only... he couldn't get hold of it. The Pharaoh's hands shook as he tried to grasp the cup, threatening to knock it out of Semerkhet's steady grip. And slowly, with a sigh, he let his hands fall in defeat.

"Would you... help me?" he asked softly.

Semerkhet's face had remained quiet, calm, but even Tut's tired eyes could see a glimmer of sadness shining in his friend's eyes.

"Of course," he said, sitting down beside the Pharaoh. And slipping an arm behind his shoulders, he raised his friend's head, gently holding the cup to his lips. Defeated but grateful, Tut drank until he was satisfied. And he let Sem settle him back into bed, the dying King who could no longer eat or drink without help.

"Where's Meritaten's necklace?"

Meresankh looked up from putting away the Queen's wigs to see Ankhesenamun striding into the room with purpose on her face. "Which one, My Lady?"

146

"Meritaten's, you know, the one that's mostly blue, with the little lotuses on it— you're the one that keeps track of all my stuff; don't you know where you put it?"

The handmaiden just smiled to herself. This was just one of those days.

"How is the Queen?" Semerkhet asked.

Meresankh looked up from her beer. They were sitting in her chambers together, sharing a short break on that chilly day, halfheartedly playing *seega*.

She smiled. "We're wondering. She's had some nausea, and been thirstier than usual… and there are other signs, too. She's taking the teas Granny's making her to keep her strong, and she's eating the right foods and not the wrong ones, not drinking wine, being careful not to carry anything too heavy. But we're still… waiting to be sure."

Sem reached out and took her hand. And Meresankh smiled.

"I'm praying," he said softly. "To Whoever's listening."

Meresankh nodded gratefully. And as she reached up to touch her necklace, Semerkhet wondered if the image of Isis meant anything at all, or if it was just a tiny, sweet portrait of a character from a story.

They were crying more, Ankhesenamun, Semerkhet. They almost always excused themselves before the tears began to fall, but the Pharaoh could tell. He could see the tears welling in their eyes, the way they held their bodies, the way they shielded their faces with their hands or the tilt of their heads as they muttered thickly that they needed to go check something. He understood why. Slowly, they were being forced to let him go.

147

The best thing he could do was to let them mourn, sometimes wiping away his own tears.

Bastet never cried. But there was something new in her expression… a sadness. And she stayed closer to him than before, purring as she comforted him with her soft, warm presence. She, too, was struggling to let him go.

She shouldn't have been short with Meresankh. The Queen shook her head as she thought of all the hard work her friend did to keep track of all her things. And of how ungrateful she had been; how demanding. She promised herself that she would do better. And she resolved to make sure Meresankh knew how grateful she was.

He was sleeping more. Ankhesenamun and Semerkhet had long since gotten used to the routine of spending their days and nights in the Pharaoh's chambers, solicitously attending to his every need. But, other than during the horrible first two days of the ague, and the day that he'd been afflicted by the Vizier's poison, they had spent those days talking. Light conversations, serious ones, reflections on times gone by, random bits of palace news. Tutankhamun had not been able to get out of bed, but he had been able to chat. And, on most days, he had wanted to.

But now… Ankh, Sem, would turn to their brother to say something, but instead of petting the cat, he would be quietly drowsing in the bed, eyes wearily closed. And silence filled the hours that used to be occupied by a steady stream of conversation.

The Queen was grateful for Meresankh. Faithfully, her friend, her sister, walked this hard road with her. The smiles and brief

148

hand-clasps she offered in the hallway warmed Ankhesenamun's heart, and when the weight of discouragement and questions of international importance that refused to be answered threatened to force her to her knees, Meresankh would take her turn as the one that gave orders and tell her Lady to take fifteen minutes for herself.

And Ankh would follow her friend into her own chambers for a much-needed break, and, lying back in her favorite chair, she would sit and listen as Meresankh told her one of the stories that she had first told her— stories of Neith-Hotep, Iput, Ahhotep. Sometimes, Meresankh would even rub the Queen's weary shoulders, and even as Ankhesenamun felt her tired body relax, she would chuckle to think that in comforting her brother through touch through the endless days and nights, she had almost forgotten how good a simple shoulder rub could feel. And Ankh would smile, grateful for the friend who would see her through this long, hard journey, one way or another.

He had grown so weak. Semerkhet bit his lip, fighting back tears as he remembered holding the cup of tea to his friend's lips, gently placing his other hand behind Tutankhamun's head, raising it so he could take a sip. Tut's weak hands could no longer hold a cup. And he could no longer feed himself, maneuvering a spoon from a bowl of soup to his mouth, keeping hold of a piece of bread or keeping grapes or jujubes from slipping from his fingers. Every day, he grew worse. And Semerkhet wondered... how many days he had left.

"Do you want to be turned?"

Tut opened his eyes to see Semerkhet bent over him, a friendly little smile on his face. Slowly, the Pharaoh put a smile onto his own face. "I am stiff," he admitted with a little nod. Semerkhet just nodded. He took Tut's hand, and slowly, began to pull him from his back to his side.

Fire raced down each of the Pharaoh's broken legs like lightning. He heard himself give a strangled yelp as tears of pain came to his eyes, his stomach somersaulting. Every part of his body was screaming at him to stop moving.

Semerkhet stopped pulling. "I'm sorry—" he cried, bending worriedly over his Master to stare into his face. Tut was gasping, coughing, struggling to get his breath back as the searing pain in what was left of his legs slowly, slowly ebbed away.

"'S fine," he whispered, shaking his head. "Doethn't matter." He closed his eyes, taking a deep, shaky breath as he felt a cold sweat running down his face. "Maybe… maybe later."

Even with his eyes closed, he could almost hear Semerkhet nodding enthusiastically.

"Later," the valet repeated. And he was gone.

Again Ankhesenamun sat looking through the Queens List. And again, it was Hatshepsut she turned to for strength. She thought of what that long-ago Great Royal Wife had gone through. Losing her husband, her little brother, after watching over him his entire life, left to lead her country herself, through marriage, motherhood, and politics the likes of which the world had never seen.

Softly she placed her hand on her belly. Was there a baby? Was there? And was it a boy… or a girl? If it was a girl, even if Ankh somehow managed to succeed Tut as Pharaoh, would she really be able to make her daughter her own heir? Or would it be her

150

marriage to Zannanza; her placement of the Hittite Prince onto the throne of Egypt, and the sons born of their union, that continued the dynasty of Grandfather Thutmose?

She didn't know. Didn't know what the future held. But as she read the history of Hatshepsut, who had taken what life had given her and courageously made herself into the Pharaoh Egypt needed her to be, Ankh knew that she would find a way.

He hadn't done anything wrong. He hadn't. Semerkhet went over it again and again in his mind; the way he had grasped the Pharaoh's hand and slowly begun to pull him from lying on his back to resting on his side. Three days ago, it had worked. Three days ago, it had been fine. Painful, yes, challenging, yes, but doable. But this time… this time Tut had all but screamed in pain, and he'd been left gasping and coughing, practically in tears.

Maybe Semerkhet should have known. The night of the sixth, Tut hadn't been able to roll onto his stomach, and had slept on his side. Last night, they hadn't attempted to get him onto his stomach; he'd slept on his side by choice. And here, on the eighth of Tybi, moving from his back to his side was too painful to bear.

Semerkhet pressed the heels of his hands into his tired eyes until he saw stars. And he prayed that if he had to, his friend would be willing to take the poppy medicine.

There was a knock at the door. Semerkhet opened it to see five servants, all looking nervously down at their feet.

"Yes?" he asked quietly, glancing back into the room to make sure that he hadn't woken his brother, who had slipped into a nap.

"We were sent," one man said softly, a heavy sadness showing on his face, "by the Vizier."

Semerkhet straightened up, feeling revulsion shivering down his spine. "What does he want?" he asked a little less politely than he'd intended.

"He said it was time…" a woman said, "to begin preparing the Pharaoh's tomb. To begin gathering the things he will take with him to the next life."

The valet's stomach clenched. And he bowed his head as her words burrowed into his heart like an arrow.

"Come in," he said in a choked voice, stepping aside to let them enter. "But keep it down."

Tut woke up to see that around the edges of the bedroom, servants were working, putting things from his storage room and sitting room into plain wooden boxes as if they were packing for the twice-yearly move from Memphis to Thebes or back again. Tut saw them take some bright, shining jewelry, an armful of walking-sticks in a dozen colors and styles, a box of shoes, his special iron dagger, even a stack of neatly folded loincloths.

"Where are you…" he started to ask one of them, but the servant just looked at him, tears in her eyes. Silently beckoning to her companions, she scurried out of the room with a whispered wish for his life, health, and prosperity, leaving him to wonder.

He understood. Tut lay his head back down, closing his eyes. They were gathering up the things he would need to pack for the next world. These were the items that would be placed inside his tomb. And in beginning the preparations early, the Grand Vizier was thrusting another dagger into the Pharaoh's breaking heart.

Soon, Tutankhamun knew, he would be dead and buried.

"They've begun preparing your tomb," Ankh whispered to her brother, sitting down beside him to stroke his head. "Well, the Vizier's tomb. For you."

He looked up at her. "I know. I saw them."

She sighed heavily, looking down at the bed. "Why have the gods done this?" she whispered.

He looked up at her with half a smile. "I don't know…" he whispered back. "But I've been thinking. Even… even before all thith. Whenever I go outside, whenever I stand in the Sun, I feel something. And sometimes I wonder… if Father was right. I know it's crazy, but… *what if* Father was right? And the Aten ith I-AM… maker of Heaven and Earth? What if Ra and Horus and Osiris are the stories, not the Aten?"

His sister shuddered. "Mother took us back afterward, and so did the priests," she said, still looking down. "Why would she have done that if the Aten was real?"

"Because she didn't want anyone to be forthed to worship in a particular way," he said. "She wanted everyone to be free to worship according to their own convictionth." Tut looked at his sister. "Ankh… what do you believe?"

She closed her eyes, feeling another shudder pass through her. This was the same thing Meresankh had said. And yet she felt a hint, a strange, fleeting hint of something, of purpose, of… Truth. Of Light.

"I'm… not ready to decide," she whispered finally. "It's too much… to even think about."

Tutankhamun nodded. "I'm not sure either."

The Queen went to go get herself a cup of tea. She sat in her own room for a few minutes, sipping it slowly. And thinking. Her

153

little brother had just told her that he was no longer sure the gods were real. That maybe the Aten of their father was not only real, but was the only God, another name for I-AM.

They had talked about it before. And she had thought about it. And even agreed that there was something missing in the way they worshiped.

But the way things were going… now Tut had more than questions. He had doubts.

And… Ankh's hands tightened on the cup. So did she.

She had always trusted in the gods of Egypt, ever since they had been returned to the forefront, Father's Aten banned. Although their silence hurt her, a dissatisfaction squirming in her heart as her pleas echoed back to her in silence. Silence so complete that she sometimes did wonder if they were actually listening. And they had never… Ankh put her hand on her stomach. Had never given her what she asked for. Begged for. Wept for.

She thought back to the warmth and Light she remembered from those long-ago days in Akhetaten, worshiping alongside her parents. And to the Light she had just felt, only moments ago, and in moments here and there over the past year, moments of need when a loving warmth had filled her heart. To the Light she saw in Meresankh's eyes, in Merneith's. And to the conversations she had had with Meresankh; her handmaiden's simple, satisfying faith.

Now the Queen of Egypt was beginning to wonder.

And wonder… what she was going to do. She blinked back tears. Because they were preparing his tomb.

"Are they going with me?"

Ankh looked over at her brother, who had a question on his face. And as their previous conversation echoed in her heart, she knew what he was asking. Knew of whom he was speaking.

With a sigh, she got up from her chair, climbing up onto the bed to sit beside her brother, taking his thin, fragile hands in hers.

She looked down, feeling the tears fill her eyes. And she nodded.

"Yes," she said softly. "I… I told the planners to… to move them. And they'll… they'll be with you. They'll be… with their Daddy."

Tutankhamun blinked back tears of his own. And he gave her a sad smile.

Tut reached up to put his arm around her, and Ankhesenamun lay down beside him, feeling his warmth, his strength. So many questions remained. But somehow, she knew she had spoken the truth. Someday soon… someday very soon, her husband would be reunited with their daughters.

# 15   The Heir

Tut lay in bed, breathing in the fumes of the hemp incense, the taste of the poppy medicine still in his sand-dry mouth. He'd been feeling slightly better, but someone had spooned the medicine into his mouth without giving him a chance to refuse, held a cup of peach-pit wine to his lips until he accepted a sip, and lit the incense without asking. As a consequence, his stomach was growling, his heart was pounding, his head was aching, and he felt dizzy, hazy, and intoxicated. And now, someone had just come into the bedroom.

"Who there?" he mumbled with a thick tongue and a dry mouth, unable to see clearly enough to tell. But he could see, that in her chair, his sister was sitting quietly. Although, the way that her head was resting on the back of the chair, she seemed almost to have drifted off. And it was strange that the Pharaoh's bodyguard had not told this visitor to come back later.

"Only me, Your Majesty." Tut recognized Ay's voice, although it seemed strangely fuzzy and distorted. "How are you today?"

"Don't like thith… medithine," he groaned, putting a hand on his aching forehead. "Feel… drunk."

"The medicine is behaving as it ought," Ay said calmly. "If you don't mind, I have something for you to sign." Tut reached out clumsily where he thought Ay was holding out the piece of papyrus, fumbling for it and eventually catching it in his fingers. He squinted at it.

"What ith it?" he asked, giving up and closing his eyes. Ay took the document back.

"Approval of your successor, My Lord."

"Approval… what?" he mumbled.

"Of your heir, My Lord."

"Don't have an heir," Tut muttered.

"I am your heir, My Lord."

Tut shook his fuzzy head, fighting, swimming through the inebriation. Just like Ay to try to get him to sign something he wouldn't be comfortable with when he was high on two types of mind-altering painkillers. Painkillers he had never expected to be given again since firing the Chief Physician. Slowly he gathered enough mind-power to understand what Ay was trying to get him to do. And to know that his answer was *no*.

"No, you're not. Pr... Printh Thannantha is. Hittite. Gonna marry Ankh. Not you. Not Nakhtmin. And not Horemheb, either. Write that down. Horemheb ith not my heir."

"If, however, I were to marry the Queen..." Ay began.

Tut managed to raise an accusing finger amid the blurriness in his mind. He shook his head emphatically, then stopped when it made him even dizzier. "No, Ay. You can't marry the Queen. Not allowed. Nakhtmin can't either."

The Vizier's nostrils flared. "I don't see how you'll have much say over that, My Lord."

"Juth try marrying her if she doethn't want you to." Then the Pharaoh paused. "Why should I lithen to you after you killed my parents and Meritaten and Pentu and Uthermontu and Raherka and Amenmoth and who knowth who elth?"

The Grand Vizier looked at him in silent shock. Tut gazed back steadily. Now another secret was out of the way.

Ay gave an impatient sigh. "May I have your authorization or not, My Lord?"

Tut swiped for the papyrus, and Ay handed it to him again, along with a pen. Of course, he had already prepared the proclamation he was about to recreate, but calling for the Queen to ask her to bring it would be a waste of time. He scribbled out Ay's name and scrawled "Queen Ankhesenamun with Prince Zannanza." Underneath he clumsily pressed the signet-ring, which had not left his hand since Granny had recovered it, into the waiting wax. "Here," he said, thrusting it back out at Ay. "Thigned it."

"Thank you, My Lord," Ay said delicately. And he was gone.

Tut lay back, closing his eyes and pressing his palms into them until bright colors bloomed before his vision. He was never taking those medicines again. *I would rather suffer than not be in my right mind and risk doing something that will hurt my country.*

Perched on the end of the bed, Bastet began to cough as though she had a hairball. Then it turned into an angry snort. His little lioness would protect him no matter what.

"Who in the Ten Plagues lit this? And is that poppy that I smell?" Merneith bustled into the King's room, quickly snuffing the hemp incense and confiscating the bottle of poppy medicine. "And…" She stopped, ancient face crumpling in fury as she smelled the contents of the wine-cup. "Peaches," she spat, the word sounding like a curse. "Oy, vavoy." She looked up at the King. "You may want to talk to your bodyguard, Your Majesty."

He nodded weakly. "Good idea."

Semerkhet came back into the room after a ten-minute break. Something had happened. The hemp incense had been burning, and Merneith was angrily shaking her head as she cleared away a wine-cup and a bottle of medicine.

Sem sat back down in his chair. Maybe he would have to be more careful about his breaks.

The Queen sat up in her chair with a blink. How had she drifted off during Semerkhet's break? She sniffed. And who had been burning that hemp incense?

Soon, Tut was sitting up to vomit, reeling with the familiar symptoms of lightheadedness, dizziness, and an uncomfortable thirst. But he knew they would soon pass. That poison had gotten into his system for the last time.

"...so that's five foolish decisions the Vizier will overturn when he takes the throne, and you still won't admit that he'll make a better Pharaoh than the boy?"

Semerkhet paused on his way back inside with a fresh bouquet of daisies he'd gone to pick himself in the interest of stretching his legs.

"But the Vizier will never take the throne," a second voice said. Two men were standing in a dark corner of the atrium Semerkhet had entered, lowering their voices as they argued. "The Hittite will come, and the Queen will marry him."

"The Hittite may never arrive," the first man said. "And if he does, and he moves for the crown, then we'll see if Hittites have red blood. And anyone who tries to protect him will regret it with their dying breath."

"Then the Queen will take the throne," the second man replied.

The first man scoffed. "You really think the Vizier would let a woman rule? We saw how things went when Nefertiti became Smenkhkare."

"The father of the Heretic wrecked the economy, not Smenkhkare," the second man said protectively. "But what about the General? He is technically Crown Prince as we speak. And as a great General, he can protect himself if those who follow your Grand Vizier turn on him."

"Maybe he can, maybe he can't," the first man said. "All I can say is… when the General gets home, it's going to get messy."

The Sole Companion shuddered. And he kept walking.

Merneith was an excellent asset. Her herbal preparations kept Tut more comfortable than those the Chief Physician had made, and most importantly, he knew they could trust her. She had helped them solve this murder mystery in the first place. Even… even if she couldn't save him, she would do her moral duty as a doctor. Granny would take care of him until the end.

He followed her advice and told Minnefer not to admit the Vizier if he showed up again. And breathed a sigh of relief to know that in this, he was safe.

The Queen was ashamed. Protecting her brother was her responsibility, and she had failed. Failed to take care of him; failed to use the authority she wielded. And she promised herself that as Queen, Pharaoh, wife, sister, and mother, she would do whatever it took. For her baby brother. For her child. And for her country.

Meresankh didn't see her Mistress or her Pharaoh very much. Semerkhet, too, was always occupied. But she prayed while she worked. Prayed for her Pharaoh to be healed; prayed for her Queen to be strong. Prayed for the baby to be real, and for it to be strong and healthy and safe. Prayed for Semerkhet to keep being everything that he was. Prayed for herself to be as helpful as humanly possible.

Prayed for her friends to find the Light.

They had turned another corner. That morning at breakfast, Ankhesenamun had watched Semerkhet feed Tut his porridge one slow, exhausting bite at a time, then bend over the Pharaoh to help him take a sip of tea from the cup Sem carefully held to his lips. The thin hands that had grown too weak, shook too badly, to hold a cup or a spoon lay quietly on the blankets as Tutankhamun patiently opened his mouth again and again for each bite of porridge; gave a soft, sad smile as he allowed his valet to raise his head and shoulders to offer him a drink.

The Queen turned away as tears filled her eyes. But even as the unfairness ached inside her heavy heart; the unfairness of the fact that her nineteen-year-old brother was now as helpless as the oldest grandfather, she was grateful. Grateful for her brother's friend.

"I want my other pillow; the one from Amenia!" Tut whined. Even for as rotten as everything was on average, he was feeling awful. His head was still swimming from the hemp the Vizier had forced on him, his fever and chills were making his very bones ache, and there was literally no comfortable position in which to lie. And now Semerkhet was dawdling as he sorted through the Pharaoh's collection of pillows for a fresh one. The first replacement he had brought had not sufficed.

"I'm looking," Semerkhet said, a hint of exasperation creeping into his tired voice. It had been a long day already, and it was barely lunchtime.

"Well, look faster!" Tutankhamun moaned.

"I'm trying," Sem said shortly. "You're all right."

"No, I'm not!" Tut wailed, angry tears coming to his eyes. "You don't care. You wish you were a scribe! Well, sometimes I do, too!"

Semerkhet paused. And very stiffly, he brought the pillow to the royal bedside.

"Your Majesty," he said, moving to replace the pillow Tut was lying on.

And the angry tears in the Pharaoh's eyes became tears of shame.

"I'm thorry," he whimpered, reaching for Semerkhet's hand. "I didn't mean it... I know you care... I know you do your best... I know I'm hard to deal with..."

Semerkhet just shook his head with a forgiving little smile, giving Tut's hand a friendly clasp. "It's all right," he said. "I understand." He gave a sad little chuckle. "I am doing my best... and so are you."

And the Pharaoh blinked back even more tears; tears of gratitude. Semerkhet understood.

Ankh stood out in the garden just after lunch, breathing in the cool, crisp air, feeling the breeze, listening to the birds. It felt good to get outside for a bit; to have a few minutes to think about anything and everything but what was going on inside the palace. Just a few minutes.

A soft sound behind her, a swish of heavy fabric like the wings of a bird of prey, made her turn around. And she gritted her teeth.

"My Lady," the Vizier said, "time is running out."

Ankhesenamun forced herself to look at him. "It is," she said stiffly.

162

He had something in his hands, a tiny object he kept fiddling with between his fingers. A jujube? A piece of jewelry?

"My Lady," he said again, "my Queen. Egypt needs you. Needs you... to remain Queen. And I would be honored... if you would become my Queen when I take the next throne." As the gorge rose in Ankh's throat, she watched him reveal the tiny object he had been holding— a ring made of blue glass. Glancing at it, she could see that it was inscribed with two names— *Ay and Ankhesenamun.* And her stomach turned.

Haughtily, the Vizier continued. "Nakhtmin will become my heir, of course, but we will not exclude your son... perhaps he will become Treasurer, or even Vizier himself one day. But I'm sure you can see how it would be best for everyone for your son... the son of Tutankhamun... to find his place in the royal court... a place where he may never take the throne, but he will surely be able to make a difference... in his own way."

He shook his head. "For a woman to become Pharaoh, for a Queen to become King, unbalances the world, threatens *ma'at* itself. In Egypt, there is a place for everyone, and everyone stays in their place. Scribes and peasants, Pharaohs and Queens. These systems have sustained us for millennia, My Lady. And maintaining them... is best for everyone."

Anger began to pound in the Queen's head as her heart raced in her chest. But she fought it back down. If she lost her temper, everything else would also be lost. Snapping would destroy her credibility. She had to be courageous and cunning, civil and sneaky, sweet and deadly. And she could not tell Ay to go jump in the Nile. That was not an appropriate thing for a Queen to say to even the most obnoxiously tenacious suitor. So she bit her tongue and thought of what she could say instead.

"No, Vizier," she whispered with a dangerous little smile. "I will not marry you. And you will not be the next Pharaoh. I will continue leading my country with or without Zannanza… with or without an heir… with or without anyone or anything. But not with you. I promise you that. Good day." And leaving him, she returned to her walk.

The Queen had refused the Vizier again. Meresankh hugged her Mistress, her friend, as Ankh told her how courageously she had told Ay that she would never be his Queen. The future was yet to be written. But Meresankh was proud of her Lady. She had fought her battle and won.

Tut woke up for a little while. And yet, lying there in bed, he did not feel peacefully grateful for all the love and care Ankh and Sem were providing to him day and night. He felt angry.

Ankh had slipped away for a moment; Semerkhet was improvising softly on his lute. Painfully, Tutankhamun extended an arm, beckoning to his cat. Bastet hopped up onto the bed, padding over to him and lying down beside him.

Gently he petted her, knowing that she would listen to what he was about to say.

"It'th not fair," he whispered. "None of it. I shouldn't be here right now. I should be running my own meetingth; leading my own country. I should be showing the world the warrior King. I…" Now he blinked back angry tears, resentment beginning to burn inside his heart as his next thought came to him. "A strong… a strong Pharaoh wouldn't be lying here on his deathbed." He looked at Bastet, who was blurry beyond the veil of tears that dimmed his

164

vision. "Why can't I be the strong Pharaoh I was born to be? Why can't I fulfill my destiny?"

He looked at his beloved cat, and calmly, she looked back. But Bastet had no answers.

The Queen sat watching her brother sleep, his chest rising and falling gently with each breath, cat curled up warmly against his side. Sleep was becoming the only time that he was comfortable.

The King's valet stepped into view, and she smiled up at him. "Semerkhet?" she said, standing up.

He dipped his head respectfully. "My Lady."

"Sem…" She had never addressed him by his nickname, but just now, it felt fitting. "I just… want to thank you. For everything you've done in all the time you've been here."

Semerkhet dipped his head again. "It's been my honor, My Lady."

She smiled at him. "I really don't know what we'd do without you. You've been so dedicated. And I just want to say…" She swallowed back a tear. "That whatever happens, we're grateful. I'm grateful. For everything you've done for my husband… my little brother."

Ankhesenamun extended her hand. Semerkhet looked at it, then slowly met it with his own, sharing a brief clasp. His hand was strong, and warm, a bit like the Pharaoh's but not quite as big, powerful and delicate all at the same time.

Slowly she nodded. "I'll never forget you."

Semerkhet gave a small smile. "And I'll never forget you."

Semerkhet gave the King a little bow, then excused himself with a sniffled wish for life, prosperity, and health, carrying away the half-empty bowl of soup and hiding his face. Because if he was about to cry, he didn't want his Master or his Lady to see it.

He'd sat down on the side of the bed with the soup, but the King hadn't even been able to move himself upward in the bed so his head was elevated. He stayed flat on his back, too weak to move. And when Semerkhet had offered to get more pillows to prop him up, he had shaken his head. He thought he might get dizzy. So Sem had struggled to feed him the soup flat on his back, pausing after every bite to wipe his chin with a bit of linen.

And when the Pharaoh turned his face away from the still half-full bowl of soup, not full but simply too tired to keep trying to eat, Semerkhet had barely been able to get away before the Pharaoh saw his tears. Time was running out.

"We didn't get to do all of it," the Pharaoh said heavily as he lay there in bed, trying to have a conversation with his sister between naps.

"Hmm?" She picked up a bowl of fresh, cool water, dipping a cloth into it so she could bathe his face.

"The new policieth," he continued. He sighed, giving a little smile as the cool cloth washed away a little of the heat of the fever. "We did motht of it, but we didn't... didn't get to resettle Goshen. It'th still... still ath empty ath ever."

Ankh shook her head. "Well... that may be true. But what else is true?"

Tut thought. And his heart warmed. "New schoolth. Better taxes. Good wageth. We did... we did make Egypt a better plathe, didn't we?"

Tears sparkled in the Queen's eyes as she bent forward to kiss him on the forehead. "Yes, love. Yes, we did."

166

Still Ankh and Sem faithfully fetched things for the Pharaoh, bringing him a fresh cup of tea, a bowl or plate of whatever sounded good at the moment, another blanket. He was still a bit sorry that he was making them work so hard; that he was so helpless to do anything for himself. But then... he let it go. Minimizing how much of an inconvenience he represented to his loved ones was no longer a reasonable goal. Because as his fever rose and his body weakened, he was, as always, only responsible for doing what he could do. And as for the rest... he was grateful. So grateful. And his gratitude would have to be enough.

He went over the days in his mind; the days he'd been trapped in this bed. Tut had been home for five weeks.

The Queen sat with her brother on the afternoon of the ninth day of Tybi, reading Ay's account of what he had done the previous day.

"Ordered shipment of cedar-wood, in exchange for five hundred sacks of grain, approved completion of new wing of servants' quarters for cooks and gardeners and housing for laborers— and that's all right," Ankh said. "Meresankh said they both look fine. He's not being funny. So," she said, "ready to sign it?"

Tutankhamun yawned, looking sleepily up at his sister. He was so drowsy... he had barely heard what she had just said. Hadn't grasped the implications of what Ay was suggesting. And didn't feel competent to give a *yes* or *no*. "You sign it," he said, taking off his signet-ring and offering it to her. "You decide."

Ankh frowned, taking the ring and looking at it. "What?"

"Ath Pharaoh, I'm deputizing you," he yawned. "You read his notes; tell him *yes* or *no*. You know what to do better than I do

167

anyway. And I don't… don't fink I can make those decisions anymore." He gave her a little smile. "Effective… for her husband.
Juth like Mother."

With a sigh, the Queen put on the ring. "Assignment accepted,
Your Majesty." And seeing nothing wrong with the day's
proposals, she signed them into effect.

# 16  Despair

The Pharaoh lay silently in bed that afternoon, feeling like his left leg was resting on a bed of hot coals. Nothing he could do could relieve it; no matter what he did, sweat dripped down his body with his rising fever; yellow pus continued staining his bandages; his whole leg remained red and hot. There was no escape.

Merneith was examining him, her wise, gnarled old hands delicately probing the angry wound as he hissed in his breath, clenching his hands into fists. The slightest touch was agony.

Granny touched him gently, carefully; as tenderly as she always did. But there… was an uncertainty in her manner. Or rather… an unwilling certainty of something she did not want to see.

She reached for his hand, and he let her take it, holding it in her grandmotherly old fingers that pointed every which way. He just closed his eyes. Then he felt her other hand touch his wrist, taking his pulse. Gently she placed one old hand on his sweaty forehead, listening carefully to every painful breath he took. Granny closed her eyes, seeming to sense his condition, feel out how he was. Slowly, she released a heavy sigh, which surprised him.

Opening his eyes again, he looked up at her, at her solemn face. "My dear boy," she said gently, "it's too late. Even if we might have amputated your entire leg, at this point, such a measure would only speed your passing."

She shook her head, pausing. And she swallowed, as if she did not want to say the words that were rising in her heart.

"Time is running short, dear boy," she whispered sadly. She paused again, bowing her old head and clenching her hands for an instant before looking up again. "It is no longer possible to contend

169

with the damage and the infections. At this point, it is time to prioritize pain management. If you choose, I can provide you with hemp… or mandrake… or even poppy. We can… minimize your discomfort… for as long as necessary."

Tutankhamun closed his eyes again. Even Granny was offering him poppy. This was serious.

But that was not all. The old woman shook her head solemnly, then said softly, "Based on what I see… I would estimate… a week. At most."

The Pharaoh shuddered. Today he could see the remainder of his life stretching out before him. And it would be days, not years.

Ankh sat there on the end of her brother's bed, silent pain slowly filling her heart. Merneith's words echoed in her mind… *It's too late. Too late.* Even the greatest midwife in Egypt could no longer do anything but help him manage his pain.

The Queen wrapped her arms around herself, curling into a ball. But there were no tears. The pain was too deep for tears. And she lay there, trying to breathe as it cut through her, body and soul.

The end was coming.

The Queen got up as if in a dream, slowly stepping out into the hallway. *A week. At most.* Words that tore at her gut, reverberating into the confusing nothingness that was going to be her life without him. The life she could not bear to think of.

The life that would be here for her by some point next week. Because she, even in her authority as Queen, could not command it to stop.

She hardly noticed she was crying until she felt Meresankh's arm around her shoulder, gently leading her to her chambers and closing the door behind them. Slowly Ankh sat down in a chair in

170

the sitting room, shaking with sobs. Meresankh stayed at her side, putting her arms around her Mistress.

"It w-won't be much longer," she sobbed on her handmaiden's shoulder. Meresankh was so tiny that even when the Queen was sitting down, she was just as tall. "G-Granny said she c-can't… and his f-face… I c-could just see…"

Then there were no more words, only the wailing; the wailing torn from the place in her heart where she held her sisters, her parents, her tiny precious ones. A place in her heart that would be torn open again when her brother, her husband, fell asleep for the last time.

Tut lay there in bed in a silent, stoic haze of shock, not thinking, not feeling. Right now he had no tears. Right now it was all too much to take in.

It wasn't helping, Ankh decided. Even weeping, letting it out. Wasn't making a difference.

She had to talk to the ones who had let this happen. Wiping her face, feeling her makeup smear, she stumbled out of Meresankh's arms, out of her bedroom, down the hall, past the study, and out into the courtyard. She squinted in the unfamiliar brightness, finding the temple in the distance. And she made her way toward it.

The Queen ran all the way to the temple, sobbing as she ran, feeling the muscles of her legs burning, her red outer robe flying behind her. Already weak with exhaustion, Ankh ran inside, into the cool, dim sanctuary, collapsing before the image of Amun-Ra. She lay shaking on the cold stone floor, sobbing as she fought to pray.

"Why are you doing this?" she moaned into the cold stone. "Why? *Why?*" Her question became a scream, and she turned her face up toward the cold, silent face of the god that stood above her, solemn and impassive. *"Why?"* she shrieked, her whole body wracked with pain. "Which one of you did this? What did he ever do? What did I ever do?" Maybe it was blasphemy, but she didn't care. She was beyond blasphemy.

But there was no answer. Only a cold stare from cold stone.

Now rage filled her heart as every promise her mother and grandmother had ever made to her about the power a Queen could wield; every moment in which she had ever taken pride or satisfaction in what she could accomplish through her authority, echoed back as an empty lie.

"And why can't I change things?" she cried. "Why can't I protect anyone? Why does nothing I do, nothing I say, even matter?"

Now the wailing came again. Slowly the Queen collapsed again on the floor, slapping her hands against its unyielding chill as her body shook. She clutched her flat stomach as pain wracked through her, remembering the pain of those days, the answers that had never come, Tawaret's silence toward her endless prayers.

Why had her children died? And why was her husband about to join them? They had been so loved. Why didn't that matter? Shouldn't the gods and goddesses who loved them respond to their love for one another?

Then the answer hit the Queen squarely in the heart.

The gods were not ignoring her. Nor were they withholding love. They were not there. And they never had been.

And on the cold stone floor of the temple, the Queen of Egypt sobbed until she lay exhausted. There was nothing inside her. And there was nothing above her.

Was that purpose even there? Had it ever really been there? Or was that gone too?

As she lay there shivering, the life she knew and loved torn from her unwilling grasp, an image gently touched her breaking heart. Her and her brother, months ago, so many years, it seemed, standing on the balcony, looking down at Memphis. Looking into the future. And she remembered the hope that had filled their hearts. Slowly, Ankhesenamun felt the tiniest bit of hope touch her heart now. Egypt was still out there, waiting for her to guide it into the future. She had promises to keep.

Life… was dealing with what was, one day at a time, with what you could change, and what you couldn't. And hoping tomorrow would be better.

For the first time, she felt she truly understood the words she had used so many times to encourage her little brother. And she clung to them, pressing herself tight against them as to a camel in a sandstorm.

She had come through before. And she would do it again. What choice did she have? She would keep going… because she had to.

Slowly, Ankh got to her feet. She had to get back. Whatever happened next, whatever was true, they needed her. And she was going to have to be strong. Gods or no gods.

The Queen wiped her bleary eyes and runny nose, swallowing back the rawness in her throat. Smudged makeup came away on her hand. She would have to hope no one looked too closely at her until she got inside.

Slowly she walked out of the temple, back into the sunlight. She was shaking slightly; with exhaustion, with the cold of the dark temple.

She paused. She felt something, in the warm Light of the Sun, which was sliding toward the horizon as afternoon passed into evening, its warm rays touching her face like a whisper of Love. Something... good. Something... encouraging. Something that told her that there *was* Someone up there. And that the purpose she was searching for remained. She touched her belly. Maybe.

To her surprise, Ankhesenamun smiled. She had a mystery to solve.

If the priests were wrong; if Amun and the others were meaningless statues, what was the truth?

Walking back to the palace through the warm sunlight, Ankh promised herself that she would find out.

The Queen realized with a shock that she had sprinted from the palace without a guard; a guard she knew she could trust. But there was Hannu, a concerned smile on his face as he calmly approached her, loyal, brave, and true, ready to safely escort her back inside.

But she wasn't ready to return to her post. Not yet. She was tired, confused, too overwhelmed to be able to begin pouring her love into her brother again. First she needed a cup of tea.

Leaving Hannu with a grateful smile, she crept inside, down a few hallways and back to her familiar room. Meresankh was there, quietly untangling a wig that the Queen had worn for one too many days, resulting in a number of snarls. When her Mistress entered the room, she looked up with a quiet, gentle smile. But she didn't say anything. She especially didn't say "Are you all right?" She just poured a cup of tea as the Queen slowly sat down.

"Thank you," she said quietly. Meresankh smiled again, the same quiet, gentle, sisterly smile. And slowly, she extended her hand.

Ankh reached out and squeezed it. They didn't need to talk about what had happened. Meresankh understood.


Ankhesenamun came back into her brother's room an hour later. Her eyes were puffy and red and her makeup had been washed off; she could hardly seem to look directly at him.

Tut held out his hand, and she sat by him, gently taking his head and shoulders into her lap. He looked up at her.

"I know," he said softly. "I know."

She just nodded. For now she had no more tears.

And he closed his eyes and let her hold him.

"You're right," she whispered a few minutes later. Her voice was hoarse; her throat sore. "What you said... the gods... they're not there." She shook her head, heart aching. "Not there at all."

He looked up at her calmly, shaking his head back. "No..." Then he sighed. "Who *is* there is the question. The question I've been athking mythelf for a long time. And how we find Them."

Ankh sighed, looking out the window. The sun was shining, one gentle ray streaming into the room. In spite of herself, she smiled. "We'll keep looking," she said finally. She shrugged. "And I suppose we can still pray... that Whoever it is, whether it's Aten or I-AM or Someone else entirely, will reveal Themselves to us."

The Pharaoh nodded. "I think that sounds like a good plan."


"They're not real," the Queen announced as she sat down in her private sitting room for a short break before dinner.

Meresankh looked up from arranging a bouquet of chrysan-themums sent by Mutnedjmet as her heart began to pound. "Who, My Lady?" she asked in a breathless whisper.

Her Mistress glanced toward the unseen sky. "The gods," she said simply. "Any of them. When I..." She bowed her head, folding her hands tightly. "When I sort of ran out, and I'm sorry if I scared you, I... I ran to the temple. And I tried to pray, but... they weren't there. None of them." She swallowed back a tear. "And it broke my heart. But..." Now she smiled, even as tears glimmered in her eyes and her voice broke. "I know Someone's there, because when I came back out of the temple, I could feel the Sun, and I knew... I just knew that I wasn't alone."

The Queen looked at her handmaiden. "So if Amun-Ra and Isis and Osiris and all the others aren't real, Who is left? Who *is* real?"

Meresankh just smiled back, offering a silent prayer of gratitude for the discovery her Mistress was slowly making her way toward. "Who indeed, My Lady?" And she turned to open the curtains, letting the bright, warm evening Sun shine into the room.

Semerkhet sighed over the dinner he was sharing with Meresankh in her chambers; a dinner of roast beef, onions, and beans with a cup of beer.

"Hard day?" she asked, reaching across the table to gently rest her tiny hand on his.

He looked up at her with a wan smile. And with a heavy sigh, he nodded.

"Granny said..."

"I heard," Meresankh said with a sigh of her own. She shook her head. "I'm sorry."

"I just feel so… helpless," he choked, pressing his free hand to the back of his mouth as he suddenly found himself fighting back tears. "There's nothing… nothing…"

"There's always something," Meresankh said softly, squeezing his hand. "Always. Even… even if it seems small. Even if it's as small as a cup of his favorite tea; as small as you getting Bastet for him or reading to him." She sighed. "Maybe… maybe you can't change the future. But you can make the present… a place where he knows how much you care."

And Semerkhet gave a watery smile.


It hit the Pharaoh that evening. It was too late. Tut fought back tears as he lay there, left leg burning, body shivering and sweating, every moment wracked with pain. Too late to do anything but try to control his suffering until the day the gods… or Whoever was up there… decided to take him away. If even Merneith had admitted it, it must be true. He was dying. Now the question was how many days he had left. And what he would manage to do with them. With what he could change… and what he couldn't.

The sun was setting on his life.

Then… he let the tears begin to flow. Covering his face, he lay shaking with sobs, disturbing the cat, who jumped from the bed onto the floor and hurried out of the room. Half a minute later his sister was hurrying into the bedroom from the sitting room, frowning in concern as she saw her brother weeping.

She didn't say "What is it?" Just sat down beside him, gathering him into her arms and holding him. Letting him cry.

He didn't want to die.

Again, the anger filled him. Anger at himself, for having foolishly put himself at such risk. Anger at life for the unfairness that had seemed to come at him from every direction from the moment he had been born. Anger… anger at the One Who had let it happen; the One Who had put him on this Earth with mismatched feet and a twisted spine, holding him back from becoming the mighty warrior-heir of the great Thutmose the First, establishing a legacy that would echo through the centuries. The strong Pharaoh he was supposed to be.

"Why?" he hissed under his breath. Weak as he was, he struggled with his bedsheets, forcing them aside to reveal his broken legs; the feet that had always been twisted and bent; one an ugly, misshapen appendage more like a fist than a foot, the other as flat as a goose's.

The Pharaoh shut his eyes with an angry sigh. "Why?" he moaned again. "What'th the point? Why did You put me here like thith? Weak, scrawny, pathetic, just like Grandfather Thutmose said. What can I accomplish in a body like thith? How can I be the thtrong Pharaoh I need to be? Why— why didn't You want me to do anyfing important? Why didn't you let me? Why shouldn't I make Grandfather Thutmose proud? And what'th…" He blinked back angry tears. "What'th been the point of my life if you're juth going to take it away? And why…" Now the tears began to flow down his cheeks as he felt a lump build in his throat. "Why did you take them? Mother, Father, my sisters, my precious little girls? If You love us, why have you taken everything away?" Tut wiped his eyes with a heavy sigh. "I wish I knew Who you were. I wish You would tell me. Tho pleathe… pleathe tell me."

He lay there in silence, the pain still simmering inside his aching heart. And yet, even as outside the window, the afternoon

178

sky was dimming into twilight, he felt a warmth inside his heart like the touch of the Sun on his face.

And as he had in the past, he knew, somehow… that he had been heard.

Ankhesenamun swallowed back tears as she looked down at her husband trying to rest early that evening, fighting the pain of his infected leg, sweat dripping down his body as he shivered and burned. Soon, she knew, his life would be over. And yet, he was still here, every instant of life that remained to him full of suffering. Suffering that thanks to modern medicine, could in some ways be eased, even if his life could not be saved.

And that was all she wanted, goals or no goals. For his pain to stop. Whatever it took. Looking at him lying there in burning misery, politics no longer seemed so important.

"You can let go," she whispered through her tears, stroking his sweaty forehead. "We can give you that poppy medicine again. Just let you sleep through it. You don't have to make any more decisions. You gave me your signet-ring, remember? You can just rest."

But he shook his head. "I don't want to be out of my mind," he whispered. Then he tried to give a little smile. "You're all the medicine I need."

Meresankh hugged her Granny. There was nothing to do but hang onto her; her ancient strength, her limitless wisdom. Gently Merneith patted her back with her gnarled old hand.

"Even the Red Sea has two shores, dearie," she whispered.

And Meresankh gave a little smile. This nightmare would not last forever.

Semerkhet watched his friend resting, the Pharaoh's face pale, thin cheeks still streaked with tear-tracks. And he swallowed back his own pain. And he thought. And he remembered.

Remembered his own baby brother, Nedjes. Who he had not been able to protect. And now, a second little brother lay before him on his deathbed.

Semerkhet bit his lip to think that he could not protect him either.

# 17   The Shadow

"**W**here will I go, Ankh?" Tut whispered as she fed him a bowl of yogurt, a bit of a bedtime snack. She closed her eyes. And she shook her head.

"All I know… is how much I don't know," she whispered. She set down the bowl, taking her brother's cold hands in hers. "But I do know this… you will always be in my heart."

Tut swallowed back tears. "And you will always be in mine."

As he slept, she wondered. Where *would* he go? What would be his fate? He would be remembered… but would that be enough to bring him peace?

She shook her head. The space the gods and goddesses had left when they had disappeared from her heart felt raw, empty. The Queen knew she had found the truth; the truth that told her that the gods and goddesses of her people were nothing more than stories, but she still did not know what to think. Only… only that a greater Truth existed; a Truth greater than any human attempt to reach out to the Divine. And she wondered… truly wondered… to Whom she was praying.

But amid all the questions that remained, the Queen shook her head as the answer to one of them began to form inside her heart, slowly coming into view like the Sun emerging from behind a cloud. Months ago, when her brother had gotten the ague after that hunting trip, she had wondered if the next time that illness struck him, he would recover.

Ankhesenamun closed her eyes as the answer settled into her heart like a heavy millstone. The answer was *no*.

What time was it? Ankhesenamun sat up with her brother, letting Sem drowse on his cot. After painfully being turned onto his side by both Semerkhet and Kamose— successfully, this time, as she'd been glad to see—, her brother had slept for maybe an hour in all that night; a few minutes here, a few minutes there. But mostly he lay stiffly, body tensed against the pain in his legs as she slowly, methodically moved her hand up and down his bony back, feeling every rib, every vertebra. As she sat, she was humming the ballad about the turtledove, the same melody she had been humming for the past fifteen minutes.

The Queen sat there in the darkest depths of the night. Morning was so very far away. So very, very far away.

She couldn't help but bite back a yawn. How long had it been since she had slept in her own bed? At least half of every long, cold night was spent taking turns with Semerkhet, hour by hour, one getting up to sit with Tut, stroking his head, humming to him, rubbing his back, while the other tried to catch a few minutes of their own sleep. Letting him know with gentle, reassuring touch that they were with him; that he was safe, that he was loved. Back and forth they went, lying down, getting up, sitting quietly beside him, hour by hour until morning came. Sem had a little cot next to Tutankhamun's bed, and the Queen usually lay back in her chair when it was her turn to drowse, pulling a blanket over her body and closing her exhausted eyes.

She shivered. Tybi nights were cold. She had a blanket wrapped around her shoulders, but she was still chilly. Just another reason she wanted to curl up again in the chair under her warm blankets and go back to sleep. Or even in her own bed.

It was beginning to weigh on her. She could hardly open her eyes when Semerkhet gently patted her hand to tell her it was her turn. Even now she sat staring into space as she gently, absent-mindedly stroked Tut's back. Would he ever fall asleep?

She bent and looked down at him, the tightness of his jaw, the tiny line between his eyebrows. He was in so much pain. And if she could do anything to help him sleep, it was worth it. Even at the expense of her own sleep.

And her own words came back to her, the words she had taught her brother. *There is always something you can do. No matter how small it may seem.*

And she gave a little smile.


Finally, Tutankhamun drifted off, feeling loved and safe under his sister's watch; the touch of her gentle hand. With her hand on his back, he was still him. And some things... would never change. Slowly, he descended into sleep.


*It was dark. When Tut opened his eyes, he did not know where he was. Pain made him gasp, and he looked down to see that his legs lay unwrapped, unsplinted. Where was he?*

*The Pharaoh felt about him, his hands exploring smooth, cold, dripping stone walls. A prison?*

*"Hello?" he called into the empty blackness. His voice echoed off the damp walls, reverberating into silence.*

*There was no response. Tut swallowed, his throat becoming dry. His heart was pounding, his palms slick with sweat. And his empty stomach twisted within him. Suddenly, he was very hungry.*

183

*And he was alone. Completely alone. He put his arms around himself, shivering with cold, and with fear.*

*Then, at a great distance above him, he noticed something. A tiny pinprick of light. He squinted up at it, trying to see what it was. It shone above him, encouraging, loving. Tut reached up a hand, but there was no way for him to reach it. He could not stand on his broken legs, there was no walking-stick in sight, and even if he had been able to get up, it appeared that the Light was shining from higher than the top of the Great Pyramid.*

*He sank back, defeated. And he began to cry like a child.*

*The Light was there, and It loved him. But he was separated from it forever.*


He awoke with a gasp. Tut looked around him; he saw his own room, with its familiar outlines. In the chair beside the bed, Semerkhet was sitting silently, watching over his rest, and in her chair, his sister was sleeping.

It had all been a dream.

Silently, Tut reached up, pressing his hands into his eyes and wiping away the tears that had gathered. He released a deep, shuddering sigh. All a dream. He was safe. Through the crack under the door, he could see lamplight from out in the hall.

He was not dead. Because suddenly, he could see that that was what he had dreamed. The fate that awaited him if after his final breath, he awoke unto darkness.

If he could not find the Light, he would be separated from it forever.

"O Great Light," he whispered, not knowing to Whom he spoke, but knowing that that was the best he could do, "help me

184

find You. Help all of us find You. Reveal Yourself to us. Don't let me die in darkness."

And as he relaxed again under his blankets, his faithful cat at his side, he smiled. Because a tiny bit of peace had touched his heart like a gentle ray of sunlight in the middle of the night. And he knew that he had been heard.

It was time for his break. Semerkhet stood in the doorway of his Pharaoh's bedroom, ready to go get his lunch and sit down for a few minutes. He had seen something in his Master's face... a shadow. And he needed to think. The King was asleep for the moment, breathing slowly, the cat curled up under his arm.

Semerkhet bowed to him anyway, and to the Queen, who sat quietly beside him. "All life, prosperity, and health," the valet whispered as he left the room. As he walked out, he hoped it would come true.

The valet walked down to Meresankh's suite. He hadn't been invited, but he needed her right now. Blindly he made his way down the halls that separated the Pharaoh's chambers from the servants' quarters, and a few minutes later, felt his knuckles gently rapping on her door.

A moment later, the door opened, and there she was, the silver necklace gleaming over her heart— although he was almost too distracted by the pain in his own heart to take note.

"How's your day?" Meresankh asked, stepping into the doorway to squeeze his hand. It still made him feel like locusts were whirring inside his stomach when she touched him. "I was going to bring you something if you didn't come down."

He shook his head, biting his lip. Even to say the words... If he told her what he thought, would that make it come true?

185

Loving concern on her face, Meresankh pulled at his hand. "Come on. Let's sit down." He stumbled through the door, and she closed it behind him. They made their way into Meresankh's living area. On the table, he could see two plates filled with flatbread, beans, a bit of spiced mutton, and a few dates. Semerkhet could smell the fresh bread, the spicy meat, even the mild, vegetable fragrance of the beans. But he wasn't hungry. This was not a time for food.

Meresankh guided him to a chair, sat down next to him, and looked up at him earnestly, taking both of his hands in hers.

"What's going on?" she asked, frowning up at him. He looked down at her, her sweet brown face going blurry with the tears that were filling his eyes. He swallowed them back down.

"Time is running out," he choked out. "Won't be much longer." He glanced around nervously, hoping that even through the walls and doors, none of the other servants had heard him; he hoped he wasn't about to start a mass panic by bringing news of the impending death of the god-king. But no sudden wails echoed through the hallways. No one had heard them. No one knew the terrible secret.

Meresankh's blue-painted eyes slowly filled with knowing tears. Then they closed as she bowed her head, holding his hands even tighter. He felt his heart warm, as though she was sending him strength through her grip.

He waited for her to say, "Are you sure?" or even, "I'm so sorry," but she didn't. She just wrapped her warm little arms around him and held on tight, her strong heart beating in time with his. And sitting there holding him, even the palace gossip was silent.

186

Semerkhet held her as she held him, finally letting the tears flow. She let him cry. And she didn't say anything. Right now, no words were necessary.

As Semerkhet wept, he felt himself going back in time, to when he had mourned at Nedjes' funeral. And his body went weak as the pain overwhelmed him; the guilt.

"I couldn't protect him," he whispered to Meresankh.

"Who?" she asked, although there was little question who he meant.

"Nedjes," he choked. "All those years ago… we lost him on his first hippopotamus hunt… *I* lost him, Meresankh. It took him. And I couldn't save him. And I let the Pharaoh fall at Kadesh; I let them poison him. I can't protect him either. And it's my fault… my fault he's going to d-d-die…"

Then there were no more words; only the tears ripped from his breaking heart. And Meresankh sat with him, her arms wrapped around him, and let him cry.

"Why do you say it was your fault?" she whispered. "You know it wasn't. Not Nedjes; not the Pharaoh. Life—"

"Life happens," he cut in, his voice harsh. "I know. And I know I stood by and watched my little brother go to his death. Twice. How… how is that not my fault?"

She just shook her head. She knew that she did not have the words to convince him of what was true.

"Think of all the ways you've protected the Pharaoh," she said. "You brought him home from Kadesh. And you're protecting him now. You've risked your own life to protect him; so many times and in so many ways. That… that outweighs whatever may have happened. He needs you. He really does. Now… now more than ever." She swallowed. "He always has. And he always will."

Finally Semerkhet nodded, wiping away his tears. He gave a heavy sigh, standing up and straightening his warm outer robe. Whatever was true, whatever was his fault, she was right about one thing. His Pharaoh needed him.

"Thank you," he said softly, reaching out to squeeze her hand again. "Thank you."

Eventually Semerkhet was ready to go back; back to his place at his Pharaoh's side, to guide him through the next few hours. He walked quietly down the hall that led back to the royal suites, past a multitude of other servants working on various activities. People nodded respectfully at him, and when another man bumped into him, he heard, "Forgive me, Your Excellency."

Would he ever get used to it?

Suddenly from behind him, there was a gasp. Semerkhet's stomach lurched and he whirled around; was his Master's pain becoming too much to bear?

He blinked. He wasn't in the King's bedroom; he was in the middle of the hallway, surrounded by other servants. Then who had made the noise? He scanned the hall to see a young man helping an older one stand up; he had tripped over a pomegranate that had somehow rolled all the way from the kitchen. But he seemed perfectly fine. Better than fine, actually— as Sem watched, the old man gave a chuckle, and his friend joined in. Soon all the servants were laughing at the spectacular clown-like acrobatics that old Hori had performed. Everyone was fine. And as the laughter faded into cheerful smiles, the servants went on their way, ready to return to the day's work.

Semerkhet shook his head and kept walking, back to the familiarity of his Pharaoh's room. This hypervigilance that he was developing had its advantages and its disadvantages.

Meresankh closed her eyes with a heavy sigh. There was nothing she could do but be there for the Queen... and Semerkhet.

And pray. Always pray.

She bit her lip. And she reminded herself... even the Red Sea had two shores.

There was a knock at the door.

"For you, My Lady," Semerkhet called.

Ankh got up from sitting with her brother and stretched, then made her way to the door to see her visitor.

It was a young male servant, a boy she didn't recognize. He held a platter with a cup balanced on it; a cup that looked like it was full of tea.

"From a secret admirer, My Lady," he said, dipping his head. "With his salutations to your son."

Ankhesenamun took the cup, peering into it suspiciously. No snake jumped out to bite her; no spider or scorpion scurried out.

"Thank you," she said. And she closed the door in his face. "Granny, what's in this?" she asked, showing the cup to the old midwife.

Merneith looked up from mixing another poultice and took the cup in her wrinkled hands. She smelled it. And she frowned.

"Don't accept anything anyone gives you," she said solemnly. "This a blend of bitter cucumber... parsley... caraway... jasmine..." She took another deep inhalation, discerning the fragrances of the ingredients. "Fennel," she continued, "sage, and

189

celery seed. If you are carrying the Pharaoh's heir... one sip of this, and we would have a second death to mourn."

The Queen covered her belly protectively, watching in horror as Granny went to dispose of the lethal tea. Ay was taking no chances.

And neither was she. Nothing not brought for her by Meresankh or Semerkhet would pass her lips.

She bowed her head, offering a silent prayer of thanks to Whoever was listening. If her prayers had been answered... a life had been saved today. A precious little life in whose hands the future of Egypt lay.

And then she shuddered, still hugging her belly. The Grand Vizier had attempted to murder an unborn baby. This was war.

She decided not to tell Tut. She had fought this battle herself; fended off this attack on their legacy using her own best judgment, just as she always had. And soon, she would be fighting every political battle completely alone, one Queen against the rest of the world. He didn't need to know that someone had tried to kill their child. Not now. Not when his own survival was his first priority.

But she told Meresankh. And they cried together, that someone could be so cruel. And then in gratitude that the murderous plot had been foiled.

And Semerkhet agreed not to admit anyone. Not even servants bearing gifts.


The Queen bowed her head and tried to pray for strength. But she no longer knew Who to address. The gods had left her; abandoned her when she had suddenly realized that they had never been real at all. Who was left? Aten? I-AM? Someone else completely?

190

She was not sure.

The Pharaoh also tried to pray, wishing he knew Who to address. Ankh had confirmed it. The gods were not real.

But they were not alone in the cosmos. And the Creator was great and powerful enough to hear his prayers, even if he didn't know Who to make them to.

He sighed, looking out the window as he had a thousand times before. Seeing the Sun.

Could it be the Aten?

Had Father been right? Had he?

And would Tutankhamun ever know? Or would he be gone before he ever found the Truth?

How could he find out? Who could he ask? Who in the palace knew the things he needed to know?

And so to his prayers, the Pharaoh added a request that the Great Mystery would reveal Their identity to him and his sister.

Before it was too late. Because time was running out.

# 18   Perseverance

"I just realithed something," Tutankhamun said slowly. His wife looked up from petting Bastet. "Hmm?"

He sighed, shaking his head. "I juth realithed…

that I won't get to meet the baby. I mean, I knew, but I just… it juth now hit me."

Ankh got up from her chair, carefully sitting down on the bed and taking him in her arms, holding him to her heart. She didn't say, "You're right," or "I'm sorry." She didn't have to. She just held him.

He felt her heart beating; her small strength. And swallowing back the lump in his throat, he continued.

"That's the thing I want most," he said in a choked whisper. "To be there when it's born… to hold it and sing to it and watch it grow up… all the things we never got to—" He swallowed again, remembering that for all his pain, hers was greater. So much greater. "And I'm thorry that I won't be there."

"But you will be," Ankhesenamun whispered back through her own tears. "Whenever we tell your story. And we will, every day. I promise."

And all he could do was smile as his heart filled with warmth.

"But what will happen when the General gets back?"

Semerkhet stopped halfway down the hall as he saw three other servants crowded together into a knot, whispering together with their heads down.

"He'll do the right thing," a second man said, "and step aside. And *our* Glorious Lord will finally sit on the throne."

192

"What about the Queen?" a third man asked. "She has to marry him to legitimize his claim."

"There are ways around that," the second man replied. "And if he has to… Horemheb will help clear the way for the Vizier to take his rightful place."

"But there are so many of them," the first man said. "So many who love the dear young boy and his wife. So many who won't want to see the Vizier take the throne. Horemheb is the boy's heir. If the Vizier makes a move, many of them won't accept it. What will happen then?"

"That's when those of us who care about Egypt's economy and her place in the world will step forward… and those with weak stomachs will step back," the second man sneered, fingering the knife at his belt. The first man went pale. And Semerkhet put his head down and kept walking.

The Queen sat down. Meresankh looked up from the sorting and tidying that never seemed to end and walked over with a smile.

"You'll never guess what Persenet and Rekhetre have been up to," she began, barely able to keep her laughter in check as she remembered the crazy scheme the two had concocted to engineer events so that the entire team of handsome hockey players all wound up in the easternmost storage room. What was supposed to transpire after that, she could only guess.

Ankhesenamun looked up. And there was no smile on her face.

"I don't want a story right now," she said heavily. "Or a song, or a joke, or a random fact about something completely irrelevant. I just want to take my break."

Meresankh bit her tongue. And with the words, "Yes, My Lady," she made her way into the Queen's storage room to give her Mistress space.

Once she was alone, she blinked back angry tears. What was that about? The Queen didn't want a story? What was wrong with her? What was wrong— with Meresankh? What had changed? And why… why were her stories no longer bringing joy?

Meresankh's heart ached as she thought of it. The moments that brought her the most pride, the most joy, were the moments when she made her friends smile. But— the Queen hadn't smiled. And she had all but told Meresankh to go away.

Meresankh had failed. Failed to cheer up her best friend; failed to make a rough day better. But she did not know what needed to change.

"Will they believe us?" Ankh asked. Bastet was curled in her arms as she sat in her chair next to the bed, wrapped warmly in her yellow outer robe, and Tut was trying to read a papyrus recording Ahmose-Nefertari's successes as regent for Amenhotep the First. It was not easy, but it passed the time.

Tutankhamun looked up from the papyrus. "Hmm?"

"The Hittites," she said. The cat hopped down from her lap, going on the hunt for ants. "Princesses… and Queens… don't marry outside their own families, and they certainly don't marry outside of Egypt. Will they think I'm lying and trying to kidnap the Prince instead of marrying him?"

Tut shrugged. "If anything, they'll see that it'th true because it's so strange," he replied. "Why would you lie about a thing like that… why would you make a move like this unless it really wath… an emergency?"

194

Ankh squeezed his hand. "I hope they see it that way."

Tut sat up a little. "You'll make them thee it that way. Even if they don't believe this letter, you can send another one. You can convince them. I know you can."

The Queen smiled. "Maybe that's what I'll say... *why would I lie?*" She shrugged, shoulders moving under the fabric of her white gown, her warm, yellow outer robe. Then she gave half a wry chuckle, half a cynical smile. "I suppose what will happen... remains to be seen."

"What if Ay happenth?" Tutankhamun whispered solemnly.

Ankh looked down, squeezing his cold hand. "Then Nefermaatet the Lioness will take the throne herself," she said.


"What am I going to do, Meresankh?" Semerkhet asked softly. They were sitting outside together for a few minutes that late afternoon, tossing flower-heads into a reflecting pool from where they sat on a bench.

She tossed in the last flower in her hand and put her arm around him. She didn't say anything. She didn't need to.

"I've already lost one brother," he said. "And now... now another one."

Meresankh reached out and squeezed his hand. It was a cool day, but her hands were warm.

"You're going to be brave," she said. "And you're going to take one day at a time. And take good care of yourself. And I..." She looked up at him, regarding him calmly, that mysterious Light shining in her eyes. "I will be praying for you."

Semerkhet sighed. He didn't know Who the One she prayed to really was... but he knew that her prayers had been answered when his hadn't. "Thank you," he whispered.

195

She just smiled. And the chattiest member of the palace staff didn't say anything. She just put her arm around him again. And they watched the warm, loving Sun shining on the water.

Meresankh sighed. Again, she was unable to help her friends; unable even to make them smile. Sadly, she wondered what she was doing wrong.

A wild idea arose in the Queen's heart. What if… what if she said *yes?* What if, the next time the Vizier proposed to her, for surely there would be a next time, she agreed? Of course, she would not go through with it, but could pretending to accept give her leverage; throw him off the scent and give her time to work against him from behind his back?

She shook her head as revulsion rose in her throat. And she thought of the possibilities that that choice— or apparent choice— would bring. Standing at the Vizier's side, pretending to be his willing bride, she would still carry the hope of her brother's possible heir inside. An heir who might be legitimized, as the son of the Pharaoh's wife.

And, having accepted the Vizier's proposal of marriage, she would be able to get closer to him than ever, keeping her friends close and her enemies closer. Close enough… to do some damage? She imagined it— giving the order for poison to be added to the Vizier's wine, just as he had poisoned the Pharaoh; offered her tea intended to kill her child.

And she imagined the outcome. He was an old man, but such a death would be too sudden to be set aside as tragic but natural. And she would be the only suspect. Those who had supported the Vizier

196

would rise up against her, baby or no baby, and she wondered if even Horemheb could protect her.

Accepting the Vizier's proposal as a means to having him assassinated would be fruitless, she could see. And besides that possibility… she could see little purpose to announcing her acceptance. Yes, such a marriage might facilitate her appointment as a widowed Queen Mother to her son, but even after the death of the vulture she had agreed to marry, she would be surrounded by those who had once followed him. Would she really be able to lead the country as she saw fit— update laws, build schools, fight poverty, promote education— standing alone among those whose hatred of the Pharaoh whose new policies had ultimately been hers had caused them to wish her brother dead? Or would their hot breath down her neck hem her in, force her into silence, put her very life at risk every time she did make a move they did not like?

She shook her head. She would leave the Vizier's proposal where it was— with the blue ring inside his pocket. He could take that ring, and all his hopes for their future marriage, and throw them in the Nile.

Ankh had unseasoned lentils, plain flatbread, and peppermint tea for dinner. Anything else made her stomach do somersaults. Something was changing, two weeks after she had been united with her husband. And she hoped she knew what it was.

The Pharaoh could barely breathe. So Granny made a mustard-plaster for him, gently applying it to his chest and waiting with him while it slowly grew warmer, drawing heat to his lungs and helping him expel the congestion.

Even having a mustard-plaster put on was an exhausting hassle, especially with the half a bath it took to get the mustard oils off his skin afterward. But it was worth it, if it meant that for the next hour, he would be able to breathe easily.

Tutankhamun looked toward the window, seeing the warm brightness of the early-evening Sun shining in through the fine linen curtains. And he ached to feel it on his face. He was so weak that he could barely sit up; he had not been out of bed even once over the twenty long days that he had counted since the last time he had sat in his chair, but he longed… he longed to go out into the garden again. Even if it was for the last time.

Could he?

Swallowing, Tut struggled to push himself up slightly against his pillows, raising his head. And he cleared his throat.

His sister looked up from the papyrus she was reading at the little table they'd brought in, giving him a smile. "Yes, love?"

He returned the smile. "I want… I want to go outside," he said softly.

Ankh set the papyrus aside, getting up and walking to his side, gently stroking his face with her tiny, warm hand.

"Oh, darling," she whispered, a sad smile on her face. "That does sound nice, doesn't it?"

He nodded. And his smile didn't disappear. "I mean it," he said. "Just for a few minutes," he insisted before she could provide an extremely reasonable argument for why it wasn't a good idea. He looked up at her, reaching for her hand and giving her the pleading face that had always gotten Setepenre what she wanted. "Pleathe. One… one more time."

198

Ankhesenamun looked at him, then sighed. She looked him up and down; his splinted legs, his weary, wasted body. And slowly, she nodded, a soft smile coming to her face.

"Let's do it."

Tut waited in heart-pounding anticipation as his sister went to get Semerkhet and Kamose. And he smiled as the three of them entered the room.

They didn't say anything, but their eyes lit up. And Tut locked his arms around Kamose's neck as with Semerkhet's help, the soldier transferred him to a stretcher padded with soft pillows.

The Pharaoh lay back, already exhausted. He smiled as he felt Semerkhet tuck a blanket around him; then he was in the air as Kamose and Sem took their places and lifted the litter.

The litter swayed gently as they carried him out of his room, down the corridor, into the grand front hall. It wasn't as exciting as it had been the other time, but Tut smiled. Because it would be so lovely to go out again. So very lovely.

His sister was beside him, keeping pace with the litter as they made their way to the door. She was coming too.

Then the door opened. Tut smiled with a little thrill as the fresh air filled his lungs; the bright, loving sunshine warmed his face. Blinking in the brightness, he opened his eyes to see the bright colors of the flowers, the lengthening shadows, the sparkle of the setting sun on the lotus-pools, pink, red, and orange splashed over their glittering surfaces. Among the flowers, whose sweet fragrances filled his nose as he breathed, little birds were twittering and fluttering, pecking for seeds. And on his face, Tut could feel the cool Tybi breeze.

It was lovely out here. It was beautiful. It was perfect. He closed his eyes, drinking it all in, the Sun and wind on his skin, the fragrances of the flowers, the cheerful sounds of the birds, immersing himself in the feel of the world around him. And he smiled. What a gift to be able to see, hear, smell, feel their beautiful garden… one more time.

And to feel the Sun on his face. As its loving rays touched his skin, he smiled. And again, he felt a whisper of love.

He shivered, pulling his blankets closer with weak, emaciated arms. And Ankh came to stand beside the litter, putting one warm arm around him in a gentle hug.

"Thank you," he whispered.

She just kissed him.


Tutankhamun looked carefully around the garden, taking in every detail, remembering every walk he had taken along its paths, every game of *seega* he and his sister had shared in their pavilion, Ankh's story of gathering a bouquet of purple lotuses, pink jasmine, early chrysanthemums, and the last roses of the year just for him. He memorized every flower, every tree, every lotus-pool. And silently, he made his grateful goodbyes to the garden.


They didn't stay out much longer. When Tut began to yawn as the evening deepened into twilight, Kamose and Semerkhet lifted the litter again and began the short journey back to the palace, back to his room, back to his bed. And as Semerkhet tucked him in again, safe among his soft pillows and warm blankets, he felt himself drifting off. Such a short adventure, and he was exhausted.

But satisfied. Because he had gone out into the garden. And it was just as beautiful as he had remembered.

200

Ankh and Sem sighed sadly to themselves as they watched the Pharaoh drift off. The three of them had spent a beautiful half-hour in the garden, watching the birds, smelling the flowers, feeling the Sun, listening to the breeze. And it had been glorious.

But half an hour had been all he could handle. And it had worn him out so completely that now he lay sleeping, body exerted to its limit.

It was painful to see what he... or his body... had become. But they were glad that he had gotten what he wanted.

One last trip to the garden.


Ankh sat at her dressing-table, adjusting her sleeping-tunic. She would be in her chair in her brother's room in a few minutes, ready to begin the long night of taking turns with Semerkhet in sitting with Tut, but she needed a moment.

Something touched her heart. Something heavy. A realization. Yesterday, her brother had been too tired to make any decisions. And... She looked down at the signet-ring that was now hers. And at the proclamation that now lay on her desk; the proclamation stamped with that very signet-ring, formalizing the Pharaoh's decision. He had deputized her. Now she was the one making the decisions in every capacity— signing them herself, as well as offering her wisdom. By her authority as Queen, specially deputized by the Pharaoh, their country was under her command... and her protection.

She was, in effect, regent. But as great of an honor as that was... it meant that time was becoming short. That... She clenched her hands. That, and what Granny had told them.

For so long, ever since the moment they had carried him in after the long journey home from Amurru, every waking hour had been spent taking care of him, or taking strategic breaks that would allow her to continue taking good care of him. Now even her nights were spent sitting with him, sharing the load with Semerkhet. But now... the wall of activity, busyness, and hard work that had protected her since he had told his secret was falling.

Time truly was running out.

She closed her eyes as she felt the cold void of the future. Life would be so empty. Who she was would not change, but life would be unrecognizable.

How would she get through?

Then, gentle as a whisper, the answer came to her. She would draw on the strength of the past. All through the reigns of her parents, Ankhesenpaaten had learned at her mother's knee; her grandmother's knee. Learned how to be a woman in the realm of politics, following the example of the great female Pharaohs and Queens Regent who had gone before them. How to foster diplomacy, shore up what they had rather than thinning the Empire's influence by stretching it from sea to sea, how to spot a lie and how to tell an advantageous truth. How to be sweet and deadly, civil and sneaky, courageous and cunning, getting one's way without one's opponent even noticing.

Ankh had learned political science, international etiquette, how to read others better than they read themselves, smelling out their intentions and motivations by their gestures, posture, expressions. How to be a woman in a man's world, not denying who she was but showing herself equal to every man she looked at. She would be Queen herself one day, and she needed to know how the women of old had led, whether from beside the throne or sitting on it themselves.

Little could Ankh have known as she learned from Nefertiti and from Tiye that in only a few short years, her own mother would be standing in the gap between dynasties, gracefully managing power and authority as she guided her nation from the end of one era into the dawn of another. And that she herself… would also stand gazing at an unknown future with her husband no longer beside her and no son to raise up into a strong, wise king. She had been only a little girl.

So she knew what to do, Ankh told herself. She knew she did. She would get through by relying on the same strength that had sustained centuries of women before her; the strength they had passed on to her. And the strength… She looked down at her belly. That she hoped to pass on to the next generation.

# 19   Strength

They had not answered, Semerkhet thought as he stepped into his own room to get ready for bed after the long, hard day. The gods, Amun, Osiris, the others. Had not answered any of his prayers. His brother was still going to die.

And for the hundredth time, the question pulled at his heart. Who was up there?

Not anyone he had been raised to worship, he realized with a heavy sigh, fully recognizing what he had been trying to wonder since the Pharaoh had been hurt. And with a heavy sigh, and a few tears, he felt his old religion fall away. Not real. Osiris, Horus, any of them. How could they be real, when they had never answered him in any meaningful way, even back in the days before all this?

But if they were not real… then what was the Truth? And where was the Light?

Meresankh stood in her Lady's chambers, ready to call her day's work complete and get ready for bed. Although the Queen had found her smile again, it had still been a long, hard day. The Pharaoh's pain grew worse hour by hour, and both Meresankh's Lady and Semerkhet were working day and night to look after him. She could see the weariness in their faces; hear it in their voices. Almost… She bit back what was almost a sad chuckle. Almost like new parents caring for a newborn baby. But this beloved person had not just entered the world. This person was preparing to leave it.

And Granny… Granny knew that his time was becoming very short.

204

Sadly, she smiled. Even from across the hall, she could smell the musky perfume of spikenard, the calming sweetness of frankincense; the massage lotion Semerkhet always used to try to soothe the Pharaoh to sleep. She smiled to think of her beloved's caring heart and healing hands; a caring heart and healing hands that someday, in the not-too-distant future, he would be using to treat the aches and pains of people he didn't even know; people from the wide world outside the palace walls. And she smiled to think of the love and loyalty that one day... would make him the greatest husband and father in the world.

The Light was there... but it was hard to find. Especially at night. Tut shivered through the dark watches, wishing he could ask his sister or his brother to light an oil lamp to bring even the smallest flame of warmth into the room. But if he did that, none of them would sleep. So he lay there quietly under his warm blankets on that Tybi night, feeling very small and alone in the darkness of the bedroom, a great big nineteen-year-old boy afraid of the dark.

And wondering. Wondering what darkness awaited him if he could not find the Light in time.

The Pharaoh was afraid.

Ankhesenamun lay there in her chair, drowsing while Semerkhet sat with her brother. Then a sudden thought touched her heart. Soon... she would be sleeping in her own bed again. Because her brother would no longer need her to sit up with him.

The Queen got out of her chair, joining Semerkhet at Tut's side. Because with the days and nights slipping by, how much did she really need to sleep?

Nights were hard, but the hours the three of them spent in silent wakefulness did not mean they got no sleep at all. Tut found that it was more effective to take short naps here and there throughout the day than to expect himself to be able to sleep through the night. And while he dozed on and off through the long, quiet, weary afternoons, Ankhesenamun and Semerkhet could take turns catching their own little naps. Any bit of sleep any one of them could get was a blessing.

Out in the hallway, they could hear the servants praying and smell the incense they were burning as they begged the gods to heal their Lord and Master. But even as prayers sounded in their ears, the mundane had to happen too.

It hurt to be washed. Tut let Sem wash him in the interest of smelling decent and keeping his skin healthy, but getting jostled around was exhausting, and the reward was not worth the work.

Semerkhet had just washed Tut's left arm, and turned away for a moment to dip his cloth back in the bowl of warm water he was using. As he took Tutankhamun's right wrist to lift that arm, Bastet jumped onto the bed. Tut gave a startle, and the ring of the Sole Companion collided roughly with the back of the Pharaoh's hand.

"Watch what you're doing!" Tutankhamun hissed, snatching his hand back and rubbing at it with the other one. "When did you get so clumsy?"

Sem's body went stiff, and his jaw tightened. Silently he rinsed out the rag again, then offered his hand. Carefully, Tut let him have his right arm again.

"My Lord," Semerkhet said quite formally, avoiding eye contact as he focused on carefully dabbing the cloth up and down the Pharaoh's right arm.

206

And suddenly Tut's heart was aching. Because this was not his best friend Sem. This was the Semerkhet who had worked for him for a year, stiff and formal; the Semerkhet he had vaguely known before they had become friends.

The valet got the Pharaoh cleaned up to his satisfaction, then set the bowl aside and rose, offering a deep bow. But before he could leave, Tut reached out, gently pulling at his hand.

"Sem," he begged, almost feeling tears in his tired eyes. "I'm thorry. I didn't mean it. I'm just so…"

Semerkhet looked at Tut, and his face changed. There was the good friend, the dear Sem, that Tut had come to love as the only brother he'd ever had.

Sem gave half a smile. "I know," he said softly. "And I *was* clumsy."

Tut just shook his head and chuckled.

The Pharaoh was ready for a nap after so much activity. But as exhausting as it was, it felt good to be fresh and clean and looked after.

Much had changed. But the Washer of Pharaoh would faithfully do his duty… to the end.

The month of Tybi went on. And the Queen waited. Waited to see if she would bleed. Waited to see if there was hope for an heir. And prayed and prayed that she would not bleed; that her womb had become the home of a child who would grow big and strong and carry their family into the future.

But… even if she didn't bleed, her question would not yet be answered. Because a single cycle missed was a clue; a hint that it might have happened. Until conception was confirmed by the wheat and barley test, a test no man or nonpregnant woman could pass, a missed cycle was a "definite maybe."

But it was something.

Had their prayer been answered this time? And even if it had… would her husband ever know?

And what kind of father would Zannanza make?

"Why?" the Pharaoh whispered.

His sister looked over. "Why what?" she asked softly.

He gestured at the legs that lay immobile under his blankets. "All this. And all… all the way back to the beginning. Why… why wath I never the thtrong Pharaoh I should have been?"

The Queen shook her head, beaded braids chiming sadly. "You've always been strong," she said softly, reaching out to run a gentle hand over his hot head. "You know that. But…" She paused, pondering the words that were rising inside her heart. *Physically going into literal battle did not make you stronger*, she wanted to say. She shook her head. Maybe that was true. But to say it out loud would not be kind, necessary, or helpful.

Ankh sighed, shaking her head again. "You are strong," she said again. "And I know… I know there's a purpose… for everything we've been through. We just… have to find it." She nodded. "And we will."

Her brother gave her half a smile. Was there anything else to say?

"Meresankh?"

The handmaiden paused on her journey down the hall with a basket of clean clothes to put away. The Queen was standing in the doorway of the Pharaoh's bedroom, beckoning to her.

208

"Yes, My Lady?"

Balancing the basket on her hip, Meresankh joined the Queen in the doorway.

But that wasn't enough. Smiling, Ankhesenamun reached out and gently took Meresankh's hand, drawing her into the room. And she closed the door behind them.

Quickly Meresankh set her laundry basket in an out-of-the-way corner of the room. Rising, she looked around the royal bedroom with almost as much awe as the first time she had seen it. It was still as glorious as ever, and the Pharaoh, drowsing in the bed, looked worse than ever. She bit her lip as she looked at him, but didn't say anything. Just offered a brief bow.

"Yes, My Lady?" she asked again.

Her friend grinned. And she took Meresankh's hand again.

"I really... really... really think I might be," she whispered, face glowing like the Sun. "I still haven't bled, spicy food makes me sick to my stomach, and my breasts and my belly are sore. I talked to Merneith the other day... and she couldn't say I wasn't. I know most women get really tired, and cry really easy..." She paused, considering. "Although that might actually be happening. I just..." She bit her lip, voice breaking. "Have a lot to cry about right now." Meresankh squeezed her hand with an encouraging smile as the Queen wiped her eyes with her free hand, smearing her eye-makeup. "And goodness knows I haven't been sleeping. But anyway..." She gave an exhilarated sigh, and Meresankh almost thought she could see the baby glow shining from her face. "The signs are there. The signs..." Gently, she rested Meresankh's hand on her belly. "Of hope."

Meresankh blinked back happy tears. If her Lady was having that many signs, how could it not be true?

"Praise be," she whispered. The Queen just hugged her. And Meresankh was on her way again.

She kept praying, kept hoping, kept bringing her Lady the teas that Granny made. And every day, she asked her how she was. And how the baby was.

His friend was in pain, Semerkhet reminded himself. So much pain. So it stood to reason that he'd be sensitive. Unreasonable, even. Didn't mean that Semerkhet's heart hadn't run away to hide, to curl up inside its shell again; that he hadn't been catapulted back a few months, back to the days before he was the Sole Companion, Unique Friend. But his friend... his friend had apologized. And Semerkhet had forgiven him.

He understood.

His sister's words warmed his heart. And her faith that there was a purpose for it all was encouraging. But still... Tut shook his head sadly. Just because she thought of him as strong didn't change how his heart ached whenever he thought of the legacies of Thutmose the First and the other great warrior kings; the shame he felt whenever he compared his crippled frame to the power and vigor with which they had led Egypt to glorious victory on the battlefield. Just because there was some sort of good reason for all this misery didn't mean that there was anything at all about the life he had that satisfied him.

Her words were kind. But she could not truly understand how he felt.

Ankhesenamun sat and thought about the tea the Vizier had sent her and her baby. And she continued to think about her options.

210

She had determined that assassinating Ay with a deadly drink of her own would catapult her into a war she could not win, not even if Horemheb proved loyal. But what else was possible? What other moves could she make to stop him?

She thought of the signet-ring Ay had stolen from them and used to forge the proclamation that would have placed him in power the moment Tut's life ended. And she tapped her chin. What... what if they stole his signet-ring and forged a few proclamations of their own? She shook her head, imagining sending Semerkhet to sneak into the Vizier's office, the office of the Priest of Ma'at, to borrow their signet-rings. And she envisioned the proclamations she would write.

She could see them in her mind's eye. She would compose several, in case one or more of them were stolen or destroyed. She would write one announcing that the pregnant Queen was to be made regent for her son, another stating that the Pharaoh was appointing his Great Royal Wife his co-regent and successor, a third declaring that the Pharaoh's child was to succeed him regardless of its gender, and a fourth telling the world that Horemheb was no longer Tutankhamun's heir— Prince Zannanza was, through marriage to Ankhesenamun.

The Queen smiled. Could... could that work? And would it be a risk worth taking? A lie worth telling?

And she thought of what her mother would say.

*Be brave*, Nefertiti would say, *and don't let anyone stop you from doing what is right. Be everything you are, and don't let anyone talk you into being less.*

Ankhesenamun shook her head. Sometimes, as Granny Merneith had said, a lie could save a life. But the lies she was considering telling would not save any lives. These lies... She touched her stomach. These lies would end her life, and that of her precious, innocent child. And would most likely end her brother's life, even sooner than it was already fated to end. Because the moment he discovered their ruse, the Vizier would decide that all three of them were worthy of death.

The Queen closed her eyes. There was no way that forging proclamations of her own would fix any of this. All it would do was obliterate her family line once and for all.

She would have to wait for her letter to reach Hattusa. And find out, along with the rest of the world, what answer the Hittites sent in return.

Having a grandmother around was a comfort. Merneith brought Tut calming herbal teas (a different one every night, as they were still searching for the perfect blend), prepared poultices to lower his fever and dull his pain without dulling his thoughts, offered tinctures and plasters that would help him clear his lungs. And sometimes Granny would take a watch, peacefully sitting with him for an hour or so while both Ankh and Sem took a break. Sometimes she would even hum to him, old songs he didn't know, something about a lamb, a fire, a journey. But even when the pain still wracked him despite everything she did, she would pat his hand with her old gnarled one and murmur, "Yes, dearie. Granny knows."

That almost made it better.

"Fank you," Tut whispered as Semerkhet sat with him, dabbing his hot face and neck with a cool, damp cloth.

Sem dipped the cloth back in the bowl of water and squeezed it out, then smiled at him. "You're welcome. Is it helping any?"

212

Slowly the Pharaoh nodded. He coughed, cringing in pain as he fought to fill his lungs with air. And slowly he reached out a hand, almost clumsily, toward Sem's free one. His friend took it, squeezing it gently. "Feelth good," he whispered. "You read my mind."

"That is my job," Semerkhet said, raising an eyebrow. And they chuckled together. Remembered together. Too many memories for words. Or no words to express them with. But a little laugh shared between them said it all.

"Had a thought," Tut said a moment later with another smile.

Semerkhet was patting the cloth over his forehead. "Hmm?"

"Since you're my… brother now…" he said, struggling to get the words out, "theemth only fair for you to uthe my… name." He chuckled at his friend, raising his eyebrows.

Sem chuckled back. "As you wish, Your Majesty. Tutankhamun."

Tut smiled and closed his eyes as Semerkhet ran the cloth down one side of his neck and throat, then the other side. It felt good to hear his name.

He could do so little, Semerkhet thought sadly as he sat with his friend, gently bathing his hot head with a cool cloth. Bring his brother a snack, a drink, tuck him in among his blankets, play a song for him on the lute, tell him a story. Such small things; merely the resolution of uncomfortable details, the improvement of the next few minutes. And with everything he could do, he could not heal his friend. Tutankhamun was going to die no matter how many honey-cakes Semerkhet brought him; no matter how many bedtime stories he told.

Pain filled his heart; frustration at his helplessness, anger at how meaningless all his small gestures of care and loyalty had become in the face of the Pharaoh's impending death. It was so unfair. Why should it not matter that he would have given up his right hand to save his brother from this fate?

"Why?" he whispered under his breath, too softly for Tut to hear. And unexpectedly, he felt an answer warm his heart. Blinking back both joy and surprised confusion, he listened to what it was saying.

*Life is full of things you can change, and things that you can't,* it reminded him. *And you... you are changing everything you can for the better. You are not helpless. What you are doing matters... and it is enough. Just... just keep being the best brother anyone ever had.*

Gratefully, Semerkhet accepted the words of the Unknown One that softly touched his heart. He knew that they were true. And he knew that he would faithfully care for his little brother until the last.

Even as he sat with his friend, offering companionship and comfort, Sem still had work to do. Even here, so close to the end.

Semerkhet couldn't spend every moment sitting with his beloved brother, even if that was what he wanted to do. Because he was his valet. And as such, he was the director of the Pharaoh's care and everyone who contributed to it. And there was administration to be done. So the Sole Companion, the Unique Friend, would do it.

But there were still plenty of moments to be shared. And when his friend was hungry, Semerkhet would help him eat— a little porridge or broth, or a few bites of yogurt or lentils. Just like always,

214

the faithful valet would take the first bite of anything he was about to serve his friend, protecting his Pharaoh from poison.

Although… now that he knew that the gods of Egypt were nothing more than stories, Semerkhet could no longer bring himself to address his Master as the son of Ra. So with the words "I taste your food, Great Morning Star," he fed his brother when he was hungry.

# 20 Days

The Queen blew her nose. The days were growing colder, and she seemed to have caught a sniffle. But it was as though she had blown a trumpet to herald the arrival of her cold; no sooner had she tossed her handkerchief into the dirty laundry than Meresankh appeared, a cup of tea in her hands.

"Colds are going around," she said with a sympathetic little smile. "I made this for you."

Ankh sniffled again and accepted the steaming cup. "Thank you, Meresankh. What did you put in it?"

"Licorice, basil, peppermint, and ginger," she said. "Ought to fix you right up."

Ankh took a sip of tea, feeling her stuffy airways open up as the warm sweetness soothed her throat.

"Thank you, Doctor," she said with a grateful smile. Meresankh just smiled back.

Ankh fell asleep quickly that evening. But it didn't last. Because he was there in her dreams, the Hittite Prince, taking her horseback riding, bringing her flowers, kissing her, giving her one, two, five, ten strong sons, ten identical Princes to carry their family into the future. And again she woke, shaking her head. Was it right to be feeling this way? About the husband who might be about to come into her life; the husband who would not be a brother, who she could love freely? It was the right thing to do politically; she knew that. But was it really the right thing to do?

She looked at her brother, sleeping in the bed. And she wondered.

Meresankh kept praying. But just as Granny's goals had changed, so had her prayers. And she asked I-AM that their Pharaoh and their Queen would find the Light… while they still had time. And that they would be strong. And that it would not hurt so much anymore… either the Pharaoh's dying leg or the Queen's breaking heart.

And Meresankh prayed for Semerkhet. Prayed that he would see the truth of the miracles that had happened; that his heart would be opened to the Light. She couldn't marry him until they were standing together in their beliefs.

She prayed for herself, as well. That she would have the strength to carry on and continue supporting the ones she loved. And her heart warmed as she remembered… even the Red Sea had two shores.

"My Lady."

Ankhesenamun stopped short on her way down the hall, returning to her husband's room after a short midmorning break on the twelfth day of Tybi. And she gritted her teeth. Sweet Osiris, when would that man learn to take a hint?

With a deep breath, she turned to him. And she gave him a smile.

"Yes, Vizier?" she asked sweetly.

The old man fiddled with something hidden in his hand.

"My Lady…" he said softly, "my offer still stands. My offer… that would allow you to remain as Great Royal Wife. *My* Great Royal Wife. I would… I would be honored to have you beside me when I take the throne. Honored to claim you as my bride."

He opened his wrinkled hand, revealing the blue glass ring resting on his palm. "And that is the last political decision you would ever have to make. As my Queen, the only decisions you will have to make are what to wear. And all you will have to do is be beautiful. You are beautiful, My Lady. And that's all a Queen, a wife, a woman, should be. I want you on my arm, My Queen, not making decisions." He sighed. "My dear wife Lady Tey always told me that I made her feel safe. Knowing that all she had to do was be my beautiful bride. Knowing that she could trust me to make all the decisions." He smiled, reaching out his wrinkled hand again. Ankh just looked at it. "Let me do that for you, My Lady. You've worked so hard, for so long. So please... trust me. Just be my Queen. Just leave the decisions to me. And let your son... be my son."

A shiver of revulsion ran down Ankhesenamun's spine. But even as her stomach roiled, she forced herself to smile again.

"I told you before and I'll tell you again, Vizier. No. I will not marry you. I will not make you Pharaoh. I will not make my child call you *Father*. And I will not be your trophy. After Kadesh, that tea, Meritaten's ague, Father's fennel medicine, and Mother's horse, there is nothing you could ever do to make me trust you. Good day."

And she walked away, leaving him and his ring. Only through marriage to her could he legitimately become Pharaoh; she knew. And she would keep refusing, no matter how many times it took. What she did, she did for Egypt.

Tut grew weaker. He never called for a wig or makeup anymore; he hardly had the energy to let Semerkhet bathe him or change him into a fresh sleeping-tunic. Just drowsed when he

218

could, and accepted a sip or two of broth when Ankh or Sem offered it. But not usually more than that. Semerkhet still took a ritual sip of whatever he was about to serve to the Pharaoh before presenting it, but vaguely, Tut noticed something different about the phrasing he used. He had always said, "I taste your food, Son of Ra, and if there be harm in it, let the harm fall upon me." But now he said, "I taste your food, Great Morning Star." Vaguely, Tut wondered what had changed.

Every day it grew harder to breathe. And every day he expended a little more of his fading strength in coughing, fighting to clear his lungs. Every day, he expended a little more of his strength fighting the infection that raged in his leg; the ague that clung to him, propelling him through an endless cycle of fever and chills. Every day, his chills and fever grew worse. Every day, he grew closer to the end he knew was coming.

Merneith kept doing her best; High Priest Parannefer brought the entire priesthood into the palace and they implored the gods to restore him to health, but Tut knew they would not listen. Why would they, when they had never done anything for him in his life that didn't make life harder for him? And, to be honest, how could they, now that he knew none of them were real or ever had been?

Meresankh rolled her eyes in indignation as the Queen described yet another attempt by the Vizier to propose to her. Oy vavoy. That man. And she prayed that her Lady would continue to be strong, in the face of questions, options, and the pigheadedness of certain other politicians.

When their conversations fell silent, Sem brought out his lute. And the music he played continued to touch their hearts.

"That's so lovely, Semerkhet," the Queen said softly, swallowing back the lump in her throat. "Just… just beautiful. It's just… what we need right now."

Softly, the valet smiled at the Queen. And quietly, he continued to play.

Every day the Queen considered the reports and requests the Vizier's secretary delivered, analyzing them for any hint of deceit. And with the signet-ring that was now hers, she signed some into law; returned others for revision. By her authority, she would decide what to allow. What she did, she did for Egypt.

The Pharaoh felt different. He hadn't been able to sit up for days, but now, it was almost tiring just moving his head to look from one side of the room to the other; to move his hand to pet the cat. He felt… as though when he looked down at his hands, he should be able to see through them. As if he were slowly fading into invisibility. He kept drifting off at odd moments, all through the day, every hour or two, for five minutes here, ten minutes there. Resting in bed all day and he could hardly keep his eyes open.

The pain was always there, though. And the fever and chills, which had stopped coming and going every two or three days, instead settling firmly into every inch of the Pharaoh's exhausted body as though they would never let him go. Always there.

And he knew… he knew that Merneith was right.

Time was indeed becoming short.

Meresankh looked after her Queen faithfully. Every day she asked her how she was; tried to make her smile. And she brought her the best food and the best herbs, and every day, she prayed that Egypt would have an heir.

And when she was sad, when she was discouraged, Meresankh reminded her of Nimaathap, Ankhesenpepi the Second, Ahmose-Nefertari, Sobekneferu. And the Queen would smile. And she would take courage.

And then Meresankh would smile. Because her Lady was the strongest of them all.

And someday… someday, Meresankh would be the one teaching Nefertiti, her new little sister, the stories that Ankhesenamun had taught her, passed down from Nefertiti the Elder. Women taught one another, passing on their stories to their daughters and granddaughters, favoring the togetherness and spoken word of storytelling to the carved stone edifices, engraved statues, and dusty papyrus scrolls of the men. They didn't need inscriptions to remember the stories they had recounted so many times, the stories that blurred the lines between the generations, the knowledge of each grandmother preserved in her granddaughter's memories of her stories, her memories recounted decades later by her own granddaughter.

And, in a poetic sense, those wise mothers would never die. After all, to speak the name of the dead was to make them live again. Their wisdom, certainly, would live forever, as long as their stories were told. With each telling, the link to the women of the past grew stronger, and the women of today grew wiser, inspired by the accomplishments of their grandmothers. That wisdom became an unbreakable link stretching back to the days of the pyramids, handed down through each generation, a legacy of beauty, power, stability, and endurance.

And now, Little Nefertiti, *Nefertiti-Tasherit*, as they might call her, was part of that legacy.

Ankhesenamun went for a short walk after lunch. And she gathered another bouquet of flowers for her brother.

She buried her face in the bouquet, breathing in the fragrances of the lotus blossoms. The fragrances… which were suddenly so strong… Coughing, Ankh took her nose out of the bouquet, gasping for air. The heady perfume of the lotuses was almost making her dizzy; almost making her gag with nausea.

Shaking her head to clear it, she held the bouquet at a comfortable distance and made her way back inside. Time to try to brighten up her brother's day a little.

Ankh set the bouquet into the vase on the dressing-table, rearranging the flowers for the best effect. That looked nice.

She looked over at Tut. And he smiled at her, thanking her for her small gift, her gesture of love. In his smile, she could see the last dimple that still remained in his thin cheek. And as she turned back to the bouquet, moving the chrysanthemums so they didn't hide the cornflowers, she felt a thought touch her heart as gently as a ray of sunshine.

*You are not helpless,* it whispered to her. *You are making a difference. What you are doing is meaningful. You need to let it be enough. Because no one… no one could do more. Some things no one can change. But you are changing what you can. And the rest is not your fault.*

She remembered the lessons she had taught her brother so many long months ago, of the positive ripples one small act could send out into the universe. And Ankh wiped away tears as she realized

222

that that was what she was doing— doing the right thing, over and over, in a thousand small ways. Each of those choices, words, gestures, would make its own small difference, echoing out into the lives of those around her. And with each day that passed, she would change everything she could for the better… without burdening herself with the things no one could change. The Queen sighed, feeling the truth of the words she had taught her brother filling her heart with warmth. And she accepted the thought as a gift.

Semerkhet gritted his teeth. Some landscaping was being done in the corner of the garden closest to the royal suites. So that meant that large numbers of gardeners kept trooping up and down the hall, laughing, joking, a few even singing. The noise was happy. But it was still noise.

Sem kept glancing at his Pharaoh, lying in the bed. He was drowsing, one thin hand clasped around the Queen's as she sat by him. It didn't seem as though the noise was bothering him.

But— it should be. Or— it was wrong, that they were making this much noise this close to the Pharaoh's bedroom, when they and everyone else in Egypt knew that he was wounded and seriously ill. This was unacceptable.

Semerkhet crossed to the door. And wrenching it open, he bellowed,

"If you haven't got anything better to do, you can go jump in the Nile!"

Silence descended. Terrified gardeners scurried out of the hallway as fast as they could, fleeing to the safety of the outdoors. As they ran, he thought he caught the words "life, prosperity, and health."

Semerkhet stood there in the doorway, heart pounding. And from behind him, a soft voice said,

"Well, that thertainly told them."

Semerkhet's insides seemed to melt like a wax cone. Stomach twisting, he slowly turned around to see his Pharaoh opening his eyes to survey the interesting events that were unfolding. And he dropped his gaze to his own feet.

"A thousand apologies, Great Morning Star," he whispered, bending in a deep bow as his original palace training tempted him to grovel on the floor. "I'm… I'm ashamed."

He heard his Master give the slightest of chuckles. "I'm not," he said. "I'm grateful. Grateful that you thaw a problem and took action to tholve it. For nektht time, though, I would juth thay… If the perthon you're protecting ith athleep, try not to wake them up."

And Semerkhet looked up to see a smile on his Pharaoh's face.

"Yes, Master," he said. "Yes… my friend."


It was difficult to be patient. So many things needed to be done; things large and small, from the delivery of fresh pots of tea to the removal of laundry baskets full of dirty cloths. And Ankh felt herself bursting with frustration at all the small details that refused to be caught up with. Even with all the work that Semerkhet was doing.

"I can't believe we're out of the frankincense-and-spikenard," she grumbled, peering into a nearly-empty ointment jar. "Go tell them we need more, will you? And bring another bowl of pomegranate. Er, thank you."

"Of course, My Lady." And with a bow, he was off. Ankh shook her head as he left. There was no reason for her to have been

224

short with Semerkhet. But he probably wanted to take a walk anyway.

Meresankh came in to bring Semerkhet and the Queen some tea early that afternoon, and Ankh told Sem to take two minutes with his friend. Meresankh led Semerkhet to the Pharaoh's private sitting room, and they sat down together.

"Sem," Meresankh said with half a little chuckle, fiddling with her necklace, "This is going to sound funny... but I have a question... on the subject of succession."

He looked at her. "Hmm?"

"Do you think... do you think that our Pharaoh will make you his heir?" she asked, twisting her little hands together. "You are the Favorite of the Pharaoh and the Sole Companion."

Sem smiled and took her hand. What a sweet idea... but not a real option.

"Being our Pharaoh's valet has been... such an important part of my life, and I wouldn't exchange it for anything. But I am afraid... that if he nominated me as his successor, that it would go all wrong. We were only able to switch the letters to the Hittites because the switch happened outside of the Vizier's reach. If our Pharaoh made me his heir, even if he sent me straight to Thebes, I would still be in danger."

Meresankh frowned. "Even in Thebes?"

Semerkhet sighed. "Zannanza is only safe because Hattusa is so far away. Although... I wouldn't be sure it'll go smoothly until he gets here. So I think that our Pharaoh might see me as a good person to be his heir, but he knows the Vizier would go straight after me. And if he has Ay executed... we'll have civil war. The only way for any sort of stability to continue is for the line to continue through the Queen's marriage to Zannanza."

Meresankh just shook her head.

Semerkhet sighed again. "So… it's for my sake that he won't do it. He's setting me free… setting *us* free… to be safe and to live the life we choose to. He wants what's best for me, and he's letting me… us… decide what that looks like."

Semerkhet paused. "Of course, there's still Horemheb."

Meresankh nodded. "Do you think we can get him back on our side? And do you think…" She bit her lip. "Do you think he'll get home soon enough for it to matter?"

Sem squeezed her hand. "I don't know. But if he does help us… that could change everything." Sem gave a little sigh. "He was actually the Pharaoh's heir in the absence of a son, technically, anyway. If he hadn't gotten mixed up with the Vizier, if we knew he was loyal, we wouldn't have this succession crisis. And if we can turn Horemheb around…" Semerkhet shook his head. "But I just don't know. I just don't know."

Meresankh squeezed his hand. "I don't know either. But I know that I'm praying. For all of us."

Sem smiled again. "So thank you, Meresankh. It would be a great honor… and if it wouldn't get me killed, I think he would consider me."

She just nodded. So the Pharaoh wasn't going to make Semerkhet his heir…

But it was to keep him safe.

# 21 Patience

*The Queen stood on the balcony of Grandfather's palace, looking down at the city of Thebes. Beside her stood her husband; at their elbows, three children. Three little boys. Ankh looked up to smile at the Hittite Prince who had become her husband, who now stood beside her as the Pharaoh of Egypt. But as more than her puppet. As her partner.*

*Her husband.*

She woke from her brief catnap with a sigh. And an ache in her heart. Would she love him? And would she call him... *husband?*

The Queen closed her eyes again. Somehow... somehow she did not feel the same guilt; the same conflict that all the other dreams had brought her. Now, amid all the grief, all the strangeness, all the questions that remained to be answered, she had peace.

To make Zannanza her husband was the right thing to do.

"I hope they're all right," Tut said out of the silence of a short, cold day. Chilly rain was pattering against the roof of the palace, and he was wrapped up in blankets, Ankh huddled up in one of her own as she sat with him, the cat in her lap.

"Who, love?" she asked, looking up from petting Bastet.

"The people," he said simply. "It'th all tho... unthertain. What kind of future they will have. Could be very different bathed on who..." He sighed heavily, then coughed into his hanky. "Who winth."

Ankhesenamun reached out and took his hand. It was cold, and even thinner than last time.

"They will be," she said with a solemn little smile. "I'll make sure." And she kissed him on the forehead.

Tut smiled and lay back. Whatever lay ahead of them… he could trust his sister to do what was best for their country.

She was so strong. So brave. His sister had come through so much, and now… now she was facing another loss. The loss of him.

But she would endure this loss as well. He knew that Egypt was safe in her hands.

Semerkhet shook his head. What was the matter with him? Shouting at those poor, innocent gardeners; scaring them half to death for a crime no more serious than walking down the hall. Those gardeners… who had threatened to wake the Pharaoh from his nap. Which Semerkhet himself had done rather skillfully. Semerkhet sighed. He knew why he had done it; he wanted to protect his little brother from all that was annoying in the world. But shame on him for becoming one of those very things himself.

A cup of tea. A cool cloth for his burning head. A warm blanket for the chills that made his teeth chatter. A new position in which to lie, relieving some of his aches as his tired eyes found a different part of his room to stare at. So many things Tutankhamun could not get for himself. Even a cup of tea was more of an undertaking than before; his weak hands shook so badly that he could no longer hold the cup, only smile wanly as Ankh or Sem held it for him, patiently helping him take sip after sip until he silently turned his face away, too tired to drink any more.

He could no longer do anything for himself. So… when he needed something, he asked for it. And he always tried to say *thank you*.

"And so Satiah bumped into little old Hori, and Persenet dropped her laundry basket and clean cloths went everywhere, and Khenut was so mad because it all had to be done again—"

Semerkhet rolled his eyes. Today hadn't been easy; the Pharaoh grew weaker by the hour, and Semerkhet himself was still ashamed at how he'd mishandled the noisy gardeners. And now, during the break he'd decided to spend with her, Meresankh simply would not stop yammering on about the theatrics, gymnastics, and miniaturized politics that comprised the social life of the palace staff. And he set down the cup of tea she'd poured for him with an audible thump.

"Will you stop for just one minute?" he groaned. With a gasp, she stopped short, looking at him with confusion on her face. And she held her tongue. "Your stories are great, but it's been a day and a half already, and I just— I don't want a story. Not right now. I just want to take my break."

Meresankh swallowed loudly. And stiffly, she refilled his teacup.

The Queen closed her eyes. And she focused her senses.

It was much, much too early to feel the baby's kicks. But she listened.

There was… there was something. Whether it was only the echoes of her own hopes or the beginning of a new life deep within her, there was something. And there was the breast tenderness…

the moments of nausea… the sensitivity to the flowers… the missed bleeding…

And the Queen smiled. Maybe.

Meresankh blinked back her frustration as Semerkhet left her chambers after finishing his tea, pausing to lovingly clasp her hand, but not smiling as warmly as he usually did. He'd shut her up. Because he hadn't wanted to hear her stories. She was annoying. And the reports on palace life that usually made him smile were tiresome.

What was going on? Why did he suddenly hate something that made him smile; why was he exasperated at her? What had she done wrong? Why was the smiling storyteller— who she was as a person, by the Ten Plagues— suddenly not good enough?

Then she thought of what he'd said. *It's been a day and a half already.* And she nodded. She understood. It wasn't her. But at the same time… it was. And she shook her head as she felt I-AM telling her something.

*Not every hour of every day is perfect for storytelling.*

She nodded to herself, gratitude for her realization filling her heart. He didn't hate her stories. And he wasn't rejecting her as a person. But she… she was the one who needed to think twice. And carefully consider whether Semerkhet or the Queen wanted to hear the latest palace gossip… or whether they wanted to sit in companionable silence.

There was a soft sigh. And Tut smiled at Semerkhet as he slowly woke up. Semerkhet fetched a bowl of lukewarm licorice tea, then helped him sit up enough to have a sip.

230

"Fank you," the Pharaoh whispered as he lay back on his pillows.

Semerkhet tried to smile as he set aside the tea, but his breaking heart betrayed him. And it was with tears in his eyes that he turned back to his friend and whispered,

"It's coming, isn't it?"

The Pharaoh gave a heavy sigh, looking away. And silently, he nodded.

"It ith," he agreed softly. "And we can't do anyfing about it."

"How am I ever going to let you go?" Semerkhet whispered through the lump in his throat. He took Tut's hand, holding it tight. And as the tears spilled over and ran down his face, he did not turn away to hide them. He let them fall. "I've already lost one brother."

Tut just shook his head. He had no answers. "I tried," he said finally.

Semerkhet gave a sob. "It's not you," he choked. "It's them. Those snakes that sent you off to die and then poisoned you and—why didn't you have them executed?" he asked harshly.

Tut shook his head again. "I didn't want another war," he said softly.

Semerkhet bowed his head. He knew his Master was right.

"So if it's coming…" he asked more softly, "how do we prepare?"

The Pharaoh paused. "I don't fink we can," he said with another sad sigh. "Just…" He looked up at his friend with a poignant little smile. "Make every moment count."

Semerkhet nodded, blinking back more tears. And he helped his friend take another sip of tea. He knew that he would never be ready.

But he could try.

Again, the Queen looked at the dwindling stack of clean cloths; the diminishing levels of the pot of tea from which she kept serving her brother. And again, she bit back annoyance that these frustrating details never disappeared. There was always more laundry to do. Always more tea to be made.

She got up. Semerkhet was on duty, so she kissed her brother on the forehead and made her way out into the hallway, finding her way down to the laundry department. She knew they were working hard; knew they couldn't really get out another batch of fresh cloths any faster than they were. But she could at least get a status report.

The Queen approached the doorway behind which the magic of laundry took place. But at that moment, Khenut appeared, whistling merrily as she carried an enormous basket of neatly-folded cloths, freshly washed and ready to go back to the Pharaoh's room. She was happy in her work. She knew she was doing all she could. And she knew she was making a difference.

Ankh just shook her head in gratitude. And silently, she followed Khenut back down the hall.

Ay seemed to be gone. The Vizier had not tried to visit them in several days. Instead, his secretary brought the daily reports he was still preparing, still pretending for all he was worth to be a loyal servant to the crown. Nothing exceptional was to be found in them anymore, just shipments of stone, occasional hiring— decisions that the Queen approved with her signet-ring without fear for the future. He was biding his time. Staying in the shadows, keeping quiet, avoiding any sudden moves, keeping things looking normal.

232

But they knew he was there. Waiting for the opportunity he hoped would come.

He didn't come back. That was good. Right now, dealing with him was something they didn't need. He was waiting, they knew. Waiting to find out what would happen. They could let him wait.

They were waiting too.

One thing they were waiting for was Horemheb's homecoming. If they could reclaim his loyalty, get him on their side for good, he could help them more than almost anyone else. With him at their side, they had a chance to win.

The days continued to pass, the days until the seventeenth of Tybi, when, as Amenia and Mutnedjmet had learned, the General was expected home. They were counting them down, the days until Horemheb would get home, and everything would change. For good...

Or for ill.

Because when he got home, he would either save them...

Or betray them.

Meresankh's heart ached. She knew she was doing enough. She knew that everything she did mattered. But she wished she could do something particular, something special; a gift from her to the Pharaoh, from her to the husband, the brother, of Meresankh's best friend.

She thought of what he would like. Tea... Granny was already making gallons of tea for him; blends that fought infection, recipes to help him sleep. And on the same note, he was stocked up on his favorite frankincense-and-spikenard lotion.

What, then? Meresankh tapped her chin, thinking. And then she thought of it.

Heading down to Granny's workshop, she sorted through Merneith's library of dried herbs, gathering lavender, valerian, chamomile. She placed the herbs on a square piece of fabric, carefully tying it with a ribbon into a neat little bag. There. A sleep sachet. The Pharaoh could tuck it under his pillow, and maybe the sweet, sleepy fragrance would help him get just a little more rest. Maybe.

"Darling? You have a visitor."

"V-visitor?" Feebly, Tut tried to sit up against his pillows, squinting around the room for the new face.

He smiled as he saw who it was. "Hello, Merethank." He bit his tongue in embarrassment as he botched her name, but she didn't so much as bat an eye.

"Hello, Your Majesty," she said, offering a polite bow. Quietly, she stepped toward the bed. Did she have something in her hands? "I… I made something for you," she said. She offered her gift, and he accepted what appeared to be a small bag of something. Something that smelled delicious.

"It's a sleep sachet," she explained. "You can put it under your pillow… and I hope it'll help you sleep. I thought you already had enough tea, and enough lotion, and everything else, but you might not have a sleep sachet."

Tut brought the little bag to his nose, breathing in the sweet, calming fragrance.

"Fank you, Meresankh," he said, offering a thin hand. She kissed it, then held it for a moment in a friendly clasp. "What a nithe gift."

234

And as he lay back down with a yawn, Meresankh excused herself with a wish for life, health, and prosperity... and a little smile. Her gift was working.

Nearly three weeks had passed since their union. Silently Tut wondered if they had conceived; if a tiny child now lay curled inside Ankh's graceful belly, the heir that would continue the dynasty. With a pang, he wondered, if that prayer had been answered, if his wife would suffer again through the same pain and grief that she had in the loss of their two tiny, perfect baby girls, whose tiny caskets were being placed inside his tomb, moved from the chapel where they had rested. Would she again say hello only to say goodbye?

He thought back to those terrible days barely halfway through his sister's first pregnancy, when a day and a night with no movement from the child had kept Ankh awake, worrying and praying. The next afternoon, bleeding and contractions had seized her, and the tiny, tiny baby girl she had delivered had been still and silent. At fifteen, Tut had been unprepared to become a father, but even more unprepared for the loss of a child. Together they had laid their daughter to rest, marveling at her tiny, perfect hands and feet, her delicate nose, the eyes that lay so gently closed. And they had given her all the love that had been growing in their hearts since the moment she had been conceived. And they knew that somehow, she would know how much she was loved.

Time had passed. And the day had come when they had begun to feel that they could truly smile again. Then, two years later, Ankh had recognized the signs of pregnancy again, and they had spent the next six months watching and waiting, hardly daring to hope, their joy and excitement tempered by fear. Ankhesenamun had crossed the halfway mark and they breathed a sigh of relief, fear beginning to give way to hope.

Only a few weeks before the child's birth was anticipated, the pain had come again, and Ankh had gone to the birthing pavilion with her attendants, leaving Tut to wait and worry, hearing her cries ringing out, praying in his heart for his wife and for the child. Then they came to tell him,

"It's a girl." But there was no smile, and there was a hush. Tut crept in to see Ankh in the bed, holding a tiny, tiny baby carefully wrapped in soft blankets.

But she was not well. There had been a strange sac attached to her curved back, which had become detached during the difficult delivery, and her tiny feet did not kick. Her head was large and round, larger than was typical for a newborn. The doctors worked to protect the lesion on her back from infection, a wound with no apparent source, but they could not heal her legs, or her head. Tut remembered the pain that had filled his heart when the doctor had finally said that her condition was not treatable. And he remembered seeing his wife's pain.

The tiny Princess' parents loved her and held her, but their love could not heal her. All they could do was fill the hours they had together with love, showing her what it meant to be loved. It was only days before she slipped away in their arms, joining her sister. Now their tiny coffins lay in the Pharaoh's tomb, the two baby Princesses waiting for their father to join them.

And for many months, trying again had been too painful to think about. But now there was hope.

Tutankhamun knew in his heart that even if they had been blessed, and the child had been blessed with health, that he would

236

not live to rejoice over its birth. He wondered if he would live long enough even to know if their prayer had been answered. Even now, he prayed that it had been.

*Bless my wife,* he asked the Unknown One Who was listening. *Give us a child. And let it be healthy and strong.*

For a moment, he caught a glimpse of his own parents' dilemma. Despite all their desperate politics, for their line to continue, his wife had to have a baby, and it had to be a boy.

And so he found himself praying for something he never would have imagined.

A strong son.

Then he thought again of his two little girls, whom he had waited so long to meet. And even as his eyes filled with tears, he gave a little smile. He would be seeing them again soon. Somehow, with everything he was no longer sure of, he knew that.

# 22 Time

Tutankhamun lay in bed, turning his head fitfully as he lay with his fists clenched, tears of pain in his eyes, every particle of his body fighting against the pain. He was many miles from Kadesh, but he was in battle just as surely as he had been on the day that had broken his legs and stolen his future.

"Why don't you take the poppy?" Ankh whispered through her own tears, stroking his sweaty face. He was so hot, but she was cold, wrapped warmly in her blue outer robe against the chill of the day.

He just shook his head. "Don't want to be out of my mind. Don't know what Ay will do nektht. Got to... got to keep Egypt thafe. Keep you thafe." It was getting harder for him to speak clearly; more and more lisped words slipped out without him being able to stop them. He smiled, brushing shaking fingers over her flat belly. "Bowf of you."

The Queen gave half a sad smile, gently shaking her head. "Darling... we'll watch him. I promise. We won't let him do anything. We're safe. And... and Egypt's safe. We just... can't bear seeing you like this. If you take some... even just a little bit... you might be able to rest."

*Rest.* Sounded good. He didn't want to surrender, but it never ended... *never... ended...* and how much longer could he last before his mind snapped or the pain itself killed him, rather than the infection?

He tried to think back to how it felt not to be in pain. And he realized he barely could. It had been so long. So very long.

Then he nodded. "I'll take thome."

238

Half an hour later, Tut felt like crying with relief. The pain... it wasn't gone, not entirely, but the relief... was one of the most beautiful things he had ever felt. He could... he could actually ignore the pain that was left.

Now he was sleepy. That was a side effect of the poppy, he remembered from the trip home from Amurru. And he could feel his heart beating very, very slowly, pulling him down, down, down into sleep. Well, that was all right. He needed to rest.

And now he could. Gratefully, the King closed his eyes. And he smiled as he felt himself peacefully drifting off.

They stopped hiding their tears. There were still tears to be shed, but Tut, Sem, no longer ducked behind a papyrus or floundered for a task to do when they felt a lump in their throat, tears welling in their eyes. Because there was no reason to hide it. This, all of it, was a family thing. And they were family.

The Queen beckoned to Meresankh.

"Yes, My Lady?" The handmaiden set aside the jewelry she was cleaning and approached the chair where Ankh was lying back, taking a short break.

Ankhesenamun sat up, reaching out to take her friend's hand. Meresankh offered it with a smile.

"I just want to thank you," she said earnestly. "For everything you do. And... for being so patient. I don't mean to get short at you. I'm just..." She trailed off, the words *worn out, stressed, overwhelmed*, written on her face.

Meresankh just shook her head. "You're the one doing all the hard work," she said. "It's only fair that I should be able to read your mind."

And the Queen and her friend laughed together.

*Thank you for everything you do… and for being so patient.* Meresankh thought of the words her Lady had just spoken. And she smiled even as sudden tears prickled in her eyes. She hadn't made the Queen laugh today. But she had been helpful. And her Mistress was grateful. The smile she had given Meresankh hadn't been the grin she wore when Meresankh told a funny story on a good day, but it had been happy, in a way. Maybe… Meresankh swallowed back the lump in her throat. Maybe there was more than one way to bring joy.

Laundry never ended. And neither did dirty dishes. Life piled up— items to be sorted, cleaned, put away, brought back. But not in a single, smooth, organized, streamlined process. In little bits and pieces here and there throughout each day, one problem being solved as another arrived.

But it wasn't just dishes; wasn't just laundry. It was life. The endless stream of chores was nothing but a metaphor for the problems that no one could fix.

The Queen straightened the diadem that she had chosen to wear today. And snapped her fingers as frustration filled her heart. She was the Queen, the most powerful woman in Egypt, one of the most powerful women on Earth. And with her wisdom and the signet-ring she shared with the Pharaoh, she should be able to solve any problem that came her way.

Meresankh stepped quietly into the Pharaoh's room, offering a cup of tea to her Lady. Gratefully, Ankh accepted it, nodding toward her brother's private sitting room. And Meresankh followed her.

"What am I doing wrong, Meresankh?" the Queen asked with a heavy sigh.

Her friend looked at her in surprise.

"What do you mean, My Lady?"

She shook her head, tapping her fingers restlessly on the teacup. "I mean... all this. Everything. I'm doing what I can, but— I'm the Queen. I should be able to do more." She looked down. And as the irrational questions, the brick-wall arguments filled her heart, she understood how her brother felt. "I know it doesn't make sense, but it's not fair— we're all working so hard, and it feels like it doesn't even matter. And— I can change the fates of two countries with a single letter, so why can't I make a difference for him? What's the point of being a Queen if you can't protect the people you love?"

Meresankh looked at her, a sad, sympathetic little smile on her face. And gently, she reached out and squeezed her friend's hand.

"I don't have all the answers," she said softly. "But I know... I know that what we're doing matters. All of us. No... no matter what the outcome is, what we're doing is important. It's worth it. And it is making a difference."

Almost unwillingly, Ankh felt herself return her friend's smile. Meresankh was right. And right now, she was the wise one, reflecting the lessons Ankh had proudly taught her friends back to her.

And all she could say was "Thank you."

"Do you really believe in I-AM?" Semerkhet asked later that day, seeing Meresankh walking down the hall as he took a moment, just a moment, to stretch his legs by taking a basket of laundry down to the washerwomen.

She stopped, looking up at him. And he saw that she was still wearing his necklace.

"Yes," she said confidently, looking up at him and meeting his eyes. "How else can you explain what Merneith saw?"

He sighed. "I don't have an answer for that. But what I'm wondering is… if Ra and Osiris and all the others are only stories, can I-AM… help our Pharaoh?"

Meresankh nodded, blinking back tears. "If He can do everything we know He has done, I'm sure He can."

Semerkhet swallowed. "Will you pray for our Pharaoh?"

She nodded again. "Yes. I already am. And so is Merneith." Her voice was a whisper, aching with sorrow and hope.

He gave a little half-smile. "Thank you."

Meresankh gave a little nod at the basket that Sem was carrying. "I was going down that way, if you want me to take it," she said.

Semerkhet sighed. "Would you?"

She held out her hands for it. "Of course. I really… really don't have much to do lately. So if there's anything… anything at all… I want to help."

He nodded gratefully. "Thank you. I… I will… let you know if I think of anything."

He kissed her cheek, and he was on his way back to the Pharaoh's room.

Meresankh started down the hall with the laundry basket on her hip, a little smile on her face and a flutter in her heart. Her prayers were being answered. Semerkhet's heart was opening.

242

If she closed her eyes, she could still feel the gentle brush of his lips on her cheek.

"What will we do… if he doesn't get here?" Meresankh asked. "The Prince?"

Ankhesenamun looked up from staring into space during a five-minute break in her chambers. And with a heavy sigh, she reached out to squeeze her friend's hand.

"You're a politician, you know that?" the Queen said softly. She looked away sadly. "You're right, though. There's a chance… that he might not." Then she raised her head with a confident, peaceful smile. "But you know what we'll do." Fingers laced with her friend's, Ankh gently raised their hands, an unbreakable link that would see them through the unknown future, whatever it might hold. "Get through."

Semerkhet stopped letting himself think ahead beyond the next hour. There was work to be done— tea to be made, pillows to be fluffed, medicine to be given and blankets to be put on and taken off as the Pharaoh's mood, and fever, required.

He knew it was coming. No matter what they did, no matter how hard they tried to fight it, it was coming, and it grew closer every day. But there was a strange freedom… a strange peace… in knowing that it was coming. And knowing that neither he nor anyone else in the world could do anything about it. If there was no fight to be fought, he could stop fighting.

Bringing Tut his favorite tea wasn't going to save his life. But it would make the next half-hour a little better. And at this point… Semerkhet could remind himself that that was enough.

All he could do was be helpful and cheerful and loving… right until the very end.

And treasure every moment they had left.


What could she do, to protect the Prince? Ankhesenamun searched through her options, the orders that she, as Queen, could give.

And then she shook her head. To whom could she give them? Horemheb, the only one they could still potentially trust, was not yet home from Kadesh, but even if he agreed to meet Zannanza and escort him safely to Memphis, who knew if even he could outrun or outfight the assassins the Vizier would surely send after the Hittite.

What would happen remained to be seen. But Ankh shook her head to think that even through her authority as Queen, she could not protect everyone.


He couldn't stay awake. Tutankhamun drowsed in the bed, the cat beside him, Ankh and Sem moving gently around the room. When he woke for a few minutes here, a few minutes there, they would offer him a sip of water or tea or a bite of yogurt or fruit, or they would sit down with him and bathe his face and scalp with a cool cloth. And out of the corner of his eye, he could see the flowers that Ankh always brought, a bright-colored blur his fuzzy vision couldn't quite make out, but a gift that made him smile all the same.

Sometimes they told snippets of old stories, or Semerkhet would play the lute. All to keep him entertained. But he could never listen for long. He would smile at their gentle voices, the

244

familiar words and sweet melodies, and he would drift off again into a vague dream full of warm sunlight.

But that meant that the pain was manageable. Granny gave him low doses of poppy throughout the day, keeping him at a steady level of pain control. It felt so good not to spend every moment fighting. Felt so good to truly rest. And now that he could truly rest… that was all his body wanted to do.

He didn't want to spend so much time asleep. Because he knew that with every hour he spent napping, that was an hour he didn't get to spend interacting with Ankh, with Sem. And so, with every last remaining particle of strength, he fought to keep his eyes open.

But he couldn't help it. His body was too tired. And so he would find himself drifting off in the middle of a halting conversation; the middle of a lullaby or a sweet, simple report on daily life in the staff quarters or on how dramatically Semerkhet's teammates had crushed the hockey team from On last week and how badly they were going to destroy Iuny next week. Sometimes… sometimes he would find himself waking up, and he would not know what time it was… or even remember having fallen asleep. But even as he found himself drowned in sleep, he smiled. Because they were there with him, Ankh and Sem. And they loved him so much.

*Why was the Great Someone doing this?* Ankhesenamun wondered with an ache in her heart. Allowing him to get worse every day; fade a little more each day. Why was the Creator, for Whose Name she was still searching, about to take her brother away from her?

She thought back to her conversation with Tut from so many months ago, out in the garden, about their childhood in Akhetaten;

245

to their more recent conversations about what they believed. And about how their father had believed so strongly in the Lord of Light. A simple faith, a faith of love and light. The Light she had always seen on her parents' faces reminded her of the light she saw on Meresankh's, on Merneith's.

She thought back to her moment in the temple, shaking her fist at Heaven as the gods had disappeared from her heart, her life. And the way that when she had come back into the sunlight, a bit of her hope had returned. And she thought back to sitting with Meresankh, waiting for her brother to come home from Kadesh, and the conversation they had had... the way that she had told Ankh that Aten was just another name for I-AM.

Was it possible... was it just possible... that Father had been right?

And now, now that her brother was facing death, was it time for them to reach out to the Aten?

Was the Aten, in fact, the unknown "You" to Whom she had been struggling to pray?

Was the Aten I-AM?


"What are we going to do?" Semerkhet asked Meresankh as they ate dinner together in her suite.

She sighed, looking up from her plate and reaching across the table to rest her warm, little hand on his. As always, the little silver necklace gleamed over her heart.

"Live one day at a time," she said.

He smiled. "I know. But I mean... us... together... what are we going to do?"

She looked away with a little blush, her dimple appearing as she gave him a sideways smile. "I suppose there's a question you could ask me," she said.

Semerkhet chuckled. "I want to. All I want is to spend the rest of my life with you. But what... what kind of life is it going to be? After..." He bit his lip, clenching his free hand as he thought. "What will I do? I know I have skills; I know I can get a job, especially after I've studied with Granny. But... how long will that take? For me to graduate, and then for me to find a job? And how will I get a house, and get it set up so we can make it our home?

"And who..." He looked down again; the next problem was the most serious. "Who will we get to speak for us? My mother's gone... and my father never wants to see me again. He'll never give his blessing."

"And both my parents are gone," Meresankh said sadly. "So my father can't write our marriage contract with you. And I don't have a dowry." She smiled up at him. "I know I can earn my own living as an herbalist. But it probably wouldn't buy us a house."

Closing their eyes, they sat there together, hand-in-hand. No dowry. And no families to give their blessing. How could they ever marry?

"I'll wait for you," Meresankh said softly. "We'll wait as long as we have to."

Semerkhet nodded. He was grateful that she felt that way. But this wait... this uncertainty... wasn't something he wanted to ask of her.

Granny patted Meresankh's hand. And together, they prayed. For the Pharaoh; for the Queen. And for an answer. A way forward. So that when the page of history turned, the Queen would find joy in the strange new life that awaited her… and that Meresankh and Sem could begin their life together.

# 23   Curiosity

There wasn't a lot for Meresankh to do; her Lady's room was as tidy as it needed to be, and organizing and reorganizing the Queen's shoes and jewelry was nothing more than busywork. So, during the long hours when her Mistress didn't need her to be doing any particular thing, Meresankh threw herself into helping the rest of the staff, parceling out teas, ointments, and poultices and treating headaches, backaches, sore throats, indigestion, burns, sprains. And she smiled as she identified what they needed, felt her heart warm as she prepared a remedy and sent it home with them, found joy as she brought them joy with a kind word or even, if the time was right, a funny story. Because through it all, she knew she was making a difference.

"What's wrong, Meresankh?"

The Queen walked into her room for a short break to see her handmaiden sitting quietly in one of the chairs. She looked like something was bothering her.

Meresankh looked up, then gave Ankh a smile. "Oh, just thinking," she said. "About… about Semerkhet. And how much I love him."

"There are things you can do," the Queen said, "solutions for couples who don't have anyone to speak for them or who don't have a lot of savings yet. I'm sure I could do something to—"

Meresankh shook her head, visibly restraining herself from interrupting. So Ankh stopped. And listened.

"It's not your problem," Meresankh said. "But I would... I would like you to listen. Without trying to fix it. Just listen. As my friend."

Ankhesenamun nodded. And she listened.


Merneith sat down beside Tut early that evening after checking his bandages, seeming to quietly drift away into her own thoughts as she stayed just present enough to jump into action if something went wrong. He looked up at her. She was the oldest person he had ever met. So old that she must have been around his age when the Hebrew slaves had all disappeared. And with her simple faith, and her old songs, she seemed to know something.

He had to ask.

"Granny?" he whispered. She looked up, then bent over him with a smile.

"Yes, dearie?" she asked, softly stroking his hot forehead with her wrinkled old hand. Her fingers were crooked, but they were gentle. And still nimble enough to tie a bandage.

"Are the stories true... were my Father's stories true... about the plagues... the insects, the frogth, the Nile turning to blood... I-AM setting the Hebrewth free from my grandfather?"

Slowly Merneith nodded, taking his cold hand in hers. "Yes, dearie. I was there. And I saw it all." She smiled. "Your father... came very close to finding the Light."

Tut's heart began to pound. "Tho the Aten... really was I-AM all along?"

"The Aten... is a metaphor for I-AM," she said, nodding thoughtfully. "But that does not mean your father was wrong. The Creator of Heaven and Earth does not change based on what we

250

call Him." Merneith smiled. "So yes, dearie. All your father's stories were true. I remember."

"But what about our traditions?" Tut asked Granny. "If your traditionth are true... are ourth not?"

She started to answer, but he pressed on, his lisp taking over. "So what will happen to me when I die? What about the forty-two judgeth a perthon hath to anthwer to; tell them they lived a good life? I've been a nithe perthon. If there'th only one God, what doeth He want? If being a nithe perthon ithn't enough, what elth ith there?"

"You have been a nice person," Granny said gently. "But I-AM doesn't want us to try as hard as we can to be 'good.' He wants us to realize that we can't, and come to Him for help. Only He can free our hearts from the weight of our sins. And this forgiveness isn't offered on the basis of whether a person can remember all of the 'negative confessions' they have to recite before the tribunal of the underworld. And it's not limited to being given once a year, on a day like the Opet Festival, or from a particular place, like a temple. Whenever anyone reaches out in repentance, wherever they are, I-AM... the Aten... is there. And He will set them free from the burden of their sins. Whoever calls on the name of the Lord of Light will be saved."

"And what about the lambth?" the Pharaoh asked. "That the Hebrewth thacrifithed on the night my uncle died? What did all that mean? Doeth I-AM require thacrifitheth?"

Merneith sighed. "I-AM told Moshe, Prince Moses, that the night of the Death of the Firstborn, each Hebrew household should sacrifice a lamb, cook it, and share its meat with one another. And they should take the blood of the lamb and put it on the lintels and posts of their doors. Then when the Angel of Death came, it would

251

see the blood… and pass over. The blood stood between the people and their sins, the sins for which I-AM was judging Egypt. Blood must be shed to atone for sin. But not in order to maintain the cosmos itself. The Creator of Heaven and Earth sustains His Creation no matter what we do… and no matter what we call Him. His Love is enough for us all."

Granny smiled, wise old eyes disappearing into smile wrinkles. She bent and kissed Tut in the middle of the forehead. And then she went to make him a cup of tea.

The warmth that he remembered from leaving the cold, dark Temple of Amun-Ra; remembered from every time he had simply stood out in the Sun, seemed to touch him.

She had given him a lot to think about.

But even as he pondered these profound thoughts, he chuckled. Because Granny had kissed him… without even asking. He was the Pharaoh— technically, touching him in any way without asking permission was against protocol. But he wasn't offended. Of course he wasn't. She was his Granny.

And he was glad that she had kissed him.


Semerkhet watched Merneith look after the Pharaoh, checking his bandages, sharing a short conversation with him, and disappearing to make him a cup of tea. And the valet observed just how… just how much pus there was.

But even if he couldn't make his friend's legs any better, he could help with this housekeeping issue. Sem found an extra bedsheet, and with the Pharaoh's permission, carefully slipped it under his destroyed left leg. There. That was… well, it really wasn't any better.

But it was something.

252

He wanted to talk. Tut wanted to keep up his conversations with Ankh and Sem; hear about the ins and outs of daily life. He was just aware enough to be bored. But not conscious enough to keep a conversation going. So he lay there as they talked at him, letting their words flow over him, helping him feel both connected and entertained for the next few minutes.

And he had just enough mind-power to be vaguely annoyed that he heard the beginnings of a great number of stories and lullabies... but never the endings.

It was bedtime. Meresankh finished her daily work, then stepped out into the hallway to make her way to her own chambers. Again, she paused. And again, her heart warmed. Because she could smell the frankincense-and-spikenard ointment, the sweet, calming fragrance that heralded bedtime... or at least the beginning of the long night. And she hoped, how she hoped, that Semerkhet would be able to help the Pharaoh fall asleep.

Ankh settled into her chair that night as always. Slowly, she drifted off. And she dreamed.

*Ankhesenamun looked down at the baby in her arms. The beautiful daughter she had named* Meritsenmut, *after her father and uncle. Because Tut, dearly beloved, dear departed, was her father. Not Zannanza. The Hittite Prince had never arrived. Only a message that he was not coming. But Ankh knew why. And the Vizier knew too. The Vizier... who after eight months of political back-and-forth had taken the next throne. But the Queen, who had given birth to her daughter under the watchful eyes of Merneith and Meresankh, would not marry him. Ever.*

*No husband. No throne. No son. Her options had narrowed. And now, it was time to begin a new chapter of her life. A life that she and her daughter would share as private people in the city of Sais.*

*Before her stood Horemheb, tall and strong and faithful. Hannu was there too, his spear in his hand as he stood a few yards away, continually scanning their surroundings for any spies of the Vizier. And Semerkhet... dear, wonderful Semerkhet, face haggard and full of pain, chin unshaven in mourning, but the ring of the Sole Companion shining proudly on his finger. All three of these faithful men had gathered to ensure her safe escape. The Queen suddenly realized that it was the middle of the night, and they were standing by the stables.*

*"Your horse is ready, My Lady," Horemheb whispered. "Ride hard. Ride to Sais. You'll be safe there. Both of you. I'll cover your escape. Go now, before it's too late."*

*She smiled at Horemheb. Horemheb, who had proven himself faithful to her and the memory of her husband. Horemheb, who had protected her escape by lying to the Vizier and claiming that he had killed the Queen and sent her body to the bottom of the Nile. And Granny... Granny, too, had lied, solemnly informing the old man that another royal child had left this world. Believing them dead, Ay would never look for them. And they would be safe in a town a day's journey from Memphis.*

*Adjusting the baby in the sling that held her to her mother's bosom, Ankhesenamun mounted the horse with the General's help. She clasped hands with Hannu, then with Semerkhet, seeing his faithful smile one more time. "Thank you," she whispered to both*

*of them. And she began to ride north as the Sun illuminated the*
*horizon. The Sun, which, as it rose, its warm, friendly rays bathing*
*her face, gave her strength. Gave her hope. Because as she rode*
*out of Memphis, away from everything she had ever known, away*
*from the city where she had been Queen, she had a sense of*
*adventure. Of safety. Of a Love that was greater than any fear.*
*And of a future.*

She woke up. And she wiped away the tears with a sigh. It had only been a dream. But a dream with a good point. A dream that forced her to ask herself a question; a question she had not yet fully explored.

What *would* she do if Zannanza did not come? What would she do if despite everything, all the politics and strategy and desperate engineering, the next person to sit on the throne of Egypt was Ay?

She would not marry him; that much was certain. She would not become his Queen. But if she refused to marry him… what would he do… to her, to those she loved? To… She touched her stomach, remembering the tea sent by her affectionate "secret admirer." To the baby?

If she could not become Pharaoh; if she could not keep Egypt going in the right direction by remaining Queen, what could she do? How could she protect herself and her child?

Ankh closed her eyes. And she pictured a map of her country. Memphis in the Nile delta; Thebes in the center of the nation. She thought of the cities of the delta. Per-Bast, On, Sais… Sais. The name echoed back from the dream from which she'd just awoken.

She smiled. Because she could hear her mother's voice, teaching a history lesson to her and Meritaten eleven or twelve years ago.

"The city of Sais is renowned for its school of women's medicine," Nefertiti had said. "Women come from far and wide to learn from the female professors, and they take what they have learned from one end of Egypt to the other."

Ankhesenamun sighed. And she nodded to herself. She and the baby would go to Sais.

Ankh chuckled. She had never really thought of going into medicine, but it was actually quite fitting. Over the past two months, she had learned more about nursing than she ever could have anticipated. And with all the experience she had gained over the past ten years… she could spread the news of how important good shoe design was. Maybe… maybe her familiarity with her brother's challenges would provide her with an opportunity to help others.

But wherever she worked, whatever she did, her education and ability to read would be an incredible advantage. And wherever in Egypt she lived, she would have the right to earn her own living and raise her child as a single parent, until the day she found someone… if she ever did. And when she returned to Memphis…

Ankh smiled again. Because she knew what she would do. She would work at one of the schools that she and her brother had had built. And she would be… Now Ankh blinked back hopeful tears. She would become a history teacher. And teach the little girls of Memphis about all the great Queens of the past.

Ankh thought of the lessons she had taught her brother, her friends Amenia and Mutnedjmet, her friend and sister Meresankh, over the past year. And she smiled to think that it had come full circle. She had been a history teacher all her life, but now… now that could be her life. And amid all the darkness and chaos and misery of death and uncertainty that they were facing, that thought brought her one small spark of joy. If she became a history teacher, she could only imagine the ripples she would be able to create in the lives of her students. Even if she was no longer Queen, she could change the future.

The Queen of Egypt nodded. She had a plan. She did not like what the future looked like, but at the same time… it was something. She had a plan. And she had hope. And she hugged her belly and went back to sleep.

Tut slept on and off throughout the next day, a gentle slumber offering temporary freedom from his pain. And again, his sister was glad to watch him sleep. Even if that meant that they could not spend every one of these final moments "together."

She wanted what was best for him. And what was best was for him to sleep.

As her brother slept, Ankh sat and thought. About her sisters; about the legacy of their family. She had outlived all her sisters, even Meritaten, who had always been the oldest. Before turning twenty, she had become the oldest surviving child of Akhenaten and Nefertiti. What a strange, awful gift to be one of the only two survivors of their family of nine, and how terrible to look back on the moments when their days had suddenly ended, one by one, snuffing out the lives that had been so bright and strong. She should not be the only remaining sister, the oldest remaining child. She should not. But she was.

Ankhesenamun looked down at the Queens List. Sobekneferu had taken the throne as the last person standing. Hatshepsut had become regent for her husband's tiny heir and retained her position, becoming a great King who had led her nation into a golden age. Ankh's own mother had served her country as a powerful co-regent, succeeding her husband as Pharaoh to lead it through one of the bumpiest periods in recent history.

If Zannanza never arrived in Egypt, Ankhesenamun would become the next Pharaoh. Except... It hit her like a cold raindrop, like missing a step in the dark, like the hard ground her brother had slammed into when he'd fallen from his chariot.

She wasn't next. She should be; she stood in exactly the same spot as the female Pharaohs and powerful Queens Regent of the past, at what felt like the darkest point of her family's beloved dynasty. She had the right to claim the next throne; carried a potential heir in her womb. She had the moral high ground.

Except... if she did that, she would die. And so would her child.

The Queen let out a shuddering sigh as the truth echoed through her; the truth she would face if Ay and those loyal to him stopped the Hittite Prince from joining the wife who had called him to Egypt. If that happened, she could not "hang on" for the moment that she would become Pharaoh. Because Ay, and all the weight of his followers, was against her. No matter how much paperwork her brother prepared, no one who mattered would accept her as Pharaoh.

Even Horemheb's homecoming, if he proved loyal to them, would not change things. If he returned to an Egypt in which Pharaoh Zannanza had not taken his place on the throne beside Queen Ankhesenamun, it would be too late for him to help them. Or too late... for the great General to do anything but help the Queen escape in safety.

If Zannanza did not come, then trying to take the throne herself would sentence the Queen and her child to death. Ankh swallowed.

258

And opening her hands, she let go of the future that should have been hers. All she could do was carry her crown with her in her heart, in her bearing, in her attitude. And bring up her child as a Prince or Princess.

It was so unfair. But it was the way things were. She felt like she had during the long, hard hours before she had revealed her letter to the Hittites to her brother. Agonizing over a decision she had to make, a decision that would cut her off from the future she wanted, the future that belonged to her by right. And Ankh knew that if the Prince did not come before her brother's funeral, she would have no choice but to take the path that was before her. The path that led to Sais.

# 24   Hope for the Future

**M**eresankh saw her Lady sitting in her chair, resting her tired head on her hand. And she saw that tears were sparkling in her eyes. Quietly, she approached. And gently, she rested a hand on her friend's shoulder.

That was all. But Meresankh smiled as she felt her heart warm. Because she felt a thought, an idea, a realization gently rising within it. Other people's emotions were not her responsibility. Her job was to be compassionate and supportive, but she should never assume that a bad day someone else was having was her fault. Her empathy, her love, were enough. And she poured all of her empathy and love through the hand that rested on her sister's shoulder.

Tut had not thought to see Nakhtmin again. But the little General popped in again for a brief conversation. As he clearly posed no threat except for being fatally annoying, Minnefer had let him in apparently without a second thought.

"I still don't know what the Queen's thinking, refusing to marry me or my father," Nakhtmin drawled, crunching an apple as he slouched in the Pharaoh's favorite chair. Tut's sister was on break, and Semerkhet was putting clean blankets away in the Pharaoh's storage room.

"I fink she's doing what she feelth ith best for Egypt," Tutankhamun responded. And he left it at that, declining to further the conversation.

Eventually, Nakhtmin got bored, getting up to leave with a mumbled wish for prosperity, leaving his apple core and a miasma of perfume behind. The Pharaoh let him go.

There was a sneeze. And Tut looked around to see Semerkhet emerging from the storage room with a grimace.

"What did the little jackal want this time?" he asked.

Tut rolled his eyes. "A future where Queenth can't become King, basically."

Semerkhet shook his head. "Shame on him."

Semerkhet collected the apple core, wiping up the flecks of sticky juice that had landed on the desk. And… He smiled. Because he was proud of himself. Somehow or other, Nakhtmin had gotten into his Pharaoh's room without Semerkhet's permission, but despite his indignation, Sem wasn't fighting the expected urge to strangle the little General. He wasn't even fighting resentment at the fact that his friend had not summoned him to get rid of the offender. He wished that he could protect his friend from all that was annoying in the world, shut down everyone who bothered him or got in his way, but he knew that he could not. And he was… he was just proud at the way that his little brother had not needed him this time.

"Do you really think she is?" Meresankh whispered to her Granny as they sat in the Pharaoh's private sitting room, Meresankh holding a small jar steady while Merneith used an unguent spoon to fill it with a fresh supply of the Pharaoh's favorite frankincense-and-spikenard ointment. He seemed to be going through rather a lot of it lately.

The old woman sighed, tapping the spoon against the lip of the small jar so the last chunks of the solid coconut-oil paste fell away.

"She could be," she said finally. Merneith shook her head slightly. "That's all I can say. It hasn't even been a full month.

Even I don't want to say she is or isn't until we do the seed test…"
Granny looked up, looking at Meresankh. The old woman sighed
again, taking her granddaughter's hand. "Sometimes there is no
way to answer a question but to wait."

Meresankh nodded. There were things that even the greatest
midwife in Egypt didn't know.

*What if it didn't work?* Meresankh wondered as she set her
Lady's freshly-cleaned wigs back on their stands. What if the letter
to the Hittites never arrived in Hattusa, what if they said *no*, what
if they said *yes* but Zannanza never made it to Egypt? What if, in
the end, they were left with no help from Hattusa?

And what… She bit her lip. What if there was no baby? What if
the Queen's body was so full of hope that the first signs had appeared, but in another month or two, they would disappear again?
And what… what if somehow, after all their hard work, all their
scheming and secrecy and politicizing, Grand Vizier Ay still
managed to claim the next throne of Egypt?

She asked I-AM inside her heart. *What if?* And she felt an echo
of a thought; the warmth of reassurance. What if? What if the
Mitanni attacked Memphis and the Nile dried up?

Meresankh didn't know what was going to happen next. But she
knew, no matter what, that I-AM was with them. And that the God
Who had done so many signs and wonders in Meresankh's own
Granny's youth held the future of Egypt in His hand.

Prayers always resounded from the palace. The servants knelt
beside the priests, imploring the gods to preserve their King as
sacred incense burned and livestock was sacrificed. Outside the
palace citizens stood weeping, praying, waiting for news. Courtiers

whispered who would succeed him if the gods did not heal him. Ay, they said. Or maybe Horemheb. Or perhaps the Queen would remarry, putting a new Pharaoh in place… or even take the throne herself, following in her mother's footsteps. Or maybe all of them would rule, one after the other. Would they lead the kingdom well? The people of Egypt could only hope.

The King and Queen listened to the prayers of the priests and the servants, shaking their heads silently as they wondered if the gods were even listening. But they were grateful that those around them cared so much. And they knew… somehow… that Someone could hear their prayers. And that Someone loved them.

As Semerkhet walked to the kitchen for a bowl of grapes, passing yet another angry conversation between servants whose political differences were simmering into unrest, he remembered what his Pharaoh had told him. Sleep with a knife under his pillow… and tell people to put unity before anything else.

"Hey," he said abruptly, stopping a few feet away from the argument, which was beginning to get testy. The four participants fell silent immediately, two dropping into deep bows, the other two offering grudging nods. "Hey," he said again, more gently, "I know it's hard right now. I know no one knows exactly what's going to happen. But right now… right now we need to stick together. We need to put Egypt herself first. And hang in there as we wait to see what the next chapter of our lives looks like. As… as Sole Companion, I can tell you that if you can't stand it around here any longer because of all the politics, you have permission to resign. You're not being fired," he said hastily as their eyebrows began to rise toward the bangs of their wigs, "but in all honesty, the Pharaoh and the Queen don't want to hold anyone here against their will. But please," he said, "put Egypt first. We're all in this together."

The four men stared at him, and slowly, smiles touched the faces of three of them. The fourth, at least, looked a little less grudging. And as they offered their wishes for life, prosperity, and health, he kept walking, his heart just a little lighter.

"My Lady?"

"Yes, Sem?"

He approached the Queen, who was organizing empty teacups and bottles of medicine on the little table, wondering how to say it. "My Lady... I've made a decision."

She looked up at him in curiosity, setting aside a stack of fresh bandages and stepping around the table to stand beside him, looking into his face.

"Yes?"

Crossing the room, she locked the door, then nodded toward the Pharaoh's private sitting room. Semerkhet followed her into the other space, sitting down across from her.

Semerkhet swallowed, looking down at his feet. "After... when it... happens..." he said slowly, hardly able to make it true by saying it out loud, "I don't think... don't think I'll stay here. By your leave, of course. If you need me, I'll go exactly where you need me to be; do exactly what you need me to do. But with your permission... I've been thinking, and I think I would do well studying with Granny Merneith, and then... finding work out in town. Use what I've learned here at the palace to help... other people." He chuckled. "With my, uh, gifted hands."

264

The Queen smiled. Gently she took his gifted hands in hers, holding them for just a moment.

"They are miraculous," she agreed. "Whoever you work with will be very blessed." She winked. "And will sleep very well."

The valet laughed, then gave a sigh. He looked down at his hands, now folded in his lap, then met her eyes again a bit shyly. "H… how is it, by the way? The baby?"

The Queen smiled. "It's doing just fine," she said. "In another month… in another month, I should be sure."

"Will you be all right?" he asked softly. "The two of you?"

Ankh looked up at him courageously. And she nodded. She wasn't ready to tell him about her plan to flee to Sais, but she could still tell him the truth.

"I have a lot of hardship behind me. And I know there is plenty more ahead. I don't know exactly what will happen… but I know I'll get through. I always have. And I always will."

Semerkhet dipped his head respectfully. "I hope the letter goes through."

She sighed. "So do I. But even if it doesn't… I'll figure out a way. Just like always." Ankh looked up at him. "So, yes," she said. "You have our royal permission, when the time comes, to resign your role as valet and begin a… a new chapter of life in Memphis, or Thebes, or wherever you choose to live." She smiled. "You and Meresankh."

Sem blushed. "You know?"

The Queen just smiled. "I hope you're very happy together. Although… even if you're no longer valet, you'll still be Sole Companion, Favorite of the Pharaoh, and Unique Friend. Whatever happens. And you can…" She paused, biting her lip as she struggled not to choke up. "You can wear your ring and your sash, wherever you live, and people will see, and they'll know… what you did for the Pharaoh."

Ankhesenamun swallowed, reaching out to squeeze Semerkhet's hand again. "He's lucky…" she said. "To have had a friend… a brother… like you."

And Semerkhet blinked back tears as he smiled.

The Queen watched him go, getting back to work, the endless stream of small tasks that filled his day and ensured that everything went as smoothly as possible. And she sighed. He and Meresankh were not the only ones setting out on a new chapter of life.

He told the Pharaoh. Semerkhet told his friend that when the time came, he and Meresankh would resign their posts at the palace and begin a new life in Memphis. But he reassured the Pharaoh that he still had a good career ahead of him, as he would study under Merneith and become a doctor. And that someday… that someday, he was sure that he and Meresankh would get married.

Tut nodded. And he took his brother's hand with a sad smile. And he said that he agreed. As Tutankhamun had told Semerkhet so many days previously, the safety of his Sole Companion was his priority.

Meresankh brought her Lady, her friend, her sister, another cup of tea as the Queen took a short break in her chambers. And with a soft smile, Ankhesenamun accepted it, slowly sipping it as she gazed into her own thoughts.

A story was dancing inside Meresankh's heart, just like always. But gently, she held it back. And took a chair of her own to sit in

266

companionable silence with her friend. Sometimes, silence was all right.

"Granny?" the Queen asked.

The midwife looked up from setting a hot cup of the herbal tea, the same blend as before, on the table for her.

"Yes, Your Majesty?"

Ankh picked up the teacup and took a sip. It was good. Then she sighed. She'd locked the door, for her own peace of mind, so she could speak freely. "Do you think I could be?" she asked finally. "With all the signs?"

The midwife gave a wistful smile. "Your Majesty…" she said slowly, "I pray that you are. But we can't be sure yet. Not until we do the seed test."

The Queen bit her lip. "But why can't we do the test now?"

Merneith shook her head. "These things take time," she said gently. "We need to wait for your body to be ready to answer our question."

Ankh gave the midwife a tired smile. "Thank you," she said softly.

Merneith bowed her head. "Of course, Your Majesty. Keep drinking the tea, keep eating the right foods and getting as much rest as you can, and time… time will tell."

The Queen gave a heavy sigh. Now it was time to ask her other question. "And if I am…" she said slowly, "will you lie?"

The old woman looked at her strangely. "About what, dearie?"

Ankhesenamun held out her hand. And gently, Granny took it, looking up at her with her wise old eyes as she waited for what Ankh was about to say.

"If the Prince doesn't come…" she said, "and I still refuse to marry the Vizier, both the baby and I will be in danger. So, if he doesn't come, then, after it's born, I'm going to move away to Sais, and teach history until it's safe to come back. I'll have Horemheb tell the Vizier that he killed me, so he won't look for me. But…" She touched her belly, feeling tears coming to her eyes. "If you would be willing… I want to ask you… will you tell him…" With a sob, she covered her face. And Merneith understood.

Gently, she squeezed Ankh's hand in her old, wrinkled one, and the Queen seemed to feel strength flowing into her. "I'll tell him, dearie," she whispered. Wiping her eyes, Ankh looked at her with a grateful smile. "After all, sometimes…" Now Merneith smiled, old eyes sparkling as she continued the legacy of Shiprah and Puah of old. "Sometimes, a lie can save a life."

The Queen swallowed. And the Light that shone from Merneith's eyes just as it shone from Meresankh's pushed her forward. Now, of all times, was the time to ask.

"Granny," she said.

"Yes, dearie?"

Ankh paused. "Will you… will you pray for the Pharaoh?"

Merneith smiled, the Light growing stronger as her face crinkled in smile wrinkles. "I am praying for him, dearie. And for you. And for the little one."

Ankhesenamun just smiled.

With a deep bow, the midwife was gone.

The Queen sighed, looking down at her flat belly. Even the midwife was not sure. There was no way to know… other than to wait. And to pray. It was possible, she reminded herself. It was. They would just have to wait and see.

That was one of the strengths of women, she reflected. To be able to sit in the stew and get through until the coming change arrived or the big question was answered. This was… this was a season of waiting. Of waiting for one sun to set… set on her brother's life. And for another to rise.

But what future would it rise on? One in which she became the wife of Zannanza and raised the strong son born of her brother's seed to become the heir of Egypt? One in which she became Pharaoh herself? One in which she lost her crown and fled into exile? One with a child… or one without a child?

There was no way to know. Except to wait and see.

But Merneith was praying for her, and so was Meresankh. To Whomever they were praying, and whoever was right or wrong, it brought the Queen comfort.

Now she had another secret. The Queen shifted uncomfortably in her chair, as though the pillow at her back was filled with pebbles, rather than wool. It ached in her heart almost as badly as the letter had; the plan she was holding inside until the time came to reveal it to her brother. Soon. She would tell him very soon. As Queen, she would know when the time had come.

Meresankh continued helping Ankh, Sem, with a kind word, a sympathetic hand, a plate of honey-cakes. And she continued helping her other coworkers. As Granny met with the pregnant or nursing mothers under her care, Meresankh met with her own patients, checking in on recurring migraines, dental problems, aching joints. And as she worked, somehow she knew that the things she was learning in this chapter of her life were preparing her for her future.

People were whispering. Semerkhet walked down the hall to the kitchen, past staff members huddled in groups of twos and threes, talking softly to one another, wrapped up in their warm robes. He caught the words "Hittite" and "General."

And then he saw Nakhtmin. Parading down the hall like he was a Prince. With what looked like fear, several servants dropped their eyes when he went by, a few even bowing.

Semerkhet sighed. He knew what was going on. The staff, and, Semerkhet was sure, the general population of Egypt, didn't know what to believe; didn't know in whose hands the future would lie when the page of history turned. And they were afraid. All except Nakhtmin. He was excited. After all, he thought he was guaranteed to become a Prince.

Sem shook his head and kept walking. And he remembered the conversation he had had with his friend a week or two previously; the words with which he himself had sown peace among at least a tiny fraction of the staff. All he could do was continue to be courteous to everyone and encourage them to unite for the sake of the future of Egypt.

And... He bit his lip. Sleep with a knife under his pillow.


Ankhesenamun wondered why she was watching so intently. Slowly Granny unwrapped Tut's leg from its bandages, revealing the gaping wound that got worse every day. But Merneith had half a century of experience, and a strong stomach.

So the Queen was surprised to hear the midwife gasp, just as Tut hissed in his breath with pain.

"What is it?" she asked, stepping closer to the bed.

270

Merneith set aside the pus-stained bandages, bending over what was left of Tut's left leg to gently probe it with her old fingers. Tut gave a tiny groan of pain, and Ankh took his hand, letting him squeeze hers as Granny explored the wound. Now the Queen stopped observing, looking down at her and Tut's hands while the midwife completed her exam.

Finally Granny raised her head, stepping away from the Pharaoh.

"The infection is spreading well beyond the wound," she announced grimly. "I fear it has entered the channels of his body. These red streaks…" Granny pointed to a series of angry red lines radiating from the wound— "indicate how far it has spread."

Tut almost asked what that meant. But he knew. So he said nothing.

Silently, Merneith took his hand, placing her fingers against his wrist to check his pulse. What it told her seemed to make her even more solemn.

"But we can control the fever, for the time being," she said gently, "with cold compresses on your forehead, and under your arms. We can at least relieve some of the heat. And the poppy… the poppy is doing its job."

The Queen closed her eyes, feeling the weight of the news settling upon her shoulders; her aching heart. This was beyond even Merneith's skill to heal.

Then Ankh stiffened her shoulders, even as Granny herself seemed to admit defeat. And she bore up under the burden. It was painful. It was heavy. But it would not crush her. She had carried similar burdens in the past. And she would carry this one as well.

She would not carry it alone, she reminded herself with a sad little smile. She had Meresankh, she had Semerkhet, she had Merneith, and she had the Creator Whose Name she was still searching for. She was not alone.

As she had when she had decided to write to the Hittites, she felt her broken heart mend itself, joined back together by a will of iron. There was no time for tears. Not this time. She had to stay tough. Her brother needed… his strong big sister. And Egypt… Egypt needed its strong Queen.

# 25   Preparations

For what felt like the eighty-fifth time that week, Semerkhet sat and watched his friend sleep. And as the Pharaoh drowsed, chest slowly rising and falling with each gentle breath, Semerkhet realized… that he missed him. It made his heart ache to think that because his friend was sleeping so much, they were not able to make the most of the fleeting moments they still had. But sleep was the only thing that protected Tut from his pain. And so, as he watched his brother sleep, Semerkhet was grateful.

He got up, finding his lute and returning to his seat. And too softly to wake his friend, he began to play.


"Meresankh?" the Queen called. Her handmaiden hurried across the hall, joining her in the Pharaoh's room.

"Yes, My Lady?"

Ankh glanced at her brother, drowsing in the bed, the cat curled up by his gently moving chest. And quietly, she locked the door.

"Sit down with me," she said, welcoming her friend into the Pharaoh's private sitting room. The Queen picked a chair, and Meresankh clambered up into the one across from her, feet not touching the floor.

Reaching out, Ankh took her friend's little hand. Meresankh looked down at their entwined hands, then back up at her Mistress.

"What's going on?" she finally asked. "Is our Pharaoh all right?"

Ankh sighed. "Not really. Merneith's doing her best, but…" She gave Meresankh half a smile. "Actually… it's you I'm thinking about right now."

"Me, My Lady?" Meresankh gave almost a little frown.

The Queen smiled. "Yes. And about… the future. Sem told me… he told me that when this is… over… that he planned to study with Merneith and then find work in the city. Not work at the palace anymore. And I know… how much you love one another."

Meresankh reached up, fingers gently stroking the little silver necklace at her breast. And her dimples appeared as she smiled.

"So," Ankh continued, "if, when we… enter the next phase of our lives… Sem doesn't work here anymore, but the two of you want to get married…" Meresankh blushed furiously, but the Queen went on. "I want to tell you that your working here is completely voluntary. The moment the two of you are ready to move… forward, I will wish you well."

Meresankh bit her lip. And to the Queen's surprise, her handmaiden's face fell. "Thank you, My Lady," she said softly, her words halting. "We want to; we really do. Maybe someday. I hope."

Ankh frowned in confusion. "I know he loves you. What will stand in your way? I thought you wanted to get married right away."

Meresankh shook her head with a sad smile. "You forget, My Lady, that common people have to follow the law. You were a child when you got married, and the adults basically did it for you. Granny, Little Nefertiti, and I could do well in town, but I can't speak for Sem. I love him… but without a dowry and someone to speak for us, we won't be able to get married."

The Queen shook her head with a heavy sigh. And she looked down at the signet-ring that was now hers. Was there anything she could do to help her friend?

"I'll talk to the Pharaoh," she promised. "We'll figure something out."

Meresankh just nodded.

Ankh felt tears glistening in her eyes. She sighed again, a lump growing in her throat. "But I want you to be happy, whatever happens here. And safe. So you are not bound here, not a minute longer than you want to stay. I've treasured our time together, but I want what's best for you. And with all the… changes… that are coming, the safest thing might be for you and Sem to get as far away from the palace as possible."

Meresankh frowned. "Is the Prince…"

Ankh shook her head. "We don't know. But I wonder. I've been thinking some more," she said, "about the timing. And about… about how much of a risk we're taking. And I have… I've made a plan, another plan… for if it all falls apart— the Prince, even taking the throne myself. Because I have to know what I'll do if all my options disappear. I have to have a plan… that will keep the baby safe."

"Tell me, My Lady," her friend said, forehead wrinkling in curiosity.

"I'll leave Memphis," the Queen said simply. "If we can regain his loyalty, then Horemheb can keep the Vizier off my trail, and it won't be long before he succeeds the Vizier. And the baby and I will stay in the city of Sais until it's safe to come back."

Meresankh nodded. "Granny's told me about Sais. Such an amazing school they have there… I always wanted to visit there. Although Granny knows more than any of the midwives who teach there."

Ankh smiled. "And then…" She sighed. "I'll see what I can do about becoming a history teacher at one of the Pharaoh's new schools. Teach… teach the little girls of the next generation about the Queens of the past. And show them that they are the Queens of the future. I… I won't be Queen anymore, but I can still make a difference for the future of Egypt."

All Meresankh could do was blink back tears.

There was a slight sob. And before the Queen knew it, a small, soft pair of arms had been thrown around her neck as Meresankh fell into her arms, hugging her for all she was worth.

Ankhesenamun smiled through her tears, wrapping her arms gently around her friend. "Thank you, sister," she whispered into Meresankh's wig. "Thank you for everything. I'll never forget you."

Over her shoulder, she could hear Meresankh sniffle. "And I'll never forget you, My Lady."

The Queen chuckled. "You have royal permission to call me by my name."

Meresankh seemed to go stiff for a moment. She paused. Then Ankh smiled to hear, "I'll miss you… Ankhesenamun."

Then Meresankh sat back with a little smile that looked rather determined. "Going to Sais… that's a good plan. The women's college there will help you get established until you can come home to Memphis. But… how much time does that leave you? If you go… when will you go?"

The Queen sighed. And she bit her lip. Because she remembered… remembered the tea the Vizier had sent. And her heart ached as she realized that the baby would not be born at the palace. Granny's promise to lie and claim that the child had died at birth would not be relevant. By the time it was born, Ankh and the baby would have to be long gone.

276

"I can't wait around," she said slowly. "The Vizier has... he has no qualms about hurting other people's children. He already tried to poison the baby, and I wouldn't put it past him to try to stage an accident. Even... even for a pregnant woman." Meresankh bowed her head solemnly, and the Queen continued. "And if it's a boy... if it's a boy, then my brother's dynasty continues. And the Vizier can't have that. So I'll... I'll need to be there at the... the funeral..."

She paused, reaching out to squeeze Meresankh's hand. And then she went on. "But I'll have to disappear within the next couple of days. I can't stay here one minute longer than I have to." She shook her head. "If the Prince doesn't arrive before the funeral, I can't even wait for him, can I?"

Meresankh blinked back tears. And she opened her arms, pulling the Queen in for another hug.

Sadly, Ankh smiled at her friend. "I wanted you to be there when it's born," she said softly. "Hold my hand. And Granny... the greatest midwife in Egypt. I need you both."

Meresankh returned the sad smile. "I wish I could be there."

The Queen gave another heavy sigh. "I'll ask Horemheb, and if he is loyal, he will lie for us, so the Vizier won't even think of looking for us." She smiled sadly at Meresankh, whose deep sigh and little nod showed that she understood, then continued. "And when Ay's gone, we'll come back, and I'll work at one of the schools. But..." Ankh paused, a horrible thought rising in her heart. "If the Vizier becomes the next Pharaoh... what's to keep him from shutting down the construction projects? What's to make him finish the schools at all?"

Meresankh just shook her head and squeezed Ankh's hand. Then a small smile spread over her face. "Could you write another letter?" she asked.

The Queen nodded, her own face breaking into a smile as relief filled her heart. "Never forget what an amazing politician you are," she told her friend. "That's perfect. We could write to Nubia, the Mitanni; all the countries that came to Tribute Day. And we could announce the opening of the schools, and formally invite them to send as many students as possible. If he knows that students are coming from all over the world, expecting the schools to open on time, the Vizier won't be able to shut down construction. Back in Paophi, the Pharaoh sent messengers throughout Egypt to spread the word; we just need to expand it to another level." She smiled. "I think that might work. You, my friend, are a genius."

Meresankh just smiled.

Then the Queen sighed again. "Usually having a son is considered an advantage," she said, "but right now, it doesn't even matter if it's a boy. Even if I technically continue the dynasty with a little boy, he'll never be the legal heir. And there's nothing I can do about it. If we just killed the Vizier, then I could serve as regent for my baby, but if we did that, we'd all be dead the next day." She shook her head. "So if the Prince doesn't get here before the funeral.... leaving town really is the only way forward."

"The only way for both of you to stay safe," Meresankh emphasized.

Ankhesenamun paused, tapping her chin, then shook her head as an idea presented itself and failed just as quickly. "And there is no way to make Horemheb promise to make my son his heir, if and when *he* becomes Pharaoh someday, because someday, he could have a healthy son of his own. Sometimes heirs come from other

278

places, like a brother or a Vizier, or even…" She smiled as she thought of her parents. "Even a wife, but I don't think we can hold out hope for an arrangement like that."

Meresankh sighed, giving her Lady a brave smile. The choice the Queen would have to make if the Prince did not come was clear. The handmaiden nodded again, at Ankh's belly. "So, in the event that the Prince doesn't come to Egypt, that makes seventy days, counting from… after," she said. "Seventy days to prepare."

"Prepare?" the Queen asked, cocking her head.

Meresankh chuckled. "Do you know how to make beef stew? Or even porridge? If you're going to become an everyday citizen, there are some things you need to learn to do. Like laundry."

Ankh found herself wrinkling her nose. "Laundry?" Then she chuckled too. "I can't believe I've never thought about it before. But you're absolutely right. Laundry, cooking, grocery shopping… I'd better start learning." She smiled, reaching for her friend's hand again. "Will you teach me?" she asked.

"Teach you?"

The Queen shrugged. "Cooking. Laundry. How to run a house. How to do my own makeup. I really… really wouldn't know where to begin. And I need your help."

Meresankh nodded with a sigh. "You do, My Lady. You do. How are you going to manage? You can reason circles around any other politician in the world, and you know more history than anyone but Granny, but cooking… laundry… they're just so different from anything you've ever done before." The handmaiden sat up straighter, rolling up her sleeves. "I'd better come with you. It's not right to sit around waiting for something that may never happen when my friend needs me." She swallowed, then went on. "Until we get a dowry, and find someone to speak for us, Semerkhet and I can't get married. Maybe someday, I hope, but as for right now… I can come with you. I can't leave you alone and pregnant, running a house for the first time in your life. I don't want you burning yourself making dinner with no one around to bandage you up."

The Queen shook her head with a grateful smile. "I don't want to make you take care of me your whole life. I can do it."

"I know you can," Meresankh said. "But I want you to be safe. For example, on the subject of laundry… you do remember that babies generate dirty swaddling? Swaddling… that has to be washed?"

The Queen wrinkled her nose as she chuckled. "I remember the existence of dirty swaddling… but that's just when you hand the baby off to the nanny. But that… that will be my job." She shook her head with a little smile. "Have to get used to that. And maybe… maybe I can practice with Meryt's baby, Tjauenmaya. Even… just practice holding her; carrying her around with me. The more experience I can get beforehand, the better prepared I am, the better I'll feel."

Meresankh just sighed. Practice would make a big difference. But she could not justify leaving her Queen alone in the world.

"This is a new chapter of life for me as well," she said, feeling herself choking up. "I won't be the Queen's handmaiden anymore. With you going into exile, I'm losing my job as your handmaiden and my home here at the palace."

Ankhesenamun grabbed Meresankh's hand again, face crumpling as words of regret began to leap from her tongue. "No, don't feel bad," Meresankh said, cutting off her Queen's apology. "I have no doubts that I can earn a living as an herbalist, and Granny and I don't need a big place. But I will also be moving away. So wherever you go, maybe I can come too, and be your neighbor, at least. And see you and help you every day. If we do get to get married, Sem will be delighted to be neighbors with you. There would be plenty of relevant work for him in Sais." She smiled. "I'll talk to him about it soon."

Ankh smiled. And she nodded, grateful for her friend's faithfulness.

"As long as this is what the two of you really want," she insisted.

Meresankh squeezed her hand. "Don't tell me to abandon my best friend," she said. "Where you go, I'll go. And where you live… I'll live in the same neighborhood." She shook her head. "Semerkhet and I want to get married… I want to come with you… but how can we do both at the same time? Except… not at the same time. Not until we get a dowry." She shook her head. "We'll figure it out. Sem can work in town— he has so many skills; I'm sure he can find a job right away. And I'll talk to Granny; see if we can find work and a place. With all the changes, I'm sure she will want to move, too." Bravely, she nodded. "We'll figure it out."

"But what about before I start working at the school in Memphis?" the Queen asked. "I'll be a student… but what will my income be? I won't have time to go to school, work, and take care of the baby. And who will watch the baby while I'm at school or at work? Especially early on, what am I going to do until it's weaned?"

Meresankh was about to say "I'll do it, of course," when her heart glowed with another idea. "What about Nefertiti-Tasherit?" she asked.

The Queen smiled. "How is she?" she asked.

"Doing all right," Meresankh replied. "Granny's fattening her up, and teaching her her herbs, just like she taught me. Be quite the doctor someday." She blushed. "Actually, I'm teaching her, too. And we're teaching her to read. But what I was thinking was… what if you took her with you? What if she watched the baby and helped run the house while you were at school or at work? And she can go to one of the new schools, too."

Meresankh swallowed. "She doesn't… doesn't have anything tying her to Memphis. And she talks about you all the time. About how kind you were to give her your shawl. Granny knew she could be trusted, and she is so excited about the baby. I think…" Meresankh shook her head with a little smile. "I think she likes you even more than she likes me." The handmaiden smiled. "So you would be giving her the home she always wanted. And she would be able to help you. I think… I think you need each other. She doesn't have anyone else… and if you have someone by your side who you know, who you love…" Meresankh blinked back tears. "The three of you will be a family. And…" Now the handmaiden chuckled, even as peace filled her heart. "To be honest, I'd feel a lot better knowing she's with you. The skills you're still developing are ones she has already, and the other way around, so you'll be a good team."

Ankh sighed. And she thought back to the conversation she had had with her brother. About whether they could adopt that little girl. They had decided that with everything up in the air, it wouldn't be a good idea, for her sake. But now… The Queen nodded. Everything was more up in the air than ever. But maybe… maybe this was a door that was opening.

"I think that's a wonderful idea," she whispered. "Can you bring her, later today? So I can ask her what she thinks?"

Meresankh nodded. "Of course. But I already know what she'll think. Because you'll be making all her dreams come true." Meresankh sat up straighter. "But as for what to do until the baby is weaned…" She sighed. "I wonder… if you could take some of your jewelry with you. And sell it. It's some of the most beautiful jewelry in Egypt. And I'm sure that even one piece of it would feed you for a month."

The Queen nodded. "That sounds like a good plan." She smiled. Even as she found herself blinking back tears. "And I would be honored… if you would pick some pieces for yourself. For my friend."

Meresankh just smiled.

Meresankh walked down the long hallway just to stretch her legs. As with the past week or so, it hadn't been a very busy day. But she paused when she heard a familiar voice; a voice that made her scalp prickle. And in the shadows of the hallway, she stopped to listen, silently taking in every word.

"What other choice does she have, really?" Nakhtmin was drawling to some sycophantic underling. "My dad will ask her one more time after the funeral, and if she says no…" He made a slashing motion across his throat, accompanied by a guttural hiss. The son of the Vizier gave a heartless snicker. "She's not showing yet, but since everyone knows, he can't have her executed for treason. But there are plenty of *accidents* a person can have… I mean, how many flights of stairs are there in this palace?

"And, yes," he continued disdainfully, "I know that General Horemheb is technically the boy-king's heir, since the weakling never had a son, but there are ways around that. Simplest way, of course, is for the Queen to marry my dad… see if she really has a boy or not, and… go from there. Marrying the Queen will put him on the throne, easy as that. But even if she won't… Horemheb may be the heir right now, but if the Queen won't cooperate, my dad will make the General an offer he can't refuse. And banishing the Queen won't be enough," he sneered, "even if Horemheb would try to convince my dad to go easy on her and just kick her out. Could you imagine if she had a baby boy in Greece or Babylonia or some such, and came back with an army to reclaim the throne? Heirs in exile are the last thing my father wants to deal with. She will make an awful lot of work for him in any case, if she won't do the smart thing and marry him. Anyway," he said, scratching his nose ostentatiously, "one way or another, two months from now, my father will be Pharaoh and I will be Crown Prince."

Sweating, Meresankh stepped back further into the shadows, hands clenching into fists. Her friend had no time to waste.

She told the Queen. And amid her horror that her darkest suspicion, the awful realization that the Vizier would indeed try to have a pregnant woman killed, had come true, Ankh was grateful. Grateful that with this information, she would be able to keep herself and her child safe.

"I have something to tell you," Ankhesenamun whispered to her brother. Slowly he opened his eyes, looking up at her with a little smile.

"Yeth?"

"I don't think I can wait for the Prince."

He sat up a little, forehead creasing in confusion. "What do you mean?" he asked.

Ankh looked down at her hand and her brother's, entwined on the bed. And she thought of her dream, of Nakhtmin's words, and of the plan she had made with Meresankh.

"The Vizier... the Vizier has no common decency," she said with a sigh. She squeezed Tut's hand. "I didn't tell you what he gave me."

And she told him about the tea. And about what Meresankh had heard.

"...so, I'll wait for the funeral," she finished. "And if the Prince has arrived by then, I'll marry him. And Egypt and Hattusa will be married as well. But if he doesn't get here by the funeral, then the next day... I'll disappear."

The Pharaoh unclenched his jaw and the fist he'd been making with his free hand. And he looked up at her.

"So, if you're only thafe here until the... the funeral, where will you go?" he asked.

"To Sais," she said softly. Ankh went on, describing her plan to flee and study at the medical college, then to wait for Ay's life to end and Horemheb's reign to begin.

Ankh gave a deep sigh, thinking of just how she would escape. "When Horemheb gets home... I'll ask him to lie for me. I'll ask him… to tell the Vizier that he killed me and threw my body in the Nile."

Tutankhamun looked up at his sister with a little gasp. "What?"

She gave a sad little smile. "It's the only way he won't look for me— if he thinks I'm dead."

"But you're the nektht Pharaoh," her brother interjected with a frown. "You're everything Egypt needth— you'd be ten timeth the Pharaoh I ever wath. The next throne should be yourth."

The Queen bowed her head, gulping back tears as she nodded. "I know," she said in a choked voice. "It's all wrong. It should be me. But it… it can't. I know I could do it," she said before he could ask why she was suddenly doubting herself, "but they'd kill me. And I can't…" Gently, she laid her hand on her belly. "I can't put our little one at risk."

Tut nodded. He understood. The precious little life who might be growing in his sister's belly could not be endangered. Not even for the sake of the moral high ground they both knew Ankhesenamun possessed. Both wiped away tears as they saw the throne that had belonged to their family for generations torn away from their unwilling grasp.

Bitterly, the Queen sighed. "It's all wrong… but it's just politics."

The Pharaoh just shook his head. *Just politics* indeed.

Swallowing, Ankh continued. "So I'll hide out until the Vizier is gone, and Horemheb takes the throne. Because we both know it won't be Nakhtmin. And then… we'll come back to Memphis, the baby and I. We'll be safe; I know Horemheb will let us live in peace as… ordinary, anonymous citizens. And no one will know that I used to be the Queen of Egypt."

"But what will you do?" Tut asked. "How will you earn a wage?"

"Well…" Ankh scooted closer to her brother, reaching out a hand to stroke his face. "I'll find something. First I'll be a student— I'll go to the college of women's medicine in Sais, the one Mother taught us girls about. And then…" She smiled. "When I come home to Memphis, maybe I'll work at one of the schools we're building. Become… become a history teacher."

Tutankhamun smiled. "You'll be good at that."

The Queen sighed, looking into the future. "A history teacher," she said wistfully. "Teach the girls of this generation about the great Queens who brought us to where we are now. Teach them… teach them to become the Queens of their own lives. And I… I can still influence the future of Egypt, even if I'm not Queen anymore." She bent her head, wiping away a tear. "And maybe… maybe I'll find someone," she said, her voice breaking.

"I hope you do," Tut said earnestly. "I hope you do."

She touched her stomach, imagining the baby she hoped and prayed was inside, and hoping it was listening.

"And our baby…" she whispered, "will be a Prince or a Princess. I promise. Maybe it'll never see the palaces we grew up in, but it's her heritage, or his heritage. Its father… and both its grandparents… were Pharaohs."

"Tho was its mother," Tutankhamun whispered, reaching out to squeeze his wife's hand. She squeezed it back.

Then she smiled. "Remember Nefertiti-Tasherit?" she whispered. Her brother just nodded. "I'm going to invite her to come with me," she said. He gasped, and she nodded. "She'll take care of the baby while I go to school or work, and we'll run the house together. And we'll… we'll be a family."

Tut just smiled.

Ankh swallowed, setting aside her tears. "So we'll be all right," she whispered. "I promise."

He smiled back at her. "I know."

And she bent and kissed him on the forehead.

"Meresankh will be moving too," the Queen said a bit wistfully. "Along with Granny. Maybe we'll be neighbors in Sais. And if she and Sem get to get married someday, he'll be there, too."

"If?" Tut asked, concern twisting inside his heart. "I thought they were going to get married right away."

"I was talking to Meresankh earlier," Ankhesenamun said, "about the future. Her future. And she told me… about how she and Sem won't be able to get married right away, because they don't have a dowry or anyone to speak for them." Gently she took his hand, looking down at the signet-ring that shone on her own finger. "What do you suppose we might be able to do to help them?"

Silently the Pharaoh nodded. Slowly, the beginning of a plan was beginning to tiptoe around his heart.

"I'll fink about it," he said, pondering the signet-ring shining on his sister's hand. He smiled. "I know…. I know there must be somefing I can do."

His sister just gave him a proud smile.

"We found a way, by the way," Ankh continued a moment later, "to keep Ay from shutting down work on the schools if he ever does become Pharaoh."

Tut raised his eyebrows. "How?" he asked.

"I'm going to have Nuya write letters to all the countries that came to Tribute Day and invite them to send students. Just like you did from Tamiat to Napata, but as far and wide as we can go. So,

288

with that many people coming, he'll be obligated to go through with the schools."

"Why don't we go even further?" Tutankhamun asked his sister.

She looked at him with a curious smile. "How?"

"Well," he said, "we could invite all the Kingth and Queenth to come early, to thee the progress on the building projectth. Or to thend ambathadorth. And we…" He smiled. "If we're afraid of what Ay will do with our Egypt, how many promitheth can we make in this letter? Promitheth he'll have to keep?"

Tut coughed. Slowly and painfully, he took a deep breath, refilling his stubborn lungs. And he squeezed his sister's hand.

Ankh smiled. He was doing it. Her baby brother was practicing politics… figuring out what needed to be done and doing it; applying the lessons he had learned from so many sources and fearlessly making the decisions he knew were right.

Even if they were coming to the end, she was proud. Because she truly had worked herself out of a job.

The ideas kept coming. Now Ankh was the one tapping her chin as another bit of inspiration came to her.

"And what," she said, "if we invited the other countries to actually invest in these schools? That way, maybe… maybe we could build more than five. And maybe they could open more quickly. They could be…" She smiled. "They could be a celebration of our alliance— we built them together, and each country can send teachers, each country can send students, and each country will benefit. It's like…" She blinked back tears, biting her lip as she hoped her brother would understand what she was thinking of.

"A legacy of peace," he whispered with a smile.

She just squeezed his hand.

Ankh found Nuya. And she gave him the draft she had written; an invitation to the known world to come and study at the five new schools that would be opening over the next five years in Egypt. An Egypt that boasted moderate taxes, a generous minimum wage, freedom from the abusive practice of slavery, and the opportunity for men and women to study at the same college. Faithfully, the scribe copied her letter out over and over, and together, the King and Queen stamped each copy with the royal signet-ring. And the Queen watched out the window as the post went out. To the Mitanni, to Nubia, to Babylonia, Alashiya, Assyria, Retjenu, the message went out. In a year, Egypt would be flooded with students excited to study at the first of the new schools.

Ay would have no choice but to give them what they wanted.

Meresankh blinked back her tears. And as always, she prayed. She prayed that her Lady and her little niece or nephew would be safe in Sais. And that one day soon… they would see one another again.

Then she sighed. The bright bubble of excitement that had been building in her heart at the thought of having a new little sister was slowly, gently deflating, going dim. Because now, if the Prince did not come, Nefertiti-Tasherit was going to go with the Queen when she moved to Sais. Meresankh would not get to have the same hand in teaching her that she had hoped.

But… they had the next seventy days, in addition to whatever time I-AM blessed them with. Meresankh would make the most of those seventy days, pouring into Ankhesenamun and Little Nefertiti, preparing them for whatever future lay ahead of them. Over those two months, she would continue teaching Nefertiti to read; teach her Lady how to cook and clean. Proudly she smiled to think of the difference she would be able to make as she taught them everything she knew, readying them for the next chapter of their lives.

And when the throne once again changed hands, both Ankh and Little Nefertiti would come home to Memphis. With a sigh, Meresankh smiled again. One day, they would all be together again. And… if I-AM sent Zannanza to them safe and sound before Ankhesenamun's brother was laid to rest, the Queen would retain her place beside the throne, and none of them would have to leave Memphis at all. There was nothing… nothing to do but wait and discover which future lay ahead of them.

But through it all, Meresankh reminded herself… even the Red Sea had two shores.

The Pharaoh's heart ached as he thought of the future his wife was facing; the choice she was having to make for the safety of their child. She was giving it all up, the rank of Pharaoh that should have been hers. Only… she was right; he knew she was right. Under the circumstances, the crown would never be hers. Even if it should have been. And now… now she was planning a strange, new life; a strange, new life that would take her, the baby, and Little Nefertiti to Sais. If the Prince could not come, that was her only way forward. The only way to keep herself and their child alive.

Tut swallowed back the lump in his throat. But his heart warmed as he remembered that she was strong, she was wise, she was brave. She had come through things that others would not have survived. And no matter what happened, he knew she would find a way.

Then his mind turned to the other person he cared about most in the world. What... what would become of Semerkhet, when this was all over? Tutankhamun bit his lip as the question troubled him. His friend had many transferable skills— administration, team leadership, makeup artistry, household management, nursing... The Pharaoh knew that Sem could find a meaningful career in Memphis or Thebes, especially after studying medicine with Merneith.

But would he be all right? Would he be safe? And would Meresankh, who had become Ankh's sister just as Sem had become Tutankhamun's brother, be all right?

A little purr made Tut smile. Dear little Bastet had hopped up onto the end of the bed and was making her way over the blankets toward him. Gratefully, he held out one arm, giving her a space to settle in right next to his body. And he smiled as he felt her purr again.

He bit his lip. What would happen to Bastet? He... wouldn't be around much longer, and Ankh... who knew what political drama she would be facing as his widow. She did not need to be burdened by the responsibility of a cat.

But who could he entrust her to? Who would love his furry little friend just as he had? Who would keep her safe?

Tutankhamun held Bastet close and wondered.

Taking a moment in her room, Ankh wrote two letters; one to Amenia and one to Mutnedjmet. And she told them that she was moving away to Sais. Maybe the Prince would get here early and they would have ten sons; maybe she would never have to send these messages. But just in case... she wanted to let her friends know.

292

Then she looked down at the letters she had written. And she remembered the paperwork wars and document-stealing that she and the Vizier had been engaged in. A paper trail was the last thing they needed. And she had just prepared two pieces of written evidence that would probably convince the Vizier that she should be executed for treason, baby or no baby. So she got up and placed her letters in the incense burner.

She would have Meresankh deliver her message, if it became necessary. In person.

Then there was a knock at the door. And as she unlocked it, she smiled to see Meresankh leading Little Nefertiti.

"You wanted to see me, My Lady?" the little girl asked.

Ankh got up with a smile, holding out a hand. Shyly, Nefertiti shook it. "I have a question for you, actually," the Queen said. "An idea. You said the things you wanted most were a home and a family... and that's all I want, too."

Nefertiti looked around the beautiful room. "But you have a home, My Lady."

Ankh sighed. "Well... things are changing. And it's possible that I'm going to be moving away. And if that happens, I won't... won't be Queen anymore. And the baby and I..." She put her hand on her belly, and Nefertiti gave a delighted gasp, "are going to move to Sais for awhile. So I want to ask you... if you will come with us."

The little girl blinked. "Come with you, My Lady? You mean..."

Ankh nodded. "As my companion. As my mother's helper. As... as my friend. I'll go to school, and you can watch the baby. And then someday, we'll come back to Memphis, and I'll work at one of the schools the Pharaoh and I had built as a history teacher, and you can study at one of the schools." She smiled. "I need someone to help me. And I was hoping it could be you."

Slowly a smile spread across Nefertiti's face. "Go to school? Thank you, My Lady," she whispered. Then she paused. "If you're not going to be Queen anymore… is the Pharaoh coming with us? Is he not going to be Pharaoh anymore either?"

Ankhesenamun bowed her head. Out of the corner of her eye she saw Nefertiti's forehead crinkle in concern as the little girl watched her new guardian's face fall. Ankh swallowed. And she looked up again.

"The Pharaoh…" she said slowly, "he won't be able to come with us." The child's eyes filled with tears, but Ankh continued. "He's very sick. And his legs are never going to get better. I've written a letter to the Prince of the Hittites, asking him to come to Egypt to be my husband." The Queen paused. "But we don't know if he'll say *yes*, and even if he does… we don't know if he'll get to Egypt safely. So I will wait for the Pharaoh's… funeral, and see if the Prince is here yet. And if he's not, then after the funeral, it won't be safe for me to stay here anymore, because the people who didn't like the Pharaoh don't like me even more. So, to keep myself and the baby safe, I'll move away."

Slowly, Nefertiti nodded, eyes filling with sadness as she took in the news that the Pharaoh was dying. "I understand, My Lady," she said. Then she paused. "But what if the Prince does come, and you don't have to move away? Do you still want me to come live with you?"

The Queen's heart warmed. "Yes," she said gently. "If I get to stay Queen, I would be honored if you would stay here. I'll still need your help. And you'll be able to go on learning from Lady Merneith."

294

Little Nefertiti smiled. "Yes, My Lady."

Ankh tapped her chin. This child was so respectful. But if they were going to be living together, she didn't want Nefertiti to feel like she was a servant. So she said,

"If you want to… you can call me *Auntie*. And you… you will be Auntie to my baby."

Nefertiti just grinned. Cautiously stepping forward, she reached a shy hand toward Ankh's belly. Gently the Queen took her little hand and let her feel. There was nothing to feel yet. But someday soon, they would be rejoicing together over every little kick.

"I know all about babies, Auntie," Nefertiti said confidently. Ankh smiled at how comfortably she had slipped into the name. "I helped with my baby sisters, and my baby brother." She blinked back tears, and the Queen reached out a hand for her to clasp. The little girl swallowed, eyes clearing. "But I know how to feed them, and wash them, and change their swaddling, and get them to sleep, and help them when they have colic…"

Ankh nodded with a smile. This child knew more than she did. And she was happy to do it.

"It sounds as though you're exactly the helper I need," the Queen said appreciatively. She chuckled. "Because I don't know how to do any of those things."

Nefertiti blinked. "You don't?"

Ankh shook her head with a smile. "Not yet. But I have a… a friend who just had a baby, and another friend who's going to have one, so I'll be able to practice before we leave. Even if the Prince doesn't come, I won't have to move away until— until the funeral, which makes at least two months," she clarified. "So you… you would be staying with Granny, like you have been, until Phamenoth or Pharmouthi. And you can learn as much as you can about herbs and medicine, and I can learn as much as I can about cooking and cleaning and doing laundry and being a mommy."

Nefertiti's eyebrows rose. "You don't know how to cook? Or wash clothes? Or do dishes?" She gave a little chuckle, and under her air of respect, Ankh could sense a devilish sense of humor. The child shook her head. "You palace people... you *have* everything, but you don't know how to *do* anything!"

Ankh laughed. "No, I don't. Not yet. But I'll learn."

This time, Nefertiti reached out to take the Queen's hand. "I'll help you." She nodded at Ankh's belly. "And I'll ask Granny to teach me how to take care of you. And Baby. Because I don't..." Again, the little girl blinked back tears. And again, Ankh squeezed her hand.

"Neither do I," she whispered. "But I know how much it hurts."

Nefertiti looked up at her, bright, catlike eyes shining with unshed tears. "You do?"

Ankh nodded. "My sisters died, too. All five of them. And I have..." She gulped. "I have two other daughters. Precious daughters I haven't seen for a long, long time."

"I didn't know," Nefertiti whispered. "Did they..."

"They were very young," the Queen said simply. "Very, very young. And I miss them every day." She swallowed. "The past hurts. And it will never disappear. But we have a future, too. A future full of hope."

Nefertiti nodded, a small smile returning to her face as she wiped away her tears. "And I'll help you. And Baby." As the child looked up at her, so courageously ready for anything, the Queen felt a sudden surge of recognition. Meresankh had become a sister to her, but speaking with Nefertiti... also felt like the conversations Ankh had shared so long ago with her sweet sisters. And Little

296

Nefertiti… she was just about the same age as Meketaten had been. Looking at her new friend, Ankh could almost see an echo of her own older sister.

The Queen sighed. "Thank you. Thank you for saying *yes*. I don't know exactly what adventures we'll have… but we'll do it together. I promise."

She opened her arms, and carefully, Nefertiti stepped into them for a hug. "I promise too."

# 27   The Vizier

Ankh stayed in her room for a few minutes after Little Nefertiti had gone back to Granny's workshop. She needed another moment to think… about the future.

About the friends she would be leaving behind if she and the baby moved to Sais. And the things she wanted to leave with them.

She reached for her copy of the Queens List. The Queens List that she would take with her to Sais; that one day, she would share with her child and with Little Nefertiti, just as her mother and grandmother had shared it with her and her sisters.

And she wiped away tears. Because the chain was not broken. As her niece, Nefertiti-Tasherit would hear, alongside the baby, the same stories Ankh had grown up hearing; the stories handed down from the days of her grandmother's grandmother's grandmother. And when she grew up, she would teach her daughters, her granddaughters. And this legacy would never die.

In her own hand, Ankh copied out the Queens List. Four times. For her friend Meresankh, for her friend Amenia, for her friend Mutnedjmet, for her friend Meryt. And she smiled. Because even though they might be separated by time, space, and uncertainty, this powerful legacy would connect them. And all of them would continue to grow, learning from the wise Queens of the past, using the lessons of ages past to guide their own choices, help them forge their own paths. And they, too, would raise up the women of the next generation, their daughters, nieces, and students. And these truths, these lessons, would go on and on, outliving them all.

It was because they had a past that they had a future.

298

As the afternoon wore on, Tut was glad when his moments of wakefulness coincided with a brief visit from a servant or two— Shepset, Kamose, Tentamun, bringing pitchers of water, bowls of fruit, fresh linens; taking away used cloths and dirty dishes. He smiled at them when he could, acknowledging their hard work with gratitude; recognizing them as human beings like himself. And he smiled when they smiled back, dipping their heads in respect without feeling that they had to prostrate themselves on the floor.

He thought back to before his birthday, when he had first realized that the servants were as human as he was. And even with everything that had happened, he was so, so glad that he knew it.

Meresankh sighed. And with a purposeful smile, she sat down with her Granny to write down every word of the precious stories Merneith had told Meresankh a thousand times; every word of the priceless religious histories that had always given them the strength to face whatever tomorrow might bring. From the arrival of the future Canaanite Vizier in Egypt as the slave of Potiphar to the departure of the Children of Israel from the wrecked remains of the Land of the Nile after the ten deadly miracles I-AM had sent to free them, Meresankh wrote down the precious chronicles, praying with every word she wrote that they would bring her friend the same courage they had always brought her.

She imagined her friend learning from these pages; imagined her, one day, teaching the timeless truths they recorded to her child. And she smiled. No matter how long it was before they saw one another again, these words would keep them with one another.

Then she shook her head with a sigh. The Queen knew that the gods and goddesses of Egypt were only stories, but she had not yet embraced the Light of I-AM. So Meresankh would wait, and pray, and ask the Lord when the time was right to give her friend the histories that would guide her in solving all the mysteries of life.

Then she got out her Granny's collection of recipes. And Meresankh kept writing, detailing the many teas Merneith had prepared for the Queen to support her and her child, preparations that would help minimize uncomfortable signs like morning sickness, even Granny's famous spicy chicken. And again, she smiled. They might be separated in time and space. But with these words, these truths, these recipes, her friend, her sister, would be all right.

"She said *yes*," Ankh whispered. Tut opened his eyes to see his sister smiling, a smile that was satisfied… and the tiniest bit excited. "Nefertiti-Tasherit," she went on. "So if the time comes… she'll come with me to Sais. And I'll be her Auntie… and she'll be Auntie to the baby. And even if the Prince comes, and we get to stay here, she'll stay in the palace as my companion."

"Good," he whispered back. "I'm glad. Tho glad… you have each other. Won't be alone."

"So am I," the Queen agreed. For half an instant she wondered if she should go get the little girl, bring her to see the Pharaoh one last time, give them a chance to say goodbye… but already, her brother's eyes were closing again. With a sad little smile, she bent to kiss his forehead. Her question was answered.

Ankhesenamun smiled as she thought of Amenia and Mutnedjmet and Meresankh poring over the Queens List as she herself had so many times. And she felt a little ache in heart as she hoped that Meryt would accept them. And that one day,

Mayamenti and Tjauenmaya would learn from them too, and that they would know, truly know, that the world was theirs.

Meresankh gave a sad sigh. She wanted to talk to her Queen, her best friend. Wanted to pour out her heart to her, her frustrations, her pain, her sadness that she and Semerkhet might be barred from joining one another in marriage. Wanted to ask her friend for help.

But just like when they had been waiting for the Pharaoh to come home from Kadesh, the handmaiden felt the warm, gentle touch of the Sun inside her heart; a whisper that now was not the time. And she deferred. She knew that things would either work out or they would not. But as the Queen's husband lay dying, it was not time for Meresankh to burden her friend, her Mistress, with her concerns about her own hopes of marriage.

So she said nothing.

Semerkhet fed Tutankhamun a bowl of beef broth for dinner, or at least as much of it as he would eat. And the Queen had a simple plate of beans and a few small pieces of unseasoned chicken. Because nothing tasted quite right. And anything with a strong smell made her stomach do somersaults. This was beginning to feel very familiar.

"The rumors are getting bad, My Lady," Meresankh said softly as she stepped into the Pharaoh's room with a tray, ready to clear away the dinner dishes. This was far beneath Meresankh's station, something a lower-ranking maid would usually do, but she wanted to. It felt good to know that she was helping. How strange it was, though, to enter her Pharaoh's chamber with a simple knock; to actually consider it normal to walk in and out of his royal room ten times a day. Everything about life was so strange now.

The Queen looked up from staring at the Pharaoh's hand, wrapped around her own as he drowsed, the cat beside him. Slowly she stood up, softly kissing him on the forehead and gently placing his hand back on the blanket.

"Hmm?" she asked. Ankh nodded in the direction of her brother's sitting room, and Meresankh followed her, taking the chair across from the Queen's.

The handmaiden gave a little frown, then began. "All kinds of questions are going around the staff... and people are thinking up answers, whether or not they make sense. Some of them are saying the Vizier will be the next Pharaoh and General Nakhtmin will be the next Crown Prince, some of them are saying something about you marrying into the Mitanni royal family, and some of them are saying that General Horemheb will never come home or that Ay's already killed him, or that the Hittites are about to take us over. None of them really know what's going on, but they're all scared. And they're trying to answer their own questions... but oy, vavoy, are they doing it wrong."

The Queen gave a little sigh. Then she smiled at her friend. "Sounds like I need my effective communicator." Meresankh grinned, looking at her Mistress for whatever her instructions would be. "Why don't you start another story," Ankh said. "Tell them that the Queen has a plan. Several plans, in fact. And that she won't let Nakhtmin become Pharaoh or the Hittites destroy us. We still have options. And whatever might still fall through, we'll figure something out. Tell them... not to lose hope. Because even though things look bad... it'll be all right."

"What about the staff that are loyal to the Vizier?" Meresankh asked quietly.

"Tell them too," Ankh said with a shrug. "We're at war, Meresankh. And the allies of our enemies need to know where we draw our line in the sand. And which side they're on... and which side we're on."

The handmaiden nodded, squaring her shoulders. "I'll tell them," she said. "What they do with the message is up to them."

Ankhesenamun smiled. Her friend was right. "Yes. It is."

"But we have courage," Meresankh said. She reached out and took Ankh's hand. "Like your mother."

Ankh just smiled again.


"Not that it matterth tho much," Tut murmured a little while later, and his sister bent closer to hear his soft voice, his voice that seemed to grow weaker every time he used it. "Not really... but what ith... what ith my legathy? How will they remember me... if they remember me at all?" He knew he was lisping, but he didn't care. Trying not to no longer seemed to matter. So he didn't try any longer. Just let the words come out the way they did. His sister could understand him.

Ankh felt tears coming to her eyes. She took her brother's cold hands, holding them tightly as she gave him a smile. "You will be remembered," she promised. "No matter what they do. Even if history hides you... a day will come when everyone will remember you. And they will remember you for your courage, your strength, your determination. For how you never let anything hold you back from being a great Pharaoh... a strong Pharaoh. For rebuilding Egypt from the ground up after our grandfather's slaves left, through education and expanding the workforce, not on the backs of slaves.

"For building schools so everyone could learn the skills they need to live their best life, regardless of their background. Giving the people an economy where they can be sure of supporting themselves with a good job and a fair wage, and only fair taxes to pay. For seeing all people as human; seeing men, women, rich, poor, freeborn, slave-born, Nubian, Egyptian, Mitanni, Hittite, as worthy of receiving the opportunity to get an education and build the lives they want. And they will remember you... as a King of peace."

Tutankhamun just smiled up at his sister through his own tears. It warmed his heart to hear that no matter what happened... he would not be forgotten.

Ay came in again that evening, standing in the doorway like a ghost, tall, spindly, bringing death wherever he went. Bastet growled like a lion, ears flattening against her skull.

"They've begun painting your tomb," Ay said quietly. "The picture of you being greeted by Osiris is particularly nice. And my secretary has just seen to the hiring of the wailing women for your funeral. I shall be honored to perform the Opening of the Mouth ceremony for you before taking my place as Pharaoh."

Tut rolled his head, fixing his bleary eyes on his Vizier. The poppy was working, but Merneith's carefully measured dose was controlling his pain without making it impossible to think clearly. He smiled.

"That remainth to be theen," he whispered, refusing to elaborate.

"You're not allowed in here," Semerkhet said angrily, standing up with his fist clenched. "Brother, would you like me to summon a guard?"

"I think you'll find that my power around the palace is difficult to curtail, as long as I am Grand Vizier," Ay said smoothly. "Your bodyguard has known me longer than he has known you, for example."

Tut just stared at the broken legs under his blanket. He was going to convey his royal displeasure with complete silence. *If you try to use that hemp incense again to make me sign something, I may have to set Semerkhet on you,* he thought. But something told him it wouldn't be productive to say it out loud.

Beside him, the Queen was also expressing her royal displeasure with icy silence, a deadly glare that might have turned a lesser man to stone. But she said nothing.

"And I am sorry to hear that your joyous announcement was nothing more than a front," Ay continued smoothly. "After so much pain, I almost would have wished you joy. Your handmaiden was very helpful."

The Queen went white. The Pharaoh watched her face fill with horror. And his stomach clenched as he wondered just how the Vizier had exploited Meresankh.

"And so I talked to Kemsit," the Vizier went on, voice dripping with poisoned honey. "That was enough. That is almost always enough." He gave a simpering sneer. "She admitted to preparing the pregnancy test for you. Kemsit is the wise one. She knows when she is beaten. She knows who is truly master of Egypt."

Tutankhamun released a deep breath, blowing out his growing anger with it. His only hope was to be more mature than the Vizier. And to be sweet and deadly. Civil and sneaky. Courageous and cunning. If he lost his temper, everything else would be lost as well.

"And whether our announcement was a front... only the future can say," Ankh said, covering her belly protectively. "Thank you for the tea, by the way. I had the herbs in it identified and disposed of it. You'll want to make sure that the next time you send a gift to a pregnant woman, it isn't one that might endanger her child. Imagine what might have happened if I had drunk it."

The Grand Vizier just looked away, picking at a loose thread on his sleeve.

"And may I offer my congratulations on stealing back your signet-ring, as well as the proclamation I had prepared," he said smoothly, nodding at the ring that gleamed on the Queen's hand. "And, of course, switching the two letters to the Hittites. You've become quite the politicians— I must say, I taught you well. You've won yourself back those seventy days, and for that I salute you. Of course, I still may send a... welcoming party to greet Prince Zannanza, but if the Hittite King agrees, he should make the journey to Egypt, just as you planned."

Ankhesenamun clenched her fists. She knew what battle re-mained for her to fight after Tut was gone. Were enough guards loyal to her and her brother for her to send a squadron to protect the Hittite from the assassins the Vizier surely meant to send? Or would defending her own life, and that of her child, force her to turn her back completely on the danger the Prince was facing? The danger... into which she had invited him?

"Nuya made a bad decision," the Vizier said softly. "I'm not going to execute him," he said, "not so soon before your own tragic death... but once your funeral is complete and I have taken

306

my place as the next Pharaoh, there will be no place for him in my palace."

Inside his heart, the Pharaoh sighed. So Nuya's job would be eliminated. His heart ached with regret that the faithful scribe had been punished for his loyalty… but he was thankful that Nuya was still alive. And grateful beyond measure for the loyalty with which Nuya had helped ensure that the Queen's letter made it to Hattusa.

"General Horemheb should be home tomorrow, or the nektht day," Tut pointed out. "And you won't be on the throne when he getth here, like you thought. Once he theeth what you've done, and what a terrible Pharaoh you'll be, what'th to keep him from beating you to the throne, other than the threat of a civil war he would be willing to fight?"

"His love for his wives," Ay said dismissively. And again Ankhesenamun clenched her teeth in silent fury. "I haven't harmed them… yet," he said, lip curling in a sneer. "But when he arrives, he will find them both in the dungeon. And if he refuses to cede the throne to me, he will never see them again."

The Pharaoh's stomach twisted. So Horemheb's wives were the bargaining pawns the Vizier had spoken of all those days ago.

"Where are they?" the Queen was about to ask, but she knew that would be a bad move. As would… as would trying to free them. If she jumped in, then if their lives were in danger now, she truly might be condemning them to death.

So she would do something else. After the Vizier left. And she let out her anger with a deep breath. She had to be calm. Crafty. Use all her wisdom. Not leave any openings.

Then the Vizier's hand disappeared into his robes. When it reappeared, he was holding the blue ring inscribed with his name next to hers.

"One more chance, My Lady," he whispered. "To remain Queen. *My* Queen. Your image is nowhere to be found in your brother's tomb. Let me be the husband you share eternity with."

She looked at him calmly, eyes hard and deadly under dark eyebrows. Again, she had no choice but to turn herself to stone; resist the urge to raise her voice; to get up and slap him across the face. Only as a calm, collected, calculating politician would she defeat him. "My answer has not changed, Vizier," she said quietly. "And it will not change."

"Very well," the Vizier said softly. "So be it." Slowly, he replaced the ring inside his robes. "I'm also sorry to inform you that when I take the throne, construction on your expensive new schools will halt immediately," he sneered. "We cannot justify expending such high levels of resources building and staffing five new institutions for the education of peasants."

"Well, the people of Babylonia and Alashiya and Retjenu sure will be dithappointed," Tut said with a sigh. "We juth thent invitations to them, and three or four other countrieth ath well." Tut smiled. "Post juth went out, in fact. Thertainly would be a shame to have to tell them that there wouldn't be any schoolth."

Keeping his face impassive, he took a shuddering breath, struggling to fill his now-empty lungs with air even as the pain of the inhale cut like a knife. Interpreting his pause, his sister stepped into the gap.

"Or," she continued, "to have to tell them that the decent minimum wage, ban on slavery, moderate taxes, and educational opportunities for women that we promised them were no longer the case. We also informed them that the first school will open next year, and invited them to send us some ambassadors in the meantime, so they could see our progress. And we asked them to partner with us in building the schools, and to send us teachers as well as students."

The Vizier just looked at them as though he was trying to decide what to say. And Tut smiled to himself. Was it just possible that they truly had him cornered? He prayed it was so.

Then Ay looked at Semerkhet with narrowed eyes, Semerkhet, who was beginning to look dangerous. Was he actually looking at the dagger on the wall? "Be careful, Your Excellency."

"Thank you, Semerkhet," the Pharaoh said gently. His valet had sunk back into his chair, holding his head as if in exhaustion. "I think the Vizier is wise enough to know when he's not wanted." Now he glared up at the old man, thunder rumbling in his gaze.

And Ay was gone, robes rippling behind him like the wings of a vulture.

The cat snorted furiously.

Tut shuddered as the Vizier left. Somehow, he had a strange sense that they would not meet again.

And what would happen remained to be seen.


The Pharaoh looked at Semerkhet, having seen his anger, heard his sigh, and now seeing him bent with exhaustion, his head in his hands.

"You all right?" he asked.

Slowly Semerkhet looked up, trying to give his friend a smile. The rage had passed, leaving him weak with exhaustion. But satisfied, because he had defeated it.

"I'm all right."

"You?" Tut asked, looking up at his brave wife; his brave wife who had just fended off the proposal delivered right in front of her soon-to-be-departed husband.

She nodded curtly, giving him a grimly satisfied smile. "Just fine."

"What in the Ten Plagues does that man think he's doing in here?" an angry old voice asked, cutting through the reflective silence. Merneith came creakily into sight, a steaming cup of some new tea in her old, wrinkled hand. She set it down on the table. "Doesn't he know he's not wanted?" As the three of them watched, she stomped to the door through which Ay had just exited and called, "And stay out!"

Slamming the door with a satisfying bang and an angry mutter of "Oy, vavoy," she turned back into the room, brushing her hands off as if even that interaction had dirtied them.

"Some people need more forceful handling, Your Majesty," Granny said with a creaky chuckle. Tut shook his head with his own chuckle, and was pleased to see that Semerkhet was laughing too. Ankh's icy glare, too, melted as she smiled. That had been just the medicine they had needed.

How many more times did they have to laugh together?

"Now where was I?" Merneith said, picking up the cup she had set down. "I made a new mixture for you. Chamomile, lavender, and valerian, all together." She smiled. "The one combination we haven't tried yet."

Tutankhamun smiled as Ankh gently held the cup to his lips, letting him take a sip. Already he was beginning to feel a little sleepy, even aside from the poppy he'd taken, a higher dose calculated to see him through the morning. What a relief.

# 28   Courage

"Just... tell me... what happened," the Queen whispered, leaning forward in her chair to rest her head on her hands, her elbows propped on her knees. Ankh had marched across the hall to her chambers shortly after the Vizier had left her brother's room, full of questions for her handmaiden. And safe behind locked doors, they were going to talk.

Beside her, Meresankh swallowed, digging her toe into the floor as she clasped her dimpled hands in front of her.

"I'm sorry, My Lady—" she began, but Ankh cut her off.

"Just tell me," she repeated.

"I tried to be careful," Meresankh cried, voice rising in pitch and volume as a sob caught in her throat. "I didn't gossip. I just wanted to thank Kemsit for doing the seed test for us, and I tried to be quiet— he must have sent someone to spy on me; I never, never would have said anything if I thought anyone was listening—"

"I know you wouldn't," Ankh said tonelessly. "I know you didn't. It's not your fault. It's just... just politics." She blew out a heavy breath, pressing her fingertips against her temples. "Just politics. Just like everything else. And all we have to do is figure out what to do now..." She shook her head, sitting up. "It doesn't really matter," she decided. "He knows that the test was faked. But it is still possible that we were telling the truth. There's still hope."

"Can you ever forgive me?" Meresankh whispered, a tear running down each cheek and taking her makeup with it.

The Queen sighed. And standing up, she opened her arms. Bowed down by the weight of her mistake, Meresankh stepped into them. Gently, Ankh put her arms around her, holding her close.

"It's not your fault," she whispered. "It's not your fault."

The Pharaoh's bodyguard had betrayed him, letting the Vizier into the royal bedroom against orders. So at his brother's instruction, Semerkhet went and fetched Hannu, installing him as an immediate replacement. And then the Sole Companion told the traitorous Minnefer that he could pack his bags. Sem didn't tell him how they knew what he had done; just told him he was done at the palace. And Semerkhet allowed himself a proud little smile of satisfaction. He had used his authority as Sole Companion to fire the traitor and protect his little brother. Sem had not asked royal permission before making this decision. But he knew that he had done the right thing.

Now Hannu stood in Minnefer's place. And they knew they could sleep safely tonight.

Sem didn't come back to the Pharaoh's room the moment he had finished talking to Hannu. He sat down on a bench out in the hallway, slowly letting his back bend, lowering his head until his forehead almost touched his knees. Because he felt so lightheaded, a strange rushing inside his skull.

His heart was still pounding; his stomach still roiling. His palms were slick with sweat, and his teeth were chattering, even though he was wearing a warm outer robe. And it was good that he had sat down, as his knees had been shaking as badly as the rest of him. He had almost committed murder.

He closed his eyes, burying his face in his hands. And he tried to pray for strength.

Semerkhet bumped into Meresankh just as he was bringing a bowl of fruit to the Pharaoh's room.

"You all right?" Meresankh asked, looking at him in concern. She set aside the basket of wigs she was taking to the cleaners', then took Semerkhet's hands once he had found a place to set the bowl of fruit. She looked into his face, waiting for what he would say. "I heard about the Vizier coming in. That snake."

He gave a heavy sigh, looking down. "I am now." Sem shook his head with another sigh, then nodded at a nearby bench. "Can we sit down?"

Meresankh picked up the basket again, setting it beside the bench as she sat down next to him, taking one of his hands in both of hers. "So, what happened?" she asked gently.

Semerkhet frowned. "Snake is right. Barging in when he knew he wasn't allowed in; standing there and telling the Pharaoh how nice his tomb looks..." The valet's voice shook with anger, and he had to check himself before crushing Meresankh's fingers in an angry grip. He swallowed and closed his eyes, letting his returning anger dissipate. "So, the Vizier was standing there, and I just... just felt so angry... I felt like I... like I wanted to kill him. And not just that I wanted to— like I really could. In that moment, I... I thought I could. Thought I would." He swallowed again, looking down at his hand, held in Meresankh's. "And I saw that the Pharaoh's dagger was hanging where it always was... and I thought... I could do it. I could get up, take that dagger, and end it all. And that snake would be dead."

Meresankh listened silently, letting him tell his story. Taking a deep breath, he went on. "And I was going to do it," he said. "I really was. But..." He smiled as he remembered the feeling that had touched his heart, as gentle as a tap on the shoulder, as the warmth

313

of the Sun on his face. "Something stopped me. And I thought... thought of what would happen if I did. If I killed the Vizier, I'd be arrested again, and this time, I would be executed. And then... I would never see my brother again. And I wouldn't... wouldn't be able to protect him. He'd be in danger. And it would be my fault.

"And I thought..." Semerkhet gave a little chuckle. "I thought what he would say. What he did say when he told us that the Vizier had killed Princess Meritaten, and I told him how I was willing to kill Ay for it. The Pharaoh asked me... asked me if I would trust him. And that's what I heard him say. In my mind. *Trust me.* And then it was over. I mean, I was still angry, but I wasn't..." He shook his head. "Wasn't going to pick up that knife and kill the Vizier. And I... I let the Vizier go. And then..." This time he really did laugh. "Granny came in and said he should know he wasn't wanted. And that... that was it. He left. I... I got through it; I suppose. But there was that one moment..." Semerkhet clenched his free hand into a fist. "When I was going to."

Meresankh looked up at him. And slowly, she smiled. "I'm proud of you," she said softly. "That was hard. So hard. But you did it. And now..." She smiled, squeezing his hand. "You can keep doing what you do best. Right until the very end."

She gulped back tears, and he shook his head with a sniffle of his own. "Don't you start," he said with a sad little chuckle. "Or we'll be here all day."

Meresankh wiped her eyes, then scooted forward and opened her arms. And silently, Semerkhet accepted a hug. He knew that no matter what happened, they would face it together.

Meresankh's heart seemed to glow with gratitude as she thought of the story Semerkhet had just told her of what he had nearly

314

done. He had grown so much over the past year… and I-AM had been there with him, as surely as they breathed, gently holding him back from a violent revenge. He had listened, even when walking away was the hardest thing he had ever done. She was so proud of him.

As Semerkhet helped Tut drink his tea, Ankhesenamun sat and thought of Amenia and Mutnedjmet; prayed for them, even if she wasn't sure anymore to Whom she was praying. She would not stop praying for her brave friends.

She thought of them, shivering with cold in the dungeon. She hoped they were together, and wondered how miserable they were if they were each alone. Poor pampered flowers of the palace garden, she thought. Sitting there weighed down by their elaborate wigs, unable to get comfortable on the benches they were expected to sleep on, still hungry after a simple, insufficient meal of plain gruel or stale flatbread. Wondering… wondering if they were going to be executed. Hoping and praying that their husband would be home in time to save them.

Her heart ached as her stomach twisted. Her intuition from all those days ago had been correct. The Vizier was treating human beings as pawns in this horrible game of *seega*. Just like her own brother, just like the General. Ay was maneuvering the people around him on the gameboard of life, plotting in every direction at the same time to scheme himself toward the throne.

The Queen sighed. And she wished she could let her friends know that she was thinking of them. And how much she cared about them. Just… Ankh clenched her hands, fingernails digging into her palms. Just like she had felt a few weeks ago, when they had sent their notes to her, telling her that they missed her, wanted

315

her to know that they were thinking of her, praying for her. She wished she could send them that same warmth, that same feeling that they were not alone, that they had sent to her.

She shook her head. Right now, she couldn't communicate with them. But when he got home... the General would rescue his twin trophies.


Meresankh's heart ached as she went over and over her terrible mistake in her mind; the way she had carefully drawn Kemsit aside one day at lunch, speaking so softly as she had thanked her for what she had done for them. She had checked their surroundings first; she had not spoken until she had been sure she recognized everyone around them and that none of them were paying attention to her conversation. She had been careful.

Just not careful enough.

But she was forgiven, she reminded herself. And for good or for ill, there really was nothing to do... but keep moving forward.


"What can we do?" Tut asked his sister. "For Amenia and Mutnedjmet? I'm the Pharaoh; I should be able to thnap my fingerth and set them free. But... what would happen if I did?"

The Queen shook her head. "You're a politician; do you know that?" she said softly. She squeezed his hand. "If the Vizier would order the doctor to poison you for caring about people... would try to poison the baby to keep me off the throne... what would happen, if you ordered them to be released?" She sighed. "What indeed?"

"Hate to thay it... but they're probably thafer in prithon," Tutankhamun said thoughtfully. "They've helped uth tho much, and they'd want to help uth again. And that would— would make

316

the Vithier angry. Tho to make sure they don't try to help uth, maybe they should… should stay until Horemheb getth home. I'm thorry… but I fink they might be thafer that way."

Ankh's wig jingled as she gave a heavy sigh. "I think they might be, love. I think they might be."


The King lay on his back, breathing slowly as he struggled to fill his lungs. Every breath was pain, every movement, every thought. Hot, roaring pain. It was so cold out. But he was so hot, the fever burning through his body.

But it was almost bedtime. And Semerkhet's bedtime routine always got him to sleep. There was hope.

Even if Kamose stood there beside the valet. Because the Pharaoh was too weak, and yet too big, for Semerkhet to be able to safely move him without help. His legs were destroyed, lying wasted in their splints, the left one oozing pus onto the bandages and the extra bedsheets Semerkhet had placed under it. But thanks to Granny's poppy, his legs were not literally too painful for him to be turned from his back to his side.

"You ready?"

Tutankhamun gave his valet a tired smile and a grateful little nod. Semerkhet nodded, setting two large, wool-filled pillows at the foot of the bed, the ones from Horemheb's wives. Standing at the King's side, Semerkhet and the soldier worked together to carefully help him slide to the edge of the bed. Kamose put a hand on his bony shoulder and Sem placed a hand on his prominent hip, preparing to roll him onto his side. Taking a deep breath, they began to press their hands into the King's body, starting to roll him toward them.

The Pharaoh winced.

Semerkhet took his hands away, frowning down at him with a wince of his own. Kamose also backed away.

"Are you sure you want to do this?" Sem asked softly. "We don't have to, if it's too hard on you."

The King just shook his head with a small chuckle. "How elth am I thuppothed to get to sleep?"

Sem returned the smile. How else?

They placed their hands against Tut's side again. "One, two, three…"

And with a grunt, the Pharaoh flopped onto his side. Semerkhet got the pillows and arranged them against the King's chest and under his thin arm, making sure his friend's body was supported. Another sheet and a pillow went between Tut's splinted legs.

With a bow, Kamose excused himself. And Semerkhet opened up the little jar of frankincense-and-spikenard ointment that was Tut's only hope. The Pharaoh smiled at the sweet, familiar fragrance. It smelled like bedtime.

Semerkhet gave a little smile as he looked down at the King, lying quietly in the bed. Time to try to get him to sleep. He hoped it would work.

Tonight it was his turn to settle the Pharaoh into bed. Yesterday it had been the Queen's, and it would be her turn again tomorrow. And yet tonight, Sem had a strange feeling. And a question chilled his heart.

Would he be doing this again the night after next?

Would he need to?

Tut sighed, giving a little smile as he tried to relax. So many days, good and bad, had ended with his valet rubbing his back.

318

Sem had taken care of him for a year and two months. Tut thought back over that time; the way that at the beginning, he hadn't even seen Sem as a real person, only one of the semi-anonymous servants who dressed him, bathed him, helped him through his day. So much had changed since then.

And now it was ending. The King felt a lump in his throat as it hit him again that every time he saw Semerkhet, that was one time fewer to see him in the future. One time fewer to talk to him, to hear his cheerful laugh, to hear his chipper "Yes, Master," to see the sweet smile that always seemed to make things a little better. Even right now... was this the last time Semerkhet would rub his back?

He gave a deep sigh, releasing all those deep thoughts at the same time. If this was the last time, he had better enjoy every moment.

*How many times have I done this?* Sem wondered silently. *Too many to count.* Semerkhet tucked the King in and silently got up. There was a certain satisfaction in seeing his friend fall asleep because of the comfort he'd just brought him. Just like Tribute Day, a lifetime ago, it seemed, and the solid hour he had spent patiently ironing out the king's stiff muscles at the end of the long, long day. And... He bit his lip. Just like putting Nedjes to bed, all those years ago. It felt good to be a big brother again.

Then the valet sighed. Every day that went by, he knew, meant that one fewer was left in the future. The strange feeling came back, stronger. Even now... could it be possible that this had been the very last time that he would hear that soft, satisfied sigh as he ran his fingertips down the King's spine, feeling him fall asleep?

The sun was setting on their time together.

He sat down again, adjusting Tut's blankets for no reason other than simply to do it; to be near him. It would do no harm to sit here and watch him sleep.

Then he wondered. If I-AM, the God of the Hebrews, was real… could He help Tutankhamun?

# 29   The Wedding Gift

Morning came. Semerkhet saw Meresankh and Merneith praying together at the foot of Tut's bed as the Pharaoh continued to sleep; heard their soft voices.

They looked so peaceful; so full of deep and abiding joy. As if they knew in the core of their being that they were being heard by Someone Who loved them.

How he wanted that. He had worshiped in the Temple of Amun-Ra, of Isis, of Horus. He had knelt before the images of the gods and goddesses of Egypt and prayed.

But not once had he received a response. Life had gone on, some of the things he had prayed for happening, others not; some of the things he had asked to be spared from not happening, others coming just as if he had never made the request. And those prayers had never brought him peace. The only prayers that had brought him peace had been those he had desperately murmured in the darkness of the cart that had carried them home from Kadesh. Those prayers, he remembered with an ache of longing, had filled his heart with a warmth as loving as the Light of the Sun.

But as he watched Meresankh and Merneith, that was what he saw. Peace and blessed assurance.

Something twisted inside him. Suddenly, that feeling of direction, of being heard, that warmth that he had always longed for but rarely felt, filled his heart, his whole body. And it pushed him toward Meresankh and her Granny.

Slowly, quietly, he approached the two women, who stood hand-in-hand, heads bowed, surely praying for their Pharaoh. Very, very gently, he touched Meresankh's shoulder, and she looked up at him with tears in her eyes but a smile on her face.

And a Light, such a light, shining from her heart. He could feel it shining from Merneith as well. Even as she stood here praying to the God of the Hebrews, the little silver necklace still gleamed on Meresankh's neck, and he knew that she was right. Isis was only a story, but the necklace had meaning as a symbol of love.

"Can I pray too?" he whispered.

They nodded, and he took their hands. As he joined the circle, he felt connected— to them, and to something, Someone, bigger. And he opened his heart and let the Light in.

A soft murmur gently roused Tut from the long, gentle sleep he had been enjoying. Slowly he opened his eyes, wondering who was talking, what they were saying. Were they telling a story; were they telling secrets?

From where he lay on his side, he squinted around the room, and a sudden warmth rose in his heart. Sem, Meresankh and Merneith were standing by the foot of the bed, hands linked, heads bowed. They were... praying for him. And a light seemed to be shining from their faces, a Light that looked familiar— he had seen it in his parents' faces all those years ago, in the faces of the five sisters he had not seen for so long. And even as tears welled in their eyes, he could see a greater joy there than anyone else in the palace seemed to possess.

Tears sprang to his own eyes as he listened to their words; heard phrases like "Heal him... We love him... Help us find the right herbs... Let him sleep through the night... Help him breathe... Please take away his pain," and, finally, "Great I-AM."

He didn't want to interrupt them. Maybe they didn't need to know that he had woken up; that he was listening to them praying for him.

His parents and sisters had prayed to the Aten, and Semerkhet and Meresankh and Merneith were praying to I-AM. But the Light was the same.

Tutankhamun closed his eyes again, feeling their love surround him, touching him just like the gentle rays of the Sun on those two beautiful days they had spent out in the garden. And again… he wondered what was true.

Meresankh smiled and squeezed Semerkhet's hand as they finished the prayer. She could see the Light in his eyes. He had found the Truth. Her prayers had been answered.

"Thank you for not giving up on me," he whispered.

She chuckled and shook her head. "It's I-AM Who doesn't give up on us."

And she stroked her necklace, a simple symbol of affection from a man to the woman he loved.

"Lady Merneith?" Sem asked when the prayer had come to a close.

"Call me Granny, dearie," she said, shaking her head with a smile, her sparkling eyes almost disappearing under all the happy smile wrinkles.

"Granny." He smiled down at her; the tiny, ancient doctor who had seen so much. He extended his hands slightly, and she took them in hers, her gnarled, bent old fingers closing gently over his. "Can I study with you? I want to be a doctor too. But not like the Chief Physician was. I don't want to give anyone crocodile eyeballs."

She chuckled, a creaky old chuckle like a shoe crunching on crumbling stone. "I don't go in for crocodile eyeballs, or giving

323

dead mice to mothers with sick babies." She brought his hands closer to her face, peering at them as she examined them with her own. "You've got good hands."

He laughed, thinking back. "I know."

"Th… thank you for praying," the Queen said softly as Meresankh brought her a cup of tea and a hot bowl of porridge for breakfast. Ankh had not eaten in the royal feasting hall in days, but Meresankh always brought her her meals. The Queen could trust her sister to protect her from poison.

Meresankh paused, giving her friend a little smile that showed the dimple in her cheek, then a blush. "You're welcome… Ankhesenamun. It's my honor."

Gently Ankh reached out and took Meresankh's hand, giving it a friendly little squeeze. Meresankh looked down with a smile. It felt good to hold hands with a friend, a sister.

"Meresankh…" Ankh said slowly. She wondered how to begin. They had talked about it before, but somehow, she needed to hear it again. "Tell me… tell me about your Lord of Light again."

The handmaiden smiled again. "His Name is I-AM. The God of the Hebrews. My Granny taught me about Him, about how your father the Pharaoh found His Light in the Sun and called Him the Aten."

A chill passed through the Queen. "So the Aten *is* I-AM?" she whispered.

"Aten is what the Pharaoh called him," Meresankh said. "But he wasn't wrong. My Granny saw everything He did in Egypt— the Nile turning to blood, the frogs, the insects, the darkness. Everything that made the Pharaoh turn to Him." She smiled. "The

324

God Who created the world is bigger than any name we might give Him."

Ankh closed her eyes. She was getting very close to something. Very close indeed. It felt almost… like purpose. Like a purpose she had been searching for for a very long time.

"Thank you for praying," she said finally. Then she smiled with a little sigh. "Please don't stop."

Meresankh shook her head with her own smile. "Never."

Meresankh went back to the Queen's room, ready to get her daily work started. Her heart was pounding, and she could almost feel it glowing with the Light that filled it. Semerkhet, her beloved Semerkhet, had accepted I-AM. And the Queen was asking questions. Her prayers were being answered. And she would never stop praying.

Semerkhet went to his own room to get dressed, choose a wig for the day, and check on his knee. Sitting down at his dressing-table, he rested his right foot on his left knee, examining his right knee. Slowly he untied and unwrapped the linen bandage, peering at the healing abrasions. A healthy scar was forming, and only occasionally did it give a twinge of pain. Satisfied, he began to wrap it back up again.

Then he paused. He looked at his knee again; the scar that was forming, a thin, pale line against the warm brown of his skin. The wound was healing, and soon it would stop bothering him at all. But the scar would be there forever.

Wounds healed. But scars remained. Scars didn't disappear. They reminded those who bore them of the things that had happened. Helped them remember. Sem ran his hand over his knee almost lovingly; almost like he would touch the Pharaoh's hand. He would think of his brother whenever he looked at his scar.

Gently he wrapped it up again, putting it away. He would heal. But he would never forget.

The Pharaoh felt better that morning. Really did. He ate a proper breakfast; had the energy to talk, even laugh, with Ankhesenamun and Semerkhet. He felt... he felt as well, or close to it, as he had an entire week previously. And he couldn't help but wonder... had the past few weeks been only a nightmare? A nightmare that was about to end as he resumed his recovery? Were his prayers being answered?

"You're chatty this morning," Ankhesenamun said after enjoying a surprisingly animated conversation with her brother. His eyes were brighter this morning; he had the strength to sit up a little in the bed, and he had had more of an appetite at breakfast. He looked better. Almost... Ankh couldn't let herself hope. But almost as if... everything was turning around. As if he was going to get better.

"I feel better," he agreed with a smile. "*Seega?*"

And shaking her head with a confused but happy sigh, the Queen set up a game. Whether he was simply having a good day or this was the sign she had been hoping against hope to see, the sign that he was going to get better and rule for forty years, she was going to enjoy every moment of it.

They played two games, Tut winning the first by keeping his pieces in a tight formation that prevented his sister from capturing them, and Ankh winning the second through setting a series of

326

traps, luring him into what looked like an easy attack on one of her pieces and capturing his once it was too late. And then Semerkhet came to sit with him, gently bathing his face with a cool cloth as they chatted comfortably about the latest victory of the Stallions against the hockey team from Tamiat.

As the boys talked, Ankh sat and thought. About the future she and her child were facing. And she swallowed back the lump in her throat to think that her days in her beautiful home might be limited. So many memories… and now, each day she spent here meant that one fewer remained in the future. She thought of the houses she and her brother had seen out in Memphis. She knew that wherever she and Little Nefertiti lived, they would make it a home. But she wondered, with a small, wry chuckle, whether it would be larger or smaller than her royal bedroom.

Semerkhet sighed as he pondered the unknown future those left behind were facing; felt the ache in his heart that reminded him that he might never be able to marry his true love, because how could he ever secure the means to support a family? And even if someday he could, how long would they have to wait?

"What is it?" the Pharaoh asked softly. He had heard the sigh; seen the frown that touched his friend's face.

Semerkhet put on a smile and adjusted his brother's blankets. "Just thinking about love and marriage."

Tutankhamun smiled and raised his eyebrows. "You'd better athk her," he said teasingly. "Or she'll fink you're not theriouth."

Sem returned the chuckle, rather sadly. "She knows I'm serious. But things… things are hard. And we're not going to be able to just write our marriage contract and move in together like everyone else."

"Why not?" Tut asked. His sister had told him of the obstacle Semerkhet and Meresankh were facing, but he wanted to give his friend the space to tell him.

His friend sighed again. "Well, for one thing, I don't know what I'm going to do next. I have to get my education from Granny before I can become a doctor, and how long will that take? And if my... my job here at the palace will be... gone... in the meantime... where am I supposed to live while I go to school? I can't ask Meresankh to marry me until I can put a roof over her head. She doesn't have a dowry, either. And I'm not going to get an inheritance from my father. So we wouldn't be starting with much in the way of savings. And then..."

Semerkhet looked down sadly at his hands. "Someone has to speak for us. Write the contract with me... witness the marriage... and give permission. It should be my father. But he'd never do that for me. And there's no one else with the authority. So... we're stuck. If we move in together without a contract, we'll love one another just the same, but it wouldn't be right... and we'd never forget that it wasn't right. But I don't know how long we'll have to wait... because I hardly know what we're waiting for."

The Pharaoh had listened quietly to his friend's explanation of his problem. And now... now he smiled. Because the Lord of the Two Lands, the king of the known world who could change a law with the snap of his fingers, knew how he could help. Even as he pondered this rise in energy, this liveliness he had not enjoyed in days, he still had to continue preparing for the future that might be coming.

"Bring me my signet-ring," the Pharaoh said softly. "And Nuya." Tears began to glimmer in Semerkhet's eyes as he did as he was asked.

As the faithful scribe recorded his proclamation, Tutankhamun dictated the words that would create his friend's future.

*The marriage of Semerkhet, Sole Companion, Favorite of the Pharaoh, and Unique Friend, to Meresankh, Handmaiden to the Queen, is hereby witnessed by His Majesty the Pharaoh on this, the fifteenth day of the month of Tybi. The Sole Companion and his wife are tasked with composing their own marriage contract, which by the authority of the Pharaoh, shall bear full validity.*

After Semerkhet, again fighting back tears, had placed a drop of soft wax on the papyrus, the Pharaoh applied his signet-ring and scribbled his name. He handed the document to his friend with a smile.

"Congratulationth, Sem. You're married. All you have to do ith both thign it." Before his brother could do more than give a shaky laugh of gratitude, the Pharaoh had continued. "We're not done yet." He paused. And he smiled again. Because suddenly he knew, beyond any shadow of doubt, who he could trust to take care of his cat. "But first I have a question." Tut smiled wistfully at Semerkhet, then glanced down at the cat, who was drowsing at the foot of the bed. "Will you and Meresankh take Bastet for us? I'm... I'm out of time, and the Queen... doethn't know what her life will look like, even where she'll live, next. But I... we... would like to know that she'th wiff thomeone who will love her and who we can trust to take good care of her."

With a pensive little sigh, the valet nodded. "It would be our honor," he said softly. Gently he put out a hand, and Bastet padded over to sniff at it. The Pharaoh smiled as slowly, Semerkhet picked Bastet up, holding her close as she purred. She was in good hands.

"Tho that'th settled," Tut said in satisfaction. And paused, covering his mouth as he began to cough. Rolling as far as he could, he grabbed a hanky, clapping it to his mouth as he brought up more of the blood-red stains. When he was finally done, Semerkhet sadly but silently tossed it into the pile of dirty laundry in the corner.

Slowly, Tutankhamun caught his breath, even as pain seared in his chest. And he continued. "Now… on to the nektht order of business." Whatever this rise in energy, improvement in his clarity of thought, meant, he was going to make the most of it as he secured his friend's future.

And as Nuya recorded his words, Tutankhamun issued another royal proclamation.

*By order of His Majesty the Pharaoh, a sum of two hundred measures of gold is to be provided to the Sole Companion, Favorite of the Pharaoh, and Unique Friend Semerkhet, on the occasion of his marriage to Meresankh, Handmaiden to the Queen. Such jewelry, furniture, and other personal possessions of the Pharaoh as he may choose are also bequeathed to him. Furthermore, ownership of such belongings as were possessed by Semerkhet and Meresankh as palace employees, including furniture, is transferred to them, to make use of as they choose. Finally, guardianship of the Royal Cat, Bastet, is entrusted to Semerkhet and his family.*

And as Nuya excused himself with a bow and a murmured wish for the Pharaoh's well-being, Tut signed and sealed the second document.

Semerkhet was still gazing wide-eyed, struggling for words as he let the cat go. Tutankhamun just reached out and took his hands.

"B-b-but— w-what— I d-don't—" Semerkhet was stammering, eyes overflowing with tears. "What are— I don't un—"

Tut just smiled. "Be still," he whispered to his friend. "Pharaoh speaks." That stopped Semerkhet's stumbling words. Bowing his head, the valet waited for his Master's next proclamation.

"I'm not going to need any of thith," Tut continued softly, gesturing toward his room in general. "I'd be honored if you'd pick a few thingth. Anyfing you want. Anyfing Meresankh wants. To liquidate… or to remember me by. I don't need any of it," he said again, "but it'th my honor to put it to good uthe. Tho my brother… tho my brother can get off to a good thtart in life."

And as gently as he could, Semerkhet put his arms around his friend and hugged him for all he was worth.

Semerkhet continued to blink and chuckle at the gift he and Meresankh had been given; the riches they had been promised. And Tut silently smiled at him. *Let me set you for life*, he seemed to say. *Let me take care of you. Let me leave you knowing that you are provided for and will be all right.*

And Semerkhet smiled. He would be all right.

# 30   Plans

She had to ask him. Now that Meresankh knew that Sem had found the Light, that they were standing together in the Truth, she was ready to ask him. Because as life as they knew it came to an end, as one chapter of their lives ended and another began, she had to know for sure.

Even… even if she didn't know when they would be able to make it official. They could still make their promises to one another.

She held the tiny scarab pendant for which she had traded her favorite hair accessory. The body was blue, its outstretched wings formed of tiny pieces of inlaid glass in yellow, blue, and green, and the round solar disc it held between them was red. It was perfect. And she smiled, hope bubbling up in her heart. Hope, even now. Because together, she knew they would be able to find happiness. Even in this.

Their Pharaoh was resting; the Queen sitting quietly beside him, browsing a papyrus and occasionally fighting back a yawn, rubbing her tired eyes with her free hand. Semerkhet was sitting too, staring quietly into space. He looked exhausted, his back curving in a weary slouch, his face a little pale, his eyes bloodshot and underlined with dark circles. His makeup was smudged, and his wig was tangled and a bit lopsided.

The guard nodded at Meresankh, giving her permission to approach. Quietly she knocked, and Semerkhet blinked, sitting up as he looked to see who it was. And his tired face smiled.

Slowly he got up, stretching his weary body as he came to greet her. Meresankh opened her arms, and he stepped forward, gratefully accepting a hug.

"Come here a minute," she said softly, gently taking him by the hand and leading him out into the hallway that led to the Queen's room, the royal study, the grand feasting hall. He paused, as always, wishing his Pharaoh life, prosperity, and health before leaving his side. And the Queen nodded her royal approval of his break.

Meresankh looked both ways, making sure they were alone, Hannu out of earshot. And she smiled up at Semerkhet. Her heart was beginning to pound.

"Sem," she said breathlessly, "I know there's a lot going on right now, but I have to know…" She gave a little laugh, squeezing his hands. "Semerkhet…" she said. "Will you marry me?"

Semerkhet's exhausted eyes went wide as he looked down at her. For a heart-stopping instant she wondered if she had hurt his feelings by moving forward too quickly, being pushy. By being the one to ask, had she changed everything?

And then he smiled. Meresankh grinned again as Sem smiled at her, tired eyes now shining like the Sun as his weariness fell away, replaced by joy. "Yes," he whispered. "Yes. I will."

A happy sob catching in her throat, Meresankh threw her arms around him, holding him tight as he hugged her back, lifting her off her feet and turning, turning, dancing with her like this was their wedding day. And they laughed together. Because whatever happened next, whoever took the throne, they knew that they would be able to find joy in this strange and uncertain future. They would find it together.

There was hope.

Setting her down, he bent so she could slip the necklace over his head, the little scarab resting against his heart. And he laughed again.

"I was just going to tell you," he said, his face shining. "Look at this." And he handed her a papyrus. "We're already married, Meresankh. The Pharaoh witnessed it, and told us to write our own marriage contract. And he's giv… he's given us enough to start our lives together. We're set for life. As soon as we sign our contract… we're signed and sealed."

She just gave another happy sob. And they stood together in one another's arms, exploding with gratitude. They were married.

As he held his wife, Semerkhet felt locusts hopping inside his stomach. Now that they were married…

"May—" he began to ask, but as he reached out to softly place a hand on her cheek, she popped up onto her tiptoes again, gently drawing him close. He felt her lips brush against his, and they were kissing, kissing, the world disappearing as they clung to one another, knowing that whatever their future held, they would hold one another through it.

A little breathless, they broke apart. And all they could do was stare at one another, laughing for pure joy. And hand-in-hand, they walked down the hall, ready to face whatever came next. Together.

Then Semerkhet paused, and Meresankh looked up at him in curiosity.

"What is it?" she asked.

Her husband smiled again. "He's also giving us Bastet."

Meresankh just chuckled.


There wasn't much time. But Semerkhet rushed to his chambers and got a piece of papyrus and his best pen. And the husband and wife put their heads together and composed the contract that would outline their promises to one another.

334

One by one, they signed it. And they smiled. They were married.

Tut opened his eyes again, taking another look at Sem, who had reappeared after a short break. Something was new. Although… two things were new, actually. Because the Pharaoh's heart ached with a strange combination of confusion and hope as he noticed a new Light in his friend's eyes… a light that reminded him of the Light in his own parents' eyes.

Then he saw what else was different. And he set aside the deep philosophical questions as he smiled.

"New necklathe?" he whispered.

Suddenly Sem laughed, reaching up to touch the little scarab much like Meresankh always touched the necklace he had given her. "Well, Meresankh and I are married," he said with a grin. "Thanks to you."

Slowly Tut smiled. And he winked. "It'th about time."

And Sem laughed again.

Meresankh flew down the many hallways that separated the royal suites from Granny's workshop, yanking the door open and racing in without even a knock.

Merneith was stirring a small terracotta bowl of some new preparation that Meresankh suspected would become a poultice for the Pharaoh's poor leg. And she gasped as her granddaughter flew into the room and threw her arms around her.

"We did it— he did it—" Meresankh panted, face glowing as she stepped back, giving her Granny a breathless smile. "Granny, we're married. The Pharaoh witnessed it. And he gave— he gave Semerkhet enough gold to build a big house and see us through for years. We're married, Granny! Whatever happens next… we're married. And we'll be just fine until Sem can get a job. Just fine."

Wise old eyes filling with happy tears, Merneith set aside her spoon. And she turned to Meresankh. She took her hands, looking up at her with a smile that was beyond any words.

"Congratulations, dearie," she whispered. "Our prayers have been answered."

The Queen looked up. Because she had heard… what sounded like a laugh. What a… strange… sound. But a welcome one, certainly. Who was laughing, she wondered. And what was so funny?

There was a knock on the door, and it opened to admit Meresankh and Semerkhet. They were the ones who had been laughing; hand-in-hand, they were chuckling over something that had set their faces alight with joy.

"Your Majesties," Semerkhet said in his most formal voice, standing as straight as a statue, "we beg leave to present an announcement."

"Proceed," the Pharaoh said grandly, and as she glanced at her brother in slight confusion, Ankhesenamun thought she saw a glimmer of a chuckle on his face; the deepening of the last remaining dimple in his cheek. Did he know something she didn't?

"Your Majesties," Semerkhet said again, "it gives me great pleasure to present my wife Meresankh. Through the magnanimity of the Pharaoh, we were married this afternoon." Laughing, Meresankh stepped forward, still holding Semerkhet's hand, and as he took a step to join her, the Queen could see that the valet was wearing a necklace of his own, a little scarab with bright-colored

336

wings and a red solar disc held between them. A gift of love from a woman to the man that she loved.

"Who spoke for you?" the Queen asked softly. "And approved your contract? Without your parents being here... and without a dowry?"

And Semerkhet just smiled at the Pharaoh, who was wearing the royal signet-ring on his thin hand. The Queen understood. The king of the known world could sign a marriage into law as easily as a treaty or a trade agreement. And from all the riches he was about to leave behind, he could provide his friends with the grandest dowry in history. She smiled. So that was what he had needed the signet-ring for.

And then the propriety was gone. With a squeal, Meresankh sprang forward, throwing her arms around the Queen. And the men chuckled as the ladies hopped up and down in their excitement, Ankh congratulating her friend over and over as Meresankh gushed over how excited she was.

Above the squeals and laughter and questions about how and when they were going to set up house, Semerkhet smiled at his friend, silently thanking him. And the Pharaoh smiled back. Leaving his friend a married man, he could go in peace.

And Tut thought of his legacy. He was a King of peace, yes. And now... he was a King of joy.

"Not only that," he said to the Queen, "but I've also given them an important assignment."

His sister looked at him in curiosity. "What?"

With a sigh, he looked down at the cat, who was snoozing at the end of the bed. "I've plathed Bastet in their care. I won't be here... and thith way, you won't have to worry about her, with whatever cometh next. She'll be thafe. And they'll love her ath much ath we have."

As her brother seemed to choke up at the thought of being separated from his beloved cat, the Queen reached out to pet Bastet's soft, gray fur.

*Thank you*, she said inside her heart as she gazed into those calm, golden eyes. *Thank you for being there for him. And thank you for telling me about Kadesh. You helped me prepare for what was coming.* Bastet gave a long, slow blink. Ankh sighed. *Like you're preparing me now.*

But the conversation was not over. Meresankh turned to her new husband, taking his hand.

"Actually, there was something I wanted to tell you," she said softly. He raised his eyebrows, inviting her to continue. "The Queen... the Queen has made a decision." Meresankh looked at Ankh, and her Mistress nodded, taking up the story.

"If... if Zannanza doesn't get here before the funeral... or if he can't come at all..." Ankhesenamun outlined her plan, moving herself, her child, and Little Nefertiti to safety in Sais, where, protected by Horemheb's lie, she would study at the medical college and continue to impact the future as a history teacher.

Silently, Semerkhet nodded. And he gave his friends half a smile. "Well, I'm glad you have a plan."

He looked down at the ring of the Sole Companion gleaming on his hand. And his stomach plummeted.

"What about us?" he asked his wife. He looked at the Pharaoh and the Queen, asking them as well. "If they'd... if they'd do this to you, Brother, if they'd do this to your parents, your sister, if

338

they'd threaten the Queen and the baby... what about me and Meresankh?"

Semerkhet swallowed. And he described the whispers he'd heard; the rumblings of the deadly conflict that might break out between the servants who were faithful to Tutankhamun and those who were loyal to the Vizier if Ankhesenamun and Zannanza's succession did not go as planned.

Tut closed his eyes. Had he condemned his friend to the life of a wanted man through wanting to honor him for his heroism? And was the palace doomed to become a battlefield on the day the unknown future arrived?

But it was Meresankh who spoke next. Warmth was rising in her heart, a warmth that told her that now was the time to talk to her beloved about where they might make their home, just as she had promised the Queen she would. Now that she knew they would be making their home together, it was right to speak of it.

"What if..." she said, looking from Semerkhet's face to Tut's to Ankhesenamun's, "what if we come too?"

Sem blinked. "What do you mean?"

Meresankh smiled. "Just listen. If the Prince doesn't come, the Queen won't be safe here in Memphis. And when everything... everything changes, we won't be either. Ankhesenamun needs a fresh start. And so do we. So what... what if we move to Sais with her?" She blinked back tears as she smiled at the Queen. "After all, she wants me there to hold her hand when the baby's born. And what..." Meresankh chuckled. "What if Granny came with us? She could teach at the school of women's medicine in Sais. She is the greatest midwife in Egypt, after all. And you could study there, Sem. And so could I. You can become a nurse, and I can keep building on what I've learned from Granny and become an

339

herbalist." She looked at the hopeful faces around her; faces that were beginning to smile. "So? Do you think... you think it could work?"

Slowly, Ankh's smile turned into a grin. Tut nodded. And Sem laughed.

"I think we have our answer," they all said at once. And as they squeezed one another's hands, they knew their prayers had been answered.

Tut smiled as he watched Meresankh offer a little bow and excuse herself after sharing another special little smile with her husband. A great sense of peace was settling over his heart. Because the people he cared about most in the world had a plan for their future. And they were going to be all right. Because they would be together.

Granny agreed. She said she would be proud to teach her craft to the next generation at the school at Sais; honored to pass on her wisdom. She said that she could feel it in her bones— I-AM was telling her that the time was right to leave the palace. Her mission was to go where she was needed. And right now, she was needed in Sais.

They had a plan. And it was a good one. But the way that she was failing to take her place as the female Pharaoh or Regent Queen-Mother, standing in the gap between Dynasties, ached in Ankhesenamun's heart, turning her tea bitter, the honey-cakes Meresankh brought her sour.

Her brother was visiting with Semerkhet. So Ankh went to her own room for a few minutes, lying back in her own chair. If she could take a catnap, there would be nothing wrong with that.

But she couldn't fall asleep. Couldn't even keep her eyes closed. Because the guilt followed her. It twisted in her stomach, filling her with shame. And anger. Because she was angry at Ay, at Horemheb, at all the people and all the situations that were preventing her from fulfilling her destiny and being who Egypt needed her to be. It was her job. Her birthright. The only right way forward. She was the Queen. And she would become the next King. It was her duty.

Ankh turned her head, shifting in the chair. But if the Prince didn't come... she couldn't stay. Couldn't. Because if she did, she and her child were guaranteed to die. The only way for them to survive was for her to forsake it all. Her crown. Her throne. Her country. Her authority to write laws that could change the future for everyone. Everything she had ever worked for.

She was breaking her promise to lead Egypt out of poverty. And she was breaking every promise she had made to the little girls of this generation; the little girls of the future. Fleeing into exile... she would not be leading her country into a glorious future, either on the throne or beside it. Fleeing into exile, she would be abandoning the country that so desperately needed her guidance; her wise leadership. The nation she had sworn to protect; had spent the past year guiding from beside the throne as she advised the brother who sat on the throne.

But if Zannanza never made it to Egypt, leaving her throne behind would be the only way to protect her child. Ankh hugged herself. She wondered what would happen. And she wished, wished that there was another way.

341

"He's so much better," Meresankh announced to her Granny as they sat together at Merneith's sturdy old worktable, grinding herbs to be made into tea. She gave a blissful smile. "He's so much more awake— he's talking more, making decisions, he's got so much more energy— Granny, we think he's going to get better! Our prayers are being answered!"

The old woman reached out and took her granddaughter's hands. But her smile was restrained. As if… as if she knew something she was hesitant to share with the excited young bride. "Prayers are answered in many different ways, dearie," she said. "Many different ways."

# 31   Inheritance

"What did you pick?" Tutankhamun asked with a little chuckle. He had just finished his simple lunch of poppy-seasoned broth, a step up from lukewarm poppy-flavored gruel. This was hot, and had garlic, onion, and thyme in it.

Semerkhet bent over him with a questioning little smile, running a cool, damp cloth over the far side of his neck. He was burning, and there was so little they could do. But the valet knew that the gesture was almost as important as how much it actually helped.

Except... except for the way that today, although the Pharaoh still had a fever, was still stuck in bed, he seemed to have some energy today. He was downright talkative. And he had had the energy and mind-power to make the major decision of approving the marriage. He truly seemed to be feeling better. And Semerkhet couldn't help but wonder... *was* he getting better?

"What do you mean?" Sem asked softly.

Tut nodded vaguely at his whole room, raising his eyebrows meaningfully. "I thaid you could pick a few thingth. W... wedding giftth. To remember me by... and tho your children will have nithe inheritantheth. We have to take care of your grandchildren." He nodded at his friend, looking up at him earnestly. "I want to know what you picked."

Semerkhet realized that he meant it. He was being instructed by the Pharaoh to get up, look at all the marvelous treasures around him, and make a little pile that he was claiming. So that his brother could enter eternity knowing that he had provided for his best friend.

Obediently, Semerkhet got up, walking into his friend's storage room, where even he had not been in days. And he looked around. So many indescribably beautiful pieces of artwork, any one of which would be worth a year's wages. Except… that they would be priceless, as each one would carry the memories of a year of service; a few precious months of brotherhood.

There was… there was a necklace almost as large as his hand, a graceful golden hawk holding a red solar disc between the tips of its colorfully inlaid wings and the symbols of life and infinity in its talons. Of course the hawk represented the god Horus, but to him, it was just a beautiful bird; a delicate piece of artwork made precious by memory. He picked it up, feeling its heft, its craftsmanship. The weight of the legacy of the man who had owned it.

He would wear it with pride.

He also picked a pair of earrings, a necklace, and a bracelet for his bride. How proud he would be to be able to present them to her. They, too, were heavy, with the weight of the memories of every time he had put them on the Pharaoh. And… three fabulous rings. For the next generation. Somehow… somehow, three felt like a good number. A few other pieces Semerkhet picked as well; things he would run his fingers over one last time and then sell, grateful for the way in which his best friend was continuing to provide for him and his family even after Tut was gone.

Then he looked around again, and felt his eyes film over with tears. Because he was gazing at his brother's rack of walking-sticks. Slowly he walked over, gently reaching out to run his hands over their lengths. Remembering.

He picked one. A simple one; a simple staff with a classic lotus motif. Somehow, he remembered it from Tribute Day. Toward the

344

bottom, it had a metal cartouche. And he could see his brother's name, written in three hieroglyphics. *Aten, Ankh, Tut.* It was an old staff. From the days of the Aten. And he smiled as the Truth of the name of Aten, I-AM, touched his heart like a gentle ray of sunlight.

Semerkhet held it in his hand. And it was as if he could feel the imprint of his brother's hand on its handle. Preserved proudly in Semerkhet's home, it would carry his friend into the future. Because when his children… He bit his lip, feeling a lump aching in his throat. When his children asked him who the staff had belonged to, he would tell them. And they would know. And his friend's name would live on in the minds and hearts of another generation.

Taking this staff home was a promise. A promise that the Pharaoh would never be forgotten. After all, to speak the name of the dead was to make them live again. He would live forever in their hearts… in their memories… in the stories they would tell.

Turning around, Semerkhet bit his lip again. Shoes. The Pharaoh's rack of eighty pairs of shoes looked back at him. And with a heavy sigh, he approached. He looked at them. He remembered. And he chose a pair. Not for him or his descendants to wear… but to put away somewhere and bring out when he needed to remember.

He smiled, sniffling back his tears. Good choices. Time to show the Pharaoh what he had picked.

Tutankhamun looked up as Semerkhet came back out of the storage room, hands full of treasure. And he smiled. Sem had done as he was told.

"What did you pick?" he whispered.

First, his friend chuckled. "I don't need anything more to re-member you by," he said. "I have this." He showed off his ring, the red jasper gleaming in the soft lamplight. "And this." He patted his own knee, and the Pharaoh nodded. He had not seen it, but he knew that his friend had a scar. Sad... but beautiful... to think that that scar would connect them when here on Earth, he was nothing more than a memory.

Then Semerkhet sighed. "But I did pick some... some beautiful things." And he showed the Pharaoh the fabulous jewelry that he had selected for himself and for his family, and the items that would one day allow his children to go to school. And they blinked back tears together as they looked at the walking-stick and the sandals. And remembered.

"I have thomething elth for you," Tutankhamun said softly. And Sem watched as his friend reached out toward the table beside the bed, picking up the familiar blue lotus cup with which Semerkhet had served him so many countless times. Silently, he offered it to the valet.

And the words echoed again in Semerkhet's heart. *I taste your drink, Son of Ra... and if there be harm in it, let the harm fall upon me.* He had been faithful to the end. And whenever he looked at that cup, he would be proud.

The Pharaoh nodded across the bedroom, where Semerkhet was amazed to see four graceful chairs, long stowed away in the storage room. There were also two elegant tables, crafted of wood from a faraway forest, inlaid with delicate patterns of glass tiles and precious stones. On one of the tables was the most luxurious *senet* game Sem had ever seen, inlaid, like the tables, with precious

346

stones. And there was a bed, the end of which almost stuck out into the hallway.

Semerkhet looked at the furniture. And he looked at his friend.

"For your houthe," the Pharaoh said simply. "You can thell them and buy a houthe, or have one built. Hope it'll be enough."

Semerkhet staggered forward on shaking legs, running his hands over the graceful furniture. "Two of these would be enough for a house," he whispered hoarsely, again blinking back tears. "I— I don't know how—"

"Build it big enough," Tut said with a chuckle. "For a houseful of kidth."

Sem looked at his friend, and there was a smile on his face. Tut smiled back. His friend had a lot of love to give. The Pharaoh knew his life would not be complete until he and Meresankh were parents.

"And all your thingth are yourth," Tutankhamun reiterated. "You and Meresankh. You can take all your clothes, all your furniture, all your other thingth, with you. And you can sleep on the new bed, or sell it and keep your own. All up to you."

Semerkhet just smiled in amazement.

As Semerkhet sat with the Pharaoh, who had slipped into another nap, Ankhesenamun took Meresankh's hand. And she led her across the hall, into her chambers. Into her storage room.

"What is it?" Meresankh asked. Tentatively, for she could see tears gathering in her friend's eyes.

"I have something for you," Ankh whispered. Slowly, she got two baskets down from a shelf. The two baskets that no one else was allowed to touch.

Meresankh's breath caught in her throat. Because she understood.

The Queen brought the baskets out into the sitting room, placing them carefully on the table. And she opened them.

"These are Mereneferet's things," she said, reaching inside the first basket, bringing out armfuls of soft swaddling, a rattle, beads that might have adorned a little girl's first dress.

Meresankh just looked.

Ankhesenamun opened the second basket. "And these are Senebhenas' things," she said. Slowly, she brought out more swaddling, a handful of ribbons, a tiny doll.

The handmaiden gazed at the precious objects; heart too full for words. "They're beautiful," she said finally.

The Queen gathered up the beads, placing them in a tiny bag. And neatly, she looped up the ribbons so they wouldn't tangle.

"I want you to have these," she said. And she offered them to her friend, her sister. "For your children."

Meresankh looked down at the precious gifts in her friend's hands. Slowly, she felt the tears fill her eyes. And she put her arms around her friend.

"Thank you," she whispered, trying to put everything for which there were no words into the phrase. "Thank you."

The Queen's heart was full as she watched her friend take the ribbons and beads to her own room. She had given them away, these mementoes of her daughters. And yet… She smiled. She smiled as she thought of them, one day, belonging to Meresankh's children.

Semerkhet closed his eyes as relief, joy, amazement, gratitude coursed through his mind... and a hundred other emotions that didn't even have names. He was a married man. And— all his worries about the future, about where he would live while going to school, how he would eat before he got a job, how he would put a roof over Meresankh's head... had disappeared as suddenly as if they had been swept down the Nile. Everything was taken care of. And he could go to school each day and come home to a house that was fully paid for, and share meals with his wife that hadn't put them into debt.

The Sole Companion wiped away tears of gratitude. Their future was secure. All thanks to his brother.

Through happy tears of her own, Meresankh admired the necklaces, rings, tables, and chairs that the Pharaoh had given to her and her husband. They were exquisite. And they were worth a lot of gold. The handmaiden smiled and shook her head. She knew Semerkhet was right when he said that just two of the chairs would have been enough for an entire house.

"But what if he does come?" Semerkhet asked the Queen.

Ankh looked up from the papyrus of history she was perusing as her brother drowsed.

"If the Prince gets here on time, and you marry him, we won't have to move away. So... what then?"

The Queen smiled and shook her head.

"Then... I will remain Queen, and you and Meresankh will be welcome to stay, a thousand times welcome. Whether you..." She almost chuckled. "Whether you become a scribe, or work with Granny, or simply grace us with the presence of the Sole

349

Companion, there will always be a home for you and Meresankh at the palace as long as I am Queen."

When he woke up a little later, after a short nap, Tut had another idea. He thought of his grandfather, Amenhotep the Third. And he thought of the Pharaoh's father-in-law, the father of Grandmother Tiye. His name had been Yuya. And from what Tutankhamun could gather, he must have been just as important to his Pharaoh as Semerkhet was to him. He, too, had been Sole Companion, Favorite of the Pharaoh, and Unique Friend. All in all, Amenhotep had given Yuya forty different titles. So it wouldn't hurt for Tut to give his friend a few more.

"Sem," he whispered. An instant later, his friend was at his side.

"Yes, Brother?" he said with a gentle smile.

Weakly, Tut smiled back. "Got a few more titles for you. Get a pen."

"What?" Sem asked, brow wrinkling in confusion.

"Titleth. Like Royal Favorite. Got a few more for you. Need you to write them down."

Finally Semerkhet nodded. "Oh, yes, yes." A moment later, he was back with a pen and a fresh sheet of papyrus. Tut lay there and thought. What titles could express everything he thought about his valet, his friend, his brother?

"Ath Pharaoh," he began slowly, "I appoint you Confidant of the King." He smiled. "You alwayth have been. About time I put it in your job description. And I appoint you Praised of the King." Clearing his throat, Tut went on, bestowing rank after rank, designations that would be more symbolic than anything else in the days that would surely follow, but would bring his friend honor for the rest of his life. Titles that thanked Semerkhet for everything he

350

was; that the Pharaoh knew would bring a smile to his face when Sem remembered that they were his and always would be.

Semerkhet blinked back more tears as he took down the titles his Pharaoh was assigning him… here, so close to the end.

"These titleth are yourth now, no matter what happenth," Tut said, reaching out to squeeze Semerkhet's hand. And he gave his friend a breathy chuckle. "You can keep *Washer of Pharaoh* if you like."

Sem laughed. "I'll always be Washer of Pharaoh."

Tut smiled, then looked wistfully up at his friend. "Don't forget me."

Semerkhet shook his head as he wiped away tears with his free hand. "Never."

"It'th been… it'th been a year now, hathn't it?" Tutankhamun asked in a breathless whisper. "Thinth you've been my valet?"

Sem squeezed his Master's hand again. "I think you're right," he said with a sad smile. "A good year," he said softly.

"A good year," Tut repeated. And again, he closed his eyes.

The cat got up and stretched, then padded across the bed to hop into Semerkhet's lap. The valet looked down at her as she got comfortable, curling up on his knees with a purr. He sighed. And as he began to pet her, he smiled.

She understood. And she was telling him that it was all right. Semerkhet and Meresankh would be happy to take care of her. And she would be happy to live with them.

The day went on. Dinnertime came and went; a bowl of sliced apples eaten one small bite at a time, a bowl of yogurt, a few grapes, a little of his favorite cheese, two of his favorite honey-cakes. Despite how hungry he'd been at breakfast, Tutankhamun didn't have much of an appetite for dinner. But he enjoyed the flavor of the food. And he appreciated the care with which it was presented to him.

"I hope you like your houthe," Tut said to his brother early that evening, resting back on his pillows with his blankets pulled up to his chin. He was tired again, the energy he'd enjoyed that day quietly fading, and he felt like an early night. Even earlier than usual.

Sem looked up from pouring a bit of tea into a little bowl. His Pharaoh hadn't had a drink for a bit, and he wanted to make sure he didn't get too thirsty.

"It'll be beautiful," he said softly as he used a ladle to fill the little bowl with herbal tea, the same blend as last night. "We'll build a big one. Might even have a garden. And I'll work in Sais, and Meresankh will use what she's learned here to run our home, and both of us will go to the medical college…"

"Fank you… for taking Bastet," Tut said. "I'm tho glad… it'th you. You'll take good care of her."

"We promise," Semerkhet said. He set the ladle aside and checked that he hadn't dripped any tea down the sides of the little bowl.

He turned to his Pharaoh, the bowl of tea in his hand. "We'll be all right," he promised.

Tutankhamun just smiled. "I know."

Sem sat down on the edge of the bed, offering the tea to his friend.

"Fank you," Tut said through dry lips. His whole mouth was so dry; his tongue wasn't behaving. Bending over him, Semerkhet

352

slipped his arm behind Tutankhamun's shoulders, gently raising his head. Carefully he brought the bowl to Tut's mouth, and the Pharaoh sipped it, feeling the sweet, warm herbal tea bring some life back into his mouth.

When Tut was done, Semerkhet set the bowl aside, using his fingertip to brush away a tiny drop of tea that had stayed behind in the peach-fuzz that was what the Pharaoh had by way of a moustache. Then gently Sem laid him back down, settling him back into bed.

The Pharaoh got his breath. And then he chuckled. "Want to go on a chariot ride?"

Semerkhet just smiled.

"Meresankh does want children, doethn't she?" the Pharaoh asked after Sem had given him another sip of tea.

Sem paused. Tut had been the one to bring it up, so it must be all right to talk about babies. "I think so," he said. Then he grinned. "I do."

Tutankhamun reached out to squeeze his hand, the red ring of the Sole Companion shining on Semerkhet's hand. "You'll have a lot of stories to tell them," he said with a soft smile of his own.

Sem just squeezed his hand. "Yes. I will."


How did Semerkhet do it? He was the expert... Sitting on the bed beside her brother, Ankhesenamun dipped out a palmful of frankincense-and-spikenard ointment with the alabaster spoon, letting it warm in her hand. Getting him onto his side had been an adventure, although a little less painful this time, because he had just received his bedtime dose of poppy— a higher dose than Granny had yet given him. Semerkhet and Kamose had worked together, slowly rolling him in a slow, controlled manner, supported with a large pillow against his chest and stomach, on which one arm rested as comfortably as possible. And, of course, a pillow between his splinted legs, covered in a sheet that could easily be laundered. He wasn't going anywhere.

"Are you comfortable?" Ankh murmured.

She heard him chuckle. "Not yet."

She knew what he meant. This was the only thing that would make him comfortable.

"Goodnight, my love," Ankh whispered.

Gently she began to rub the ointment into his bony back, smiling as she heard him sigh; felt him begin to relax. She felt connected to him, sitting there with him with her hands on his back, even as she traced each rib and vertebra with her fingertips. To her baby brother; her strong Pharaoh husband. Even... even if she was letting him go at the same time.

It was simple, what she was doing. She wasn't an expert, not like Semerkhet. But it would be enough, she knew as she hummed a lullaby in her throat, the song about the turtledove. Because he knew how much she loved him.

Tut smiled, closing his eyes as he felt his sister's warm hands on his back. There was so much love in her touch; so much care. And soon he would be asleep. The day went away; the good, the bad, what had been accomplished and what yet remained to be seen. This... right here... was the best part of today.

So many memories. So many days, good and bad, had ended well, with his sister gently rubbing his back.

That night he slept well.

# 32   Without My Brother

It was a quiet morning. The sixteenth morning of the month of Tybi. Semerkhet's brother slept late, sleeping peacefully into mid-morning like he hadn't been able to do for what felt like months. And he had slept through the night, which was a relief to his exhausted valet, who had also been refreshed by getting more sleep than he had had in a long time, a whole hour at a time. Sem smiled at the Queen, who was resting quietly in her chair as the Pharaoh continued his good night's sleep, and she told him to take a few minutes. Even after a good night's sleep, he needed a break. And so he wished his friend life, prosperity, and health, and quietly left the room.

Semerkhet made his way down the familiar hallways to his own room, stretching as he went. There was his door, right next to Nakhtmin's. On the floor in front of his neighbor's door, he saw the usual stray fruit remnants— an apple core, this time— but ignored it. Poor foolish boy. Hopefully he would grow up.

Slowly Semerkhet opened the door, giving a deep sigh as he walked into his familiar room. He looked around with a smile— it was just the same as he'd left it… bed, desk, little dining area, dressing corner. Then he caught sight of his reflection in the copper mirror on his dressing-table. He really didn't look that good; he was a little pale, and he had dark circles under his bloodshot eyes; eyes that were almost too tired to properly focus, even after a good night of sleep. He even wondered if he had lost a little weight.

Semerkhet made himself a cup of tea; wrote down a few grateful reflections in his journal. He had found the Light. The Truth; the Love that was greater than any name. But which now had a name— I-AM. This was the Creator to Whom he had found himself praying on the way home from Kadesh, to Whom he had been blindly reaching out over the past weeks. No matter what happened next in his life, no matter the twists and turns of politics, war, and betrayal, he knew he was safe.

Semerkhet gave a grateful sigh, feeling the warmth in his heart that had seemed to guide Meresankh for as long as he had known her; the peace and love that he had longed for so many years to feel. And slowly, gently, his thoughts returned to the problems and issues of this world. Returned to the friend, the brother, who even now lay dying.

Brothers... Semerkhet sighed as his heart ached. But in the ache... there was encouragement. He had survived the death of a brother before. And as much as on some days, it had felt like it could not be true, he knew there was life on the other side.

Semerkhet looked down at his ring. No matter what happened, he would remember that he was the Pharaoh's brother. And his ring and his sash would make sure that the world knew too. So even now... he knew. One chapter of his life was ending. But his life... his life would go on.

He thought back, over the long months that had separated him and Nedjes in time and space. Back to the first time he had lost a brother. When Nedjes had died, Sem had had no one left. Only the sister whose love encouraged him, but who had been so knocked down by her own grief that she had nothing left to give from her empty heart. Mother was dead, her only presence found in the sweet memories Semerkhet carried inside his heart. Father was consumed by pain, rage, and alcohol, no longer a part of Semerkhet's life. And Nedjes... Nedjes was the one who now lay in his tomb. But now... Semerkhet found himself giving a little smile. Now, he was surrounded by friends who would go through this grief, this change, along with him. Meresankh, her Granny, the Queen, even the little girl Meresankh had said was going to live with the Queen in Sais. Through it all, they would be beside him. So this time... this time, he would not be alone.

Semerkhet got up and went to his dressing corner, retrieving his kohl and an application tool. If he had a few minutes, he wanted to do his makeup. There was something that felt... special... about today. And there was no harm in looking his best.

Her brother had slept surprisingly well last night, Ankhesena-mun thought. And therefore, so had she, rising refreshed for the first time in what felt like months. She gave a little smile. It felt good to be rested.

Actually, he was still asleep. Ankh sighed, watching him slowly breathing in and out, the cat curled up at his side. Let him sleep as long as he would, she thought. Asleep, he was safe from his pain.

The Queen heard the prayers of the priests echoing through the palace; could smell the sacred incense even from the bedroom. But even as the priests and the servants celebrated their traditional religion, Merneith and Meresankh appeared to be praying too. Very quietly, without pomp and circumstance. As though they were communicating very simply, with a God they knew loved them and didn't ask much more than that they reach out to Him. She smiled to herself as memories filled her heart. Like her parents, worshiping the Aten.

The questions that had begun to move within her heart bubbled up again. And the void that the Egyptian gods had left when she had realized that they were not, and never had been, real, didn't feel quite so empty.

Someone… was there. And always had been.

She thought of the phrase she had heard Granny say, "What in the Ten Plagues." Like the story of the Hebrew Prince that no one was allowed to talk about… I-AM, the God of the Hebrews Who her father believed had revealed Himself to the Prince who had become a shepherd.

I-AM was a Lord of Light. The Aten was a Lord of Light. Meresankh had said they were the same; that the Creator was greater than any name they might give Him.

Ankhesenamun shook her head. Could that really be true? And was I-AM, the Aten, truly the Great Someone, the nameless *You*, to Whom she and her brother were reaching out… the source of the Love the Queen felt whenever the Sun touched her face?

She crept outside while he was still sleeping. The sun was still low; the morning was chilly and a mist still lay over the royal garden. The Queen pulled her robe closer, smiled at Hannu, whose loyalty, and dagger, would protect her no matter what, and gathered a few lotus blossoms from one of the pools. Then she bent and picked a few cornflowers to add to the bouquet. Cornflowers… that somehow reminded her of teardrops.

She stood there in the early-morning sunlight, shivering as a sudden chilly breeze ruffled her robe, setting the beads of her braids to jingling. She shivered again after it had passed. Because somehow, it felt like more than a breeze.

It felt like a warning. That today… something was going to happen.

But then, a gentle warmth soothed the chill of the foreboding wind. And as she raised her face to the warm rays of the early-morning Sun, she felt that amid whatever might happen, peace and joy lay ahead of them as well.

Tut woke up hungry. So they turned him again, onto his back. Tut held his breath as Semerkhet and Kamose slowly moved him from the position in which he'd slept, arranging pillows around him again so he'd be as comfortable as possible. Delicately, they replaced the bedsheets that had been tangled around his legs and were now stained with pus. Carefully, Semerkhet gave him as much breakfast as he would eat, one slow bite at a time. And they left him to rest with helpless but loving wishes for life, prosperity, and health.

He was hungry. But he was also tired— too tired to sit up; too tired to play *seega*. Tutankhamun sighed sadly as he felt the energy of yesterday slipping away; the faint hope he'd had for a new trajectory of improvement. Today… today he was as bad as he had ever been. Today, he knew, brought him one day closer to the end.

They could see it, Ankhesenamun, Semerkhet, Meresankh. Whatever had been so special about yesterday, it had passed. And they wiped away tears as they realized that even if that mysterious change had given them a few more precious hours with Tutankhamun, it was not going to last.

Still, Tut struggled to breathe. But it was not as though he had anything more important to do. So he focused his mind on the steady rhythm… in, out, in, out. And he was very grateful when the gentle rhythm of his own breathing soothed him to sleep again.

"I didn't get to tell you what happened the other day," Ankh said as she took a moment to walk down the hall and back. That was all she had time for, but it felt good to get up and stretch. "The Vizier came back. With his ring."

Meresankh just shook her head. "That man," she said.

But the Queen smiled. "But I think he got the message this time."

The handmaiden returned the smile. "I pray that he did." She paused, then smiled again. "I'm sorry for his disappointment at your refusal," she said with a wry smile.

The Queen turned and took her friend's hand. "I'm not," she said with a mean chuckle. Meresankh grinned, her dimple showing. "But I said *no*… one last time," Ankh continued. "And whatever happens, it's final. Whether I'm the Queen or the King… my decision is made."

Meresankh squeezed her hand with a smile. "And there's nothing he can do about it."

And Ankh shook her head. That he would try to marry her after killing her entire family was just insulting.


The Pharaoh fought back a cough as a sudden thought made him actually chuckle. Semerkhet looked up from browsing through a papyrus of history, intrigued by the sound.

Tut smiled at his friend, beckoning him to the bedside with a nod.

"Nakhtmin will be dithappointed," he said. A smile was playing around his mouth; amusement was lighting up his eyes.

Sem looked at him in expectation, waiting for the funny part of whatever his friend was going to say. "Why?" he asked with a smile of his own.

360

"Becauthe wiff you moving to Sais, he won't be able to make you *his* valet," Tutankhamun said in slightly vindictive triumph.

Semerkhet laughed out loud. "No, he won't," he said with satisfaction. "No, he won't."

Semerkhet watched his brother sleeping. His brother who lay there in bed, days, if not hours, from death; a death from which no one could save him. Another little brother about to leave Semerkhet behind.

He bowed his head, tears welling in his closed eyes, as the terrible guilt, the awful weight of his failure, weighed him down as it always did. His brother was dying. And he could do nothing.

*Why?* he whispered inside his heart. *Why can't I protect the ones I care about? Why am I such a failure?*

Then the answer came to him. Came to him with the same loving warmth as the gentle touch of the Sun.

He had not failed to protect Nedjes— hunting accidents happened, and they were no one's fault. He had not been *able* to protect him, no, but neither had he failed to. And he had not failed now. The web of deception, betrayal, and regicide was one that no one person could ever have untangled.

Semerkhet shook his head, biting back a sob. Not... not his fault? Not his fault that Nedjes had died; not his fault that at this very moment, the Pharaoh lay dying?

Semerkhet wiped his eyes with a shaking hand. And he let go of the burden of guilt that he had been carrying since the day Nedjes died.

He had not failed.

The Queen had another thought as she sat silently in her room during a short break, considering the past, the present, and the future. If she left Memphis and moved with her child to Sais, leaving her old life behind, she would no longer be Queen. Everything, everyone, she had always been, would die along with her hopes of inheriting her brother's throne.

But… it wouldn't, though, would it? Wistfully, Ankh smiled as she realized what her Mother would tell her. She knew what was true. *My circumstances do not define me or change who I am. Without a King beside me, without a crown, without a throne of my own, without anyone or anything, I am still Queen. That is who I am.*

She smiled as she remembered all the years she had reigned as Queen, guiding her nation from beside the throne. She thought of all the lessons she had taught her brother, taught her friends— lessons in leadership, courage, strength, how to be civil and sneaky, courageous and cunning, sweet and deadly, how to draw strength from the past. She had taught them so much. And what she had taught them, and what they would go on to teach those around them, would change the world.

She shook her head. Did her greatest opportunity to change the world lie in giving up her throne and becoming a history teacher? She would change the world as she continued to teach young girls the histories of the great Queens of the past, raising them up into the Queens of the future. She would miss her crown, her throne, the authority they had afforded her, but she smiled to think that through it all, it had been her role of teacher that had allowed her to make such a difference.

She closed her eyes as another thought warmed her heart, filling it with grateful tears that gently brimmed over, sliding down her cheeks. The lesson she had taught her brother so long ago about life. None of this was fair. None of it. But that was the way life was… full of things you could change and things you could not.

That was what she would do. She would disappear from the royal court, saving herself and her child from the things they could not change, and study nursing in Sais, supported by the community of like-minded female professionals, scholars, and intellectuals who would surround her in the city famous for its school of women's medicine. From that foundation, she would go on to become a history teacher. And she would carry that role of wise teacher with her, no matter where she went in the world, with or without a crown.

And the Queen of Egypt sat straight and tall, ready to face her future.


The pain got worse, and no matter what he did, Tut couldn't escape it. He tossed and turned in Ankh's lap, sweat running down his face as he shivered or burned, muscles and bones aching with each lung-stabbing breath he took. Every restless movement sent shocks of pain through his leg that made him gasp, wondering what it would be like to be shot with an arrow. He doubted it was this bad. These days, he hardly noticed the pain in his foot.

"Make it stop, Ankh," he whimpered through his tears, staring up at her imploringly. "Hurts…"

And with her own eyes full of tears, she lay down beside him, holding him to her heart and wiping his eyes. She could not make it stop.

"Why…" he moaned to no one in particular. "Why…"

All she could do was shake her head. Even the wise Queen of Egypt had no answers.

He tried to smile, memories from before the pain warming his heart as his teeth chattered, sweat rolling off his burning skin. "We've changed so much, you and I. Taxes… jobth… schoolth… Even if it's almost over… I suppose I have left a better Egypt."

She nodded, tears beginning to run down her cheeks. "Yes," she said in a broken voice, squeezing his hand. "Yes, you have."

A sudden realization filled his heart, and he smiled. "Have I been… a strong Pharaoh?" he whispered.

Ankh blinked back more tears. "Yes, love. Yes, you have. Stronger than any other. And with your wisdom… you've created a strong past for the people of the future."

Tut smiled as her words touched him. "Have I… been wise? I thought no one could be born wise."

His sister squeezed his hand. "Well, you weren't born yesterday. And you—" She turned her face away for a moment, fighting back the tears. "You made the most… you made the most of your time. And you have become a wise Pharaoh."

Tutankhamun felt his heart warm with satisfaction. Strong. And wise. Even if it was all ending fifty years too soon, maybe he had, in some way, become the Pharaoh he had set out to be. Then he chuckled as his weary body gave another painful, unhelpful shiver. "Fank you for teaching me to be a politician. I just wish Mother and Father and our sisters could have seen us." He paused. "Wath it all worth it?" he whispered to his sister.

She squeezed his hand again, giving a little nod. "Yes. It was."

Ankh nodded, too many feelings filling her heart to leave any room for words. He had said everything she was thinking. For a few bright, shining months, he had been blossoming before her eyes into a strong, wise, young Pharaoh, standing on his own two feet as he led his country with her at his side, guiding him with her

364

knowledge and wisdom. Taking power; not letting the older adults control him or make decisions for him any longer. Deciding what kind of Pharaoh he wanted to be, treating those who worked at the palace as the humans they were, seeking peace and friendship with their neighbors instead of war and conquest. Learning about the world around him; the many people and systems that made it function. He had been just like their sister Meritaten, using his mind and heart to guide his politics, regardless of what his legs could do.

She was so proud of what they had accomplished in a few short months. Yet now it was ending, fifty years too soon. And no one could stop it. No one could stop life and death from running their course, not even the most powerful King or Queen in the world.

*What can I do,* she wondered. *Right now… in this moment? What can I possibly do? How can I make this any better?*

And the words came back to her again. *There is always something you can do; something you can change.* Even if it seemed small. And the ripples of one small act would echo out through the future.

And then… she realized what she could change in this moment, right here, right now. And trying to smile, she began to stroke his head and sing.

# 33  Letting Go

Tut's heart continued to ache as he imagined the life that lay ahead of his sister; the pain she would feel when he was gone. How lonely she would be without him. And then it warmed... warmed, even through his sadness, at the hopes he felt for her and her future.

"I hope you're happy," he whispered. She bent closer, gently taking his hand as she leaned in to catch his soft voice. A proud smile touched her face, but she said nothing. "I mean it," he continued. "I know you'll go on... I know you'll be all right. I know... there'th tho much life ahead of you. Tho much... to accomplish. You can do anyfing. And I hope... you're happy."

He bit his lip, fighting back tears as the very idea that had pricked him with painful jealousy returned, this time with a gentle touch of joy. Maybe he had never understood what marriage was supposed to be like, but his sister did. And as the very end of their time together approached like the setting of the sun, he realized that he genuinely hoped she would find what she was looking for. As her brother, he was about to leave her behind. But now... now, maybe she could find a real husband. "You," he continued, "and Thannantha. I hope it's everything... you ever wanted."

His sister just looked at him. And softly, she whispered, "Thank you." She swallowed, giving a courageous nod. "We'll be all right, Little Nefertiti and I. And we'll be neighbors with Semerkhet and Meresankh and Granny, and I'm sure we'll see them every day. Meresankh will teach me how to do housework, and Nefertiti will help me with the baby, and they'll teach me everything I need to know about how to run the house; how to take care of the baby. And Granny will teach at the medical school, and Meresankh and

366

Semerkhet and I will all study there. And Little Nefertiti will go to school, too." She sighed, taking his hand and gently running her thumb back and forth over his knuckles. "We'll be together, all in Sais. And we'll be all right."

Tutankhamun nodded. And with a little smile, he closed his eyes again. He had to leave. But his sister had a good future ahead of her. She was prepared to face whatever came her way. She would not be alone. She would be all right.

And he could go in peace.


Tutankhamun lay very still while Merneith gently removed his splint, then the stained bandages, carefully dabbing a cloth over the open wound; the angry red skin around it. Craning his neck with his remaining strength, Tut could see that the red streaks had continued to spread over his leg, extending from his wound, some crawling down past his knee, some snaking up toward his hip. Now there was pain in his hip, and swollen lumps under the skin when he pressed his fingers into it. And his whole leg was so, so terribly hot.

At the same time, most of his body felt colder than before, although he knew that his fever was higher. As the infection in his leg and his lungs had gotten worse, his fever had continued to rise even outside of the three-day cycle of ague. And no matter how hard he tried, he could not draw a full breath. The congestion, and the new pain in his chest, were too severe.

His hands ached with cold. And as he raised them to look at them, he heard Semerkhet's voice fill with anxiety.

"What's wrong with his hands?"

Tut peered at his own hands, which were strangely mottled with purple, as the old healer gave a heavy sigh. "It's a sign," she said simply. Of what, she did not say.

But they all knew.

Gently, Granny placed a fresh herbal poultice over his wound. And carefully, she wrapped it up again and tucked him in. Then she took his thin hand, holding it gently in hers as she pressed her fingers to his bony wrist to check his pulse.

"Rest," she said, reaching up to gently touch his sweaty face with her gnarled fingers. The cold compresses on his head and under his arms were making a difference, but not very much of one. "Just rest." Her voice was gentle, kind. But she did not smile.

He nodded. And he knew what she was telling him.

The end was very near.

Ankhesenamun closed her eyes and turned her face away. There was nothing else to be done, was there? Only to wait with him, showering him with love, until he took his final breath.

How long did they have left?

But this time... she couldn't pray. Only let out a deep sigh, reaching out her hands for help. But she didn't know Who was there to help her.

And this time... she didn't cry. Didn't rush to her own room, covering her face, to take a few minutes sobbing out her pain. Many tears waited in the future; that she knew. But right now, there wasn't time.

She thought of Horemheb again. And again, she wondered... if when he got home, they would be able to get him on their side again. His loyalty was one of their last hopes; their last chances to defeat Ay. She... she would let him kill Ay, she decided, if that was what it took. She would place that decision in his hands when he got home. Even if doing so threatened civil war, he was the General, wasn't he? And he would get them through whatever was next; protect them from the fury of the courtiers and servants who were loyal to Ay. And if he was loyal to them, he could protect the Hittite Prince from the Grand Vizier and his men.

They needed him.

"Ith the Printh coming?" Tut whispered to his sister after lunch, of which he had eaten three bites of broth. He was drowsy, his thoughts garbled even as Granny carefully measured an appropriate dose of poppy. The appropriate dose was rising along with his pain levels. And so, sometimes, clear thinking was sacrificed for the sake of relief. And his tired, fuzzy mind wondered what the Hittites had decided; what reply his sister had received.

Ankh held the cat closer, Bastet purring in her arms like a tree full of locusts. "I haven't gotten a reply yet," she said. Letting the cat go, she turned to face him, taking his cold hands in hers as she bent closer to him, jingling the silver beads on her simple wig, the same one she'd been wearing for the past several days. "But no matter what happens... even if the letter doesn't go through... or even if someone... stops him... I'll be all right. The Pharaoh will manage... with or without a husband. And with... or without... an heir. No matter what happens."

Tut smiled and raised his face, silently asking for a kiss. She gave him a peck on the forehead. "I know you will. You're the withetht perthon I know.

"*You* are our last hope," he whispered with a sigh. That was all he could get his lips to say, but he placed as much meaning as he could into the words. If their prayers had been answered, she would be their last hope as she married the Hittite Prince and ruled from beside the throne, and she carried their last hope within her, the potential baby whom she would raise into a wise Pharaoh, protecting Egypt as a powerful Queen Mother until it grew up. And even… even in another future, she would be their last hope, carrying their family legacy away to safety in Sais.

She understood. And she nodded.

"I know."


Slowly, methodically, Semerkhet dabbed the cool, damp cloth over his friend's forehead, down each side of his face, over his neck. And he smiled as Tut gave a comfortable sigh, appreciating the moment of relief that Sem had brought him.

He didn't say anything. Just continued bathing his brother's face. Just focused on this moment.

"So thith ith what it's like?" he heard the Pharaoh whisper a moment later.

Semerkhet smiled at him, even as he lay there with his eyes closed.

"What?" he asked.

Tut opened his eyes. "Having a brother."

Semerkhet felt himself giving a little chuckle. "Yes," he whispered, running the cloth over the Pharaoh's jawline. "This is what it's like."

Now tears were gathering in Tut's warm, brown eyes. And he let them fall. "I just wish we had longer," he said in a choked whisper.

Gently Semerkhet wiped away his tears. "So do I," he said.

370

Semerkhet kept working. He sat with his friend for long periods, keeping him entertained and as comfortable as possible, but there were times when he had to get up, even leave the room, leaving his Mistress to sit with his Pharaoh. He had a staff to manage. Even on a day like this.

Especially on a day like this. Even as he realized that today marked six weeks since coming home.

Semerkhet was still in charge of all the servants who contributed to the looking-after of the Pharaoh— he was the King's Valet, the Attendant of the Lord of the Two Lands. So he managed the teams who looked for him for direction, telling them what laundry needed taken down to Khenut and her washerwomen, what dishes were no longer needed and could be returned to the kitchen, what herbs needed replenished.

Semerkhet went back and forth, getting a fresh basket of clean bandages from the Handlers of Royal Linen, keeping the other servants quiet as they fetched and carried, going down to the kitchens to tell the bakers to make an extra batch of honey-cakes. Just in case his brother was hungry enough to want some.

The maids even came in to clean while the Pharaoh drowsed, giving the room a quick dust; taking the wilting bouquet of daisies that had been sitting on the Pharaoh's forlorn dressing-table, replacing them with a fresh bunch of bright chrysanthemums. That did make the room look a bit more cheerful.

There was always work to be done. A thousand and one small things, one after the other, that would help add up to the best possible day for everyone. And doing them made Sem feel good. Because he knew he was making a difference.

"Meresankh?"

The handmaiden paused as she walked down the hall with a basket of laundry, having little else to do other than carry it down to Khenut herself.

"Yes, My Lady?" she said, making her way to the Pharaoh's bedroom door and setting her basket on the floor. Ankh beckoned to her, and she entered the room, glancing silently at the sleeping Pharaoh, who looked worse than yesterday, if that was possible. "Yes... Ankhesenamun?"

The Queen gave a wistful little smile. And she nodded at the Pharaoh's private sitting room. Meresankh followed her inside and took the chair her friend offered to her.

"I have something else for you," Ankh said, reaching over to her desk for a document. As the Queen moved, Meresankh looked at her stomach. If she squinted, she could almost see a slight curve. Almost.

She looked up again. Now Ankh was offering her a rather substantial stack of papyri. And there were tears in her eyes, even as she gave Meresankh a very proud-looking smile.

"These are the Queens Lists," she said, offering them. Meresankh held out her hands, carefully taking the heavy pile of documents. "The ones we've been studying together. I thought it was only right... that you have your own copy."

Meresankh looked down at the papyri in her arms, heavy with the weight of history. And she could see her Lady's graceful handwriting, tracing the names *Khentkaus, Tetisheri... Merneith.*

But one was missing. And Meresankh blinked back her own tears as she smiled up at her friend, her sister.

"I'll put you in," she whispered, holding the stack of papyri to her heart. "Everything you've done... everything you go on to do. You're just like them... just as strong, just as wise. Just as worth

372

learning from. And I'll read it to my daughters, and they'll read it to theirs…"

And then Meresankh felt the air leave her lungs as the Queen threw her arms around her.

Now that Semerkhet's heart was filled with the Light, he wondered about his Pharaoh. Worried about him. Because if he did not accept the truth about I-AM, then after he took his final breath, he would know no peace.

So Sem prayed for his friend, for his brother. That his heart, too, would be opened to the Light.

Regretfully, Semerkhet got up, crossing the room to the door. Now he had a load of dishes to take back to the kitchen.

But before he could get very far, a smiling face stopped him. Meresankh stood there with her hands out, little silver necklace shining over her heart.

"May I?" she asked. And gratefully, he handed her the dishes.

But she didn't carry the stack of dishes down the hall immediately. She stood there, face glowing.

"I still can't believe we're married!" she whispered, voice aching with joy. She sighed, looking off into the future even as they stood together in this heartbreaking present. "So many plans to make; so many things to talk about… but it can wait; it can wait," she said. Meresankh sighed again. "A bride wants to celebrate, and pack, and dance and scream for joy, and hurry up and start our life together, but we need… we need to do this first." She swallowed, reaching out to take his hand. "But my heart is so happy— I can't stop smiling… but I'm sad at the same time." She shook her head. "I want to tell everybody, but I'll wait, don't worry." She gave a thoughtful pause. "If you see me smiling, don't think I'm being inappropriate. I'm just so happy, and so grateful to him... which makes it even sadder... that he's leaving."

Now her face fell, and Semerkhet reached out and gently rested a hand on her shoulder. She looked up at him, and tenderly, he reached out and wiped away the tears that were running down her cheeks.

"We'll keep praying for him," he whispered. His heart warmed as he realized that now, he could be the one to say that to her.

And she smiled. "Yes. We will."

He returned her smile, watery as his was. "I have... have something to tell you," he said softly. He swallowed, blinking back tears again as she nodded, inviting him to continue. "You were right," he said, his voice choked.

"About what?" she asked gently.

"About Nedjes," he said, wiping his eyes and smearing his makeup. "About... about it not being my fault. I don't know... but I understand now. That things happen... but a bad thing happening... even a bad thing I couldn't stop from happening... doesn't make it my fault. A bad thing happening... doesn't mean I didn't protect my brother. Then... or now."

Meresankh nodded, tears slowly filling her own eyes. And without a word, she put her arms around her husband, holding him close. Silently she smiled, gratitude warming her heart. He had finally found the truth.


The Queen's brother was hungry. That was a good sign, she supposed. His body was requesting food. It wasn't done fighting. So Ankhesenamun sat with him, carefully feeding him spoonfuls of yogurt, a little afternoon snack. He opened his mouth, and she

374

poked a bite in, watching his Adam's apple bob as he swallowed, then wiping any excess from his mouth with a bit of linen. Over and over again.

And then… Ankh saw her brother's head slowly turn on the pillow; heard his breath gently release as his eyes drifted shut. Then she heard him snore.

Chuckling even as tears came to her eyes, Ankh set the bowl of yogurt aside and gently patted Tut's thin shoulder, feeling his bones under her hand. Slowly his tired eyes opened again, and he smiled up at her. Even with all the weight he had lost, he still had the dimple she'd always loved.

"You sleepy?" she whispered. He just smiled. She wasn't sure if he understood what had just happened. And he fell asleep again.

The Queen sighed and tucked him in. Apparently he was done eating.

He was spending a lot of time sleeping, Tut knew. More than ever. Maybe his body was getting tired. Maybe it was wearing out. Maybe he was running out of the strength he needed to fight.

It was strange; almost funny. He was sleeping so much; so deeply that sometimes he could hardly seem to wake up. If only he could have had some of this restfulness during the long, hard nights of the past few weeks; the nights when he had spent the dark watches staring into space by the hour. Now morning, afternoon, evening, night, it hardly seemed to matter. Whenever he let his eyes fall closed, he would drift off… whether or not he wanted to.

But sleep was the only thing that brought true relief. And so he accepted it as a gift.

# 34    Horemheb

The General would be home late tonight, the staff were saying, or the next day at the latest. Between the shocks of pain that jolted through his burning leg as he shivered in a painful chill, Tut wondered if he would be able to hang on long enough for one last conversation. And gauge if Horemheb was remorseful enough to deserve a place in Ankh's royal court, trustworthy enough to help continue guiding Egypt in the direction Tutankhamun had established, wise and powerful enough to limit the Vizier's machinations without starting a war.

He hoped he would have the opportunity.

It bothered him all that day. Something left; something that still needed resolved. He had left his friend a married man, set for life with enough gold to build a house; had opened his heart to the sincere wish that his sister might find happiness in another marriage. And yet, there was still something.

He thought of those he cared about; Ankh, Sem. Nothing remained unresolved between him and them. Even Bastet had been provided for. And then he smiled, giving a little nod as an image of the other person he wished was here, the man with whom he had hoped to become lifelong friends, rose in his heart. *Horemheb*. What he needed to do was to leave a message for Horemheb.

The King called for Semerkhet.

"Get a papyrus," he whispered. "And a pen. Have a... have a letter to write."

"A letter?" Sem asked, bending over the Pharaoh with a curious smile.

376

"To Horemheb," Tut said.

Semerkhet nodded. And already, Tutankhamun could tell that he understood.

The valet sat down. And Tut struggled to keep his eyes open; to form the series of coherent thoughts that would express the wishes he was commanding the General to carry out.

"Tell him… tell him I thaw him," he said. "Know what he did."

"But that you forgive him, though," Semerkhet said gently. "He needs to know that, too. We need to take… the long view."

Tut just nodded. And Semerkhet promised Horemheb that the Pharaoh had forgiven him.

His eyes drifted shut. *He was wandering in the courtyards of Akhetaten, following his Mother, who was walking just ahead of him.* Then Semerkhet's voice said,

"And what else would you like to tell him?"

Tutankhamun dragged his eyes open, resisting the sleep that was pulling him down. And resisting the pain that shuddered through him with every labored breath he took. He needed another dose of poppy, but he wouldn't take it until the letter was complete. He needed every bit of mind-power he could gather.

"Tell him… don't let me down. And to take… take…" A wave of coughing overtook him, and he bent inward, chest searing with fire as his body shook, jangling his legs until tears of pain came to his eyes. Slowly, he dragged in a breath, fighting to refill his screaming lungs. "Tell him to take…"

"To take care of the Queen, and the baby?" Semerkhet finished for him. Through his streaming eyes, the Pharaoh could see the loving concern on his friend's face. Along with sorrow that he was helpless to ease Tut's pain.

Tut just nodded. And Semerkhet continued to write.

Sentence by sentence, point by point, the Pharaoh constructed the letter he wanted to send to the General. This was his last move on the *seega* board of life— using Horemheb as a piece in the game in which he and the Vizier were still locked. But with this final move, they might still win.

If the Queen could not become King, if Zannanza never arrived to accept the throne they had offered him, Horemheb was the next best person to take leadership of Egypt. And deep in his heart, Tutankhamun knew that if he proved loyal, the General would be more than capable as Pharaoh.

It took an hour. But patiently, Semerkhet took down every word the Pharaoh choked out between coughing fits and minute-long lapses into an exhausted drowse. And as the afternoon wore on, they completed the letter that the Pharaoh hoped would secure the future of Egypt.

The letter finally complete, Tutankhamun reached for the pen, then scrawled his name at the bottom of the letter.

"Need to hide it," he whispered, "until we can thend it."

Semerkhet nodded. Carefully, he slipped the letter under the Pharaoh's pillow.

Tut lay back against the pillow, exhausted but smiling. This might be his final move in this game, he knew, but with a move like this, they just might win. Even if he was not there to see it.

He yawned. Decision-making, letter-writing, were exhausting. Even without having had his poppy, he was ready to take another nap. He settled down in bed, trying to find a comfortable spot as he took Bastet in his thin arms. He felt intuitive Semerkhet tucking

378

him in, seeing what he needed. Time for a little afternoon nap. When he woke up, he would ask Ankh to stamp the letter with their signet-ring, then hide it securely for the proper time.

Tut slept. And he dreamed.

*Ay was standing above him, taking the letter Ankh had just sent to the Hittites, then tipping a cup of red wine over it so the red stain slowly spread over the papyrus like a growing bloodstain around a knife-wound, staining the entire letter and then dripping onto the floor in a crimson puddle. Then Ay turned into a vulture, slowly circling the room with a guttural cry of triumph before flying out the window, the Queen struggling in his claws.*

*Then Tut saw the throne room, where Nakhtmin was sitting in full royal regalia, being served by a frowning Semerkhet who seemed bent and aged by grief and woe, the scars of whip-lashes visible on his skin. Suddenly fire rose in Semerkhet's eyes, and he straightened up, tall and proud as before, spitting at Nakhtmin's feet. Seconds later Tut's dream-self wanted to scream as Nakhtmin drew back his hand and struck Sem full across the face— with a cry, the valet collapsed, dead. Then suddenly, Horemheb appeared, stabbing Nakhtmin and jamming the crown onto his own head, shoving the young General's body to the floor and claiming the throne for himself.*

*Now Ankh was crying over seven bodies lying on the floor of the throne room; his own, lying strange and stiff, Meritaten's, those of their mother and father, Pentu's, Usermontu's, and that of a young man he had never seen, who looked as though he may have been Hittite, with a peach-pale face and a curly brown beard. Above them Ay stood with a bloody knife, while Horemheb silently stared,*

379

*an uncomfortable look of painful, conflicted indecision on his face. Sem, meanwhile, had stopped being dream-dead, and, hand-in-hand, he and Meresankh ran from the palace as swiftly as gazelles, following Granny Merneith to safety, three small children running along with them. As they ran, Tut saw Sem's red jasper ring of the Sole Companion and Meresankh's silver necklace catch the torchlight. What were they running toward? It looked like a burning bush. Its bright light matched the flame that seemed to burn inside Semerkhet's heart, Meresankh's, Merneith's; those of the three children, two girls and a boy.*

*Now the double crown of Egypt stood on a tall shelf. Ay, Horemheb, and Ankh were struggling to reach it; trying to push one another out of the way to win the best chance of grabbing it. But the image faded too quickly for Tut to see who managed to get it.*

*Now the Queen was holding a baby. Ay beckoned to her, but she turned away, then spat at his feet. As he raised his hand to strike her, Horemheb got between them, allowing her and the child to escape in safety as he prevented Ay from following them. But as she ran, Tut noticed that she was no longer wearing her crown.*

*Ay sat down on the throne, suddenly resplendent in the full regalia of double crown, false beard, and crook and flail, and Horemheb transformed into a lion, prowling back and forth in front of the throne as if waiting for Ay to fall into his open jaws.*

*Then the doors of the palace flew open and all the sands of the desert rushed in, sweeping everyone away in a blinding avalanche that formed a roaring tidal wave like the faraway sea. Everything he knew, everyone he loved or hated, was gone.*

*But when the dust cleared, the Sun was shining, its loving beams stretching down to Earth like gentle hands. And two little*

380

*girls he thought he recognized stood there, ready to welcome him to a place he'd never been, but felt like home.*

Tutankhamun woke with a start, dripping with sweat and blinking back tears. Only a dream. He was safe, Ankh was safe, Semerkhet was safe, Meresankh was safe, the Hittite Prince they hadn't even met yet was safe. And the heir, if there was one, was safe. Even Nakhtmin and Ay and Horemheb were presumably safe. The future was yet to be written, but for now, all of them were safe. And the letter to the Hittites was already sent.

Ankhesenamun sat with Tut late that afternoon, dabbing his head with a cool cloth while his face and body burned. He had become too weak even to let Semerkhet assist him with shaving, and a light stubble of hair was growing on his scalp, delicate little wisps that reminded her of the first time she'd seen him, the baby brother whose life would be permanently intertwined with hers.

"Make sure Horemheb gets the letter," Tut whispered. The Queen shook her head, blinking sleepiness from her eyes. She'd rested in her chair for a few minutes while Semerkhet took a break, but a moment with her eyes closed had refreshed her, and she was ready to get back to work. Although something had disturbed her rest for a moment... but she wasn't sure what it had been. It had sounded like a familiar creeping footstep; the swish of the sleeves of a robe like the heavy wings of a circling vulture. Probably just a dream.

"What letter, darling?" she asked, her eyebrows contracting in curiosity.

"Under here," he said, cocking his head in such a way that she knew that he meant it was under his pillow. "Help me?" She got

381

up, setting the cloth and bowl of water aside for a moment to poke around among his bedding, the silver beads on her short, simple wig clinking as she moved.

"I'm not finding it," she said with a little frown, pushing aside sheets, blankets, and pillows to check every inch of the bed, then checking the floor.

Tut frowned, pressing his lips together with a heavy sigh. So Ay had had one more move in this game. "Never mind." He looked up at her. "Juth… tell Horemheb… I know that deep down, he wath… faithful to me, whatever he did. And… not to let me down when he'th Vizier for you and the Printh."

She nodded sadly, squeezing his hand. "I will."

"That ith all right, ithn't it?" Tut whispered, fighting back a cough as pain twinged in his chest. "Horemheb ath Vithier? I thought that wath the only way he… would do what I thaid… if I promithed him thomefing."

Ankh sighed, giving him a little nod. "We'll manage." Then she paused with another frown. "What were you looking for, just now? What letter?"

He swallowed. "The Vithier hathn't learned to thtay out of other people'th things. I wrote to Horemheb… told him everything… but it'th… gone… Ay found it…"

Yawning, Tut settled back into bed, closing his eyes again. That was all the conversation he could manage.

Ankh sighed, guilt twisting in her heart as she realized that she had failed to keep her promise to watch for Ay and keep him from doing something exactly like this. One more plan had fallen through because of the Vizier. Even now, they were at war. And who would ultimately win… was a question no one could answer until it all happened.

Only whoever won in the end… her brother had lost.

"I'm sorry," she whispered, bending to kiss him on the forehead.

Tut closed his eyes as Ankh bent to kiss him. He was so tired… he knew he wouldn't be able to stay awake. Knew he shouldn't even try. He needed to be rested for whatever was coming next. Another little catnap would do no harm.

It was sad, though. That had been the whole reason that he hadn't wanted to take the poppy… to keep Ay from doing something exactly like this, making one last wicked move in this terrible game. Ankh and Sem had promised Tut that they wouldn't let the Vizier do anything; that they would keep watch. And so he had accepted the medicine and the sleep that came with it. But Sem had taken a break and Ankh's exhaustion had caused her to drift off at exactly the wrong moment… and Ay had had his chance.

But Tut wasn't angry at them. Not really. He didn't have enough energy to be angry. He was… disappointed. But forgiving. Because they were so tired from taking care of him so faithfully… How could they help needing a break; how could they keep from falling asleep? It was just… a shame.

The valet had a stomach full of guilt. Because he had failed. Failed to follow his Master's instructions; failed to protect his baby brother. And now the letter the Pharaoh had written, the letter that might have changed the future, was gone.

All because Semerkhet had failed to keep watch.

Semerkhet stepped out of the royal bedroom. And he had a chat with Hannu. Hannu, who had stepped away to help Nakhtmin, who seemed to have tripped on something and wrenched his ankle on the way down the hall. The bodyguard had noticed something, he admitted, but it had disappeared out of the corner of his eye like a shadow. And he was ashamed to learn the price of his deception.

But the Sole Companion forgave him. Just as the Pharaoh had forgiven him. They truly were all only human.

And Hannu promised to be even more strict. No one, not even Meresankh, would get through without Hannu's express permission.

A sick feeling settled into the pit of Semerkhet's stomach as he heard the whispering. He stopped in the hallway, dreading what he was about to hear.

One servant was whispering to another. "So, the day that the bad news arrives that the Hittite Prince isn't coming, you take out Kamose, and I'll get the Sole Companion before he can warn the Queen. The handmaiden will have to go, as well." The man smiled bitterly. "By the time our Glorious Lord can announce that with a heavy heart, he's taking the throne, everyone who opposed him will be out of the way. Except for the Queen. But he wanted to deal with her himself."

The second man frowned. "Do they know we're onto them? Do they know we have a plan for if they try to get in the way of the Vizier's path to the throne?"

"They don't need to know," the first man sneered. "They'll find out soon enough."

"But what if they put up a fight... a real fight? What if— what if they kill our Glorious Lord to put their Queen on the throne?"

384

The first man sneered again. "Then they will greet Osiris together, and Crown Prince Nakhtmin will finish what his father started and bring Egypt back to glory and prosperity."

"For the good of Egypt," the second man said, in the same tone with which Semerkhet might have wished his Pharaoh life, health, and prosperity.

"For the good of Egypt," the first man echoed, and they were gone.

Semerkhet turned away sweating, praying to I-AM, the Aten, that he, Meresankh, and the Queen would get to Sais before the axe fell.

The Pharaoh dreamed again. Of his family... his mother and father, smiling in the sunlight as his sisters danced in a merry circle.

"Come find us," they seemed to sing. "Find the Light."

He wasn't hungry anymore. And he was barely thirsty. He hadn't had to pee or anything in ages. Something was definitely changing.

Granny gave him another dose of poppy. Again he felt the strange sensation of his heart slowing down as he grew heavy in the bed, descending into a state that was restful, even if it was not sleep. He could feel the cold cloths that Granny had placed on his forehead and neck and under his arms, although somehow, being miserably hot was no longer registering. Because he was not miserable. He was just sort of "there." He lay there half-awake, dimly aware of what was going on around him; of the loved ones quietly going about their day. When he needed something, he whined for it as politely as he could, and they brought it.

The pain was there, but it was under control, and he could ignore it. And when he needed more poppy, Merneith gave it to him.

He opened his eyes at intervals, trying to smile up at Ankh, Sem. But had mere minutes passed since the last time he had opened his eyes… or hours… days… weeks? With the fever, the poppy, and the war that was raging inside his body, he no longer had any concept of the passage of time.

He just lay there in bed. He continued to breathe. And he continued to exist.


Meresankh sighed. Her heart was so full… so full of joy and sorrow, gratitude and pain. She knew it wasn't wrong to be happy; she wanted to shout from the rooftops how grateful she was to the Pharaoh for letting her marry her true love. The Pharaoh… who was dying.

Meresankh bit her lip. And she walked down to Granny's workshop.

The old woman was grinding herbs; Meresankh could smell the sweetness of the lavender; the pungency of the valerian. The same blend as had gone into the Pharaoh's tea last night and the night before; the tea that the Queen had said had worked. Now that they had something they knew worked, they would make gallons of it.

"How do I do it, Granny?" she asked with a sigh.

"Do what, dearie?" Merneith asked, brushing the dust of the herb-grinding off her hands and tipping the powder from the bowl she'd been grinding it in into a small linen bag.

Meresankh sat down on one of the stools by the table, taking Granny's old, black cat into her lap. It purred and rubbed its head against her chin.

"Be happy and sad at the same time," she said. She swallowed. "Be happy I'm married... and sad that the Pharaoh... doesn't have much time."

Granny set aside her work, stepping around the table to take Meresankh's hand in her wrinkled one.

"That is the strength of women, dearie," she said with a little smile. "That we can feel so many emotions all at once... and not explode like an overfilled wineskin."

And Meresankh laughed.

"But truly, dearie," Granny went on, "that's life. Joy and sorrow, gratitude and pain, envy and hope, grief and peace... they don't come to us one at a time. The things that happen... they make us feel so many things in the space of a single breath. And so... the key is to feel all those feelings inside our own hearts... and then choose what we reflect out to the world. You can be happy all day that you are a married woman... and you can be sad that the Pharaoh's life is nearly over. Both are right to feel. But it is your choice to show your joy to others without disrespecting their grief; show your grief without keeping them from what they need to do. You get to choose what you show."

Meresankh smiled. And she bent to kiss her Granny. She was ready to go back to work. And she would reflect gratitude, a calm joy, and the peace she felt inside her heart, a peace that was greater than any fear for their future. Or even... even for the Pharaoh's. Because as she felt her heart warm with the Light of the Sun, she knew that I-AM was at work.

# 35  Light

There wasn't much time. Sem could feel it in his heart as the afternoon wore on— an urgency, a change. His friend was sleeping more, talking less, and he just… Semerkhet wanted to push the thought away, but he didn't. The Pharaoh looked like a person who was dying. Sem thought back to the wailing he had heard from the Queen's room on the day Tutankhamun had given them the bad news and shuddered. What sounds would be ripped from his own heart when that day came? Or… that hour?

Politics never ended, Ankhesenamun thought, petting the cat while Tut drowsed late that afternoon, spending an hour or so on his side. Even now her brother had written another letter. But Ay had found it. And writing another one would not guarantee that Horemheb would ever receive it; even if it was hidden safely in Merneith's workshop, with the loyalties of the staff becoming ever more divided, even Granny's workshop might not be safe from thieving hands. And if he discovered that the headstrong Queen had made another attempt to influence the future, contacting the General to win his loyalty, the Vizier would have even more reason to do something permanent. So she would say those things to Horemheb when he came home, and hope that his heart would change. And hope that in his knowledge of that letter, that Ay would not pounce on the General first.

She clenched her fists as anger burned in her heart, tears of pain brimming in her eyes. Her brother had worked so hard to compose that letter. Here on his deathbed, he had expended strength and energy he no longer had to compose, word by word, she was sure, one last message to General Horemheb. Writing that letter had taken more than he could give.

And the Vizier had stolen it. Again, guilt twisted inside her at the thought that her failure to keep watch had given him his chance to strike. But more than that, she was angry. Angry at the Vizier, at Nakhtmin, for their cruelty. How could they do something like this?

She thought of what she would say to them; the false King and his fake Prince of a son. *The one I love is dying— just leave us alone until it's over. Just have the decency to give us some peace; some privacy. Just give it a rest with all the politics. That you won't stop; that you keep coming at us, even now— it's just evil. Vile. Picking at him like a vulture tearing the flesh from an animal before it's even dead, harrowing it, fretting it, flaying it, pecking it to death, stripping it to the bone— you've been circling since his birthday; hovering, waiting to pounce. Just flap away and give us space until it's over. Quit staring at us as he lies dying. Just go away.*

She sighed, her thoughts returning to the General. If they… if she… could gain Horemheb's loyalty, that would make a crucial difference as the next page of history turned, the next chapter of their lives beginning as the well-loved past ended. Because the page of history was going to turn whether they liked it or not, whatever they did.

Like everything else… where Horemheb's loyalty lay, who would win him, and how he could be manipulated, was still uncertain. What would he do when he got home? Could he defend them against Ay while also protecting his beloved wives? If not… who would he pick?

What a question. The Queen hoped with all her heart that the General would be willing to help them… but never, never in all the world would she want him to lose his wives to do so. They had all made sacrifices in terms of their daily lives, in terms of their hopes and dreams, but trading lives… was a horrible thing to imagine having to consider.

But that was the question— what would the General do? Even if her letter to the Hittites, her proposal to Zannanza, fell through… did their last hope lie in Horemheb?

Or… did it lie curled up very small within her?

She sighed. And again, she wondered… if the Prince would ever get here. Doubt was growing in her heart. Along with a resolve… to be the leader she was… with or without a husband. And with… or without… an heir. With or without a throne. And with or without a crown.

And then she set all the politics aside. This, right here, right now, in this moment, was where she was needed; what she needed to focus on. She needed to stay present. What would happen with her letter… and with the Hittites… and with Ay and Horemheb and all the others… remained to be seen.

Tut could hear them talking, Ankh, Sem. Sometimes he could hear Semerkhet's lute, endless melodies winding through the haze in which he lay. Their voices grew louder and softer, louder and softer, as they had done when he had first lain ill, during the very first fever of the ague. But he was much more comfortable than he had been then. Sometimes a gentle shadow would move across the bed, and Ankh or Sem would bend over him to run a cool cloth over his burning head, the sides of his face, down his neck. And he would smile. Because, through it all, they were there with him.

He would drift off to the sound of Semerkhet's lute, gently awaken to the touch of his sister's hand as she bathed his face with a cool cloth; nod off to a lullaby murmured by the Queen, rouse halfway through a story Semerkhet was telling about a recent hockey game. But it no longer mattered that he could no longer tell the difference between sleeping and waking.

Sometimes they would stroke his head, humming to him as they tried to help ease him into yet another nap. Or they would hold his hands, silently connecting with him through touch. Even as he slept, he knew they were there with him. Through it all, he was grateful. Because he knew he was not alone.


There was a knock at the door. Confident that whoever it was had been approved by Hannu, Sem went to answer it, finding Nuya standing there. To Semerkhet's surprise, he wasn't wearing his scribe's kilt; he looked like he must have on that awful day that Sem had been turned into a scribe and Nuya had been turned into a valet. So Nuya was looking a bit uncomfortable in a valet's uniform... and ready for action.

"The chef is wondering how much broth to prepare," he said softly. "For the rest of today. And the Handlers of Royal Linen want to make sure you have enough cloths. We haven't seen you for awhile to answer questions."

Semerkhet shook his head with a little smile. "I need to stay where I am," he said softly. "But as Sole Companion, I'm deputizing you to answer whatever questions you can yourself. You know most of what needs done. And I'm sure that you can use what you've learned to reason out most of their questions. Anything really specific, you can come ask me. But he..." Sem looked over his shoulder, to where his friend was lying there in bed, drowsing as the Queen silently read from the papyrus on her knee. "He needs me here. I have confidence in you, Nuya," Semerkhet said, reaching out to gently grasp his shoulder. "We need you. Will you do this for us?"

Nuya gave a little smile, then bowed to the Sole Companion. "As you wish, Your Excellency." And he was gone.

Semerkhet smiled as the scribe left. The staff was coming together, people from various departments setting aside their normal roles and duties to come help take care of the Pharaoh, ready for whatever task might be most helpful, whatever was needed. Those who loved the Pharaoh were uniting on this side of the line in the sand.

Then it was dinnertime, the short, cool day coming to a close. It wasn't convenient for Tut to eat on his side, so Semerkhet and Kamose maneuvered him onto his back again. And he lay there gratefully against his pillows as Ankh carefully fed him spoonfuls of warm broth, broth that Semerkhet had approved with the words "I taste your food, Great Morning Star." Tut wasn't very hungry, but it tasted good.

Although… it was as if he needed sleep more than food. And he could barely keep his eyes open as his sister fed him the broth.

He didn't finish it.

The day was passing, Semerkhet thought as he sat in the Pharaoh's sitting room, eating the simple dinner of flatbread, lentils, and hot dumplings with honey that Meresankh had brought him. He felt the simple, wholesome food filling his stomach, giving him strength to get through another hard night. They had made it through another day.

Soon it would be bedtime, and they would tell stories, sing songs, drink Granny's herbal tea as they prepared to settle in for another long night. Although, with how peaceful last night had been, maybe it wouldn't be so rough.

It was his turn to start off. He would see what his friend wanted; whether he wanted to be moved onto his side so Sem could rub his back, or whether he wanted to remain as he was and have Sem maybe stroke his head and sing. Whatever it took. Whatever it took to get his brother to sleep. And they would take turns, Semerkhet and the Queen, sitting at his side until morning came. By morning, General Horemheb would be home.

Although… Semerkhet paused in the middle of a bite of lentils, feeling a stray one drop into his lap. He picked it up, popping it back into his mouth and slowly chewing the bite he'd taken, carefully swallowing it down. And he chased it with a sip of beer.

There was something different about tonight. Something disconcerting. Unsettling. A change. A chill. And a strange feeling was stirring, deep within Semerkhet's aching heart. Like… like maybe tonight… something was going to happen. Something was going to change. And morning… was never going to come.

Or if it did… his brother was not going to see it.


The Queen paused as she ate her own meal at her brother's bedside, also brought by Meresankh from the servants' dining hall. And she pulled her outer robe closer. But it wasn't just the cold of the Tybi night that was sending shivers down her spine. Somehow… somehow she was feeling exactly the same as she had felt when her brother had gone to Kadesh.

And by morning… everything was going to be different.

Shadows were getting long, the day growing dim outside the window. Each day grew shorter as they entered the darkest part of the year. The twelve hours of daytime and twelve of nighttime waxed and waned with the year, so each hour of this long night would be longer than the daytime hours that had preceded them. The priests would be honoring the sunset with the nightly ceremony; the servants' work would be winding down. The day was coming to a close.

And so… The Pharaoh shuddered, giving a painful cough. So was his life. Because he didn't… feel the same. Something was going to happen; he could feel it in his bones. Tonight was going to be a milestone. And he thought he knew what the milestone was going to be.

The long night was beginning. So long. And so very, very dark. As dark as the isolation he had felt in that dream that had seemed to foretell what awaited him if he could not find the Light.

The growing dark seemed to touch him, and again, the great big nineteen-year-old boy was afraid of the dark. And what it meant. And yet, there was also the Light. And what it meant.

Where would he go, when he fell asleep never to awaken? Would he open his eyes to find himself being judged by Ma'at?

He had not addressed any of the traditional gods of his people in days. His feelings over the past year… his conversation with Merneith about what she remembered from her own youth… his memories of the way his parents had connected with the Divine… were pulling him toward a new idea… toward what felt like the Truth. Felt like… the warmth of the Sun, shining down to gently touch his face with its loving rays. And he knew that whatever most Egyptians expected to find in the afterlife, he would neither be judged by Ma'at nor welcomed by Osiris. After taking his final breath, he would experience something else entirely. And he was starting to think he knew what it would be.

As long as he reached back up into the Light.

The words his father had written and taught him as a little boy ran through his mind. Words of the Aten.

*How manifold it is, what Thou hast made!*
*They are hidden from the face of man*
*O sole God, like whom there is no other!*
*Thou didst create the world according to Thy desire,*
*Whilst Thou wert alone: All men, cattle, and wild beasts,*
*Whatever is on earth, going upon its feet,*
*And what is on high, flying with its wings*

What a thought. One God Who was powerful enough to create everything there was, exactly as He had chosen.

And the Aten, I-AM, loved everyone. No matter what they did, He still shone down His Light upon them. And even in His wrath, there was love, for in sending the plagues upon Egypt, He had set His chosen people free.

Just like Granny had told Tut, I-AM knew that all human beings had done wrong, and He would forgive those who confessed their sinfulness. He alone could take away the weight of sin; make a person's heart light enough to balance any scales He might have.

Tut thought of Merneith, the quiet, peaceful relationship she had with her God, the same God his father had reached out to. He thought of the Light he glimpsed shining from Meresankh's face, whenever he saw her peeking through the door. Thought of the new peace he had seen on Semerkhet's face as well. Thought of the questions he himself had been asking over the past year.

And here lay the Pharaoh, seeing death creeping around the corner. If there was a decision to be made, a prayer to be prayed, the time was now.

Semerkhet was resting in his chair; Ankh was taking a moment in her own room. So Tut had a private moment. The day had been cloudy, but suddenly, a ray of evening sunlight descended through a small opening in the clouds, streaming through the filmy linen curtains to touch his face with its warmth. Was this a sign?

He closed his eyes, feeling the warmth of the setting Sun on his face. And in his heart the warmth he had not felt in the Temple of Amun-Ra. The warmth of the days of the Aten… that he had felt more recently at key moments; moments that had moved him toward the Truth he now seemed to be holding in his hands. And that he had felt a hint of every time he left the cold, dark Temple of Amun-Ra and felt the Sun touch him again. The warmth he had longed for for so many years.

*O Great I-AM,* he whispered inside his heart, *Lord of the Hebrews, known to my father as* Aten, *I come to You now. And I say to You that I believe; I believe that You are truly the Creator and Sustainer of all, and I believe in the love that You show. I am sorry for turning away from You. I ask You to forgive the things I've done wrong, to pass over my sins, to give Your love to me now and take me to be with You when I die.*

Tutankhaten released a deep breath. And smiled. All one had to do was reach out and receive; accept the love that I-AM, the Aten, was pouring out like the rays of the Sun, like friendly hands, reaching out to humanity when they couldn't reach up to Him. The warmth in his heart was getting stronger, and instead of fear, he

396

actually felt joy. The Light had touched him. He knew that whatever happened, he was safe.

*He made me like this*, Tut thought. *And He did it with love. And purpose. A hale King of war wouldn't have been able to establish peace this way. If I'd had two strong legs, I would have spent all my time on the battlefield, and none making friends with Egypt's neighbors and making things better for the citizens of my country. With two strong legs, I would have been nothing but a selfish King of conquest.* In all the suffering, in all the frustration, there had been purpose. Always.

Grandfather Thutmose had been wrong. And so had Tut, he realized, in clinging to the idea that the only legacy worth creating was one of conquest. Chasing after the heroic ideal of the warrior King would never make him "more;" never make him more than what he already was. The strong Pharaoh he had always wanted to be… he already was. And always had been.

Over the nine years of his reign; the months he had spent ruling alone, he had established a legacy of his own. A legacy of Light.

# 36  Truth

Ankhesenamun looked down at her brother, sleeping quietly in the bed. He was so pale. So silent. His chest rose and fell with his steady breathing; he appeared to be free of his pain for the moment. But she felt something changing. Sitting here watching him sleep… it felt like a vigil. The time for herself was over, she decided. She would not leave his side again.

He breathed so quietly. So gently. With so little movement that there were moments when her heart began to pound, and she stared at him, watching his chest until she saw it move, reassuring her that even if all was not well, he was still with them. And his breathing had changed. He would take quick, shallow breaths for a few minutes; then would come a terrifying pause. And then his breathing would come slow and deep. But no matter what… no matter what, she could hear the terrible congestion gurgling in his chest, his throat. The rattle it made would frighten her for a moment; then he would give a little cough and his breathing would smooth out again. Right now it was so gentle she could barely perceive it.

But there was a change in his face. He was still pale, still thinner than she wanted to see, still looked like his body was barely hanging on. And yet… there was a peace on his face. Like she saw on Meresankh's face, Merneith's, even Semerkhet's. Like she remembered, so long ago, seeing on her parents' faces; the faces of her sisters. A Light. She was glad to see it… and yet it only added to her questions.

She sighed, thinking back over all those years. All that hard work. All those sacrifices that everyone had made to make sure

398

that little Tutankhaten had everything he needed the minute he needed it. Because that was their goal… to keep him alive as long as possible.

She swallowed. Had they succeeded? Was the day coming when it would literally no longer be possible?

And careful not to wake him with the tinkling of the silver beads of her wig, she bent and kissed his forehead. As she stepped back again, he turned his head and smiled in his sleep.

"He'th real," Tut whispered to his wife after he woke up, having slipped into another short nap without even noticing. She looked questioningly at him, eyebrows urging him to continue, to elaborate. "Aten," he said. "Father wath right all along."

Her eyes filled with tears as her heart began to pound. "You really think so?"

He glanced out the window, at the soft evening sunlight that was streaming in. "He heard me. Amun never heard me. Wath only ever just an idol. But Aten… I-AM… ith real. Made me… made me the way I am. Tho I could be a King of peace. And He anthwered my prayerth, even though I was praying to Amun-Ra." He swallowed back tears. "That I would be a thtrong Pharaoh."

Ankh closed her eyes as the tears slowly rolled down her cheeks, feeling a shudder pass through her. Something strange, something good, something real, ached inside her heart as her brother's words echoed through her mind. And she had no words with which to respond.

He fell asleep again two minutes after his earth-shattering proclamation. His sister sat with him, thinking about what they'd just spoken of.

Had Father been right? Was the Aten real— was He I-AM? Really? Really and truly? And was her brother... was her brother safe in His Light?

She thought of the Light she had just seen in her brother's eyes. And she thought... thought of the purpose for which she had waited so long. Had that purpose just been revealed? The purpose for all the suffering, all the pain, all the difficulty? Had her brother... been created to be a King of peace?

"Show me," she whispered, raising her eyes to the window, where the evening was deepening into twilight. "If this is real... if this is true... if You are answering our prayers right now... show me. Please."

And the Queen felt her heart fill with memories. Memories... of the love and peace her parents and sisters had known, of all the moments she had spent standing in the loving warmth of the Sun, of the cold darkness of the temple, of all the prayers her gods and goddesses had never answered, of the Truth that Meresankh seemed to possess. The Truth that Meresankh herself said had been found by Akhenaten. Memories of moments that had drawn her away from the timeless traditions of Egypt, toward something bigger. Memories of a faith that had always sustained her as she had searched for the purpose behind everything she and her brother had gone through.

And she knew that her brother had found the Truth.

"Thank You," she whispered, raising her hands in gratitude, the reverent salute her parents had always offered to the Aten. And Ankhesenpaaten opened her heart and let the Light in.

Her faith in what she had not yet seen had been rewarded. Ankhesenpaaten gave a sigh of relief, relief for which she had been waiting for so many years.

400

The Light had come into her heart. And the empty, aching space that the gods of her people had left was full of warmth; full of a Love that she knew would get her through whatever she still had to face. And more than ever before... she knew that she would see her daughters again.

The miracles of their grandfather's day, their own father's childhood, were so real, so monumental, that fifty years later, the old midwife and the Queen's own handmaiden still worshiped the God of the Hebrews. And to think that such an all-powerful God loved them... took all of Ankh's fears away. Even if her beloved brother was about to leave... he was safe. And in that knowledge, there was peace.

When the time came... she knew that somehow, she would be able to let him go.

A feeling gently touched Ankh's heart as she watched her brother sleeping; a feeling as deep and true as this new peace.

This was the last evening.

He had to tell Semerkhet where he was going. Even if he could barely get the words out. Tut swallowed, getting his thick tongue and his dry lips ready to speak.

"He'th real," he whispered with a smile. He squeezed Semerkhet's hand as hard as he could. "I-AM. The Aten my father worshiped." He chuckled. "I'll be all right."

"I know you will," Sem whispered through his happy tears. Now that he looked, the Pharaoh saw a familiar Light shining in his eyes as well. "I found Him too."

And Tut smiled.

A feeling of peace filled Semerkhet's heart as he stroked his friend's head with a silent prayer of gratitude. Tut had found I-AM, the Aten. Whatever happened, Sem's Pharaoh was safe.

He didn't want to let his brother go… but he knew he would be able to.

*Warrior king.* The words came back to him— the words that had rung in his heart as the only ideal worth pursuing; with which the heroes of the past had seemed to mock him. And another thought warmed his heart, gently brushing away the dust of the heroic image that had clung to him for so long. *Warrior.* Not *soldier.* He thought of his parents; his sisters. People he never would have expected to see wielding weapons, but the bravest people he knew, nonetheless.

Tut swallowed. Not… not all warriors were soldiers, were they? And the battlefield was not the only place where one could fight with courage.

But what did that mean?

A thousand memories filled his heart; all the times he had struggled to manage the steps that led up to the royal dais, moments when he had fought harder than anyone else could see to regally conceal the pain in his foot or the lisp that struggled to escape, tapping along with the walking-stick he relied on to get around and yet could, with the right bearing, transform into a simple staff of office, the pain of simply wearing the heavy double-crown, the yearly strain of Tribute Day. All the moments no one but his sister ever saw; all the hard work that he had to contend with every day simply through being himself.

He shook his head as grateful tears filled his eyes. Through it all, every day of his life, he *had* been a warrior King. Life had been his battlefield. And with calm courage, resilience, and determination, he had won his war.

Then he thought of the hurtful words with which the Grandfather Thutmose in his dream had mocked him. *Scrawny, pathetic Boy-King; feeble little cripple... weak... failure.* And he shook his head. Maybe he wasn't a soldier. But pathetic? Feeble? He considered the politics he had managed over the past few months; the decisions he had made and laws he had passed. He had proven himself quite capable, establishing a worthwhile legacy of his own. His time standing alone, ruling in full power, had been far too short, but his reign had been marked with success, not failure. And being crippled... if anything, being crippled had made him not weaker, but stronger. Just like for Meritaten, his feet, and the speed with which he got around, had nothing to do with his abilities as a politician.

Sheer force of will had not changed his feet; had not fixed his legs. But he had fought bravely through every one of the things he could not change. And in the legacy of peace he had established, he had changed the lives of those in Egypt, Mitanni, and beyond for the better.

Tutankhaten sighed, closing his eyes as a weight seemed to lift from his heart. He had fought the battles he had faced, each and every day of his life, becoming a warrior King as he weathered every trial he faced. And he had so much to be proud of.

Merneith gave the Pharaoh another dose of poppy. And it did its job, reducing his pain and descending him into a dull haze of drowsy nothingness. Life, right now, was neither good nor bad. Neither pleasant nor unpleasant. It simply *was,* in a very indifferent fashion. All in all, it was strangely tolerable, a fog of timeless,

403

mindless oblivion where nothing could hurt him. His pain and fever were no longer distressing; in fact, they no longer mattered.

But he had found the Light. And as he drowsed, dreamed, and swam through the rising fever, he held on tight to the only thing that really mattered.

"What will happen to thith?" Tut whispered, holding out one thin arm and running his other hand along it. "When it'th... over?"

Ankh sighed, taking his frail hand and looking down at it, running her thumb back and forth over his prominent knuckles.

"You know what will happen. The embalmers will... prepare your... mortal remains for burial over the seventy days, with herbs and spices and all the usual... procedures. And you... it... will be wrapped in linen bandages, and placed in a beautiful coffin. And the coffin will be placed inside your tomb, with a thousand other beautiful things. Wonderful things. And *you*..." she said, "won't care what happens to 'this'—" She squeezed his hand, "—because you'll be with Mother and Father and our sisters and our... our little ones... and you'll be too happy to think about it." She bit her lip, fighting back the tears that were always just under the surface. Then she gave a little smile. "And one day, the same will happen to me. And then we'll all... be together."

Tut sighed. "Thtill hope," he said with a sad little smile. "Thtill time. The Vithier can't juth take the throne until after the funeral."

"Still time," his sister agreed, squeezing his hand as tears formed in her eyes. "For me to get things settled. Still time for Zannanza to get here. Even time..." As she paused, he smiled, reaching toward her belly. She scooted closer to him, taking his cold, purple hand and gently pressing it to her stomach as they shared a moment of hope.

"Theventy dayth," he said softly, looking down at the hope that their dynasty would continue.

She nodded. "By that time… I'll be sure."

"It'th a long time. Long enough for you… to thave Egypt."

Ankh gave her brother a sad smile. "I'll do whatever it takes. Whether… whether I'm writing new laws or I'm teaching history."

Then he shook his head. "Politicth never thtopth, doeth it?"

She bent and kissed his forehead. "Neither will I."

And together they sighed. Whether Zannanza arrived before Tutankhaten's funeral would decide the future of Egypt… and the trajectory of the rest of Ankh's life.

Hannu and Semerkhet let Persenet in to light the oil lamps, their warm light casting flickering shadows on the bedroom walls. It was bedtime, the point when the one whose turn it was that night usually settled in to sit next to the Pharaoh, humming to him as they tried to ease him into sleep. It was Sem's turn tonight. But he didn't feel like he should ask Tut if he was ready to go to bed. And the Queen didn't go to her room to wash up and change into her sleeping-tunic. She stayed by her brother's side, her chair on one side of his bed, Sem's on the other. Still in day clothes, wigs, and the day's makeup they sat with him, faithfully at his side… where they would stay.

This was not a night like the dozens of others they had passed together. Tonight was different.

Tut thought of Ankh's future, standing beside the Hittite Prince, continuing to wage political war against the traitorous Grand Vizier, with Horemheb standing either on one side of the conflict or the other. He wondered how exactly events would play out. If

Zannanza would even arrive, or if something… or someone… would interrupt his journey.

And he wondered… if his wife would have a baby.

He didn't know. But he did know that no matter what happened, they were safe. And that was what mattered. With a deep sigh, he let go of all the politics as it ceased to matter.

He had grown up into a strong, wise Pharaoh; a Pharaoh who had established a legacy of peace and of well-being for his people. But now it was time to set his crown aside. And spend every moment with Ankh and Sem that they had left. Because right now, that was what mattered most.

The King drifted off again, and Semerkhet sat at his side, silently watching him. It felt like a vigil.

He wouldn't leave his side, Sem decided. He would stay right here beside Tut until… he didn't need a valet any longer.

Meresankh was restless. There was something about tonight; the long day ending, passing into night. Something different. A feeling in her heart. And a vibe among the staff. There was a hush. And whispering. Although not like the gossiping she had recently helped address. This was solemn… reverent. Like everyone knew something was coming. Something momentous.

*Tell me what's happening,* she prayed. *What's changing?*

No words rose in her heart, but there was a feeling of peace.

*Did the Pharaoh find You?* she asked. *Please… please let him find You. And the Queen. Help them find You. While there's still time.*

Because along with the peace, there was a feeling that time was passing. And that by morning… everything would be different.

Tutankhaten looked up at Semerkhet, trying to smile. But he couldn't. Not right now. Here, so nearly at the end.

"Won't... won't be long now," he said, struggling to form the words. It was hard to keep his eyes open. Even though the terrible coughs kept disturbing him just as he managed to drift off for a moment.

Sem looked into his face, eyes filling with tears. There wasn't really anything to say. "I'll be with you til the very end," he finally said with a little nod. His eyes never left the Pharaoh's face. Slowly Tut reached out a cold, shaking hand, and Sem took it in both of his strong, warm ones. Tutankhaten gave him a grateful smile. That was all he could manage. But Semerkhet smiled back, looking steadily into his eyes. It was enough. A year ago Sem would have been terrified to hold his hand. Or even look at him.

"Hail to thee, Lord of the Two Lands; all life, prosperity, and health," his valet whispered through tears. Tut just smiled. He hadn't heard someone say that sincerely for a long time.

Although... A number of memories, fuzzy and indistinct, rose in his heart. Semerkhet said those words, didn't he, every time he left the room? Even now. Even now, Tut was the Pharaoh. And for all their brotherhood, Sem didn't want to forget. Now... Tut nodded as a thought occurred to him. Now he understood why Semerkhet had changed the wording of the phrase with which he always tested a drink or meal for poison. If Ra was not real, the Pharaoh could not be his son. But it felt good to hear his friend still calling him the Great Morning Star.

Then Tutankhaten sighed, heart warming as he gave a sad smile. There was one more thing... one more thing he didn't want to leave without.

"Sem…" he said carefully, focusing on speaking clearly. Somehow it was more difficult than before. He couldn't even manage his valet's full name. But at least he had managed not to lisp. He had to show how much he thought of his friend, his brother, by saying his name correctly. Semerkhet looked down at him, waiting for what he was about to say. Tut gave a little smile, a breathy little laugh. "Give me a hug?"

Semerkhet blinked back tears as he grinned, the grin that had always cheered the King up even on the most horrible day. Silently, he nodded. And carefully bending over him, he gently wrapped his arms around the Pharaoh, lifting his friend into a sitting position and holding him to his heart. He was warm, and strong, and faithful, and Tut could feel his heart beating. Closing his eyes, Tut did his best to hug him back, putting his thin arms around Semerkhet's shoulders and squeezing him as tightly as he could.

Then, just as carefully, Sem released his hold, settling the King back into bed, nestled among his pillows. Tut gave him a grateful smile. That was all he could manage. But Sem smiled back, looking steadily into his eyes. It was enough.

"Fank you," Tutankhaten whispered, smiling up at his friend through his tears. Now Sem was crying properly, black kohl starting to run down his cheeks as he held his brother's hand tightly in his. "Thomething to take wiff me."

# 37  The Vigil

"Bedtime," Tut whispered. Sem nodded, bending slightly to smile at his friend in the dim lamplight. The valet got up to look at the clock sitting on a shelf near the bed, checking the water-level, which told them the hour.

"Second hour of night," Sem said quietly, reaching out to stroke the Pharaoh's hot head. He still had a cold compress in place. "You ready to sleep?"

"Not... now," the Pharaoh said, shaking his head softly. "Want to be... together." He reached out a weak hand, and Semerkhet took it in his, holding it gently as he gave his friend a smile. On his other side, Ankh took her brother's other hand, and he turned his head to give her a little smile.

Tonight, they wouldn't tuck him in and take turns sleeping. Tonight, they would sit together, all three of them, sharing a vigil of love. A family, waiting together through one final night.

But on the other side of that vigil was peace.

He was cold. Tut could feel the heat of the fever radiating from his skin, but a coldness seemed to have seeped into his very bones. So they tucked him in with another blanket, Ankh making sure he was covered right up to his chin while Semerkhet carefully arranged the blanket over what was left of his legs.

"Are your... are your feet cold?" Tutankhaten heard Semerkhet say. And there was a catch in his friend's voice. Tut managed to lift his head for long enough to see Semerkhet frowning at his feet, Sem's eyes filling with tears.

"What ith it?" Tut asked, unable to see what was wrong with his own feet. Ankh, who had joined Sem at the foot of the bed, was also frowning in concern.

"They… they just look cold, like your hands," Ankh said, reaching out to touch one foot, then the other, so very gently. Silently, Tutankhaten nodded to himself. That strange purple must have spread to his feet.

But they tucked him in warmly, cold, purple feet disappearing under layers of cozy blankets. And he smiled at them in gratitude for making him as comfortable as he could be.


*Ankhesenamun*, she thought as they sat together, evening growing late. "Her life is of Amun." She felt sickened by her own name; the fact that she had been carrying around an idol with her all her life, every time someone addressed her using her full name. It felt good to hear her real name again. *Ankhesenpaaten.* "Her life is of the Aten." She smiled. It was.

And now that she knew to Whom she was speaking, she felt like she could really pray. And that, according to His infinite wisdom, His perfect and mysterious plan, the Aten, I-AM, would really answer her. She was not alone. And life was not empty.

*Please*, she prayed. *Lord of Light. Let me be with child. Let me continue my dynasty. And let me lead my country well. But even if not… help me, no matter what happens, to be the leader, the teacher, the Queen, You created me to be. And help me…* She swallowed, feeling the tears that were always just beneath the surface beginning to well in her eyes, *help me let him go.*

410

The fear was gone. Tut knew that even if his earthly life ended tonight, he was safe. Far from having his heart devoured by Ammut, he would be welcomed into an eternity of peace.

And... He looked around the cozy dimness of the bedroom, softly illuminated by the gentle glow of three or four oil-lamps. Night had fallen, and was into its third hour. But he was no longer afraid of the dark. Because the Light in his heart shone into the darkness, and the darkness could not overcome it.

*Thank You,* Semerkhet prayed that evening as he listened to the steady dripping of the water-clock, measuring the final hours of their time together. *Thank You for my brother, and for our time together. Thank You for the gift he gave me and Meresankh. Thank You for opening his heart... and mine... to Your Light. And please...* He bit his lip. *Please help me let him go.*

*Thank You for Merneith,* Tut prayed silently as he found himself spending a few minutes awake, lying there in the quiet and the dark. *Thank You for making Yourself known to us. Please... bless Egypt. Bring Zannanza to us safely. Change Horemheb's heart. Stop Ay. Make my wife's child strong and healthy. And let her become the greatest Pharaoh, the strongest leader, the wisest teacher, that ever was.*

To his surprise, Tut felt his stomach growling. How many hours had it been since dinner? Three or so, maybe. He had never before really pondered what his final meal would be, but now that he was facing it... he knew what he wanted.

"Sem?" he whispered. His friend bent closer, taking his cold hand in his.

411

"Yes, Brother?" he asked, giving that sweet, familiar smile.

"Can I have… a honey-cake?"

Semerkhet chuckled. "I'll see what I can find."

Sem got up to sort through the arrangement of snacks that had accumulated on the new table— empty cups of tea, half-full bowls of pomegranate pips or little red jujubes, a plate with some flatbread and a lump of fresh cheese. Then he found it.

"Two more," he said, presenting the plate with a smile. Carefully he pinched off a corner of each of the little cakes, popping them into his mouth. "I taste your food, Great Morning Star, and if there be harm in it, let the harm fall upon me."

And of course, there was no harm.

Weak and weary as he was, Tutankhaten didn't trust his hands to be able to maneuver even his favorite dessert into his mouth. So he opened his mouth and let Sem feed him one, then the other, savoring the sweetness, the texture. What a… sweet little gift he had been given, that the very last thing he would ever eat should be his favorite food.

And two of them were exactly enough to satisfy his hunger.

With a little smile, Semerkhet gently brushed away the crumbs that had stayed behind in his Pharaoh's peach-fuzz moustache.

Tut chuckled. And he whispered, "Fank you."

And he drifted off with the taste of honey on his tongue.


Semerkhet yawned and stretched his stiff neck and arms; squeezed his tired eyes closed until bright flashes appeared before them. The sweaty hairline of his heavy wig itched, as did his face, sticky with day-old makeup. And he wanted to take his sandals off. His exhausted body and mind moaned at him to rest; to lie back

412

and drowse for two minutes… but he had a job to do. And he would do it. For one final night.

Ankh sat watching her husband peacefully sleeping, his chest slowly, gently rising and falling, the cat keeping him warm. It wouldn't be much longer. And her heart ached to imagine the days she would have to spend without him.

But she smiled through her tears; tears that were no longer helpless. Because she knew that the minute it was over, he would be better. Forever.

Her memories would keep her warm during those cold days they would spend apart. And so would the hope of one day, holding him in her arms again, never to be separated.

Fourth hour of night, the Queen thought to herself, looking at the water-clock. How many hours were left?

"I thuppothe thith meanth… I'll be meeting them firtht," Tut murmured.

Ankh gave a sad smile. Just what she had been thinking of.

"You'll get to give them their names," she said softly. "Mereneferet, *Love and Beauty*, and Senebhenas…"

"*Health is with her*," Tut finished. He squeezed her hand. "They're perfect." He swallowed. "Princess Mereneferet. And Princess Senebhenas." Then he put his hand out, gently touching his wife's stomach. "Can you tell yet?" he whispered again.

Softly she shook her head, eyes glimmering with unshed tears. "Not yet." Then she smiled. "But I am starting to wonder." She kissed his hand. "Maybe, love. Maybe."

Tut squeezed his wife's hand. "Lord of Light," he whispered, closing his eyes, "pleathe bleth uth with an heir. Let uth continue our dynathty in Your honor."

When he opened his eyes to smile at Ankh, whose tears had begun to trickle down her cheeks, making a mess of her makeup, he did not know if they had received the answer they wanted.

But he knew they had been heard.

Carefully his wife bent over him, resting her warm, soft little hand on his cheek as the silver beads of her wig jingled. Softly their lips met... and they shared one last kiss.

"Take care of Egypt for me," he whispered to her.

She squeezed his cold hand, smiling through her tears. "I will."

He smiled up at her. "Hail to thee, Lady of the Two Landth; all life, prothperity, and health!"

She just kissed him again.


"Do you want Kamose and me to turn you?" Semerkhet asked softly as he dabbed a cool cloth over his friend's burning face and dry lips.

Slowly Tutankhaten opened his eyes, then gently shook his head. "Not now," he whispered. "Fank you."

Semerkhet nodded and dipped the cloth back into the bowl of water. At this stage... moving him every hour or two wasn't important. At this stage... skin irritation wasn't a priority.


"His breathing's changed," Ankh said to Merneith as Granny came in with a bowl of cold compresses and a pot of chamomile tea. Slowly, the fourth hour of night was passing.

Carefully, the old woman set her burdens on the table, then bent over the Pharaoh to listen. She closed her eyes, taking in the new

414

rhythm that Tutankhaten's hoarse, rattling breathing had assumed. Right now it was fast and light.

"Has it been deep and slow?" Merneith asked the Queen as she took the Pharaoh's cold, purple-mottled hand, carefully taking his pulse. Silently, Ankh nodded.

"It keeps switching," she said. "And then there are... pauses. And that... that rattle. It's more than the lung infection." She bit her lip, knowing even before the healer had responded what the change meant. "And his feet," she continued, nodding at the foot of the bed, "his feet are turning purple, just like his hands."

Granny held out an old hand, gently taking Ankh's in hers. Slowly, she looked up at the Queen.

"It won't be much longer, dearie," she said softly. "With this sign... until morning, maybe. Maybe."

There were tears, but Ankh swallowed them back for later... for tomorrow. All she said was,

"I know."


Each time Tutankhaten fell asleep, it got harder to wake up. Sleep clung to him, pulling him down into the darkness, drowning him in a void of swirling dreams. And each time, it was harder work to open his eyes; to return to the world around him. Each time, it took more of his fading strength.

Although even as he swam through the darkness, the Light was always with him.


"What elth will they put with me?" Tut whispered to his sister. "Juth curious." He gave a yawn; although he was tired, he didn't feel sleepy. It was more as though his body was struggling to get enough air. The fifth hour of night was nearly over.

415

With a heavy sigh, she looked down at their entwined hands, his so cold, skin tinged with that strange purple. "Well..." she said slowly, "some of your walking-sticks, a lot of your jewelry, shoes, clothes, underclothes... some of that white wine from Tribute Day... some of your favorite perfumes; they'll probably pack you some of your frankincense-and-spikenard lotion... board games, so you don't get bored... some furniture, probably... who knows; they might even send you one of your chariots."

Tut gave his sister half a smile. "I wonder if I'll be a better charioteer where I'm going." Then he chuckled, even as he yawned again. "All those beautiful thingth... and I won't even need them."

Ankh bent and kissed him on the forehead. "Just shows how much we love you." Then she blinked back tears. She had something to tell him. "You remember those sketches we had made, back at your birthday?" she asked. Tut nodded, giving a little smile as he remembered those good old days. "Well, I decided..." Her face crumpled, and she pressed the back of her hand to her mouth, swallowing back tears. "I decided," she continued, "what they should be. The artists are going to cast them in gold, along with a few p-pictures of us hunting ducks, and some with f-flowers, even one of me f-f-fixing your necklace..." That was it; with a low moan, she bowed her head, hugging herself in grief.

All he could do was reach out and take her hand. He didn't want to leave either.

Finally the Queen's sobs stilled, and slowly, she looked back up at him. "But they," she continued, her voice a little stronger, "they're casting the pictures in gold, in big panels. And they'll form a shrine. And that shrine..." She bit her lip, then went on,

416

"will be placed around the stone sarcophagus that your... your coffin goes into. And... and our love will last forever."

Now Tut was the one who was crying.

As the night wore on, a few faithful servants made their rounds, Meresankh, Nuya, Persenet, bringing what was needed, taking what was used. Through the slow, dark hours of night the loyal members of the palace staff served the one they lived their lives for, doing whatever they could to make this final night a little less unpleasant; free up the Queen and the Sole Companion to focus all their energy and attention on the Pharaoh who lay suffering in the bed. And they would take pride as they remembered that they had helped.

Their wishes for life, prosperity, and health echoed through the quiet of the night.

As for what the other camp of servants were doing... Tut, Ankh, and Sem did not concern themselves with that. Not tonight.

It was hard to stay awake. But the Pharaoh summoned the energy to speak to Nuya one more time, apologizing for the way that the Vizier had fired the faithful scribe; expressing his regret that Nuya had been punished for doing the right thing. Nuya just shook his head. And Tut's heart warmed as Nuya reassured him that it was his honor to serve... no matter what. The forfeiture of his job was a sacrifice he was willing to make in defense of the future of Egypt.

"Time?"

Ankhesenpaaten blinked, rousing herself from the drowse into which her exhausted body was descending and pulling her blanket closer around herself. She got up and peered into the water-clock.

"Sixth hour," she said.

Tut nodded. The night was half over. Halfway til morning.

It was getting late. Meresankh stretched after setting a box of jewelry on its shelf, all the pretty pieces of wearable artwork that the Queen had not touched in weeks freshly cleaned and neatly put away. Between instances of fetching things for the royal couple, she had drifted back into her Lady's room; back to busywork. She did want to give them privacy, after all. But now, she needed to move around... needed to... what did she need to do? She listened to the thoughts rising in her heart; the guidance she prayed for. *You need to talk to the Queen.*

She left the Queen's room, ready to cross the hall that separated the two royal bedrooms. But a sound made her pause. Meresankh turned to see that just down the hall a group of servants stood, Kemsit, Nuya, Rahonem, and a dozen others, dressed warmly in thick outer robes. They stood talking softly among themselves, one crying, a few bowing their heads in prayer. They, too, were keeping the vigil.

She smiled. These were the servants who stood on their side of the line in the sand.

Meresankh stood there in the doorway of her Pharaoh's room during the sixth hour of night, silently watching the Pharaoh, the Queen, Semerkhet. They were sitting very quietly, her Lady sitting on one side of the bed, Semerkhet on the other, holding the Pharaoh's hands as he drowsed.

418

She could see it on their faces. The Light. They looked tired, they looked sad, but they were at peace. All three of them were secure in the love of I-AM. Even amid all the exhaustion, all the heartbreak, they were filled with a peace that surpassed understanding.

Ankh stood up to stretch, and she smiled when she saw Meresankh standing there watching. Squeezing the Pharaoh's hand, she made her way toward Meresankh.

Meresankh smiled through her tears as the Queen smiled through her own. "You found Him," she whispered, slowly approaching her friend as her Mistress nodded at Hannu to admit her handmaiden.

The Queen nodded as she reached out and took Meresankh's hand, the beads of her short wig tinkling, sleeve of her wrinkled gown rippling. Then she smiled at the Pharaoh, who, waking up a little, quietly returned her smile. "*We* found Him."

It couldn't be long. Meresankh hurried out of the room, running to find her Granny. And to fetch the precious Hebrew histories; the gift that she could feel aching inside her heart as the Light inside her told her that this was the time, the occasion, to give her gift to her friend. With no words, only a tearful smile, she pulled Merneith to the doorway, pointing to the three peaceful faces; the three hearts glowing with Light, filled with deep and abiding joy.

Merneith smiled through her own tears. And as she raised her eyes to the unseen sky above, Meresankh saw her whisper, "Thank You, Lord."

Even if the Pharaoh was still going to die… even if he was going to die tonight… their prayers had been answered. Because he was going to be with I-AM. And the Queen had found the Light too. So had Semerkhet. And what in Heaven or on Earth could be more important? Amid all the scheming, all the deception, all the murderous politics, what could mere mortals really do to them with the true Lord of Light watching over them?

"Fank you for your thtorieth, Granny," Tut whispered to the midwife. He smiled at her, then at Meresankh. "Fank you for your prayerth."

They just inclined their heads. Stuck in bed, maybe only hours from death, he was still their Pharaoh.

Then Meresankh looked up at him with a smile. "And thank you for searching for the Light… until you found it."

And the Pharaoh smiled at his wife's handmaiden. "Congratulationth," he whispered. "To you and Sem."

She just smiled, little hand moving to touch her silver necklace.

"Thank you," she said softly. "For making it happen."

"Congratulations," Ankh echoed softly, feeling her face lift in an unfamiliar smile. She sighed, beckoning to her friend, then reaching out to squeeze her hand. "We need some joy right now."

"I have something for you, too," Meresankh said. She held out what looked like a stack of papyrus. "These are the Hebrew histories," she said proudly, offering the papyrus to the Queen. Slowly Ankh accepted it, looking down at the neat lines of text, her friend's graceful handwriting outlining the chronicles of the Hebrews just as she had copied out her mother's histories of the Queens who had gone before. "From Joseph to Moses, every story my Granny ever told me. And you… you can teach them to your baby. And on and on and on."

Meresankh chuckled. And as Ankh's smile grew curious, she continued. "I wrote down some recipes, too," she said. "For the teas Granny has been making for you… and for spicy chicken. I couldn't let you start your own kitchen without the recipe for spicy chicken."

The Queen smiled. And she held the papyrus to her heart.

And Meresankh and her Granny turned away, sad but satisfied. After tonight, they would not see their Pharaoh again in this lifetime… but their prayers had been answered all the same.

*Thank You for Meresankh's faithfulness*, the Queen prayed as she watched her handmaiden cheerfully gather up the dishes and set a pot of tea on the table. *Thank You for my sister.*

# 38   Victory

**M**eresankh prayed as she worked late that night, taking baskets of linen to and fro, delivering fresh pots of herbal tea, tidying the Queen's room and then tidying it again. Somehow she knew that the Queen would not enter her own bedroom again until it was… all over. She had never been up working during the seventh hour of night, but she was proud to do it. *Thank You for answering my prayers. For opening their hearts to Your Light. Thank You… for letting the Pharaoh help us get married.* Then she sighed. *Please help us let him go.*

Yet, suddenly, she felt I-AM bless her with the gift of a smile. The Queen's wig, which she had been wearing for two days and nights, was so tangled… and Meresankh chuckled as she realized just how badly she wanted to get her hands on it to comb it out.

As the night became deep and still, the visits stopped, the staff leaving the royal couple to rest as well as they could.

But they knew that no one in the palace would sleep that night.

Granny didn't visit them again. She gave them privacy to guide the Pharaoh through these final hours— if they needed her, they could summon her. They had the teas, plenty of water, the cool compresses she had prepared. And they could feel her prayers. There was nothing to do now, but pray. And hope. And wait.

Tut looked to his left. And as Semerkhet gently smiled at him, he smiled back. Then he turned his head to the right and shared a smile with his sister. With the two of them at his side, he felt warm and safe and loved. However much longer this lasted, they were here with him.

Silently, Ankh gazed at her brother as the seventh hour of night slowly passed. Tut seemed to have drifted off again, and she watched him drowse; studied his graceful features as she listened to him slowly breathing in and out, loud, congested breaths that changed in rhythm from quick and light to deep and slow, sometimes lapsing into long, dreadful pauses. She tried to memorize every detail of his face… She knew that on the day of his funeral, those handsome features would not be the same. So she captured his long, graceful nose, his delicate chin, his full lips, his fine, molded cheekbones, the lie of his long, dark eyelashes over his brown face, his fine, dark eyebrows, the shape of his head, and put them away inside her heart.

And with him, she waited.

The Pharaoh turned his head on the pillow again, tired eyes trying to focus on the flickering oil-lamps on the walls, whose tiny sparks threw shivering shadows onto the high walls. Morning was so far away.

And he wondered… if he would reach it.

It was a strange echo, Meresankh thought. Standing around in the middle of the night waiting; waiting for something she knew without a doubt would happen soon… an event that would change all their lives forever. A strange echo… of waiting for a baby to be born.

Birth… death… they were similar in a way. Life began, springing from a miraculous spark created by I-AM. Out of the

423

darkness, a light was born. And then, when the sun set on a person's years, and life passed into death, it was as if that light passed once more into the darkness.

Only… amid all the darkness, she knew that the Light had claimed victory.

There were things that Tut wanted to say to his sister, to his brother. Specific things, references to particular things they had done together, particular hopes they had for the future. There were things that he wanted to say that his mouth simply was no longer able to. Things, even, that he wasn't sure how to express in words. And his hands were too weak for him to do any writing.

But the deepest parts of what he ultimately wanted to say could be expressed with a simple "thank you" or "I love you."

And those were words that he could still say.

"You're so brave," Ankh whispered, reaching out to gently stroke Tut's face as the eighth hour of night passed, four hours remaining until morning. "And you always have been. Even when you were this big." With her hand, she indicated the height of a toddler. "I'll remember… how brave you are."

He opened his eyes, giving her a little smile. And she knew he had heard her.

Semerkhet, too, was struggling to put fourteen months of service, ten months of brotherhood, into a few sentences.

"I wanted my brother back, more than anything else in the world," he finally said during the ninth hour of that long night. "And it came true when you reached out to me. I found one in you. And I wouldn't trade it… for the world."

424

Tut gave him a little chuckle. "I wath going to thay the thame fing." Tutankhaten smiled at his brother, a wistful smile, but an excited one, all the same. "I'll be meeting my little girlth thoon," he said softly. "And I'll tell them… about their Uncle Sem. My dear Sem."

And Sem had to go refill the Pharaoh's tea to hide his tears.

Tutankhaten looked at his wife's belly. And for the thousandth time, he wondered. For the thousandth time, he hoped. Slowly he reached out, gently touching her stomach. Sadly, she smiled.

"I'm thorry I didn't get to meet you," he whispered to the child he hoped was safe inside her belly; hoped was listening. "But I want you to know… your Daddy loves you."

And Ankhesenpaaten closed her eyes against the tears as for the thousandth time, she contemplated the future in which her child would only come to know his or her father through the stories she would tell.

Slowly Tut pulled himself up out of sleep, opening his bleary eyes. And he looked around his room. His chairs, tables, window… and the storage room and sitting room he hadn't been able to visit since before the journey to Kadesh. The beautiful paintings on his walls; the columns that supported them. The chest inscribed with countless wishes for his long life and health. Even the familiar old rack of walking-sticks. Not all of them were there— some of his furniture, clothing, and jewelry were gone too, packed away early into his tomb by the Vizier who had not wanted to let Tut forget that he was dying.

But what did that matter. Each piece of furniture he could see, each walking-stick, each painting, held a thousand precious

425

memories. But now… now, it was time to say goodbye. He let his eyes rove around his room, taking it all in… one last time.

It was still dark. Still night. It had been night for so long; so many hours. How long until morning, he wondered.

"Time?" he asked. Semerkhet blinked, shaking himself out of a sleepy reverie. And he squinted into the water-clock.

"Tenth hour," Sem whispered. "Two hours til morning."

Tut smiled. He just might make it until Horemheb got home.


They didn't sing. Didn't tell stories. Didn't say much of anything. Just sat with him, letting him feel that they were near.

And so they sat, keeping this vigil. Watching the moments slip past, one by one, passing through present reality into precious memory. Listening to the steady drip, drip, drip of the water-clock counting the hours as they passed by. The Queen and the valet hoped they would be able to remember every moment of this final night.


There was nothing else to clean. Nothing else to deliver. Nothing else to do. But wait. And pray. Meresankh shook herself, leaving her Lady's bedroom and walking slowly back out into the hall, where the little knot of faithful servants was still standing, whispering, weeping, praying, waiting.

She didn't see the Light shining in their eyes. But they had hope in something greater. And some of them, at least, had… openness. She smiled as she felt the Light in her heart pushing her forward. She would pray with them. And she would ask I-AM which of them He was calling her to speak to.

They would pray together. They would hold this vigil. Until morning, and whatever came with it.

426

His mouth was so dry. Tut gave his sister a little smile, raising his hand slightly.

"Can I have… drink?" he whispered through dry lips.

She got up from her chair in an instant, pouring a bit of chamomile tea into his favorite blue lotus cup, the one he had promised to Semerkhet… after he was finished with it for the last time. "Of course, darling." Perching on the edge of the bed, she helped him lift his head and take a sip. And as he sipped the tea, somehow all three knew that the Pharaoh would not eat or drink again… in this world.

Ankh sighed, struggling to stay out of a doze as they sat together so quietly, safe in the warmth of one another's presence; safe in the love of I-AM. Whatever the future held, they were safe.

Tut didn't want to leave them. Ankh, Sem, Meresankh, Merneith, even Bastet. He wanted to stay, to remain Pharaoh, continue leading his country, continue fighting poverty, promoting education. To meet the son or daughter who even now might be growing big and strong in his wife's belly. And to complete his parents' work, restoring the worship of I-AM, the Aten, even as the other temples remained open, giving people the freedom to worship as they chose. Wanted… wanted to see what would happen, with Ay, and with Horemheb. But he knew that time was running out. Very quickly. How many hours, how many minutes did they have left? *Please help me let them go*, he prayed. *Please help me say goodbye.*

Only it wasn't going to be a goodbye. Not really. Tut smiled through his sad sigh as he remembered that one day, they would be reunited. He had seen the Light shining in his sister's eyes, just as it shone in Semerkhet's and Meresankh's. He didn't want to let his loved ones go… but when it was time, he knew he would be able to. And one day… he would be the one introducing his daughters to their mother.

Soon, he would see be seeing his parents again, and the five sisters he had not seen since before he was Pharaoh. And Tut found himself smiling. He was… the tiniest, tiniest bit excited.


"Bless the world," the Pharaoh whispered to his friend. Semerkhet scooted closer in his chair, listening carefully to what Tut was starting to say. "When you work in Sais."

Semerkhet smiled. "I will," he said softly.

And they hoped together as the water-clock registered the eleventh hour of night.


"My Lord," Nuya said, standing at attention in the doorway, "a scout reports that General Horemheb will be home by sunrise. Within the hour."

The Pharaoh smiled; to get the news, and to see the smiling face of his loyal servant. Looked like he would be getting the opportunity he'd hoped for. And Amenia and Mutnedjmet would be safe. "Good. Thend him in when he getth here."

But as Nuya walked away, the King felt something stirring deep inside him. And he knew that by the time Horemheb reached the palace, it would all be over.

The Great Morning and Evening Star was setting for the last time.

"Hello, kitty." Tut smiled as a soft little furball whispered through the air, jumping lightly up onto the end of the bed. Bastet padded over to him with a little *mrrrow*, rubbing her furry face against his, touching his cheek with her wet little nose. She sniffed him, letting him breathe on her face as he petted her soft gray fur. And she lay down beside him. He put his arm around Bastet. And he closed his eyes, feeling her warmth, her love, her soft, gentle presence. So many years. So many good memories. His little cat would be with him until the end. And he smiled to think of her living with Semerkhet and Meresankh. In their care, she would be safe. And she would be so very loved. He would miss her. But he knew he did not have to worry about her.

"We didn't looth," the Pharaoh whispered to his sister as she sat by him, gently dabbing his burning face and dry lips with a cool cloth as the cold compresses on his forehead and under his arms, which she had just replaced with fresh ones, also did their best to fight his fever. That was all the comfort she could give him. But that was all right. Soon, none of this would be bothering him any longer... and none of it would bother him ever again.

She smiled through her tears, shaking her head. "No. We won. We found what really matters. More than any politics. More than whoever sits on the next throne." She patted the cloth over his neck, gently wiping away the sweat. "And whatever happens... we're safe."

Tut reached out and took her hand. His was cold and shaking, tinged with the strange purple that had told Granny that time was running short.

"No matter what happenth."

She shook her head, squeezing his hand with a little chuckle. "I-AM loves us. What's the worst that could happen?" She gave a little sigh. "And someday... we'll be together again."

He smiled. "I'll be waiting for you."

From his other side, Semerkhet reached out to squeeze his other hand. "And until then... you'll be in our hearts. Forever."

Outside the window that looked to the east, Ankh and Sem could see that the sky was lightening. Dawn was approaching.

Again, Tut was getting too sleepy to talk, too sleepy to keep his eyes open. But strangely, this time as he felt himself drifting off, sinking slowly into the darkness of oblivion, so deep and dark and faraway that it felt like drowning, he found himself fleetingly wondering...

...if he would wake up.

Semerkhet kept watch. He found himself counting his friend's breaths, in, out, in, out. Watching for any change. Waiting for any change. Tut's face was so pale, almost gray; his lips were so dry; his mottled hands were so cold. The end was so near. Semerkhet's job was almost finished, he knew. Soon his Pharaoh would no longer need a valet.

But until that moment came, Semerkhet was his faithful servant. He would stay by his brother until the last.

Down in Merneith's workshop, Meresankh blinked as her Granny sat up straighter, wise old eyes brightening. Her gnarled old hand gently closed around Meresankh's as she bowed her head with a deep breath, then looked up again with tears in her eyes.

430

"What is it?" Meresankh whispered, although as her heart began to pound, she thought she knew.

Granny gave another sigh, a little shake of her head.

"It's happening," she said softly.

He looked different. Coming back from getting some water, Ankhesenpaaten looked at her brother, lying in the bed. He breathed quietly; looked peaceful. The cat was beside him, curled close to his body. And Semerkhet was silently sitting beside him, offering his quiet, reassuring presence.

But there was something. A grayness to his face. A shadow alongside the Light. Quietly the Queen sat down, taking his head into her lap. And she smiled when he shifted in the bed as he took the sort of deep breath that signaled waking up.

Slowly Tutankhaten opened his eyes, coming to the surface as he returned to the waking world. He was grateful that he had been able to wake up.

But he felt different. Like he truly was fading into invisibility. Like even his eyelids weighed as much as the pyramids. And he was cold. Very cold. Even though he could still feel the feverish heat radiating from his face and body.

His sister had taken his head and shoulders into her lap. And Sem was very close, sitting on the edge of the bed. Even Bastet was nearby, curled up beside his hip.

All he could do was smile at them, Ankhesenpaaten, Semerkhet. And as he slowly reached out to take their hands, he whispered, "It'th all right."

And they smiled back as they gently held his hands. His tired eyes were fuzzy, but he could see that they were smiling.

431

He tried not to fade away; slip back into sleep. Slip away from them for the last time. Struggled to stay awake. His sister's arms were so warm; Semerkhet's smile, sad though it was, was so good to see. And he could feel Bastet purring. Taste the honey-cake he had eaten. Smell the last batch of herbal tea Granny had made. See, in the fuzzy distance, the bouquet of lotus blossoms and cornflowers that Ankh had gathered that morning. Feel the warmth of all the love his sister and brother had for him. And feel the safety, the security, of knowing that however many minutes, seconds, were left to them, they would be all right. Would be... together again. Someday.

"Yes, it's all right," Semerkhet whispered back, making himself smile, that smile Tut always loved to see. He nodded fervently, blinking back tears as he reassured his brother.

"You don't need to worry about us," Ankhesenpaaten said gently. She was smiling too, letting him know that he could go; that they would be all right after he was gone. In her eyes, and in Semerkhet's eyes, he could see the Light. And he knew that they were right. There was nothing to be afraid of anymore. Not for him, and not for them. His job was done. And it was time to set aside his crown.

But even if he didn't make the choice to let go, he couldn't last much longer. The choice... would be made for him sooner or later. Breathing was becoming hard work. In, out, in, out, feeling his lungs expand, his chest rising and falling. How many breaths remained?

"Love you," he mouthed silently, and they smiled even through their tears. And one by one, first Ankhesenpaaten and then Semerkhet, they bent to place a kiss on his forehead.

432

It was over; he knew that. He looked up at his sister one more time, and her eyes filled with understanding. She bent to hug him, putting her arms around as much of him as she could. He felt her lifting him, holding him to her heart, and he closed his eyes.

# 39  Welcome

He opened them again to hear two little voices cry, "It's Daddy!"

All around them, the Sun was shining. Where was he— a large courtyard, one he recognized from the days in Akhetaten? Two little girls, one about four years old and the other maybe just two, ran toward him, chubby little arms open in welcome.

"Daddy's home!"

"Welcome home, Daddy!" And on two strong, unbroken legs, he ran to take them in his arms.

They were so soft, so warm, so little, squirming for joy in his arms as they hugged him with their tiny little arms and placed sloppy kisses all over his face. He was crying; crying for joy as he finally held the daughters he had dreamed of so many nights.

"Mereneferet! Senebhenas!" Mereneferet was the four-year-old with her mother's eyes, who was squealing as she patted his shoulders with her tiny little hands, and Senebhenas was the even tinier two-year-old whose happy, busy little feet kept kicking him in the ribs as her tiny hands explored his face for the first time.

Her little feet were kicking. And her back and her head were perfectly healthy. Weak with joy, Tut held his babies as though he would never let them go.

But it wasn't just the three of them. Tutankhaten opened his tear-filled eyes to see a crowd of eight standing around him and smiling; beaming with smiles that shone with the same Light as the Sun that was so bright around them. He blinked in the brightness, trying to see who it was.

His parents stood beside him. And his grandmother. And his sisters who had gone before him.

"Welcome home, son," Father said, reaching out to touch his son's shoulder. Much to Tut's surprise, he was now taller than his father.

"We're so proud of you, Tutankhaten," Mother whispered, putting her soft, cool arms around him and the little ones who were still wiggling in his arms, hugging and kissing him as they told him about their day; about all the days they had been apart. It felt good to hear the form of his name that he remembered from the earliest days; his real name. Mother was also shorter than he had remembered— he had grown so much since last he'd seen her, ten long years ago. But he recognized her strength; that energy with which she had ruled as Pharaoh.

And there was Grandmother Tiye. Small, strong, sharp-eyed; exactly as he remembered her, only younger, glowing with health. And now smiling more broadly than he had ever seen, reaching out to touch his arm with those long, delicate fingers he remembered so well.

"Where are we?" he asked, looking around in amazement at the beautiful landscape that looked like the grounds outside the palace he had just left, but somehow a thousand times more beautiful. Absolutely perfect. A graceful garden path curved through the landscape, its destination not clear, but surely even more beautiful than what was around them. In the distance there were buildings, homes, possibly a marketplace. The Sun was warm, but the day was comfortably cool, like a perfect day in the month of Phamenoth, and the gentle breeze blowing through the trees sounded like music. There were no mosquitoes.

His father smiled. "Welcome to the City of Light, Tutankhaten."

Tut nodded. His father had been right. So right. And now he had gone from believing... to seeing it with his own eyes.

And now five sisters were crowding around him, all trying to hug him at once as their merry, birdlike voices sounded in his ears, the bright-colored beads on their wigs jingling like joyful bells. Meritaten was standing, and walking, her legs and feet perfectly healthy. Now that he could see her standing, he saw for the first time how tall she was.

He hadn't seen four of them in fourteen long years— it took him a moment to recognize who was who. And then he saw the gleam in Tasherit's eye, the dimple in Meketaten's cheek, Setepenre's graceful nose, so like their mother's, the way that Rure's ears stuck out just the tiniest bit. And even as they stood before him as adults, he could see the sisters he loved so much.

He smiled and smiled as they hugged him and kissed him, and realized something else— his teeth did not seem to be getting in his way. He chuckled, curious. Did they have mirrors here?

Everyone was perfect— Mother and Father looked younger than Tut might have expected; strong, healthy, and full of energy. Mother's face also looked perfectly normal, as beautiful as ever— as though she had never been kicked by the horse. Grandmother's wisdom shone from her eyes as brightly as ever, but she, too, seemed younger, stronger; mature yet in her prime. And his sisters, four of whom had left the other world as children, had grown up into beautiful young women. His own daughters, who, having asked to be set down, were now running down the path, trying to show him everything at once, glowed with health, every inch of their tiny little bodies perfectly formed, perfectly functional, perfectly beautiful.

Everything, and everyone, was perfectly restored.

Then he started examining his own body— looking down, he saw the perfectly healthy legs, the nearly identical feet, that he had always dreamed of. Even the way he was standing— had the curve in his spine been straightened out? Suddenly he realized that since his arrival, he had been standing firmly on his feet without a walking-stick in sight. He would have to try running later.

He looked at them again; the bones of his ankles, the lengths of each foot— which now matched. The one on the left was no longer turned inward and sideways with toes that pointed every which way. Now it was a perfect partner to the right one, which was no longer as flat as it always had been. Now both feet pointed the same direction, and both had perfect arches. His ankles were straight; his heels were planted firmly and comfortably on the ground. His feet were graceful. They were… Tut chuckled as he thought of it. His feet were indescribably beautiful. Just like the rest of him, they had been restored.

In wonder, overwhelmed delight, he found himself taking a deep breath. And again, he was amazed. Because he could breathe again. The congestion was gone; the pain that had knifed through his lungs with every breath had vanished. For the first time in days, he could breathe easily.

And maybe best of all, all the pain was gone. Not only did his legs now work perfectly; they were no longer broken. And his perfectly formed feet no longer twinged with pain with every step he took. His bruises and aches were gone. The weakness and feverish shivering of the ague had disappeared. His lungs were well again.

And somehow, he knew that he would never have another headache.

"I'm better," he whispered, more tears springing to his eyes. His parents just smiled.

"No more death," his father whispered. "No more mourning, no more crying, no more pain. The Aten makes all things new... even us. The way things were, back then... is in the past. This is now," he said, sweeping his hand over the beautiful landscape, "and this is forever. He is with us wherever we go... we no longer need a temple. We are His temple."

"I didn't know what to expect," Tutankhaten said, looking around at the peaceful, perfect courtyard in which they were standing. Birds were singing in a nearby garden; the bright Sun shone on lotus-pools here and there. And there were no angry crocodile-lion-hippopotamus demons in sight. He shook his head with a chuckle. "They sent so much stuff with me... but I won't need any of it. I have everything I need right here. Ay sure will be mad when he finds out that he won't get to use any of the things they bury with him." He smiled at a sudden funny thought. "Although I suppose, hundreds of years in the future, if someone finds my tomb, they'll learn a lot about our lives."

His mother chuckled with a little shrug. "Maybe, maybe not. Does it even matter?"

He shook his head with a laugh. "No. Not really." He smiled, closing his eyes and feeling the warmth of the Sun on his face. "What matters is that we're together."

And as he heard his own voice, another wonderful little blessing occurred to him. He was no longer lisping. And he doubted that he ever would again.

438

Then he looked down at his hands. And chuckled again. Like his feet, they were beautiful; perfectly formed, perfectly restored. Long, graceful fingers, delicate wristbones, slender but strong. No longer weak and shaking, unable to hold a cup or write a letter; no longer frozen and tinged with purple. They were ready to write, to work, to play music; to hold the hands of his parents, his sisters, his little girls. And he shook his head. Was there any part of his body that was not beautiful? Any part of his body that was not perfect?

And he knew that the answer was *no.*

Tut's sisters converged on him again; Rure and Setepenre, Meketaten, Meritaten, and Tasherit. Tall and graceful, they were now the queenlike adults he scarcely could have imagined when last he had seen them.

"I'm so sorry you all got sick," he said, heart aching as he saw the beautiful people into whom they had grown up and wished that these women could have lived in the other world. Then he turned to Meritaten. The version of Pentu in his dream had been wrong; in the afterlife, the Princess and Queen looked not worse, but better than she had in the other life. "And I'm sorry... for what Ay did to you." He squeezed his oldest sister's hand.

"It was over in a minute," Meritaten said softly. Then she gave a sad little smile. "But I heard you and Ankh say that you wanted me to be your Vizier... and oh, I wished I could."

"I think we could have beaten Ay, the three of us," he said.

"But you won a much larger fight," Mother said with a smile. "You and Ankh."

"Yes, we found the Light," he told his parents with a smile. "Just like you told me in that dream." They gave a little gasp, Mother squeezing Father's hand as they realized that it had worked. "…And so did our friends Semerkhet and Meresankh. And that's the only fight that really matters." He paused. "But Ankh… she's still fighting for the future of Egypt. She's going to marry the Hittite Prince if she can… and if she can't, she'll do everything she can to make herself Pharaoh. Or she might… she might even change the future as a history teacher in Sais." He chuckled. "She'll be a good King. She takes after both her parents."

They smiled, and Tut thought he could see tears in his mother's eyes.

"I wish we could tell her how proud we are of her," she whispered.

Tut took his mother's hand with a smile. "She knows."

Grandmother Tiye lifted her head proudly. "She's learned so well. Remembered everything we taught her."

"Sais," Mother said with a proud smile. Slowly she nodded. "The school of women's medicine." She closed her eyes. "Well done, my dear," she whispered. "Well done."

"The other politicians won't like it," Father said grimly. "Marrying out. Or ruling unattached."

Tut looked around his new home and chuckled. "What's the worst that could happen?"

And Father chuckled.

Tut smiled again as the five sisters surrounded him again, braids jingling merrily. "I missed you all so much…"

"And we missed you," they said, patting his hands, stroking his wig. "We wished we could see you again… but not too soon."

He swallowed. Nineteen years really was too soon. But these things had happened the way they had happened, and they were together again. And that was all that mattered.

440

"It's been hard," he admitted, his voice becoming choked. "So hard. Hardest two months of my life." He bit back a harsh chuckle as he stopped himself from continuing, "The last two months of my life."

"It's over now," Mother whispered, putting her arms around him again. He hugged her back, feeling her love, her warmth, her strength. Ankh had done her best, but it felt good to be hugged by his real mother again. "It's all behind us. You made it through... all the way to the end. You've been so strong... so brave... we're so proud of you. So proud of you, Tutankhaten."

He felt his father's hand touch his shoulder, then pat him warmly on the back. "We're so very, very proud of you," he echoed.

Giving his mother one more squeeze, Tut stepped back and wiped his nose.

"There is no more crying, no more death," his father said again, "but that doesn't mean that those things don't matter."

"Things didn't end the way we wanted them to; not for any of us," his mother said, tears gleaming in her eyes. "And not the way we wanted for you."

Tut gave her a sad little smile, then shook his head. "Maybe not," he said, "but I'm glad to be home. And as for the way things ended..." He sighed, thinking back over those nineteen years. "I may not be Grandfather Thutmose, but I do have a legacy. A legacy of peace. And I'm proud of that."

His parents just beamed, their smiles as bright as the Sun.

From up the garden path, Mereneferet and Senebhenas turned around and ran back to their Daddy. Squatting down, he braced himself as they approached— he hadn't really thought about it the first time, but how could he possibly catch them without being knocked over? Holding his breath and preparing to tumble, he found himself scooping them up as they crashed into him, holding them close as they settled in against his sides for another ride. To his amazement, he kept his footing.

And he laughed. In what kind of a crazy world could he stay upright when two little girls decided to run into his arms? And actually catch them? And in what kind of a world could he stand firm and straight with nothing to hang onto? In a perfect world, that was where. Like this one.

Suddenly he noticed something else. His father, whom he had always seen as Pharaoh, was not wearing a crown; only a simple *nemes* head-cloth. And reaching up around the wiggly little Senebhenas to pat at his own head, Tut found that he was wearing his favorite wig, but no crown either.

His father smiled as he realized what Tut was noticing. "I'm no longer a Pharaoh, son, and neither are you," he said gently. He looked up at the sky, into the sunlight that seemed to come from all around them, rather than from a single Solar Disc. "We are all the servants of the Lord of Light."

"I'm not Pharaoh any longer, either," his mother said with a wink. Tut laughed out loud.

"Your grandma was Pharaoh after your grandpa came here," he explained to his daughters, who were still patting his head, playing with his wig, kicking his ribs, kissing his face, occasionally poking their fingers into his ears.

"We know, Daddy," Mereneferet said. "Grandma says you did a really good job too and she's really proud of you."

"Proud of you!" Senebhenas crowed, gleefully arching her back so her father had to bend his knees and juggle her back into his arms. Although somehow, he knew that if he had dropped her, she

442

would not have been hurt. In this place, none of them would be hurt ever again.

Tut looked back in the direction from which he had come. There was a heavy mist; a mist through which he could almost see Ankhesenpaaten and Semerkhet sitting beside a very still form he almost recognized as his own body. How strange that he still had splints on his legs, now that he could move with painless ease for the first time in his life.

But beyond the mist, at the heart of each of the two figures, he saw a glowing Light. And peace, perfect peace, on their faces. And he knew that when the time came, he would be the one welcoming his sweet Ankh, his dear Sem, into the perfect and forever home in which he now stood. They were all right. And so was he.

Then he looked more closely. And smiled, even as tears came to his eyes. Because… because his sister's belly was strangely transparent. And inside, curled up safe and warm… there was a tiny baby girl.

He held Senebhenas and Mereneferet closer as he nodded toward the fog. "You have a baby sister," he whispered. He sighed. Not the politically advantageous son for whom they had prayed. Another beautiful daughter. Another Princess. And whether in Memphis, Thebes, Sais, or somewhere else completely, a future Queen. The Queen of the life she would choose to live. And even in exile, a member of the royal family.

Tut's father was looking over his son's shoulder into the same dark mist. Gently he put his hand on Tut's shoulder again. "They'll be with us one day," he said reassuringly. "See the Light in their hearts?"

His mother reached out and gently touched his arm. "It won't be forever." Then she smiled, nodding toward the courtyard and everything that lay beyond it. "This… this is forever."

"Sometimes we can see through the mist," Grandmother said, "but it's not what we focus on. We don't spend our time looking backwards." And she opened her arm toward the City of Light.

He nodded with a little smile. And slowly, he turned away, leaving his old life behind him.

"Daddy, how do you know our names?" Mereneferet asked.

He kissed her on the forehead, then Senebhenas. "Your mommy found them in her heart. Someday she'll be with us too. And you'll get to meet your Uncle Semerkhet and Auntie Meresankh and Granny Merneith."

"I knew you'd find the Truth," his father said, resting a hand proudly on his son's shoulder. "Welcome to the City of Light."

And holding his baby girls tight, his mother, father, grandmother, and sisters laughing and smiling around him, Tutankhaten walked into an eternity of peace.

He was home.


The Sun rose. Ankhesenpaaten and Semerkhet sat wordlessly looking down at the silent body in the bed. Their exhausted hearts and minds could hardly believe that it was over.

And yet it wasn't. Looking down at the Pharaoh, a single ray of morning sunshine streaming through the window to touch his silent face, they smiled through their tears. Because their brother was home.

# Epilogue

It was the big day. Semerkhet stood in the front room of the beautiful little house in Sais into which he, Meresankh, and Merneith had moved just over a week ago. Outside in the front yard, he could hear laughter, merry chatter, someone playing a flute as someone else clapped along to the beat. Their wedding party had arrived.

Only… This was the big day. A day full of joy; the day when he and Meresankh would celebrate their marriage with their friends and family. But as he listened to the cheerful laughter outside the house, Sem found himself thinking not of who was there, but of who was not.

His mother was not there. Nedjes was not there. His father was not there. Tut was not there.

Only there in his heart.

Semerkhet glanced in the mirror, checking his eye-makeup. It looked fine, as did his wig. But he still had dark circles under his eyes, what with how poorly he'd been sleeping. And… He turned his head this way and that, examining his freshly shaved chin, the tan-line that had developed over the long weeks that had passed since the sixteenth of Tybi. Only yesterday morning, he had shaved the beard he had been growing since his brother had closed his eyes; the beard that was the last thing that tied him to his friend. It hadn't looked good on him, but now that it was gone… he looked strange. He looked the way he had looked before all this. As if nothing had changed.

But everything had changed.

Semerkhet swallowed. His throat was sore; still raw after the funeral. Because Semerkhet had wailed with the professional

445

mourning women, wept like he had not wept since Nedjes had died, sobbed until he grew hoarse. Because the day he had been dreading had come. The day when he would lose his little brother.

He looked down at his hands. He still had blisters on his palms from the rope.

*He had helped pull the funeral bier with the other mourners, one of twelve men dressed all alike in white tunics, headbands, and sandals. The day had been burned into his heart— the despairing shrieks of the wailing women in their dresses of pale blue, tearing at their wigs and beating their heads against the ground as they collapsed in grief; the lowing of the six cattle that were helping the men pull the funeral bier— Nubian cattle Semerkhet remembered from Tribute Day. Tears had prickled in his eyes every time he glanced behind him to see the solid gold mask that covered the face of the mummy that was all that was left of his friend.*

*He remembered the boat ride across the Nile from Thebes to the Valley of the Kings, the wails of the mourning women echoing over the water as citizens gathered on both banks to join in the lamentations. The fragrances of flowers and incense; the prayers of High Priest Parannefer as the old vulture Ay haughtily conducted the meaningless, pagan Opening of the Mouth ceremony, resplendent in a crown that marked him as Tut's successor. Standing with the Queen and Meresankh outside the small tomb, surrounded by all the beautiful things that had been prepared to keep Tutankhamun comfortable and entertained during his afterlife— furniture, walking-sticks, baskets of clothing, boxes and boxes of jewelry and shoes that brought a lump to Semerkhet's throat as he remembered every day he had helped the Pharaoh put them on.*

446

*And he remembered wailing. None of the other men did, but they left him be. And they let him pour out the grief inside his heart.*

*He remembered standing beside the Queen within the tomb itself, finally watching as his friend's mummy was carefully placed inside three coffins, one of solid gold and two of gilded wood. Remembered watching the lid of the stone sarcophagus into which the three coffins had been nestled closing over the silent, peaceful face of the outermost coffin. Remembered watching the golden shrines being arranged around the perimeter of the sarcophagus as every moment immortalized in the scenes inscribed upon the shrines burned inside his heart.*

*The day had somehow ended with a ritual meal shared by all the mourners and the exhausted return to the home he, Meresankh, and Merneith had briefly shared in Thebes, heart wrung empty of tears. A day that kept Semerkhet from falling asleep and awoke him with nightmares of the moment his friend's massive golden coffins had disappeared forever inside his tomb.*

But today… today was not that day. Today was a day to be happy. To celebrate his marriage to Meresankh… the marriage that Tutankhaten had made happen. This was a day to honor his friend with joy.

Life… life was going on. With each passing week, he had found himself smiling more; crying less, at least. Swallowing back the lump in his throat when he looked at his brother's things, then turning away with a sad smile to get on with his day. There was life on the other side of this loss.

He thought back to two months or so after Nedjes had died. It felt similar, really. Only… he knew without the shadow of a doubt

447

that Tut had accepted the Light of I-AM. Knew that one day, they would be together again.

He still wondered about Nedjes.

Semerkhet touched the little scarab necklace his wife had given him, resting as it always did over his heart. And he looked down at the jasper ring on his finger, and the walking-stick that stood leaning in the doorway of the bedroom next to a very familiar pair of shoes. And he looked at the kitchen table, piled with fruit and vegetables he and Meresankh had bought together at the market, bread Meresankh had baked, a pot of herbal tea that Granny had brewed, and a very special blue lotus cup. And he looked at the little gray cat who lay curled on a familiar chair, enjoying the afternoon sunshine on this cool Phamenoth day. The love of those in this world and those in the next filled his heart with warmth. And he walked through the door to join the party.


Meresankh looked up from her conversation with Merneith and saw that her husband had joined the party. Smiling at her Granny, she excused herself and joined him, taking both his hands in hers and smiling up at him.

"Hello, my love," she whispered.

He smiled down at her. "Hello, my love." But his smile was not very big. And she could see on his jawline where he had nicked himself shaving the scraggly beard he had grown over the days of mourning for the Pharaoh. Life moved on. But the past still weighed heavily… on both of them.

It weighed on Ankhesenpaaten as well. She stood there among the guests, one of many, her belly just beginning to grow in a soft curve under the rather plain dress she was wearing. She was a Queen, and she would always be a Queen, but now she was a

448

Queen without a crown; a Queen who would teach the future Prince or Princess his or her history in secret. But even disinherited, this child would grow up knowing they were royalty.

Ankh was happy to be there, Meresankh knew. And it was an honor that she had chosen to attend. But Meresankh could see the shadow of grief on her face; a look in her eye that had not been there a year ago.

So much loss had invaded the Queen's life over the past year. The loss of her brother. The loss of the Prince she might have made her husband. The loss of her home at the palace. And the loss of the throne that should have been hers.

Meresankh thought back to the days that had elapsed since they had been a Queen and a handmaiden. Two long months that had brought with them more change than anyone could have imagined.

*So much had happened over those two months. Ay had happened. And Zannanza had not. He had disappeared upon reaching the border between Hattusa and Egypt. And although in the letter he'd written in response to the frantic message sent by Suppiluliuma upon learning that his son was missing, the Vizier had neither claimed responsibility for Zannanza's fate nor confirmed what his fate had been, everyone in Egypt knew that the Hittite Prince was dead.*

*But their prayers for Horemheb's heart to change had been answered. And he had come home grief-stricken and penitent, chin unshaven in mourning for the Pharaoh he had sent to his death. He had spoken with the Queen. She had forgiven him. And after formally relinquishing his right to take the next throne as Tutankhamun's heir, Horemheb went to the dungeons and took his wives home.*

449

The night everyone had returned to Memphis after the funeral, after the slow, sad journey home from Thebes, a slow, sad journey through which Horemheb had silently guarded the Queen from the threat of any additional schemes of the Vizier, the widowed Great Royal Wife had disappeared from the palace. Disappeared a matter of hours after the Vizier had stuffed the blue glass ring back into his pocket for the last time.

The Vizier had demanded a moment with the Queen, giving her one final chance to become his wife. And after he had stomped off in a huff, with no further reasons to leave Ankhesenpaaten alive, the Queen had locked her chamber door, blaming a migraine and the beginnings of morning sickness.

The Queen finished packing her things, items that had been gathered and sorted over the past few days and now just needed to be stowed in boxes and baskets for the journey. Meresankh helped her, then got Hannu and Horemheb, gathering those faithful men to assist in the great escape. Granny had packed as well, and there was Little Nefertiti, eyes wide and bright as she prepared to leave one life behind to begin a new one. Semerkhet, too, walked slowly through the Pharaoh's suite one last time before leaving it forever.

They had mounted their horses. And they had ridden through the night. And two days later, Meresankh had smuggled her sister through the back door of her new house. Meanwhile, back at the palace, Horemheb had announced that the former Queen would pose no threat to Ay's reign. That much, Meresankh supposed, was true. Although she would never forget that because of Ankhesenpaaten's refusal to marry him, the Vizier's reign could never be legitimate.

By the time the solemn announcement of the deaths of the Queen and the heir to the throne, so shockingly soon after the *departure of the Pharaoh, had begun to echo through the land of Egypt, Meresankh, Semerkhet, and Merneith had settled themselves into their little house in Sais, taking a short walk every day to the equally small house that Ankh and Nefertiti-Tasherit shared two streets away.*

*Her Mistress seemed so unprotected, living alone with her niece and her baby, still safe and warm inside her belly. But she would be all right, Meresankh knew. Thanks to Horemheb's deceit, the old man would never look for her. And praise be to I-AM, the civil war between the servants who had supported Tut and those who followed Ay had never materialized. There had been a single fistfight. But Semerkhet's words of peace had touched enough hearts that no blood had been shed.*

*But they wouldn't be in Sais forever. And until Ankh and her growing family could go back to Memphis, Meresankh would help her as a friend and neighbor, answering her questions about day-to-day household management and visiting her as often as she could.*

*And in about six months… in about six months, she would be holding her friend's hand as Granny helped usher her new niece or nephew into the world.*

Every day, Meresankh prayed that Ankh, the baby, and Nefertiti-Tasherit would be safe. And that their new life would be full of joy.

Sem had been excited last night; excited for the party. But… he had dreamed. And in his dream his friend had stood before him, standing firmly on his two feet without a walking-stick in sight. He had led Semerkhet to the house he now shared with Meresankh,

451

and opened the door for his former valet. And as Semerkhet had walked into his new home, the Pharaoh had disappeared.

Ankh didn't say much. She was afraid— wearing herself out praying for the well-being of her child, visiting Granny every single week for another examination that would confirm that just like last week, nothing was wrong. She was not yet three months along. Not yet as far as she had been with Mereneferet. And each day brought a new opportunity for something to go wrong. So every day was filled with prayer and preparation.

So Meresankh asked her how she was, and admired her belly, and simply stood with her and squeezed her hand. And finally the Queen began to tell her about the previous day's lecture at the medical college, a lecture Merneith herself had delivered, and what a wonderful job Little Nefertiti was doing in helping keep up with the housework.

And finally… she smiled.

Sem went back inside. And carefully he picked up Bastet, carrying her out into the sunshine. The Queen looked up, smiling sadly as she saw the cat her brother had loved so much. And together, they remembered.

Semerkhet danced with his wife. Around and around they spun with the music of the flutes, harps, and drums that their friends had brought, Meresankh's little silver necklace catching the afternoon light. And Sem smiled when Meresankh took his hand and laid it over her belly. They had not told anyone yet. But a new season of life was beginning, in more ways than one.

452

Friends asked him about his career. And Semerkhet found himself smiling as he told them; told them how he had been studying with Merneith, spending the past seventy days learning his herbs, learning how to look after bumps and bruises beyond the average, learning how to help minimize a pregnant woman's more uncomfortable signs of her condition. From Granny, he had learned to be a nurse as well as a valet deeply familiar with a diversity of needs. And now he was working at a medical practice in Sais. It was strange to be taking care of other people, but it was rewarding to use the skills he had learned at the palace to help strangers.

Semerkhet had a new career. And it made him happy. Even if it was a form of happiness he had never expected to find.

The Queen tried to enjoy the party; honor her beloved friends by celebrating their marriage with them. But her smiles felt hollow. And the memories of her final days in the palace ached inside her heart.

*Ankhesenpaaten had walked through her chambers, her brother's chambers, one last time, saying goodbye. She was leaving everything behind. Leaving her best friend, Meresankh, who, now married to Semerkhet, was also standing at the threshold of a new life as a private person. Leaving Amenia, Mutnedjmet, and Meryt, women whom she had poured into, watching them grow... or stay latched in place. Leaving the beautiful home where she had lived for over ten years; the ease and luxury with which she had always been surrounded.*

*Leaving the graceful chambers she could navigate even in the dark; the room where she'd spent the long days and nights of the past six weeks. Leaving the bedroom that still seemed to carry her brother's presence; the bedsheets and clothing that still held onto his smell, the bed that still seemed to hold the impression of his frail body. Leaving Bastet, the beloved pet who would live a good life in the care of Semerkhet and Meresankh. Leaving Ay and the ring he had had prepared with both their names on it, an engagement gift she had roundly refused every time he had offered it. Leaving the expected future that had given her strength during those dark days; the crown she had been prevented from claiming, the Prince she had hoped to make her husband. Leaving it all behind. But carrying it with her in her heart.*

*She was leaving it all behind. That she knew. But she was going somewhere. And she knew that, too. And together, she and her child would have a future. And in Sais, she would raise her child into the prince or princess that they were, throne or no throne. And they would keep the memory of Egypt alive. And as she told her child the stories of their family, and of the father it would never meet, they would keep the memory of Tutankhaten alive.*

Standing there at the edge of the party, the Queen closed her eyes. "It's all for you, Baby," she whispered, gently resting a hand on her belly. "Every step of this journey. Mommy will keep you safe no matter what. But we have Little Nefertiti to help us, and Horemheb to keep us safe. And one day, we'll come back. I promise."

There was music. And there was dancing. And there was laughter and joy and food and drink. And for fleeting moments they forgot; lost themselves in the moments they found themselves in and rejoiced with abandon.

454

And then a face would come into their field of view— a man with buckteeth; a young person with a walking-stick. Or a "hey, Sem" or a spluttering attempt at a whistle would cut through the chatter around them. And Sem, Meresankh, would blink as the breath caught in their throat, heart beginning to race. Was it—

But it never was. Just another member, or former member, of the palace staff who had come here to celebrate their marriage with them.

Tut was not here. Nedjes was not here. Meresankh's parents were not here. And neither were Semerkhet's.

But... but Ankh was here. Nefertiti-Tasherit and Granny were here. And Semerkhet's big sister Nofret, with her husband and little Ahmose, who was beginning to toddle. And many friends from the palace staff. All these people who loved them, and had come to Sais to celebrate the love they had for one another.

And the guests... they asked about the Pharaoh. And even on his wedding day, Semerkhet answered their questions about his beloved friend. But even as he had to choke back the tears, he found his heart warming as he spoke about his brother. After all, to speak the name of the dead was to make them live again. And somewhere... A ray of warm afternoon sunlight shone through an opening in the clouds, and he smiled. Somewhere, by the grace of I-AM, his friend was at peace.

Semerkhet looked down at his ring. Tut *was* here. In every word that Sem spoke; every memory that he shared. And he would be, for as long as Semerkhet told his story.

And Semerkhet and Meresankh smiled. Smiled even as the ring of the Sole Companion and the earrings that had once belonged to the Pharaoh and now hung in Meresankh's ears weighed them down, just a little. Right here, right now, it didn't matter that Ay had become Pharaoh, or that Horemheb was breathing threats down Crown Prince Nakhtmin's neck. What mattered was that they were together, surrounded by people who loved them. What mattered was the future. What mattered was the new life in Meresankh's belly, and the new life they would build together. And the new life that Ankh and her child would build with Nefertiti-Tasherit; the lives the Queen would change as she taught history in Memphis. What mattered was the hope they felt shining inside their hearts.

Happiness would take some finding. But they would find it. All of them.

# Author's Note

T he Bible is the starting point of all history. Many events in Ancient Egyptian history, from the arrival of the Canaanite immigrants to Goshen around the Twelfth Dynasty to the royal accession of a second-born Egyptian prince whose decisions as Pharaoh suggest that he may have witnessed the Ten Plagues firsthand, line up clearly with what the Bible tells us. Numerous Biblical quotes and concepts inspired me as I wrote, and found their way into *A Legacy of Light* in a combination of direct quotes, paraphrases, and vague allusions.

A major inspiration as I wrote Ankhesenamun's plotline was the story of Esther. Esther demonstrates all the qualities I wanted to see shining in Ankh, exemplifying being courageous and cunning, civil and sneaky, sweet and deadly. Both are strong, wise, confident politicians, and both know how to fight like a girl!

I was also inspired by the Biblical story of Uriah the Hittite in 2 Samuel. After impregnating Uriah's wife Bathsheba, King David sends him into battle with his own death warrant; he is to be sent into the thickest part of the combat, and at the signal, the rest of the army is to pull back, leaving him to die. In the same way, under Ay's orders, Horemheb signals the troops to retreat in *The Things We Can Change*, leaving the Pharaoh fatally exposed.

The celebration of a Pharaoh's birthday with a feast somewhat analogous to a "birthday party," as seen in *To Claim What is Ours*, is also Biblical; in Genesis 40:20, we learn that "the third day was Pharaoh's birthday, and he gave a feast for all his officials" (NIV).

Furthermore, a mysterious verse in 1 Chronicles provides us with a glimmer of a narrative I would love to learn more about; a narrative which, in its simplicity, can actually be connected to

Ankhesenamun's journey. In the genealogies of the ancestors of the Jewish people living at the time of the Chronicler, we find a description of a rather unique family. A man named Mered is described as marrying "Bithia," the daughter of the King of Egypt. The name *Bithia* seems to have been a name she received upon converting to Judaism; it translates to "daughter of God." But who was this mysterious Egyptian princess? As we learn in Ankh's story, Egyptian queens and princesses never married foreigners. However, both Tutankhamun's widow and the unidentified wife of Mered seem to have found themselves in dire enough straits to make that decision. Could they be… could they just be… the same person? Did Ankhesenamun flee Egypt after the death of her brother and marry into the Children of Israel?

We may never know.

## Unique Insights

My own life experiences also helped me as I sought to recreate the challenges of Tut's daily life. As a person with spina bifida, I know what it's like for something that many other people wouldn't stop to think twice about to be an accomplishment to be proud of. Case in point: getting up stairs, especially with no railing. I know what it's like to need a little extra help, to have frequent doctor's appointments, and to receive awkward questions about my legs and the braces I wear.

I, too, have a flat foot on one side and a high arch on the other, as well as mild scoliosis, and had quite the overbite until receiving orthodontia. Based on personal experience, I, too, can vouch for how useless backless sandals are! And I can only imagine how difficult my life would be if I had not had the opportunity to have the foot surgeries I've received or the leg braces I need.

Additionally, my family is affected by neural tube conditions, and by miscarriage.

Even a number of specific moments in my telling of the Pharaoh's story are echoes of my own experiences. While recovering from surgery, I once fell asleep while my mother was feeding me pudding, and I remember the strange sensation of my heartbeat slowing down when I received morphine. Other real details include the way that being turned in bed becomes too painful at the exact moment that the turn is complete (my experience after back surgery), the way that although Tut can no longer carry on a conversation, he is still aware enough to be bored and wants to be talked *to*, his vague annoyance at hearing only the beginnings of countless stories (how many movies put me to sleep after the first fifteen minutes?), and the dim awareness of drowsing in a hospital bed with cold packs lowering one's fever and morphine controlling one's pain. Even the painful moments when Tut's wound has to be cleaned have their inspiration— enduring the removal of an infected stitch during the recovery from a different surgery. Also while recovering from surgery, I discovered just how cold you can feel after a shower!

On a more cheerful note, my mother has worked in education for several years, with a specific focus on neuroscience and mediation. Her guidance has helped me develop my strategy in various board games, just as Ankh makes Tut into a winner. We have even enjoyed playing a modern version of the game *seega!*

I have described Semerkhet, Meresankh, and the other servants eating in a cafeteria of sorts, eating royal leftovers and plain food prepared for them, but this is my own conjecture. I was inspired by my experience of working at an event center, where staff lunches were often comprised of leftovers from the previous day's wedding or other event. Another source of inspiration is the philosophy of my current workplace, a large-scale music retailer, which reminds employees that every right choice is worth making, that every positive action is worth making, no matter how small it may seem, and that everything that every employee does can have far-reaching ripples.

Another experience of my own also inspired Semerkhet's duties. As he assists the Pharaoh with his daily tasks of "bed, bath, and beyond," everything from getting up and dressed to meal facilitation to showers and bedtime; fetching and carrying and helping his Master in and out of chairs, Sem functions as a direct support professional, and could be described as the Royal CNA. As a high schooler, I assisted my mother, who is CNA trained, in the care of an elderly client, and have been inspired by my memories of our responsibilities.

To sum up, our situations differ in a thousand ways, but in some ways, I feel like I can genuinely relate to Tutankhamun. I believe that my life and the experiences of my family have helped me to gain insight into what life might have been like for one of Egypt's only special-needs Pharaohs.

## The Medical Knowledge of Ancient Egypt

Numerous herbs were known to the Ancient Egyptians, and I have blended medical uses specific to Ancient Egypt with other herbs known to exist in Egypt being administered according to their traditional uses in other parts of the world, whether or not they were used in this manner in Ancient Egypt. For example, mustard-seed was used medicinally in Ancient Egypt, but we do not know whether they used it to make mustard-plasters.

Moldy bread was used to treat infections in Ancient Egypt, as was honey, but for the sake of the plot, the treatment had to be unsuccessful in Tut's particular case. Other medical treatments were perhaps not so effective, however, such as the consumption of a dead mouse by a mother who wanted to cure her sick baby.

As I have described, doctors placed injuries into three categories— treatable, able to be contended with, and untreatable— and may have been able to make a dying patient's last hours more comfortable with substances like opium, mandrake, and cannabis. Throughout my story, I have ensured that thoughts and ideas are described as arising in characters' hearts or minds, rather than their heads or their brains, as in Ancient Egypt, the heart was considered the location of thoughts.

Merneith's pregnancy test, in which a woman's urine is used to water seeds, comes from a real Ancient Egyptian practice. The sprouting of barley was associated with a baby boy, and wheat with a baby girl (though which was which was sometimes reversed). In a replication of this test performed in the 1960s, the urine of a pregnant woman did cause seeds to sprout, while the urine of a man and of a woman who was not pregnant did not. However, this test would not have provided a reliable indication of the child's gender.

The "birthing pavilion" was a real structure built in Ancient Egypt as a special space in which a woman would give birth. "Birthing bricks" were beautifully painted bricks decorated with scenes of successful deliveries. A woman would squat on two of these bricks while giving birth. Birthing chairs or stools were also an option; these stools were designed with a hole in the center, which made it logistically easier for the midwife to catch the baby.

461

The whole body was believed to run with a series of channels, which carried blood, urine, semen, and tears. Blockages in these channels were believed to cause illness. As such, I extrapolate that Granny would interpret Tut's worsening infection at the end of the story as an indication that his infection had entered the "channels" of his body— which is basically true, as it so happens, as the red streaks around his wound and swelling in the lymph nodes in his hip region are symptoms of lymphangitis, the entry of infection into his lymphatic system. The onset of lymphangitis truly brings Tut's infection to an untreatable stage, and heralds the beginning of the end.

The dangers of alcohol consumption by pregnant mothers may not have been known to the Ancient Egyptians, but in Merneith's encyclopedic knowledge of baby development, I have her instruct Ankh to avoid alcohol in the interest of her baby's health. References to Meritaten having had a specially padded chair that helped her avoid skin irritations, and the efforts of Semerkhet and other staff members to help Tut reposition himself in bed every few hours for the same reason, are also based simply on common sense.

We have no information as to whether or not Tutankhamun developed pneumonia as he lay dying, but an extended period of immobility is a risk factor. The physical signs I describe over the course of Tut's final hours, such as coldness and purple mottling in the extremities (cyanosis), alterations in breathing patterns, a loss of thirst, an increase in yawning, and the onset of the death rattle, are all indicators frequently observed in those who are actively dying. As described above, the Pharaoh also develops lymphangitis, a serious infection that tells even Granny that his life cannot be saved. The rally, a surge of energy sometimes

462

experienced by the dying, which can give them the opportunity to set their affairs in order and say goodbye to loved ones, is represented by the hours that Tutankhamun is able to spend awake and lucid, witnessing Semerkhet and Meresankh's marriage contract and bequeathing various possessions and titles to his friend.

## Massage in Ancient Egypt

Massage is attested as an element of Ancient Egyptian medicine. Different blends of essential oils, combined with carrier oils, were described in various medical texts, such as the Ebers Papyrus, as being good for different parts of the body as well as different concerns. The complex ointment I describe the Chief Physician preparing for the Pharaoh after his return from Kadesh in *The Things We Can Change* has nothing on one historical massage lotion that contained thirty-seven ingredients! And the use of oils and ointments to prevent dry skin and relieve sore muscles was so vital that when the usual ointments were no longer included in their wages, a group of construction workers is known to have gone on strike.

I also enjoyed analyzing the significance of the Pharaoh's bedtime lotion, which was inspired by the discovery of a container in his tomb containing traces of a sweet-scented ointment that may have been a combination of coconut oil, frankincense, and spikenard. Although the historical expensiveness of spikenard adds to the "royal" quality of such an ointment, I also found great meaning in the aromatherapeutic attributes of both spikenard and frankincense. Frankincense, which has long been used in incense, calms the mind and encourages contemplation. Spikenard soothes stress and relieves insomnia. In their combination, I see not only an expensive perfume; I see a perfect aromatherapy blend for bedtime massage.

Illustrations of massage as employed in Ancient Egypt focus on reflexology of the hands and feet, although the limbs and body are also seen to. Medical texts, however, indicate that the entire body was treated with massage. The massage techniques Semerkhet uses are based strongly in the Swedish tradition of massage; we have little suggestion as to the specific techniques that would have been used. Although in the absence of time-travel as a plot point, I was unable to treat or cure any of Tutankhamun's medical challenges through modern medicine, I was glad to know that I could make him feel a little better.

## Mediation, Learning, and Neuroscience

I was also delighted to see my characters mediating one another— getting between another person and a task or challenge. Together they learn and grow, encouraging one another to think about their thinking and to pause and think before making a decision. They also mediate themselves, remembering and applying what they've learned.

Little was known about neuroscience in Ancient Egypt (the function of the brain itself was not known), but I made sure to match Tut's level of maturity with the fact that he is a nineteen-year-old boy. Sadly enough, the Pharaoh catapults himself into the battle that ultimately causes his own death, because his impulse control is still developing, and when the Vizier suggests that he ride out into battle, all thoughts of caution fly out the window.

I also describe several instances of "neural hijacking," experienced by Tut, Ankh, and Semerkhet. This refers to the action of the amygdala, a brain structure that watches for danger. When it is

464

triggered, higher reasoning can take a backseat as adrenaline and other hormones flood the brain and body as you phase into survival mode. Blood flow within the brain actually redirects from the "thinking" frontal lobe to the "emotional" back half of the brain as reasoning is sacrificed for the sake of survival.

This is often referred to as an amygdala "hijack" because it grabs a huge proportion of the brain's resources, hoarding them so that it can save your life. Sometimes, also, a person does not notice the effects of adrenaline until after a confrontation is over. The pounding heart, cold sweat, lightheadedness, and chattering teeth that characters may feel in the aftermath of a moment of high intensity are based on experiences of my own. Even three thousand years before modern neuroscience, people would have seen the impact of brain development and the work of the amygdala in their everyday lives.

## A Colorful Cast

The villainous characters of Grand Vizier Ay, General Nakhtmin, and Treasurer Maya, the misguided Sennedjem, the High Priest Parannefer, the allies Pentu and Usermontu, and General Horemheb, who finds himself "sitting on the fence," are all inspired by historical figures. Little is known about any of them or their specific roles in Tutankhamun's life (and death), but these members of the Pharaoh's court bear the names and titles of real historical figures. The personalities, goals, and motivations of these characters, however, have sprung almost entirely from my imagination.

Amenia, Mutnedjmet, and Meryt, wives of Horemheb and Maya, also bear the names of their historical counterparts, although Horemheb is more likely to have married Mutnedjmet after

Amenia's death as opposed to being married to both of them simultaneously. Mutnedjmet is known to have given birth to several children, and may have died in childbirth. However, sadly enough, there is little evidence that any of Horemheb's children survived infancy. The naming of Maya's daughters after their father is also historical, and inspired my characterization of Meryt. Amenia and Mutnedjmet do become "damsels in distress," a stereotypical trope that I didn't really want to rely on, but their safety was the only priority that would keep Horemheb from killing the Vizier, as otherwise, he may have considered launching a civil war against the traitorous usurper a risk worth taking.

In terms of the Pharaoh's decisions, we don't know whether Tut really focused his reign on social justice. His generous zeal to raise the world out of poverty is as conjectural as my portrayal of his personality, but seemed a plausible goal for a teenager who wanted to use his unique power for good. We also have no information as to which members of his court may have agreed with his decisions, whatever they may have been, who may have dissented, and where these agreements and disagreements would have led.

No one knows how much Ankhesenamun, as the Pharaoh's Great Royal Wife and older sister, helped Tutankhamun devise the policies he may have passed. We also don't know if Ankh was a women's rights activist, but her powerful female legacy, which I hope she treasured as much as I describe, found a natural outgrowth in her wish to give all girls and women the opportunity to receive a full education and pursue a career they enjoy.

In my Queen's independence and strength, I was inspired not only by the Queens and female Pharaohs of Ancient Egypt, as well as Queen Esther, but by Queen Elizabeth the First of England. In Ankhesenamun's eventual move from Great Royal Wife to citizen of her own country, she exemplifies Elizabeth the First's statement that "I thank God that I am endowed with such qualities that if I were turned out of the realm in my petticoat, I were able to live in any place in Christendom."

I should point out that although I depict Ay as a lonely old widower who wants not only power, but a lovely new wife, historically, when the Vizier became Pharaoh, his wife Tey became Queen. As Pharaoh, Ay did make Nakhtmin his heir (their relationship is not known with certainty; Nakhtmin was likely Ay's son or stepson), but Ay's reign was followed by Horemheb's, after Nakhtmin mysteriously disappeared from further records toward the end of Ay's reign.

Nothing is known of Nakhtmin's death or personality, but I strongly suspect that Horemheb had him murdered. To hint at this, I sprinkled in indications throughout *To Claim What is Ours* that Horemheb hates Nakhtmin enough to at least metaphorically wish he could kill him, a wish that might become reality if the little General pushes him too far. There is, however, no evidence that Ay held Mutnedjmet and Amenia hostage to keep Horemheb from beating him to the throne. We also can't rule out the possibility that Nakhtmin died heroically in battle, was an ally and friend of Tut, and would have been a thoroughly decent Pharaoh himself.

As for the casting of Grand Vizier Ay as the power-hungry murderer of four members of the Amarna family whose greed and ambition push him to ever-crueler depths of brutality, this is conjectural. In Ay we do see, however, a rare male regent serving as guide and guardian for an underage Pharaoh; a regent who may have been unwilling to let the reins of power pass to the young man placed in his care. We cannot rule out the possibility that Ay stopped the independent young Tut in his tracks through ensuring his early death, then attempted to succeed him by marrying the royal widow and preventing her from either taking power herself or giving the throne of Egypt to the Prince of Hattusa.

Horemheb's lesser villainy, however, is historically inspired; after Tutankhamun's death, Horemheb treated his predecessor's tomb with respect, possibly because serving under Tutankhamun had put him in a position to become Pharaoh himself. He did relabel some of Tut's monuments and statues, but he didn't destroy them. Horemheb's conduct suggests to me that Ay, rather than the General, was the one who really wanted Tut dead, and that Horemheb came to regret whatever involvement he had had in the Pharaoh's death.

Horemheb is also known to have led a diplomatic mission to Nubia, although when this took place and whether it was part of the Pharaoh's efforts to restore diplomatic relations with neighboring countries, celebrated in the paintings of the Viceroy of Kush's tomb, is not clear.

The General also wrote that he could calm Tutankhamun when the Pharaoh was angry, and I allude to this in *To Claim What is Ours* when the King reminisces with Horemheb about his childhood, as well as in the scene when Horemheb mediates Tut through his episode of rage toward Nakhtmin. Horemheb's reference in *The Things We Can Change* to a young soldier named Paramessu is a reference to the future Pharaoh Rameses the First, whom Horemheb made his heir and who, as I mention, was the son of a commander named Seti. Seti and Paramessu were indeed related by marriage to the Viceroy of Kush.

Sennedjem, the "overseer of tutors" under Tut, appears to have fallen into some type of disgrace, as his name was erased from his own unfinished tomb. Nothing is known as to how he became

468

disgraced, but tomb robbing was a problem in Ancient Egypt, and the tomb robbery I describe him committing (or directing) in *To Claim What is Ours* ties in neatly with the economic problems that form the undercurrent of my story. Turning to another courtier, Akhenaten's Chief Physician was named Penthu, and he received many of the titles Tut bestows on Semerkhet in *Searching for the Truth.* It is possible that Penthu and Pentu are identical, but as I portray Vizier Pentu as being quite a young man, I describe them as father and son.

In conclusion, I enjoyed crafting characters whose personalities align with the known historical details of this period.

## Names and Laughter

Sweet Semerkhet, cheerful Meresankh, wise Merneith, grouchy Kahotep, helpful Nefertiti-Tasherit, furry little Bastet, and all the minor servants are the products of my imagination. The name *Semerkhet* can indeed be translated as "attentive friend," *Kahotep* does mean "peaceful essence," *Meresankh* means "she loves life," and the name *Bastet* seemed appropriate for a royal pet cat, as it was the name of an Egyptian goddess famously depicted as a cat.

Just like these, every name used in my story is attested somewhere in Egyptian history, except for five, *Nefermaatet, Mereneferet, Meritsenmut, Tutsenmut,* and *Kasobek,* which I have constructed according to the meanings I wanted to convey— a female name expressing "Beauty and Truth," a female name meaning "Love and Beauty," a female name meaning "Beloved of her Mother's Brother," a male name meaning "Image of his Mother's Brother" and a male name conveying "Essence of Sobek." I would like to point out that I have used names from many eras in Ancient Egypt's history, and they may or may not have all been popular during the Eighteenth Dynasty.

My use of the phrase "beauty in motion" in reference to Nefertiti is an allusion to the meaning of her name. It has been translated in a variety of ways, from "the beautiful woman has come" to "the beautiful one has arrived" to "beauty walks slowly." Additionally, the titles the Pharaoh bestows upon Semerkhet on the day that he witnesses Semerkhet's marriage to Meresankh and provides them with enough wealth to see them through the rest of their lives belonged to Yuya, an advisor of Tut's grandfather Thutmose the Third (who was also the King's father-in-law).

My translation of the name of one of Treasurer Maya's daughters, *Mayamenti*, as "Maya endures," is based on the translation of the name of a structure called Menti-Ankh as "Life May Endure." Furthermore, "Nedjes," the name of Semerkhet's deceased younger brother, was a nickname that might be applied to the younger of two people with the same name— it means "small" or "youngest." I imagine this as being similar to a younger brother being called "Buddy," or "Junior" to the exclusion of his given name.

Meritaten's nickname of *Mayati* is real, and is the name by which she is referred to in a letter from the leader of Tyre. However, the nicknames of Tut, Ankh, and their other sisters are completely hypothetical. The Hittite term *assiyant* in *The Things We Can Change*, a word meaning "dear, beloved" is historical.

The "old ballad" about the turtledove was inspired by a real Ancient Egyptian poem, and the ghost lullaby is my own rhyming paraphrase of an existing incantation sung over babies. The hymn written by his father that Tut remembers at the very end of the story is real; it is known as "The Hymn to the Aten." However, is

470

absolutely no evidence whatsoever that the song "Rock-a-Bye Baby" is of Ancient Egyptian origin. The "Nile… Crocodile" rhyme popped into my head, and I developed it from there. The same can be said with the "old rhyme" based on Humpty Dumpty. The Pharaoh who would not let God's people go certainly took a "great fall," and "all the king's horses and all the king's men" were indeed never seen again, but this reworking is the product of my own imagination. I also constructed the Exodus-era adaptation of *Coventry Carol*, inspired by the terrible symmetry of the Hebrew mothers whose children were killed by Pharaoh and the mothers of Bethlehem whose children were murdered by Herod.

Merneith and Meresankh's interjection of "Oy, vavoy" comes from the Hebrew version of the well-known Yiddish cry of frustration, "Oy, vey." I also enjoyed inventing their frequent interjection of "What in the Ten Plagues," another reference to Merneith's personal background. Finally, the poignant saying, "Even the Red Sea has two shores," evokes the same inspiration as Psalm 30:5, "Weeping may endure for a night, but joy comes in the morning," or the saying, "This, too, shall pass."

## Other Inspirations

In a way, I wrote my story in response to the cinematic confection that is the *Spike* miniseries *Tut*, taking some of the same elements while doing other parts "my way." For example, the miniseries' handling of its two main female characters, Tut's sister-wife Ankh and fictional second lover Suhad, whose jealousy of one another and one another's pregnancies devolves into murder, inspired me to take a different approach. I think it's unfortunate that in the handling of the female leads in this show, strength is equated with violence.

On a lighter note, a few moments in *A Legacy of Light* were inspired by the fantastically bad etiquette of a character from the miniseries, a soldier named Lagus. His aptitude for barging into the Pharaoh's chambers unannounced inspired the scene in *To Claim What is Ours* when Kahotep comes into Tut's room without knocking, as well as the solution Semerkhet invents in *The Things We Can Change*— what might be the first "Do Not Disturb" sign in history! In another scene, Lagus also quite casually shares a cup of beer with the Pharaoh. In my telling of Tutankhamun's story, I made sure that some propriety is maintained in terms of the sharing of food and drink, and that servants and courtiers offer more than a polite nod when the Pharaoh walks by. All throughout the show, no one treats the Pharaoh with reverence, a shortcoming I have remedied in my telling of his story. I also made sure that rather than loudly gossiping about murder plots in the middle of an open room, characters shut themselves behind locked doors before discussing politics!

The grandness of some of Tutankhamun's proclamations was fun to write. The phrase "I have spoken; all depart," used chiefly in *To Claim What is Ours* was lovingly lifted from *The Secret Garden*, where it is uttered by Colin Craven, who, as a young boy who cannot walk and who finds himself as the Master of a great house in Yorkshire, England, is a bit like my Pharaoh. Another character from this novel, Mary Lennox, also inspired me with her initial inability to dress herself simply because she had never been expected to.

Another similarity can be drawn with *Ivanhoe*. Like Sir Walter Scott's titular knight, my male lead, as heroic as he is, spends more than half the course of the trilogy in bed, wounded and under the effective care of a strong, wise female character. Ankhesenamun,

472

too, as a brave, wise politician who could be just as good a King as she has been a Queen, bears many similarities to Princess Jasmine as she is interpreted in Disney's 2019 *Aladdin*. References to "Ranofer, the great goldsmith of Thebes" allude to the character from the novel *The Golden Goblet*. As the childhood of the fictional Ranofer is set during the adulthood of Queen Tiye, he would belong to the same generation as Tutankhamun's parents.

Perhaps the most storyline parallels can be drawn between Ay and Horemheb's plot to murder the Pharaoh and the plot of Yzma and her goodhearted henchman Kronk to get rid of Emperor Kuzco in *The Emperor's New Groove*. In both stories, a young, naïve King decides that he no longer wants his ancient advisor making decisions for him, and the advisor responds by attempting to assassinate him with poisoned wine, aided during one point by a brawny secondary villain who later has a change of heart. As Yzma says, "With him out of the way, and no heir to the throne, I'll take over and rule the empire!" Of course, in *The Emperor's New Groove*, Yzma only manages to turn Kuzco into a llama, but the parallels are there.

Like the Vizier, she also delivers an insincere eulogy after Kuzco's disappearance and "death," and, in the manner of a Pharaoh, usurps his palace and all his monuments, plastering her face over all of them. Needless to say, this story has a much happier ending than that of my Pharaoh, but I was interested (and amused) to observe these strange similarities! On a more poignant note, however, Yzma's comment during her eulogy for Kuzco that "his legacy will live on in our hearts for all eternity" strongly applies to Tut.

I was also inspired by *Lord of the Rings*, in the way that a master-servant relationship warms into friendship, then brotherhood. Although I did not consciously select the name *Semerkhet* for this reason, I found it extremely appropriate that his nickname of *Sem* sounds almost exactly the same as Samwise's nickname of *Sam*. Moments when Tut addresses him as "dear Sem" serve to emphasize this parallel.

I was also inspired by *Little Women*— the way in which Beth's family, upon realizing that she is terminally ill, and after processing the "first bitterness" of the fact that her health cannot be restored, "accepted the inevitable, and tried to bear it cheerfully, helping one another by the increased affection which comes to bind households tenderly together in times of trouble. They put away their grief, and each did his or her part toward making that last year a happy one."

Similarly, Ankh and Sem suffer a first blow of grief when the Pharaoh tells them his secret, but they are able to, indeed, make those last few weeks happy ones, full of connection and love. Another image from *Little Women* appears at the very end, when the Queen and the valet look down at Tut's peaceful face and know that he is home. When Beth's journey ends, her family finds solace in knowing that she is "well at last."

Parallels incidental and intentional also exist between my story and Rosemary Sutcliff's *The Eagle of the Ninth*. Like Tutankhamun, the protagonist of this novel, Marcus, a young Roman centurion stationed in first-century Britain, is wounded in his first battle, suffering a broken femur after being run over by a chariot. During his long, difficult recovery, Marcus obtains a body-slave named Esca, who functions as a valet and CNA. Over time, the relationship between the master and the slave warms into friendship, and by their heroic return home from the grueling, life-threatening quest they embark upon together, they are brothers.

474

The scene during the Pharaoh's partial recovery when the Chief Physician has to clean his infected wound was also inspired by a similar scene in *The Eagle of the Ninth* when Marcus has to have shrapnel removed from a wound that had been struggling to heal, as well as a singularly unpleasant experience of my own— having an infected stitch removed during recovery from surgery.

I was also poignantly inspired by the lyrics to *Remember*, the song featured in the credits of the film *Troy*, sung by Josh Groban. They weren't written with Tutankhamun in mind, but they remind us of how when we remember a person, and tell their story, they can live forever. As the song tells us, *As long as I still can reach out and touch you, then I will never die.*

I also tried to give a bit of a sense of *Downton Abbey*, with the aristocracy's complete dependence on their servants, and especially the way that by helplessly relying on their staff, the aristocrats are able to benefit the community by giving the people who serve them the opportunity to work. Meanwhile, phrases like "I am the Morning and the Evening Star" and "Be still; Pharaoh speaks" were inspired by the Dreamworks film *The Prince of Egypt*, where they are spoken by Moses' prideful brother Rameses and their father Seti. Tutankhamun also occasionally uses the "Royal We," evoking Queen Victoria's mythical "We are not amused." Semerkhet's role as wine-taster, and the ritual phrasing he uses as he tests it for poison, comes from the Elizabeth Taylor version of *Cleopatra*. All in all, I found it very meaningful to be able to allude to the different sources that inspired me as I wrote.

## Marriage in Ancient Egypt

Marriage between non-royals was not defined in as much detail in Ancient Egypt as it is in today's America. Although adultery could be prosecuted, couples were considered married as soon as they moved in together, their marriage contract had been defined and signed in the presences of witnesses, and the gifts agreed upon had been exchanged by their respective families. The legal system also entered much more into the dissolution of a failed marriage (divorce was available, and could be initiated by both husbands and wives) than into the commencement of a marriage. In the event of divorce, there was also no restriction on remarriage, and divorced women could claim alimony payments from their ex-husbands until such a time as they should remarry. The exchange of necklaces is an invention of my own, although wedding rings date back to Ancient Egypt. Furthermore, although a stigma may have existed, it would have been perfectly legal for Ankhesenamun to live as a working single mother anywhere in Egypt.

A person whose father was dead was able to marry, and even tiny dowries were sufficient for a marriage to take place, but emphasizing the importance of the witness and permission provided by a husband's father, and of the dowry brought by a wife, provided one final way that the Pharaoh could help his friends—witnessing their marriage and providing them with a nest egg they could probably live on for the rest of their lives!

## The Missing Hittite

The proposal of marriage by an Eighteenth-Dynasty Egyptian Queen to a Hittite Prince is historical, and historically, the offer was accepted. However, Prince Zannanza disappeared on the journey to Egypt, and the two countries went to war. It is not known whether Ay or Horemheb had the Hittite Prince murdered, but I have Tut inadvertently sign Prince Zannanza's death warrant by telling Ay so plainly that he and Ankhesenamun had agreed to invite the Hittite Prince to become part of the Egyptian royal family. In order for Zannanza to not simply arrive as scheduled and help Ankhesenamun continue the Eighteenth Dynasty, the Vizier had to know Ankh and Tut's plan and take action to thwart it.

Although the Egyptian Queen who wrote to the Hittites has been variously identified as Ankhesenamun and Nefertiti, or possibly even Meritaten, after his correspondence with the Queen, King Suppiluliuma exchanged further letters with the Pharaoh who next took power. If this Queen was Nefertiti, there is no historical person who, upon taking the next throne, would have written the later letters to Suppiluliuma. But if this Queen was Ankh, the successor was obviously Ay. I allude to these subsequent letters when I describe how in Ay's further correspondence with Suppiluliuma, he avoids confirming that Zannanza was murdered. Historically, the Pharaoh who took up the correspondence with Suppiluliuma after the Queen reached out with her request to marry a prince acknowledged the death of Zannanza but attempted to shift the blame to the King of Hattusa for having sent his son to Egypt in the first place.

I base my assumption that a Pharaoh's coronation did not take place until the funeral of his or her predecessor on the fact that Ankhesenamun historically had the opportunity to write to the Hittites between the death of Tutankhamun and the point at which she expected the next Egyptian to jump for the throne (see "Adjusted Details," below). If Ay had been able to declare himself Pharaoh the very day Tut died (in the manner of an American vice president being sworn in mere hours after the death of his or her predecessor) the Queen would not have had time to make such an overture after Tut's passing.

It is also not clear whether Queen Ankh was forced to marry Ay when he became Pharaoh, but I acknowledge this as a concern. A blue glass ring has been discovered inscribed with the names of both Ay and Ankhesenamun, which some have interpreted as evidence that they married one another. However, when I bring this ring into the plot, I portray it as an engagement gift from the Vizier that the Queen continually refuses. Therefore, I use it as evidence that, as he prepared to become Pharaoh, Ay *wanted* to marry Ankh, and proposed to her, but not as evidence that he was successful.

In the end, whether through marriage to the Queen or not, Ay takes the throne, followed by Horemheb, and Ankhesenamun disappears from history. Where she disappears to is a question that may never be answered.

## Capturing Details

Many details in *A Legacy of Light* are based on truth, such as the frankincense-and-spikenard ointment the Pharaoh enjoys so much. Many of the specific images of daily life, from duck-hunting together to Ankh giving her brother flowers and lovingly fixing his necklace, also originated in a series of portraits of the Pharaoh and the Queen. Engraved historically on a small golden shrine, they were counterparts to the shrines that surrounded Tutankhamun's sarcophagus, a point which I have fictionalized for dramatic effect. As Bob Brier says in his book *The Murder of Tutankhamen*, these shrines, which immortalize Ankh and Tut's love, are the Queen's "love letter in gold."

Other details of Tut's earthly life that we can identify based on the contents of his tomb include his love of the game *senet*, that he enjoyed his favorite white wine enough to want to pack almost three dozen jars of it, and that he did not want to go without his favorite perfumes— containers were sent with him that would have contained over 77 gallons of perfume in total. Also found in his tomb were the many walking-sticks and pairs of shoes described in my author's note for *To Claim What is Ours*.

When Ankh promises Tut that "wonderful things" will be placed inside his tomb, I allude to the words Howard Carter is said to have uttered when he first gazed upon the contents of the Pharaoh's tomb. The Queen's reference to "a" beautiful coffin, however, is an understatement— Tutankhamun was laid to rest inside three nesting coffins, one of which was solid gold. Another detail that I refer to is the fact that there are no pictures of Ankhesenamun on the walls of Tut's tomb. It has been postulated that the Vizier made this artistic decision to ensure that he, not Tutankhamun, was the husband whom Ankh would accompany to the afterlife.

A number of specific objects referred to throughout the trilogy, such as the braid of hair belonging to Queen Tiye, the Pharaoh's two trumpets, and writing palettes from Tut and Ankh's childhood are real. References to Thutmose the First as Tut's "grandfather" are metaphorical; he lived around two hundred years before Tut. References to the Aten mercifully reaching down to humanity, extending His love like friendly hands or the rays of the sun, allude to Akhenaten's depiction of the Aten in the form of sunrays terminating in outstretched hands.

Tutankhamun was indeed likely the youngest Pharaoh ever to rule without the aid of an official regent. Vizier Nebet was also a historical figure; the second female vizier of Egypt did not serve until the Twenty-Sixth Dynasty.

My reference to a "royal post-box" is based on truth; Ancient Egypt had a well-developed mail-delivery system, at least for use by royalty. It is also true that in the city of Sais, women could attend a medical school staffed by female professors, which focused on women's medicine.

In every era of history, babies have had to be kept clean. However, the modern cloth diaper has only been popular since the late 1800s, and disposable diapers were not invented until the 1950s with the advent of Pampers. What, then, did Ancient Egyptian mothers do?

We know that Ancient Egyptian babies were swaddled; the swaddling presumably became soiled and was changed throughout the day. Another strategy used in the ancient world was for a mother to carry around a small clay pot, watching her baby for signs of impending elimination and then holding the little pot under the baby. One would guess that potty training would have happened young in Ancient Egypt.

Surprising though it may seem, a form of field hockey really was played in Ancient Egypt! Horse racing was also popular, and I have chosen, in *To Claim What is Ours*, to portray a single-lap sprint comparable to the Kentucky Derby, rather than a grueling nine-lap race like we see in *Ben-Hur*. Beer was a staple beverage in Ancient Egypt, consumed by rich, poor, old, and young. It was both a source of hydration and a source of nutrition; almost more of a thin soup made from grains than a beverage. Strong wines, on the other hand, were enjoyed at parties and favored for their ability to enhance merriment.

In the epilogue of *Searching for the Truth*, my description of Tutankhamun's funeral is based closely on specific images from his tomb. Descriptions of the Opening of the Mouth ceremony and the funeral dinner shared by the mourners are also historical, as is the short boat trip from one bank of the Nile to the other. A fabric collar found in the Pharaoh's tomb, woven with papyrus, leaves, and cornflowers, reveals that his funeral took place between late February and late April. Accounting for seventy days for the mummification process, we can calculate that he historically died between mid-December and mid-February.

Wailing women were historically hired for funerals, accompanying the funeral procession with histrionics, beating their breasts and striking their heads against the ground. As I have described, male mourners did not shave during the period of mourning, but Semerkhet is somewhat unique as a male mourner in joining the female mourners in keening during the funeral. I have found an image, however, from a funeral during the Old Kingdom, portraying mourning men pulling at their own hair or wigs in grief, one of whom seems to have fallen to his hands and knees in anguish.

In the tomb artwork depicting Tut's funeral, the mourners, who are essentially serving as pallbearers, are anonymous. If Tut historically had a Favorite of the Pharaoh or Unique Friend, that man is probably one of these (as Horemheb was actually Tutankhamun's Sole Companion, he may be among this group of mourners).

All the foods I mention throughout the trilogy were available in Ancient Egypt, and all the flowers I describe could be found in their gardens. As the trilogy moves through the year, I have described various fruits and flowers as coming into season at approximately the appropriate times. The cornflowers Ankh picks on Tut's final morning are the only flower whose blooming season I have adjusted for plot purposes.

As I have described, the Ancient Egyptians counted twelve hours of day and twelve of night year-round, but the lengths of the hours varied to account for the changing of the light at different times of year. Water-clocks gave a sense of the time, but would have been much less precise than today's timepieces. As such, on the final night, I am able to refer, for example, to the "sixth hour of night," even though each "winter night hour" is longer than sixty minutes.

Pentu's *The Things We Can Change* reference in Tut's dream to both him and Princess Meritaten "being at a disadvantage" in the afterlife, and Tut's later rejoinder to Granny's suggestion that they amputate his leg that he doesn't want to "hop around the afterlife on one leg" are based upon the Ancient Egyptian belief that if a person, for example, died in an accident where they lost a hand, if the embalmers didn't attach a false one during mummification, the person would be stuck with one hand for eternity.

Only a Pharaoh could pronounce the death penalty; therefore, in sentencing Semerkhet to death and actually having Raherka executed, Ay is definitively declaring his intention to become Pharaoh. The tax Maya refers to in *To Claim What is Ours*, levied to support the recently-reopened temples, is also historical, and is explained in Bob Brier's *The Murder of Tutankhamen*. The description of the way in which taxes paid by farmers on their year's grain yield were calculated, discussed by Ankh, Amenia, and Mutnedjmet in *To Claim What is Ours*, comes from the same book.

Late in Tutankhamun's reign, Egypt did reclaim Kadesh from the Hittites. This is the battle he is most likely to have participated in if he did indeed see combat. However, the city of Kadesh does not seem to have genuinely been brought back under Egyptian control until the reign of Seti the First, but even then, it was quickly recaptured by the Hittites. After that, Kadesh was genuinely lost to

Egypt, despite a dramatic battle between Rameses the Great and the Hittites, who retained control of the city.

Turning to the personal possessions of the characters, a land where most wood had to be imported, furniture was a luxury. Because Semerkhet and Meresankh are the personal attendants of the Pharaoh and the Queen, they own more furniture than any of the lower-ranking servants. Additionally, it is not known whether a special ring or sash identified a Sole Companion, but it seemed appropriate. I also identified viziers with special staffs and necklaces.

## Adjusted Details

Although I make the fear of Tut or Ankh being poisoned through food a major plot point in *Searching for the Truth*, and describe the meals that the royal couple eats as being made in the same kitchen that produces the food eaten by palace staff members and party guests, this may not have been the case. A Pharaoh's food was specially prepared at a temple, according to the same standards as that which was offered to the images of the gods and goddesses. As such, poisoning the royal meals would have been harder than I have described— or possibly easier, depending on who it was that wanted to kill off the Pharaoh. In the end, it is safest for Semerkhet to continue serving as the food taster, and for Ankh to stop eating from the royal table and eat the simple meals that have been prepared for the staff.

While all the politicians I mention bear the name of real members of Tutankhamun's court, the time and manner of Viziers Pentu and Usermontu's deaths in *To Claim What is Ours* and *Searching for the Truth* are fictional. They may both have outlived

Tut. At least one of them may, in fact, be depicted in tomb illustrations of Tut's funeral procession.

Inconsistencies in the royal portraiture found inside Tutankhamun's tomb suggests that he may have been buried with a combination of funeral goods commissioned for him and items originally intended for the tomb of Nefertiti as Pharaoh Smenkhkare or Co-Regent Ankhkheperure Neferneferuaten. Some images thought to portray Tut may in fact be of his mother or stepmother, including the famous golden death mask and two of the three coffins in which he was buried. A number of small golden statues found in Tutankhamun's tomb also portray a Pharaoh with a feminine body shape and facial features. Perhaps his mother or stepmother's changing roles, or the populace's changing opinion of her and her revolutionary husband, caused funerary items originally intended for her to be left unused upon her death, leaving them available for use in the burial of her successor upon his own early death. Some also theorize that because of his early death, Tutankhamun was laid to rest in Ay's nearly-finished tomb, leaving the former Vizier to be buried in Tut's original tomb.

The timing of Tut's death, discussed above, is loosely inspired by the timing of his funeral as calculated from flowers identified from his funeral dinner. Although I describe the famous mask as having been prepared for Tutankhamun while he lay dying, it actually bears an inscription suggesting that it may have originally been intended for co-regent (and possibly Pharaoh) Neferneferuaten.

The vicious paperwork battles waged by Ankh and Ay are also my own invention. There is no evidence that Ay wrote his own letter to Suppiluliuma in an attempt to marry a Hittite Princess, but

484

I found that to be an exciting way in which the Pharaoh, the Queen, and their friends could score an important victory against the evil Vizier without changing the way the story ultimately ends. The name I use, Muwatti, is that of a daughter of King Suppiluliuma. We also have no suggestion that Grand Vizier Ay attempted to insert himself as Tutankhamun's successor by forging a proclamation with Tut's signet-ring.

I also had the honor of inventing the Queens List passed down to Ankhesenamun by her mother Nefertiti. Although it is fictional, it fit in beautifully with the values I wanted to show Nefertiti encouraging in her daughters. It also created a wonderful way for Ankh to connect with her female friends and share those same values with them; values that will prepare all of these characters for the challenges that lie ahead of them. The description of a chapel in which the infant princesses lay before joining their father in his tomb is also completely hypothetical.

There is no evidence that, as his life drew to a close, Tut gave his Queen his signet-ring and deputized her to make his daily decisions for him, but such a move seemed like a natural choice for them, based on their relationship (as I have written it) and their political situation. I can also envision Tut appointing Ankh as his coregent and successor, as their father appointed their mother.

The timing of a third pregnancy for Ankh is also highly conjectural. Although she may have had three daughters in all (see "A Mysterious Future," below), we have no particular evidence that Tut's final weeks were spent desperately scheming with his pregnant wife for the sake of Egypt's future. I have also changed some of the timing in regards to Ankhesenamun's proposal to Zannanza; if she was the Queen who wrote to the Hittites in regards to her husband's death, she is not likely to have done so while the Pharaoh was still living. Altering the timeline in this way allowed Ankh to communicate her plans to her brother, and allowed him to depart in the knowledge that she had a plan. Unfortunately, their informing Ay of their letter also gave him the opportunity to interrupt Zannanza's journey to Egypt, as mentioned above.

Furthermore, when the Egyptian Queen wrote to the Hittite King asking to marry one of his sons, she did not specifically request Zannanza. Giving Ankh reason to infer which Hittite Prince would be appointed as her husband allowed her to refer to him by name, and to envision their forthcoming marriage on a more personal level than if she had only been awaiting an anonymous "prince."

I also adjusted some of the details of politics and war during Tutankhamun's reign. For example, I describe his hypothetical campaign to reclaim Kadesh from the Hittites as an attempt to free the people of the entire region of Amurru from Hittite rule and restore them to their status as contented Egyptian vassals. However, although details are murky and precise dates are hard to find, it appears as if although Egypt fought to take Kadesh back from Hattusa during Tut's reign, the vassal kingdom of Amurru had already declared its loyalty to the Hittites. I've also set the capture of Kadesh by the Hittites within the years of Tut's reign, when it may have taken place during Akhenaten's reign.

Tutankhamun has been confirmed to have had malaria in his system when he died, but I have changed some of the details. As discovered by Egyptologist Zahi Hawass, the type of malaria found in his body was *plasmodium falciparum*, the deadliest type, which can cause a dangerous scenario known as cerebral malaria. This could mean that he died more quickly than I have depicted, after

486

suffering from symptoms such as seizures and possibly falling into a coma. (Under certain circumstances, ague *can* kill strong, healthy people in a week).

The Pharaoh also suffered a broken femur shortly before his death, and there is evidence of infection around the site of the injury. According to a video by National Geographic, if gangrene had set in after his leg was broken, he may have died after only a few days. The lack of visible healing of his femur also suggests that he died before the broken bone could start to knit together again. Sadly enough, he may not have lived to get home to the palace.

Quite simply, I needed him to hang on as political battles began to rage, fighting for the future of his country even as his life neared its end. So although I incorporate both malaria and the infection of a broken femur, I show him slowly getting weaker over six difficult weeks until his body can no longer bear the strain.

This alteration of the timeline also adjusts the timing of Horemheb's actions and creates some interesting complexities. Historically, by the time the General got home from the campaign in Kadesh, he probably found Tut inside his tomb, Ay on the throne with Ankh as his heartbroken Queen, and Zannanza "missing." As such, and not wanting to start another war, he waited his turn, claiming the throne after Ay's. Because I give the Pharaoh six long weeks of survival after getting home from Amurru, and describe General Horemheb as arriving at the palace an hour after his death, I had to give the General another non-negotiable reason to allow Ay his time as Pharaoh— the lives of his wives being threatened worked well for this purpose.

I carefully researched the earliest signs of pregnancy, and sprinkled them throughout the final three weeks of the story's timeline to show that Ankh has more than hope that she has conceived; she has solid evidence. However, since the story ends only three weeks after the date of conception, I had to describe her experiencing these early signs even earlier than most women do. Even with only three weeks of survival after the child's conception, I wanted to allow the Pharaoh to depart with the hope that his dynasty may live on.

Finally, there is no information that either suggests or contradicts the idea that at the very end of his life, Tutankhamun may have recognized the Aten, the God of the Hebrews, as the one true God, but I found it a beautiful and satisfying way to bring his earthly life to a close. And as the loved ones who survive him move forward into the unknown future, secure in the love of God, what is the worst that could happen?

## A Mysterious Future

In the end, there is no particular evidence that Ankh became pregnant with a third child with Tut just before his death. There is, however, shadowy evidence that she may have had a third daughter, in another incestuous marriage before her partnership with Tut. This daughter's name was Ankhesenpaaten-*Tasherit*, or Junior, and she had a very short life, if she existed at all (it is also possible that she belonged to other members of the Amarna family, or was invented by the Egyptians to replace the child of another, potentially disgraced, member of court).

My telling, however, envisions a future in which the Queen loses her crown but gives birth to a third princess after Tut's death, a princess who will grow up knowing the truth of I-AM, the Aten. The use of the form *Ankhesenpaaten*, lines up well, after all, with the Queen's hypothetical decision to return to the Aten. What if vague legends made their way back to Egypt of the former Queen having given birth to a daughter in exile, and, without having access to the child's name, the Egyptian people simply referred to this mysterious princess as *Ankhesenpaaten-Tasherit?*

It may not be a politically triumphant ending, the happy ending I would have written if this were pure fiction merely set within the context of an Ancient Egyptian royal court, but I hope audiences find inspiration in the way my characters never stop trying, fighting for what's right, hoping, and bravely making the most of the horrible curveballs life throws at them. Ankh may not be able to defeat the Vizier, and her only hope of survival may be in fleeing into exile, but she is a heroine nonetheless, courageously making the most of the struggles she is faced with. In the end, she chooses to save her child's life, preserving the legacy of her family and using her skills and knowledge to change the lives of the next generation as a history teacher. And no matter where she goes, no matter what she does, no matter what may happen in her life, she is still the Queen. And no one can take that from her.

What happens next is harder to trace. Maybe she and the child will escape from Ay's deadly clutches and live out their lives in relative peace and safety as private citizens, while Ankh embraces her calling to teach history. And maybe she will see her friends again. Or maybe she will flee to Israel and become the mysterious royal Egyptian wife of Mered. History doesn't tell us. And maybe we will never know.

## An Enduring Legacy

*As long as I still can reach out and touch you, then I will never die… His legacy will live on in our hearts for all eternity…* These poignant lines from the song *Remember* and the movie *The*

*Emperor's New Groove* remind us that a poetic form of immortality is achieved when a person who died three thousand years ago has a place in the hearts of people all around the world. Even though half of them couldn't tell you that Cleopatra wasn't Tutankhamun's grandmother (she lived nearly 1300 years after he did), or that he wasn't born in Arizona (all right, most people probably know that one) people recognize the golden face of the Boy King.

And in a hundred books and documentaries, a thousand knickknacks and pieces of novelty jewelry and clothing, far too many historically inaccurate Halloween costumes, a song by Steve Martin, 2014's animated film *Mr. Peabody and Sherman*, and *Spike*'s 2015 miniseries, the memory of King Tut lives on. He may not have "give[n] his life for tourism," but the magnitude of the gift that his discovery has given to Egyptian tourism cannot be calculated, and truly is an important part of his legacy. And in a strange, small way, I, too, am honored to be part of keeping his memory alive in my own retelling of his story.

I enjoyed getting to know Pharaoh Tutankhamun and his Great Royal Wife Ankhesenamun. Although I am sorry for everything he went through, from the loss of his children to his early death, I have been honored to have had the opportunity to learn so much about him and write a version of his story. I hope that I have treated him as the Pharaoh he is, and that readers will enjoy a combination of fact and fiction that will inspire them to embark on their own journey of discovery.

When we remember a person, and tell their story, they can live forever. As the Ancient Egyptian proverb says, to speak the name of the dead is to make them live again.

Thank you for joining me on this adventure. All life, prosperity, and health!

# Glossary

**Ague:** malaria, a potentially deadly, mosquito-borne illness that causes weakness, fever, and chills

**Ammut:** the crocodile-lion-hippopotamus beast who would devour the hearts of the unworthy dead, preventing them from entering into a peaceful afterlife

**Bastet:** ancient Egyptian goddess with a role related to various aspects of health, depicted as a lioness or cat

**Crook and Flail:** props the Pharaoh might hold, which symbolized his or her being a loving shepherd but also meting out discipline

**Diadem:** a term for a type of crown with a lower profile than the white crown of Upper Egypt, the red crown of Lower Egypt, or the double-crown. A diadem would fit closely against one's wig, with the only protrusion being the *uraeus* in the front. Also referred to as a circlet.

**Hemp:** medicinal cannabis

**Henna:** red dye used in various cultures to decorate the skin with beautiful designs, and used by Ancient Egyptians to color nails and dye hair. Soldiers colored their nails red before going into battle.

**Hieratic script:** a form of writing; a "cursive" form of hieroglyphic script that could be written with pen and ink

**Kohl:** the eyeliner used by Ancient Egyptians to create the well-known cat-eye and to darken their eyebrows. Combined with blue-green "eye-shadow," it helped to protect the eyes from infection and from the bright sun. Both kohl and the "eye-shadow" were made from minerals.

**Ma'at:** both the name of an Ancient Egyptian goddess of truth, harmony, and justice and a term for these and related concepts. Upon death, Ancient Egyptians anticipated that their hearts would be weighed against the feather Ma'at wore in her hair; if their hearts were too heavy, it indicated that they were unrighteous, and their hearts were eaten by the crocodile-lion-hippopotamus beast, Ammut. They would not have the opportunity to advance to a happy afterlife in the Field of Reeds.

**Mandrake:** a plant used as a painkiller

**Nemes:** the head-cloth worn by Pharaohs in Ancient Egypt. The most famous example is worn by the Great Sphinx of Giza.

**Nut:** an Ancient Egyptian goddess of the sky

**Palanquin:** another word for a litter in which a member of the royal family might be carried, borne by servants

**Pectoral:** refers to a very large necklace that covers a portion of the chest

**Poppy:** medicinal opium

**Sed Festival:** jubilee traditionally celebrated when a Pharaoh reached his or her thirtieth year in power, and then every three or four years thereafter. Ceremonies included a ritual run that demonstrated the Pharaoh's enduring strength.

**Seega:** a board game played historically in Egypt

**Sobek:** an Ancient Egyptian god of fertility, depicted as a crocodile or with the head of a crocodile

**Spikenard:** an essential oil obtained from a plant of the valerian family, long used in perfumery

**Tawaret:** an Ancient Egyptian goddess of fertility, depicted as a grandly pregnant hippopotamus

**Vizier:** a sort of "prime minister;" a high official responsible for supervising much of the running of the government

# Locations

**Akhetaten (Amarna):** Pharaoh Akhenaten's capital city, which he had built to honor the Aten and to enable a "fresh start."

**Alashiya:** Eastern Mediterranean neighbor of New Kingdom Egypt

**Amurru:** Region in modern Syria and Lebanon historically subjected to both Egyptian and Hittite control

**Goshen:** Region in the eastern Nile Delta settled by the Hebrews

**Hattusa:** Kingdom of the Hittites, located in modern Turkey

**Iuny (Armant)**: Town near Thebes

**Kadesh:** Town in the region of Amurru, which switched hands several times between Egypt and Hattusa

**Kush:** Region of Nubia under Egyptian control from 16th-11th centuries BC

**Memphis (Cairo):** Northern capital of Egypt, in the southern Nile Delta

**Mitanni:** Neighbor of New Kingdom Egypt located in modern Turkey and Syria

**Napata:** Town in the extreme south of Egypt, on the Eighteenth-Dynasty border with Nubia

**Nubia:** Southern neighbor of Egypt, comprising parts of modern Egypt and modern Sudan

**On (Heliopolis):** Town in the southern Nile Delta, just north of Memphis

**Per-Bast (Bubastis):** Town in the southeastern Nile Delta

**Retjenu:** Neighbor of Egypt in the region of Canaan/Syria

**Sais:** Town near Memphis, famous for its medical college, attended (if not exclusively) by female students and run by female professors

494

**Tamiat (Damietta):** Town in the extreme north of Egypt, on the Mediterranean coast

**Thebes (Luxor):** Southern capital of Egypt, on the banks of the Nile in the center of the country

# Ankhesenamun's Queens List

**Neith-Hotep:** possible regent, possible Pharaoh (early first dynasty).

**Merneith:** regent for her son Den, possible Pharaoh (first dynasty).

**Nimaathap:** possible regent for her son Djoser (transition between second and third dynasties).

**Khentkaus the First:** possible Pharaoh or regent for her son. A title that can be translated either as "Mother of Two Kings of Upper and Lower Egypt" or "Mother of the King of Upper and Lower Egypt, *and King of Upper and Lower Egypt*" suggests that she may have become Pharaoh (transition between fourth and fifth dynasties).

**Khentkaus the Second:** bore the same titles as her predecessor, and may also have reigned either as regent or as Pharaoh in her own right (fifth dynasty).

**Setibhor:** wife of Pharaoh Djedkare. Her pyramid complex is larger, more elaborate, and "kinglier" than any other belonging to a Queen, and certain symbols and insignias were added to reliefs portraying her, which suggests that she may have succeeded her husband as Pharaoh or as regent for the next male Pharaoh (late fifth dynasty).

**Iput:** mother and possible regent for Pepi the First (beginning of sixth dynasty).

**Ankhesenpepi the Second:** sister of Ankhesenpepi the First, daughter of female Vizier Nebet, wife of Pepi the First, bore one of his successors (Pepi the Second), likely served as regent (sixth dynasty).

**Nebet:** vizier (sixth dynasty).

496

**Nitocris:** legendary female Pharaoh, considered to be final Pharaoh of sixth dynasty.

**Sobekneferu:** Pharaoh (very end of twelfth dynasty).

**Tetisheri:** mother of Ahhotep the First, powerful Queen and matriarch of royal family (transition between seventeenth and eighteenth dynasties).

**Ahhotep the First:** regent for her son Ahmose the First. Praised by her son for keeping Egypt in one piece, expelling rebels, bringing home deserters, guarding the country, and pacifying Upper Egypt (transition between seventeenth and eighteenth dynasties).

**Ahmose-Nefertari:** daughter of Ahhotep the First, mother of Amenhotep the First, may have served as regent for him. She may have founded the Valley of the Kings (early eighteenth dynasty).

**Hatshepsut:** Queen, then regent, then Pharaoh (eighteenth dynasty).

**Tiye:** wife of Amenhotep the Third, mother of Akhenaten. Worked as a politician to retain good relations with neighboring countries during her son's reign (eighteenth dynasty).

**Nefertiti Smenkhkare:** Queen, then co-regent, then possible Pharaoh (eighteenth dynasty).

**Meritaten:** Queen of Pharaoh Smenkhkare, who is speculated to have been her own mother Nefertiti (eighteenth dynasty).

# Calendar

**Season of Inundation (Akhet)**
Thoth: 19 July-17 August
Paophi: 18 August-16 September
Athyr: 17 September-16 October
Sholiak: 17 October-15 November
**Season of Emergence (Peret)**
Tybi: 16 November-15 December
Meshir: 16 December-14 January
Phamenoth: 15 January-13 February
Pharmouthi: 14 February-15 March
**Season of the Harvest (Shemu)**
Pashons: 16 March-14 April
Payni: 15 April-14 May
Epiphi: 15 May-13 June
Mesori: 14 June-13 July
**Holy birthdays**
14th of July: Osiris
15th: Horus
16th: Seth
17th: Isis
18th: Nepthys

# Lyrics

### The Turtledove Ballad

*I hear thy voice, O turtledove*
*The dawn is all aglow—*
*Weary am I with love, with love*
*Oh, whither shall I go?*
*Not so, O beauteous bird above*
*Is joy to be denied*
*For I have found my dear, my love*
*And I am by his side*
*We wander forth, and hand in hand*
*Through flowery ways we go—*
*I am the fairest in the land*
*For he has called me so*

### The Ghost Lullaby

*Away, away, o ghost of night*
*My baby do not harm*
*Your face turned back, your nose behind*
*You'll wither at my charm*
*Have you come to kiss him, or sing him to sleep?*
*Have you come to harm him, or steal him as I weep?*
*I will not let you kiss him, or in the window creep*
*I will not let you harm him*
*And I'll sing him to sleep*

### A Nursery Rhyme

*Proud old Pharaoh stood so tall*
*Proud old Pharaoh had a great fall*

*All Pharaoh's horses and all Pharaoh's men*
*Went after the Hebrews and were never seen again*

**Nile Lullaby**
*Rock-a-bye baby*
*Float down the Nile*
*Hope you don't get eaten*
*By a crocodile*
*Gift from the river*
*Sent from above*
*Drawn from the water*
*Chosen with love*

**Adaptation of Coventry Carol**
*Lai, lai, lullay, my little tiny child*
*Lai, lai, lully, lullay*
*My little tiny child,*
*Lai, lai, lully, lullay*

*O sisters too, how may we do*
*For to preserve this day*
*These poor younglings for whom we sing*
*"Lai, lai, lully, lullay"?*

*Pharaoh the king, in his raging*
*Chargèd he hath this day*
*His men of might in his own sight*
*Each Hebrew son to slay*

*That woe is me, poor child, for thee*

500

*And ever mourn and may*
*For thy parting neither say nor sing*
*"Lai, lai, lully, lullay."*

*The midwives wise*
*Deceived the king*
*And many sons they saved*
*Obeyed I-AM*
*Instead of man*
*And to them He honor gave*

*Then Pharaoh cruel*
*Who'd been made a fool*
*Another order gave*
*Throw each male child*
*Into the Nile*
*The river would be his grave*

*Jochebed brave concealed her son*
*Then into a basket laid*
*And on the Nile she placed her child*
*And for his life she prayed*

*Then to the Nile*
*Did came to bathe*
*The woman who'd take the throne*
*And to her heart she took the child*
*And raised him up as her own*

*But lai lai, lullay, my little tiny child,*

*Lai, lai, lully, lullay.*
*Thou little tiny child,*
*Lai, lai, lully, lullay*

# Selected Resources

*The Holy Bible*

*Daily Life of the Ancient Egyptians* by Bob Brier, A. Hoyt Hobbs

*The Murder of Tutankhamun: A True Story* by Bob Brier

*Empire of Ancient Egypt* by Wendy Christensen

*Tutankhamun: The Exodus Conspiracy: The Truth Behind Archaeology's Greatest Mystery* by Andrew Collins and Chris Ogilvie-Herald

*When Women Ruled the World* by Kara Cooney

*Tutankhamun's Armies: Battle and Conquest During Ancient Egypt's Late Eighteenth Dynasty* by John Coleman Darnell, Colleen Manassa

*The Tomb of Iouiya and Touiyou: The Finding of the Tomb* by Theodore M. Davis, Gaston Maspero, Percy Edward Newberry

*Amarna Sunset: Nefertiti, Tutankhamun, Ay, Horemheb, and the Egyptian Counter-Reformation* by Aidan Dodson

*Monarchs of the Nile* by Aidan Dodson

*The Mysterious Death of Tutankhamun: Re-Opening the Case of Egypt's Boy-King* by Paul Doherty

*Egyptian Non-royal Epithets in the Middle Kingdom: A Social and Historical Analysis* by Denise M. Doxey

*Life in Ancient Egypt* by Adolf Erman

*The Medical Skills of Ancient Egypt: revised edition* by J. Worth Estes

*Oils and Perfumes of Ancient Egypt* by Joann Fletcher

*Growing Up in Ancient Israel: Children in Material Culture and Biblical Texts* by Kristine Henriksen Garroway

"The Deeds of Suppiluliuma as told by his son, Mursilli II", *Journal of Cuneiform Studies, 10* (1956) by Güterbock, H.G.

*The Golden King: The World of Tutankhamun* by Zahi Hawass

*Scanning the Pharaohs: CT Imaging of the New Kingdom Royal Mummies* by Zahi A. Hawass, Sahar Saleem

*Principles and Methods of Toxicology, Fifth Edition* Edited by A. Wallace Hayes

*The Pharaoh's Court* by Kathryn Hinds

*Conspiracies in the Egyptian Palace: Unis to Pepy I* by Naguib Kanawati

*Who Killed King Tut?* by Michael R. King and Gregory M. Cooper

*Powerful Female Pharaohs of Egypt* by Jone Johnson Lewis (article published on ThoughtCo)

*Sacred Luxuries: Fragrance, Aromatherapy, and Cosmetics in Ancient Egypt* by Lise Manniche

*Ghosts: A Haunted History* by Lisa Morton

*Ancient Egyptian Kingship* by David Bourke O'Connor, David P. Silverman

*The Hebrew Pharaohs of Egypt: the Secret Lineage of the Patriarch Joseph* by Ahmed Osman

*The Oxford History of Ancient Egypt* by Ian Shaw

*The Encyclopedia of Ancient Egypt* General Editor Helen Strudwick

*Chronicle of the queens of Egypt: from early dynastic times to the death of Cleopatra* by Joyce Tyldesley

*Tutankhamen: The Search for an Egyptian King* by Joyce Tyldesley

*Ancient Egypt: Its Culture and History* by J. E. Manchip White

504

# Acknowledgments

When I began working on this story in 2017, I had no idea that it would blossom into one of the most meaningful things I have ever created; the project I am the most proud of. Little did I know that I had begun the long pregnancy and labor that would bring my story into the world.

Let me thank the many people who held my hands, encouraged me, and coached me during this amazing process. To my mother, Anne, this story would not be what it is today if you had not let me read it to you out loud three times in a row. You have cured my dependence on paragraph-length sentences, you have helped me mature in my application of balance and pacing, and you have answered questions I could not answer myself. I will be forever grateful for your support, your willingness to serve as my sounding board, and your second set of eyes and ears. Thank you for being to me everything Ankh is for Tut. And thank you for playing *seega!*

To my brave friends, thank you for reading this saga before the rest of the world. Thank you for your questions and your comments; all your wonderful observations that helped me understand what was coming across well and what needed further clarification. Thank you for helping me make this story everything it has become.

And to the Pharaoh and his family… thank you for inspiring me.

www.ingramcontent.com/pod-product-compliance
Lightning Source LLC
Chambersburg PA
CBHW070826260626
47170CB00007B/2274